The Cut

Andy Bracken

A Morning Brake Book

Copyright © 2020 Andy Bracken

ISBN: 9798575490999

First Edition.

For C & R. With love.

For Kevin and David Bolton.

x

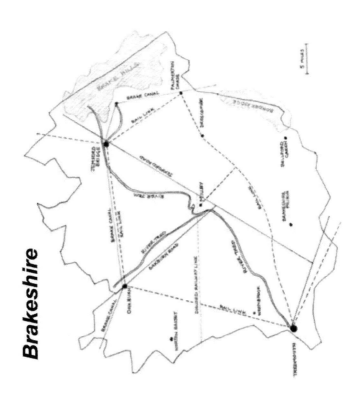

1.

It's a regular car-boot, this one, beginning now, in March, and running till October. I come every other week. I'd come every week, but it's a fortnightly event.

On the vacant weekends, I go to a different field, and see the same shite.

A row and a half is all there is, in a field just off the Oakburn Road in Brakeshire, a couple of miles northwest of Millby.

It's less than twenty miles from my home in Oakburn. Being near Millby, you see some different sellers sometimes. A lot of Millby people come from elsewhere.

Time was, I'd arrive at nine. Then it was eight. Now it's closer to seven. You snooze, you lose.

He's here before me. I can see his yellow bobble hat nodding away.

Yellow Hat is my nemesis.

There's no sense in following him. He won't have missed anything. Looping round, I pick up the stalls I might term 'new growth'.

A box of seven inches causes me to pause. It's a waste of time and effort. Mostly country music. From the seventies.

It's a positive sign, though, the fact I haven't seen that particular box of utter crap before.

"Ten pence each," the woman informs me. There's an air of desperation in her voice. It speaks of 'don't make me take the fucking things home again.'

I smile and shake my head.

Three cars down, my keen eye spies two cases standing on the hard ground. They look like they were made for records; black, plastic, silver clasps, carry-handles on top.

One of the handles is lying flat. The other is tantalisingly upright.

They might be empty, of course. Even so, I'll see if I can get them for storage.

A push-chair forces me off my beeline. The fatty whiff of bacon fills the air, as I skirt along the back of the snack van before veering sharply over to the trestle table. Beneath it sit the black carry cases.

They look right. One for albums, the other for singles.

Mind you, I've been mistaken in the past, what with portable typewriters and the like.

I pause to let an elderly gentleman pass.

"'Scuse me, mate," a voice says, and I instinctively retreat half a step to accommodate it.

The stale smell off the yellow bobble hat mouldily breezes by me.

And he's in! Nipped ahead of me, and down on his haunches before I can stop him.

Not that I'd have stopped him. Too bloody nice - that's always been my trouble.

It's tempting to squat and push in alongside him; go through one case as he peruses the other. But it would be a serious breach of car-boot etiquette.

Besides, he's cannily occupying the full space, his satchel posited in defensive formation.

He quivers with excitement as he pops a lid and his fingers go to work.

It's all punk and post-punk. Coloured vinyl is revealed on a couple he slides from their sleeves.

"How much are the records, mate?" Yellow Hat asks in a voice adopted to disguise his enthusiasm.

I've used that voice; the one brought out to imply you're doing the seller a favour by even asking.

"Quid each. Fiver each for the cases."

I reckon it up. There must be seventy-five or eighty in total.

"How much for the lot?" Yes, I'd have done that, too.

"Fifty?" the vendor suggests, making it sound like a question.

"Does that include the cases?"

He smiles, the seller. Has Yellow Hat overplayed his hand?

"Call it fifty-five?" he proposes.

"Go on, then," Yellow replies with a heavy heart that speaks of the terrible gamble he's taking.

The joker is saved till last. The crafty hatted bastard holds out a fifty and a twenty. He plays the Change Game.

Will he have fifteen in change this early in proceedings?

"Ah, got anything smaller?" comes the answer to that question.

Of course he has, but he's not going to tell you that.

"Just some loose change."

Yellow sinks his hand and emerges with about a pound-fifty in coinage.

The bright fifty pound note acts like a carrot.

"Go on, then, we'll call it evens," the idiot vendor says, snatching the fifty, and allowing the coins to drop into his open palm.

That's more than paid for his pitch.

Click-click go the catches on the cases, and he's up and away, wincing at the weight of his treasure, as his back almost straightens.

He laughs at me, as I step back to let him out.

I'd cherish those records. So much pleasure would have been mine, cleaning and playing them all, and looking each one up in the books I have, before filing them away in my collection.

And I know Yellow Hat will have them listed for sale on the internet before I can even drive back to Oakburn.

I smile and nod in the face of his laughter. It's my humble way of letting him know that the better man won.

"Mug," he sneers as he passes by, the album case catching his shin.

A blush reddens and scorches my face. I've always been a blusher.

"I wish he'd break a leg or something," I mutter to myself.

There's no point in looking at the stalls Yellow Hat's covered, so I trudge back towards the car.

Pulling out of the field, I see him struggling with his load. He parked half a mile away to save on the fifty pence parking fee.

A car indicates, Yellow Hat crossing the road in its wake.

The handle breaks off the larger of the cases. It settles stubbornly on the asphalt.

He stoops, attempting to enfold it in his free arm, but can't manage it.

Instead, he places the singles on top of the albums, and bends his spine so he can tip them towards him and get his fingers beneath the corners.

As he stands, a Reliant Robin slams into him.

I see his leg break sickeningly, the cases flopping forward to the other side of the road.

A speeding delivery truck splits them open, scattering the contents.

Records go spinning down the road at far more than the recommended revolutions per minute.

A toot of a horn encourages me on my way, as I turn left and pick up the Oakburn Road towards home.

And I wonder if I have some kind of special power.

2.

They named me Anthony, my parents. With a soft 'th'.

It was a self-appreciating nod to my mother, Anthea.

Anthony Nice, only son of Roger and Anthea Nice. Her maiden name was Pleasant. No, it really was. Nice and Pleasant.

I chuckle at that, just as I tend to chuckle at everything.

Not everything. I wouldn't chuckle at, say, Yellow Hat getting run over by a Reliant Robin.

We're in the town, playing happy families. This is my lot. My wife, Carol, and daughter, Grace. Nice Christmassy names.

Carol's teeth aren't naturally as white and pure as they appear. She goes off somewhere every few weeks to have them buffed and bleached, or something.

On reflection, that might be her arsehole. I forget which is which sometimes.

Grace's teeth are naturally that white and straight, because she's a fifteen year-old, and therefore born to a generation where dental perfection is more important than, well, education.

This is our occasional thing, eating scrambled eggs on toast together in a cafe, all smiles and best bib and tucker.

Or, in my case, a Bob Marley t-shirt.

The eggs are sprinkled with green shavings. I don't know what they are, or what they add to the meal, beyond cosmetic enhancement.

We eat in silence, the only noise being the scrape of cutlery on plates, as we all attempt to remove as many of the green shavings as we can.

"I'll take a stroll up the road," I inform my family once we've finished, and they prepare to head off to a shop with a single seat outside a changing room cubicle.

The seat is nearly always taken, occupied by a man like me, with a face that says, 'how much fucking longer?'

"Righty-o!" Carol trills.

"Shall we meet in the Red Lion?" I propose, to save me having to return and stand around pretending not to look at women I'm not related to.

"Can do. Give us an hour or so!"

Works for me.

With at least two hours to kill, I head off up the hill to the shit part of town where the interesting shops are.

About six minutes is how long it takes to walk from one end of Oakburn town centre to the other.

It takes me longer, as I pop my head in the seven charity shops I pass, to see if any sad bastard has donated vinyl to a worthwhile cause. They haven't.

Well, they have, but only after exhausting every other possible method of off-loading it.

It wasn't always like this. A few years back, you could make some really good scores by exploiting the ignorance of elderly women working for charitable organisations.

Still, I always have a quick look when I'm in town.

My spirit and lust for life are almost destroyed completely when, on leaving empty-handed, I spot a t-shirt hanging in the window. It's the same Bob Marley design as I wear. Two pounds fifty.

'There Was A Time' is the name of the only surviving record shop in Oakburn. It makes for a curious acronym.

It's not really a record shop. It's an Emporium. In the old days, it would have been called an Indoor Market.

Actually, in the olden days it would have been called The Cinema, because that was what it was.

It was gutted in the early-nineties, closed down by a much more convenient multi-screen facility twenty miles away at Jemford Bridge Retail Park.

I had my first ever date here in the 'T.W.A.T.', back when it was called 'The Palace'.

We were twelve, myself and Lucy. We'd met at school, because where the fucking hell else was I likely to meet a girl?

It was at the school disco, held every last Friday of the month during term time. I asked her to dance...

That's bollocks.

I stood leaning against a wall at the back of the hall nursing a flat fizzy drink and a semi-erection.

Her friend came over. She terrified me. It was the time of night when the smoochies were being spun, and I didn't fancy getting tangled up in that.

"My friend wants to dance with you," she growled.

"Right," I replied, "and who's your friend?"

"Lucy."

"Okay."

Lucy wasn't too bad. Fucking hell!

So we danced, me with my hands on her hip bones. She draped her arms around my neck. My semi had gone fully-detached.

Captain And Tennille's 'Do That To Me One More Time' screeched to a halt, and Lucy Michelle Patterson stuck her tongue in my mouth.

I nearly gagged as I swallowed my bit of bubblegum. It was well known at our school that you should never swallow bubblegum. If you do, it blocks up your bottom, and you'll die horribly.

"Do you want to go out with me?" I asked, as we stood outside the church hall waiting for her dad to pick her up.

"Okay. Where are we going?"

That confused me. I'd meant it in the broader sense of being together as boyfriend-girlfriend until we became husband-wife.

I sensed she was thinking more short-term.

"Pictures?" I suggested.

"Okay. When?"

"Erm, next Saturday. I'll let you know the time."

"See you then, then!" she said.

"See you then, then."

Lucy, I learned as we walked down the town eight days later, had been to the pictures on a date before. It was with a boy called Gary Nicholson. He was in the year above us, and had left for secondary education the year prior.

He asked her if she fancied a Kola Cube. She did.

When she put her hand in the paper bag he offered, he'd cut a hole in the bottom and inserted his penis.

I kept my Strawberry Bon Bons to myself that afternoon.

Despite sitting in front of the screen for about two and a half hours, I barely saw anything, and have no recollection of what was playing.

We held hands. I remember that. And in the dark, I kept looking sideways at her, so I could study and memorise her lit up profile.

That was our only date. By the Monday after Easter she was back with Gary Nicholson.

Gary, I was informed, was 'going to have me.'

I've never liked Kola Cubes since that day. Besides, they're bad for your teeth.

As was Gary Nicholson.

Ms Walsh was evil. She was the English teacher at middle school. For some reason, she took a disliking to me. I have no idea why.

That same weekend I took Lucy Michelle Patterson to the pictures, I neglected to do my homework. It was a book review, and it was due on the Monday morning, first thing after assembly.

A dreadful feeling churned within me as we mimed 'All Things Bright And Beautiful'.

Ms Walsh was witchlike in appearance, with her dank dark hair and hooked nose. Just looking at her gave me the willies.

I frequently mistook the chalk on the blackboard for her voice, and vice versa. And she'd stab-stab-stab that chalk in violent flourishes. There was no doubt that, in her mind, she was stabbing children in their eyes with a compass.

My face blushed with worry and fear, as we sat cross-legged on the floor.

"I wish her car would break down!" I chanted over and over in my mind.

Ms Walsh didn't show up for class that day.

A special assembly was called before we went home. The headmaster informed us all that Ms Walsh had been in an accident on her way to school that morning.

Her car had broken down as she'd pulled on to the dual-carriageway from Jemford, and a vehicle had smashed into her.

She had some broken bones, but was expected to make a full recovery.

Yes, I've definitely always had my special power, now I think back on it. There have been a few instances of my talent running through my life.

I like to think there are only a few because I'm a nice person. I match my name. Nice by name, nice by nature.

My mother was the same. I certainly got her personality ahead of my father's.

After all, if my father had the talent, there would be a lot more dead and injured lying around. Or sat in their cars at junctions, or crashed at the sides of roads. Or dropping down in the queue in shops. To be honest, every single neighbour we ever had would have come to a sticky end, had my dad had any kind of ability to will an outcome.

The television would struggle to find presenters, especially for the weather reports, and woe betide anyone holidaying in the same vicinity as we did on occasion.

I wouldn't have any relatives.

No, the more I think about it, my father never had the gift.

3.

Time was, there were several record shops in Oakburn. At least, there were several shops that sold records, if not exclusively.

In my youth, there was a Boots, a Woolies, and a great little shop at the bottom of town called Wesley's.

Those establishments sold new records. In addition, there were a number of places selling second-hand vinyl. They really took off after CDs came along.

If there was a utopian time for buying used records, it was the decade 89-99. Pre-internet, post-CD, to put it in historical chronological context.

They've all gone now. The last 'specialist record shop' shut down in 2012. Rate hikes did for it. It's a coffee shop now, with outdoor seating.

The irony is, they have framed album sleeves hanging on the walls, but play streamed music that never appeared on the format.

Thus, I'm left with this place.

"Alright, mate?" the owner greets me.

"Alright?"

"New stuff in," he says. He always says that.

It doesn't matter if I come every week, or stay away for six months, it's the same shit.

The record section is at the rear of the space, where the light is too inadequate to see if the records are any good or not. I think it might be deliberate.

I polish my glasses on my Bob Marley t-shirt, but it doesn't help.

A higgledy-piggledy mess confronts me, as plastic tubs accommodate crammed rows of vinyl albums that bowl as a result of the crates being the wrong spec.

The majority of the tubs are labelled with 'New In!' They fucking aren't.

Well, if they are, then they keep buying the same records over and over again, and putting them in the exact same locations as the old ones.

A lot of the containers are on the floor. I squat without letting my knee touch the carpet. It leaves a sticky mark if you do, and it can make it difficult getting back up again if you stay like that too long and allow the bonding process to kick in.

I think it might be a ploy to stop people leaving.

I also think it might have been present since I was here with Lucy.

It's a comfort, in a way, that notion.

More disturbing is how many albums are by Mantovani.

Prices appear random, and are indicated by high-tack stickers applied directly to the album sleeves. I've tried everything from washing-up liquid to lighter fuel, and the buggers won't come off clean. Well, not unless you set fire to the lighter fuel.

I once dared to suggest to the owner, Rick, that he might want to use different stickers.

He shook his head in a grief-stricken manner, drew in his lips till they disappeared, before informing me, "tried it. People switch 'em. Once, a few years back, I knew I'd priced a Tom Jones album at five quid. This bloke brought it up to the counter. You won't believe what he'd done. Go on, have a guess what he did."

"Switched the sticker?"

"Yes," he confirmed, a little taken aback, as he eyed me suspiciously. "He'd put a three on it. You remember that Dor?" he asked his wife. I presumed she was his wife, as I couldn't imagine anyone picking her as a mistress. Her name suited her, as she looked like a door.

Whatever she was, she nodded and made a face as if someone had gobbed in her soup.

I've been coming here regularly for about six years. Since they opened. I usually end up buying something. Partly because I feel sorry for them, and want them to stay in business so I have somewhere to go. And, yes, because I have an addiction problem.

After ten minutes or so, which is ample time to establish there actually is nothing new in the boxes, I approach the counter with a beaten up copy of 'The Bobby Vee Singles Album' I didn't bother with last time I was here.

The price sticker informs me it's five pounds, and always will.

It wouldn't be worth that if it was still sealed and there were two of them.

"What are those?" I ask, pointing at a box of decent looking records behind the counter.

"Those are the on-liners, aren't they Dor?"

She wordlessly confirms that they are.

He picks up the narrative. "Dor takes care of them, the web stuff. They go on the on-line auctions, where the real money is. Too good for the shop, and the customers we get in here."

I decide to let it go.

"Well, could I take a look?"

It's as if I've suggested something never before touted in the history of the world.

Rick says, "but what if we get a bid?"

"Well, you just remove it. It'll spare you having to pack and post, and you'll save on the listing fee."

"Is it possible, Dor?"

She nods that it might well be achievable.

Decision reached, Dor bends to pick up the box from the floor behind the counter. As she lifts it, she emits the loudest fart I've ever heard in my life.

And I've produced some absolute corkers in my time.

The sliding glass door on the cabinet behind her actually vibrates. I'm unsure whether it's down to wind blast or sympathetic sound frequency.

Either way, the event is completely ignored by Rick and Dor.

The records are clean, housed in plastic protective sleeves, and, crucially, are sticker free.

Beatles and Stones. U2 and Kate Bush and Led Zep. It's as if they have a list of the top twenty most collectible artists, and siphon those from the general crap that comes in the shop.

Canny Dor, I sense, also keeps her beady eye on the obituaries. The recently deceased are very prevalent.

That allows me to pull free a Fall album I don't have from the late-nineties, and a couple of Scott Walker originals.

Most thrilling and unexpected, though, is an album by The Pretenders. It's a live album, on BBC Transcription Services, and is housed in a plain sleeve with four sheets of paper tucked inside.

The track-listing reveals 'I Go To Sleep' opens side two.

I also go for a copy of Captain And Tennille's 'Make Your Move', sentimental sod that I am.

"How much?"

"Starting bid is a tenner," Rick reports, looking to Dor for confirmation.

"Well, I'll give you that."

"But what's the ending bid? That's the question!"

"When are they due to end?"

"The auctions?"

"Yes."

"Monday. We always time them for a Monday, because people are back at work, and have more time on their hands to look at the internet. Besides, they're usually a bit depressed after the weekend."

"Have you got any bids?"

Dor shakes her head.

She snatches the Captain And Tennille album from me suddenly.

For the first time in all the times, she speaks. "NM, WLP, SEW, DNAP."

Okay, they're not proper words, but I'm impressed.

"What?"

Rick elucidates. "Near mint, white label promo, slight edge warp, does not affect play."

"Okay, good to know. How about forty for The Pretenders, twenty each for those three, a tenner for that, and a fiver for the Bobby Vee?"

"Ooof, well, I think at auction..."

"Cash," I add.

"Done."

I probably have been.

Fifteen minutes later, Rick manages to tot up the numbers correctly, and write out a receipt I didn't want or need.

I emerge from the gloom a hundred and fifteen quid lighter.

Of course, as I do, it's raining. Still, it'll wash the filth off my fingertips, I think, as I make my way to the Red Lion.

4.

With at least another hour to while away, I sit with a pint of Jemford Best Bitter and look through my purchases.

To be fair, they don't look too bad. Scott '2' and '3' need a clean, and there's a split along the bottom edge of the cover of '2'. The Fall album is minty, but, I fear, may be a recent reissue. The Bobby Vee is a waste of time, and the Captain And Tennille induces buyer's remorse.

Still, playing them will give me something to do when I get home.

As a rule, I don't like looking up the values of records on the internet. It tends to reveal a price that makes me look like an imbecile for paying that much. Besides which, condition is everything, and I haven't heard them yet.

I do it, though, because the man at the next table is trying to catch my eye, and I need a reason to pretend I haven't noticed him.

I think I might have done well on the Scott Walkers and The Pretenders.

Unfortunately, a woman entering forces me to check if it's Carol. Seeing how he sits between me and the door, he's on me like a fucking limpet.

"Records," he says, and points at my bag.

"Yeah," I smile, and try to go back to my research.

He's in his late-sixties, I guess, and feels the need to wear a tan tweed jacket with brown elbow patches to nip to the pub on a weekend lunchtime.

He won't be here on weekdays. It's the same with his bit of shopping, the bag containing which sits next to him on the seat.

The sad truth of it is, he could do his shopping on the quiet days of the week, just as he could sit and enjoy a pint at those un-busy times.

But, no. He does it when the working people have no choice but to do theirs. It's all so he can have some human interaction.

The poor bugger.

They always single me out, though, the desperately needy.

"Of course, you're too young to remember," he says. It's a teaser; a maggot wriggling on a hook.

I can see the fucking sharp metal barb...

"Oh, what's that?" I bite, tucking my phone in my pocket.

"Proper music - not like all this rubbish nowadays, no, no, no - proper tunes, is what I'm talking about. See, I lived through the fifties, and we had rock'n'roll, as it was known at the time, though that was more from over there, you know? The other side of the pond. Over here, we had skiffle. Now, I bet you've never heard of that. Do you know the one I liked as a youngster?"

"No."

Fuck me, he's going to sing.

"A-little white bull," he begins, before following it up with "a-little white bull, a-little white bull... I can't remember the rest."

"That good, eh?"

"Oh, it was, back in those days when we had proper songs - songs that you could sing to - songs that remained in the memory for more than half a tick. Bet you don't know who did that, do you?"

"Tommy S..." I begin.

"Ohhh, hang on, give me a second, I know this."

"Tommy S..."

"Phurrr, I can picture his face! Blonde haired fella, with a cheeky grin! Billy-something? No, no, no. Tommy! Tommy Steele! See, now, bet you've never heard of him, have you?"

"No," I reply, because it seems like the simplest option.

"Bigger than Elvis, he was. Over here, anyway. There was him, and Donnie Lonegan, and loads of others. Then The Beatles came along! Well, they changed everything, they did - mixed things right up - altered the course of musical history. Again, you see, proper songs. You know which one of theirs I always liked?"

Oh fuck, he's going to fucking sing again...

I shake my head. It's going to be one of the shit ones.

Sure enough, he goes with "a-will you still need me, a-will you still feed me, a-when I'm sixty-four, ba-bum-dum!"

He even does a little hand-dance at the finale after patting his thighs in time.

My face blushes as a couple of blokes sitting at the bar turn to look at us. They might think we're together.

"Nuts?" he says.

"Yes," I confirm.

"Here you are then," he adds, and when I look he's holding out a bag of actual salted peanuts.

"Oh, no thanks, I've eaten. Anyway, I'd better go and see if I can find my wife and daughter."

"Yes, yes, yes, on you go! Don't keep a lady waiting. Here, I'll tell you one thing, though, before you go..."

I sit back down.

He pours the bag of nuts into his mouth. His lengthy mastications are both audible and visible. Even when I close my fucking eyes.

"You sure you won't have some?" he offers again, bits of nut flying at me like shrapnel.

"Absolutely certain," I reply, opening my mouth to the minimum.

Eventually, he says, "Engelbert Humperdinck!"

Oh fuck no, he's going to do 'Release Me'!

I wish someone would release me.

"A-please release meeee, a-let me goooooooo..."

I stare down at the floor, my face bright red with embarrassment.

'I wish he'd choke on a bloody nut,' I think to myself.

'For I don't love you...'

Hang on, that's me singing the next line in my head.

I look up and turn my face towards him.

He's bright scarlet, his mouth murderously wide. Nutty spittle drips off his protruding tongue, as his hand claws at his throat.

He gets quite into his singing.

Oh, fucking hell, he's choking!

I'm up, behind him, raising him from his seat by his elbow patches.

I can do this. I was shown how on a First Aider At Work course I attended twenty-odd years ago.

My right hand balls into a fist, my thumb poking out the side towards him. My left wraps over it

Finding the spot at the bottom of his sternum, I jerk my hand into him, performing a maneuver I can't remember the name of.

Nothing. Repeat.

Only with more force, so he almost knees himself in the face.

A partially processed nut ball flies out of his mouth and lands on the Captain And Tennille album.

He breathes again!

Applause erupts in the Red Lion.

I sit with him as he recovers. He says something, but I can't hear him, his voice being a little hoarse.

I lean in, his nutty breath on my face.

"You stopped me from dying - saved my life - kept me afloat," he croaks.

"Oh, I'm not sure about that. You'd probably have been okay."

"I wish you hadn't."

"Sorry?"

"Now I have to go home to that empty bloody house, and eat my tinned pie," he adds, tapping the shopping bag by his side metallically.

I don't know what to say.

"That's what I was going to tell you. She loved Engelbert, did my wife, Angela. First show we ever went to together that was, to see Engelbert. Late-sixties - before your time.

"Well, I proposed not long after that night - popped the question - asked her to be my wife. And she accepted!

"Engelbert played at our wedding. Well, not Engelbert in person. His record, I mean. The first dance - bride and groom - the happy couple!

"Not 'Release Me'. It was 'Winter World Of Love', being a bit more romantic - a bit more befitting of the occasion. Plus, the wedding was in the winter. November, to be precise.

"My love," he sings, "the days are colder...

"Proper song, that was. Not like the rubbish you hear on the radio nowadays."

"Probably best not to try singing just at the moment," I suggest.

He nods and clears his throat.

I pluck up courage, and ask, "did you really want to die?"

"Makes no odds to me. If I can't be with her on this earth..." he trails off.

"I'm sorry," I tell him.

"Hey, I thought you were supposed to meet your wife?" he remembers.

"Ah, she'll find me. Or ring me on my phone. Oh," I say, looking up, "talk of the devil."

Carol bustles in clutching a tiny bag the size of a greeting card. An entire outfit will be in that bag.

"Do you want a drink?" I offer.

"No time. Grace needs to get back home."

I drain my pint, stand and extend my arm to the man whose life I might have saved.

Being old school, he rises before taking my hand in his.

"George," he says.

"Anthony."

"Well, I'm in here regular, so perhaps we'll meet again."

Don't you fucking dare sing it!

A valuable lesson is learnt, I consider, as we walk to the car park. I need to be a lot more careful about how I use my special power.

5.

"Why were you talking to George?" Carol asks as I feed my entire pound coin collection into the parking meter.

"We just got chatting," I fib.

I see no sense in telling her what took place, just as I see no sense in telling my family anything about my life.

Finally, with me about a kilo lighter, the machine spits my ticket out with the same force as George spat those nuts out.

Heimlich Maneuver, I suddenly remember.

"What have you got in your bag?" Carol asks next.

"Oh, I managed to get some records from..."

"More bloody records! How many records does a person need?"

"What did you get?" I ask rather than answer her question.

"A little summer dress in the sale, just like the one I got a few weeks back. But half the price. And a new bikini."

"And they're both in that bag?"

"Yes."

"Bikini? Are we going on holiday?"

"How many times? We've been invited over to Kelvin and Sharelle's for a pool party!"

Oh, fucking hell.

"When is it?"

"When the weather's conducive."

I hope it's a shit summer.

We're in the car before I pluck up the courage to ask Grace if she got anything good.

"No," is her answer. It's quite chatty for us.

"Could you move that large bag so I can see out the back window, Gracie?"

She doesn't do anything.

"Could you move that large bag so I can see out the back window, Grace?"

"Which one?"

"The large one that's blocking my view out the back window."

She does it with a huff, and activates her phone. I'll have to listen to the fucking clicking for the duration of the drive. Please let the traffic be light. I've known it take twenty minutes to cover the couple of miles. What, with the roadworks just by the bridge that carries the cut.

Is it a viaduct or an aqueduct?

I think it's an aqueduct if it carries water over something else. I think.

Then again, being a single arch, as opposed to many in sequence, it may just be a bridge.

"It's her I feel sorry for," Carol says, and I rewind through everything said that day to find context. Did I miss something on the radio?

Drawing a blank, I ask, "who?"

"George's wife! Angela!"

"Because she died?"

"She's not dead!"

"I think she is."

"Well, she wasn't dead on Thursday when I saw her down the dance class! How she put up with him for all those years, I do not know. Nearly fifty years of it."

"Of what?"

"Of him!"

"What did he do?" I ask, and have flashes of domestic violence and kinky sex, which I quickly shake away.

"Nothing. That was the point. Well, nothing apart from his model trains and homemade dandelion wine. It's no life for a woman, that."

"No," I agree. I'd probably go elderberry myself. You see loads of them along the canal.

"At least you only have your daft records."

"At least there's that," I mumble very quietly.

I didn't live up to Carol's expectations. That's the truth of it. I thought I had ambition, but, it transpired, I didn't. What I lack, Carol more than makes up for on our behalf.

We were okay for the first few years of being together. Then she reconnected with her old school friends on the internet, and it changed her.

I honestly believe I haven't changed a bit during our years of marriage. That, it turns out, is the problem.

Apparently, I was supposed to change at the precise same speed, and along the exact same lines, as Carol did.

Worse than that, I was supposed to be the one to achieve all that Carol decided one day she aspired to.

Frankly, I couldn't be arsed.

Not that I used that precise expression to Carol when we 'discussed' our life and the direction it wasn't heading. It all led to me applying for a promotion at work.

It was all a game, and they knew who was getting the promotion long before I sat in the interview.

My lack of personnel managerial experience was the official line given for rejection. I blushed deeply and gave up any hope of Carol respecting me ever again.

I remember thinking, 'I wish you'd give the job to Lazy Susan, and you'll soon see you should have given it to me.'

And lo and behold, that was what they did!

I suppose it was another example of my special power, as I remained a Client Services Manager, rather than rise to the lofty heights of Senior Client Services Manager.

Lazy Susan, being fucking bone idle, passed all of her additional responsibilities on to me, because I was suddenly her subordinate.

I made a conscious choice not to do them, and she was too fucking lazy to check if I had.

Round and round, Lazy Susan went.

Until she went off on maternity leave, whereat I was given her responsibilities anyway. Albeit on a temporary basis, and for a lot less money than I would have received had I got the fucking promotion in the first fucking place.

Still, I did them without complaint (or job title), because what on earth would I do if I didn't?

I wasn't always like this. I was happy once. It was a long time ago. It was when I was with Juliet.

How far I didn't get. How little I achieved. How defeated I am.

"What happened with Angela and George?" I ask my eternally disappointed wife.

"He was forced to retire at sixty-five. It meant he was at home all day. She lasted nearly two years, the poor woman, before walking out on him."

"Another man?"

"Typical male thought! No, she simply worked out that being alone was better than being with a man like him."

The conversation dies at that. Carol stares off out the side window at men in shorts and hard-hats, with no t-shirts beneath their hi-vis vests.

I stare ahead at the temporary traffic light, and the 'bridge' just beyond.

A barge passes over the road, its black roof showing over the blue brick structure. The heads of a man and woman become visible as the rear of the vessel crawls into view.

Good grief, look at their miserable faces, wrapped up against the drizzle, as they chug through life and its series of locks.

I went on a barging holiday in 1983. It was the final holiday I had with my parents. We never ventured abroad. I wasn't bothered. I can't imagine Venice being any better than the Oxford Canal.

Mind you, the Oxford Canal is about the same as the Brake Canal, so we could have just stayed here in Brakeshire.

But we didn't! We ventured forth, to Oxford, before casting off and sailing north into uncharted waters. Or Banbury.

At Banbury, we parked up and visited a coffee factory. I remember the smell.

The sedate pace, punctuated by lock encounters, soon became quite rhythmic. My father handled most of the... driving, is it? But I did get to have a go when he needed the toilet.

Instructions were issued using nautical terminology, most of which I seem to have forgotten.

We picked up the Grand Union Canal at some point, and headed west to our destination - Warwick.

It was near there where I met Juliet.

The primary reason I met her was because we found the prospect of twenty-one locks in a two mile stretch too daunting. Ergo, we parked up and decided the time was right for a break of two days, before turning round and heading back to Oxford.

I was fifteen years of age, and quiet. Quieter than I am now, I mean. My blushing and shyness always held me in check. A lack of confidence, I suppose.

My dad was an angry man. That, I reason, stemmed from his lack of self-confidence, but manifested itself in that way. My mum shared the cause, but the symptoms were a nervous conservatism and a lack of adventurousness.

It explains why we never went abroad. Overseas was out of their comfort zone, where things were different, and food didn't taste the same. Language was strange and alien, and different rules were in play.

No. Better the devil you know.

Still, that holiday haunts me. Partly because dad was okay. He really tried. There was no shouting or rude gestures at another barge that was in his way. He waved and chatted with people in a manner I'd never witnessed him do before.

Mum was laissez-faire, and seemed quietly content. We ate out more than we ate in, at pubs as they happened along. The rigid planning of home life was cast off from the moment we weighed anchor and cast off in Oxford.

Mostly, though, that holiday haunts me because of Juliet.

"Changed," Carol says.

"Yes, people do," I concur.

"The lights have changed!"

"Oh, right." A blast of a horn reinforces the fact.

I think of Juliet as I pull away, and drive under the canal, the narrowboat having long since passed on.

That ship has sailed.

6.

I sit alone in my record room. I call it a record room, but it's really a dining room that we no longer dine in.

As suspected, the Bobby Vee was a waste of time and money, but the others are in surprisingly good condition.

Dor was correct. The slight edge warp did not affect play on the Captain And Tennille.

And the nutty stain came off okay.

The Pretenders is the pièce de résistance, though. That alone is worth around what I paid in total. Not that I'll ever sell it.

Once played and filed, I pick through the Ikea shelving to find Talk Talk and Human League.

They were two of the albums I listened to, having copied them to cassette, during that barge trip on the Oxford and Grand Union canals.

The tonearm is lowered manually because the mechanism can't find the run-in groove as well as I can. Besides, it's a bit clunky.

With headphones in place to minimise my impact in my home, I sink in my chair as the record begins.

Juliet.

I noticed her right from the off, my eye drawn to her trendily cut fair hair. She looked like she could have been in the Human League.

She was working as a waitress in the public house her aunt and uncle owned, and I watched her as she carried two servings of Scampi In A Basket.

I ordered Scampi In A Basket in the hope that she would deliver mine, affording me a close-up. She didn't. The delivery system wasn't based on type of food.

In a way, it was a blessing. It allowed her to serve grub to the table next to ours, resulting in me being able to look at her without being obvious about it, and, moreover, without blushing.

Was the summer of 1983 as perfect as I recall it, weather-wise? Blue skies sat over and enlightened every day of that barge trip, with any rain there was arriving in short bursts and well-timed for overnight. It was just sufficient to keep everything green and vibrant and fresh as a daisy.

She wore a short washed-out denim skirt, her smooth tanned legs ending at a pair of white strappy flat shoes. Her backside was roundly applesque - her figure curvaceously slim. Her top half was covered by a clingy black t-shirt with cropped sleeves and little slits at the fabric joints on either side.

Most beguiling of all, though, was her face. I'd never seen anyone so perfectly prepossessing.

My god, she was beautiful. And I knew, sat there with mum and dad in the pub garden - dad trapping wasps under an upturned pint glass - she was well out of my league.

Mine was a human league. She belonged with the gods, goddesses and other immortals.

Immortal she was, because she has lived on in me for the intervening years, and always shall.

It's why I like records. They remain the same. This Human League album I bought in 1982 is just as it was, save for a few crackles where the stylus connected so many times.

Dare.

I didn't dare.

Oh, I had my long swept-over fringe, as was the style of the time, but I really only had that to hide behind. A simple drop of my chin pulled that curtain over the world.

And I was skinny, always covering my arms with long-sleeved collarless shirts to hide their thinness. As a result, they never got tanned.

"Fancy a walk along the towpath, Anthony?" my father suggested, in his disarmingly agreeable temporary new persona.

"No, I think I'll sit and finish my drink."

"Suit yourself. We'll see you in a bit."

And off they went, leaving me with a sense that they were glad I'd declined.

I watched them walk away, my parents. Not arm in arm or hand in hand, but amiably enough as they chatted about something or other I'd never get to hear. My mum laughed before shaking her head. My dad shrugged and smiled.

"Want another drink?" a voice asked.

Turning, I was confronted by her; the goddess.

Oh, and I knew I was blushing horrendously, but the more I tried not to, so the worse it got.

"You look hot," she added.

"I am a bit."

"Do you want a drink? Cool you down."

"Erm, please."

"What is it?"

It was a Shandy Bass. There was no way I was going to admit to it.

"Pint of bitter," I said instead, copying my dad's beverage preference.

She held out her hand, so I took it.

What was I thinking? She was holding it out for the payment. What a twat!

I'd been fantasising, sat there with my Walkman playing and my earphones on.

Don't you want me, baby?

As my parents walked away along the towpath, I'd cast the goddess and I in their places. In my head it was real.

Just that would have been enough, I told myself. Just to walk beside her.

She hadn't pulled her hand away...

"Do you want a drink?" I dared to ask her.

"Love one. My shift's just about to finish, and I could murder a cold drink."

"What'll you have?"

"Half a lager and lime."

She still hadn't withdrawn her hand...

I pulled a fiver out of my jeans pocket with my free hand. It was awkward, because my money was on the other side, but I wasn't fucking letting go of her.

"Will you get served?" I asked her.

"As long as they think it's for someone else!" she smiled.

"What's your name?"

"Juliet. You?"

"Ant."

If school friends called at the house and asked for me by that shortened monicker, my father would close the door on them. It had to be Anthony. Replete with the soft 'th'.

I wasn't a Tony. Tony was too butch for me; too good-at-sport and popular. Nor was I a Tone. That was cool and trendy. So I went with Ant.

Antman, I'd sometimes imagine. Like Spiderman or Batman, but bitten by an ant. A red ant, like the ones that hung around the bricks on the low wall at the front of our house. That was why I blushed.

"Shall I get the drinks, then?" she asked me, as she took the note I proffered.

"Yes."

"You'll have to let go of my hand."

"Of course."

I let go, my guts churning at the loss of contact.

"I'll bring it with me when I come back," she smiled.

"Sorry?"

"My hand," she explained.

I chuckled in my nervous way, and probably blushed again. I watched her walk away, her backside seeming to wink at me as she did. I imagined the dimples in those cheeks, matching the one to the left of her lips.

She stopped to talk to another girl, looked back at me and smiled, before they both disappeared inside.

'Dare' finished, and a compilation of singles began to play, inserted to fill up the sixty minute cassette.

I was three tracks in when it dawned on me that she wasn't coming back.

She had my five pounds, too.

7.

It was the story of my life. At school they saw through me, the people who prey on such characters: The bullies.

My niceness was seen as weakness. My name something to be ridiculed. My tendency to drift away, and imagine a life preferable to the one I was living, made me an oddball - a dreamer.

They'd ask me what I was thinking about. I couldn't tell them, so I replied, 'nothing.'

And that's what I became - nothing.

How could I tell them that I was dreaming about being Antman, and having special powers?

I had friends, but they were the people like me; the people who didn't really have much of a choice as to who their friends were.

As a result, I'd often find myself cast off when a better offer came along. Even back then, most people wanted to associate with what was popular. And I knew early on, I would never be that.

It makes you shy away, after that happens a few times. Never get too close, because it'll lead to pain and rejection. And the truth is, I was always okay in my own company. My interests were solitary pursuits - music and reading.

They were right to spurn me for that promotion at work. I'm simply not a people person. Leave me to work in isolation and I'll be fine.

I sat at the grey weathered wooden table that day, waiting for Juliet to return. I imagined her looking out of the pub window, peering round a curtain with her friend, laughing at the pathetic drink-less prick waiting for her.

Three wasps explored the inside of a pint glass looking for a way out.

I wondered how long mum and dad would be.

Juliet had been gone for about fifteen minutes. The thought of her watching me from the pub induced a fresher more violent rouge to swamp my face. The mortification.

I wanted to cry with shame.

"I wish she'd just come back," I muttered aloud before rising to leave.

I shrank away with my hands buried deep in my cashless front pockets, forcing my shoulders to hunch forward and my face to hang downcast between them.

Dreamer, you stupid little dreamer...

"Ant!"

...don't tread on an ant, he's done nothing to you.

"Ant!"

I turned, a sound penetrating my headphones.

There she was, carrying two drinks, heading towards me.

Towards me!

"Sorry I took so long! I had to nip up the baker's for bread for tonight, and the rolls weren't ready."

"It's okay," I lied.

"No. No it isn't. You must have thought I'd run off on you."

"Not really," I said, keeping up my pretence of nonchalance.

"Anyway, the good news is, I have tonight off," she announced as we took a table away from the wasps trapped beneath the glass. And away from her aunt and uncle, as we sat side by side close to the water.

"What will you do?" I asked, sipping from my pint.

"What do you want to do?" she replied, almost making me gag on it.

I said it, then. I said the bravest thing I ever said in my life. "I don't care, as long as I'm with you."

And she took my hand once more.

That was it. Just like that, we became boyfriend and girlfriend.

My parents returned at some point, but I didn't notice them until they reached us. I tensed, anticipating the shame that would come from them using my full name - a telling off for drinking a beer.

It didn't happen, any of it.

Rather, my dad asked, "who's this then?"

"Juliet," I replied, before adding, "this is my mum and dad."

"It's lovely to meet you," she purred, all smiles and that dimple.

"You too, Juliet," my mum said, and they touched hands.

Hands off, she's mine!

"Will you be back for tea?" my dad asked. He actually gave me the choice, as if I were an adult.

I looked to Juliet, not wanting to make assumptions.

"It's up to you," was her response.

"We might get something out," I half proposed and half decided.

My dad slipped me a fiver then. Fucking hell! I added it to the change Juliet had given me on her return.

He wanted me absent, I realised. Moreover, he wanted my mum to himself. I'd been there, in the barge, every minute of the time we'd been away. They'd had no opportunity to be alone.

"Your mum and dad seem really cool," Juliet said once they'd walked on along the cut.

"Yes," I agreed, probably sounding a little perplexed.

We finished our drinks, chatting about life and school, and hopes and dreams. We had optimism, despite Thatcher and unemployment and things being a bit shit.

They weren't shit after all, I could see. There was a perfect life out there for me, away from Oakburn and the people who had known and judged me when I was something else.

To escape that place was to begin again - to reinvent and redefine. I could be anything I wanted to be going forward.

I was honest with Juliet, as she snuggled into me, my legs astride the bench we shared, her back to my chest. I told her about my life, as she put her feet up on the bench and further reclined so that I could stroke the exposed wedge of skin where her t-shirt didn't quite meet her skirt.

Goosebumps peppered her as I gently tickled.

"That's nice," she sighed, and rubbed the side of her face against my arm like a cat leaving a scent; marking her territory; establishing ownership.

An indelible scent that I've clung to for every intervening day.

"What's your surname, Ant?" she asked, my cassette playing Talk Talk's 'The Party's Over'.

"Anthony Nice."

"Nice?"

"Yes. My mum's maiden name was Pleasant."

"Really?"

"Really."

"That's brill."

"I've always been a bit embarrassed of it."

"Why?"

"Oh, I don't know. It's not very punk, I suppose. What's your name?"

"Juliet Hutchison. Do you want to be punk?"

"Erm, not really."

"Then don't worry about it. Nice is, well, nice."

I smiled.

"Who was the girl you were talking to?" I asked her.

"My sister."

"Oh."

"What?"

"Nothing. I thought she was a friend of yours."

"She is!"

"You know what I mean," I hastily explained.

"She's a good kid, is Jenny. She's only twelve. Life's not been easy for her."

"Why not?"

"Oh, this and that. My mum dying mostly."

"God, I'm sorry. What of?"

"Cancer."

"When?"

"Four years ago."

"Blimey, you were only eleven. That must have been rough. Did your dad re-marry?"

"No."

I sensed the subject was closed.

Today, today, it's a dream away...

Perhaps it was a dream. All of it.

If I could have described or depicted my ideal girlfriend in terms of looks and personality, it would have been Juliet.

That alone made me half believe I'd invented her. I actually doubted my own sanity. She was too good to be true - too good for me, at least. As a result, I began to think I must have dreamt her up.

Except it was a dream like none I'd had before. It was a real dream.

Was I dead?

Was that heaven?

My patient father and relaxed mother; was it all some ideal I was imagining, and as fast as I could think it, so it came to be?

No. I wouldn't have dreamt of cancer and her mum dying. I wouldn't have done that.

We were alone on that still afternoon, the pub closed till the evening. The cut lay leaden and oily, as the water barely rippled, giving it a certain solidity of form.

I could have walked on it that day. I could have walked on water. A miracle played out.

"Have I died and gone to heaven?" I said aloud.

"Mmmm," she breathed, and lay more heavily against me; more trustingly; knowing I would support her.

"I'll remember this for ever, with you, here, by the cut."

"Why do you call it a cut?" she asked me.

"I don't know. It's what we call a canal in Brakeshire."

I lightly stroked her neck and ear. She turned her face, and we kissed. My fourth ever proper kiss. With a hint of lime. And once we started kissing, we didn't stop until our tongues were tired.

She ghost-muzzled me, just the finest hairs and nerve endings on our faces suggesting contact.

It was the most erotic experience I'd ever enjoyed.

She must have felt the bulge in my jeans pressing into her lower back, but she didn't pull away.

She stretched her legs out, and I glided my hand over her flat stomach, daring to allow my little finger to slip beneath the waistband of her denim skirt.

Again, she didn't discourage me.

My fingers disappeared, the act covered by her t-shirt. Beneath the rim of her underwear they went, her soft hairs tickling my palm.

And then a sopping wetness and warmth in the trough my middle finger slid down, tracing every bump and fold of her.

My first contact with a girl's most intimate parts, as I tried to relate, braille like, that which I touched with what I'd seen in magazines, and once on a video.

It was love. No doubt.

To this very day, thirty-six years on, I maintain that it was love.

I love my mum and dad, despite their faults. I love Carol and Grace, even now, despite what we've all become.

But Juliet...

My secret I can never talk about.

How could I ever tell Carol about her, without admitting that, had we stayed together, I would not have met and married her? I wouldn't have even been looking.

It would make a sham of our life, that confession, and relegate Grace to an almost incidental result of a second best option.

Moreover, how could I ever admit that, if Juliet came calling, I would go to her?

And so I sit with my records, and spend an unhealthy amount of time reminiscing, and imagining how different my life could have been.

It's so tiring, doing that. So false and dishonest. And I'm not a dishonest person. As a result, it's such a burden, carrying the thoughts in my head.

Do others do that?

Are seemingly happy couples, long since wed, sitting every night in front of the television, because it occupies the mind that would otherwise wander to the secrets of their pasts?

Do they lie in bed feigning sleep, all the while mentally reenacting experiences they can't forget?

And does it show in other ways? Is that why Carol has drifted away from me? Is it why Grace doesn't respect me? Do they know, deep down, that I've never been fully committed to this relationship?

No, though. It's they who treat me with disdain; they who exclude me from their lives; they who have moved on, and I who has remained the same.

Well, almost the same, but with a heavy dose of disenchantment.

I remain as I was because of Juliet. By being this person, I can hold on to a bit of her.

We went to her room that evening. The pub was open, her aunt and uncle working - too busy serving holiday-makers to mind what we were up to.

Her sister was absent. It was just the two of us. All of the best times were when it was just the two of us.

We went there so that she could change her clothes, before we headed out for the evening.

She peeled off her t-shirt and skirt, and stripped in front of me. No ceremony - no flirtatiousness. She had no self-consciousness about such things.

As her perfect body revealed itself, I drank in the white patches where her bikini top and shorts had blocked the sun that had touched every other part of her.

I trembled with excitement and anticipation. And nerves.

She was the first girl I'd ever seen completely naked.

But she wasn't a girl. Not in that sense. She was a woman.

My erection was uncomfortable, contained in my jeans and tugging at the restrictive fabric.

I couldn't take my eyes off her.

She saw my discomfort, so came to me.

She knelt on the floor in front of where I sat on the bed. She deftly picked the button on my jeans, and slid the zip down.

Levering me free of the constraints, she explored me with her hand.

She smiled, seemingly happy with my reaction - happy with what she discovered therein.

It was okay!

I knew from school showers that I was somewhere in the middle scale, but one's never entirely sure.

"It's my first time," I told her.

She said nothing as she pushed me down on the bed.

I stared up at the ceiling, waiting for whatever would happen next, too afraid to look down at myself and my skinny chest.

So boyish next to her womanliness.

My jeans slid down my legs, my boxer shorts with them.

It all went away, the self-doubt. It vanished when I felt the warmth of her mouth envelop me.

I groaned rapturously, and dared to look down at her - at myself.

Her eyes were locked on mine.

An explosion boiled inside me, but she knew - she felt it coming, and so stopped.

She smiled knowingly; so in control.

Standing, she knelt over me, my mouth finding her nipples, her mouth, her neck, her ears - anything it could.

And I slid into her, so made-to-measure - so slick and perfect.

She matched my climactic pulses with little thrusts and contractions of her innermost self. It was over so soon, my first time.

No contraception. Not even the rhythm method we'd learnt at school.

What if she got pregnant? I didn't care. I hoped she would. It made no difference, because I was going to spend the rest of my life with Juliet. I believed that, despite only having known her for a few hours.

"I love you," I said to her, because there was no doubt whatsoever that I did.

I still do.

"Mmmm," she cooed, "I think I could fall in love with you, too."

8.

"I wish we could stay longer," I said to my parents, knowing that we couldn't.

It was amazing. My father rang the boat hire people, and got us an extra couple of days. It all added to a sense of unreality surrounding the trip.

All other family holidays I can recall, featured dad counting down the days until he could go home to familiarity and work.

Yet, there he was, in a public phone box, telling his boss he wouldn't be back next Monday after all.

Juliet and I spent every minute we could together. When she helped out in the pub, I waited for her.

Other families came, either by boat or car. I'd sit listening to tapes, watching her serve food and drinks. I'd see the way men and teenage boys like myself would look at her. But she was seemingly oblivious to it.

For those four days we spent together, I willed time to drag. It was the first time in my life that I'd not wanted time to pass more quickly. Whether that be so I could grow up and escape, or reach the school holidays, or get a new comic, or for a lesson to end, or whatever the reason - prior to then, I was always wishing my life away.

We had full sex seven times in those four days. Other lesser activities sustained us between those ultimate comings-together.

The hunger I had for her was terrifying. I hardly ate. I barely spoke to mum and dad, because Juliet was the only person on earth I wanted to talk to, and the only person I cared to listen to.

Yes, it was infatuation and lust, I'm fully aware of the fact. But it was more than merely that.

I taped tracks off the radio for us. For her, really, as they were the songs she liked. H2O 'I Dream To Sleep', Heaven 17 'Come Live With Me', Echo & The Bunnymen 'Never Stop', Creatures 'Right Now', Lotus Eaters 'First Picture Of You'. And mostly, on repeat, New Order 'Temptation', twelve inch version.

If there is one song above all others that I associate with that trip, it is 'Temptation'.

I really had never met anyone like her before.

Any one of those songs, though, conjures her up. Not simply a vision in my brain. But a real sense of her - her smell and feel and taste; her voice and touch and body.

Fucking hell, it still hurts...

We had sex in a field, screened by long stalks of seeded grass, a square flat patch created by the blanket we lay on. From a field away, the sound of a shovel in an allotment reached us on the breeze.

One of the seven occasions occurred in the coolness of the pub cellar, a shaft of light streaming in through a narrow window at pavement level.

Anybody passing could have stooped and looked in, but we didn't care. There was an added thrill from the danger tied to the risk of discovery.

We did it standing up, with me behind her. A 'knee-trembler' was how she described it. We couldn't get enough of one another.

She was a few months older than I, but in the same school year. Yet she seemed so much more wise and experienced.

I asked her, even though I knew the answer would hurt me. "How many other people have you had sex with?"

"Two," she told me as we strolled along the towpath, our arms wrapped around one another, thumbs hooked through belt loops on jeans.

"Who were they?"

"A boy I went out with on a date."

"What happened to you and him?"

"It was a one-off. A mistake, I suppose."

"And the other?"

"That was a mistake too."

"But not a one-off?"

"No. That one went on for a while."

"Is it better with me?" I dared to ask, and stopped walking, allowing her to swing round and take my hands as we faced each other.

"Yes!" she said, and I believed her, as she sank into me and her mouth found mine.

"Marry me!" I implored her.

"We can't get married! We're fifteen!" she giggled.

"Then will you promise to marry me as soon as we can?"

"I promise," she said solemnly, and we laughed as we carried on walking, her hand swinging in mine.

Oh Juliet!

I was her Romeo. Me! Plain, ordinary, boring, nothing me!

She was my perfect fit; my ideal in every sense. She was the piece of me that completed the puzzle and formed a full picture.

I had self-belief. I wanted to live forever, because I couldn't contemplate a day that the universe could exist with me in it, and her not be within touching distance! That would be a waste of energy on a cosmic scale.

I'd discovered the meaning of life - the answer to everything!

I'd look at myself in a mirror - whether it be my face or full naked body - and I could see, in little ways, why she would like and desire me.

She made me like myself!

We were underage, breaking the law, taking no precautions, and we simply didn't care. There were no consequences imaginable that would have stopped us.

Such was the passion between us.

They must have known, my parents. Her aunt and uncle, too. But they'd done it at our age. It had gone on for all time.

Did they trust us to be more responsible than we were being?

They either turned a blind eye, or failed to notice, as they went about their own lives for those consummate and immaculate four days.

As time passed, so things became more desperate between us.

Mum and dad went on a day trip round Warwick castle. I declined. Juliet wasn't working. It was the last of the full days we had before our departure.

We snuck aboard the barge, undressed, and slid into the single bed I'd slept on dreaming of her. She was with me, and still it felt dreamlike.

I was dreaming of her long before I actually met her.

She used her mouth to make me climax, and I saw the wonderful glint in her eyes.

"I love the way you taste," she said, lying alongside me, my scent on her breath. "You taste and smell of cake and vanilla and freshly baked bread and all of my favourite things."

"I can't leave you," I whispered, and cried in front of her, such was the emotion I felt.

I'd never cried in front of anybody but my mum and dad before.

"I want to die!" she said.

"Why? Why would you want to die?" I pleaded, cradling her face softly in my open hand.

"Because nothing will be like this ever again. Nothing can be this good and perfect. So, I choose to end it now and preserve this moment."

"I couldn't live without you."

"Then we'll both have to die," she said, and the tears cascaded from her green eyes.

"Why can't we just be together!" I almost wailed.

"Because we won't be allowed."

"Why not?"

"Because we're too young."

"I'll wait for you," I told her, "I'll wait for as long as I have to. Marry me, Juliet? Please, say you'll marry me, and we'll work the rest out. Whatever we have to do."

"I will," she said.

I wanted to burst with elation; to explode into liquid and powder, and for her to do the same so that we could merge and become one single entity, as we devoured one another entirely.

I had no clue. I didn't know feelings that strong were possible.

Nobody, I knew in the moment - nobody had ever felt the way we did about each other.

They couldn't have. If they did, I would know. I'd glimpsed and sampled a life unknown to all the people I knew in the world.

Songs captured bits of it, but not all of it. They didn't know.

We had sex that afternoon in the barge once I'd recovered. It wasn't rushed and snatched opportunistically. It was beautiful and patient, my earlier discharge allowing me staying power.

Clamped together, we employed small movements; tight little squeezes and flexes. Building up, and up and up and up.

Getting more and more energetic...

And she climaxed!

I didn't know she could. She didn't know she could.

A shuddering of release, and I felt her warm moisture drench me.

Her eyes were far away - wistful - yet close to me - loving.

With lips pale and drawn in, she whimpered softly with each rhythmic orgasm, lessening until her warmth covered us both, inside and out.

I didn't know it could be like that.

To this day, since Juliet, it's never been like that.

I got in to bed that night, and relished the dampness of the sheet I lay on. Her scent on my pillow. Her body on and in me.

We had an hour the next morning before we set sail.

We sat with our faces touching, forehead to forehead, breathing the same air over and over, back and forth between us, the oxygen content diminishing with each exchange and leaving us both with a sense of suffocation.

Blue Monday. For that was the day we left, and I sailed away from her. At about four nautical miles per hour.

Temptation came, as I seriously considered leaping ashore and running back to her. I would have walked away from my life and everything I knew for her.

If she'd called out for me, I would have gone. Fuck the consequences.

I wish I had!

She cried. She actually cried as she stood waving me off, and it broke my heart.

I felt physically sick.

"You look a bit queasy," my mum observed, "you're as pale as a ghost, Anthony."

I was Anthony again. Not Ant.

"Just needs to find his sea-legs!" dad contributed.

"I can't go," I told my parents. "I can't leave her."

"You'll see her again, if it's meant to be," my dad replied, but I saw and heard the doubt in him.

Juliet and I watched one another until we rounded a curve. And she was gone from my eyes.

The fucking agony!

Songs played all the way south to Oxford - the soundtrack to our halcyon four days of bliss.

I sat hunched on my bed, hugging myself and imagining they were her arms enfolding me.

All of those songs are in this room with me now, filed away alphabetically, lest someone should establish a link and make a connection to that glorious summer. Time was, back in the eighties and nineties, they were a section unto themselves. They were the unlabelled 'Juliet Section'.

The journey south to Oxford, and the drive back to Brakeshire are lost to me. Thoughts of Juliet obliterated anything happening in real time.

I had a photograph of her that she gave me.

Something to remind me.

And a bangle on my wrist that had been hers. They were the only tangible things.

We arrived home after that silent journey. It was as though my parents understood, and so gave me space and time.

And that very same evening, they sat me down and announced that they were splitting up, my mum and dad.

The penny dropped. That was why dad was trying so hard - that was why mum was so phlegmatic and carefree - that was why I was treated like an adult - that was why dad had been desirous of time alone with mum - that was why we went on that holiday.

That was what enabled me to meet and fall in love with Juliet.

It was one last stab at him winning her over, and an opportunity for us all to bid farewell to family life.

It had been enjoyable because all the pressure was off.

To me, it was obvious. Juliet and I had so much love for each other, that there was none left for anyone else in the world. All of the energy pertaining to love was ours. My parents' separation was part of the price.

Dad didn't convince her to stay. A couple of extra days off work and a temporarily affable disposition were never going to be sufficient.

I had no choice other than to remain with dad in Oakburn. Mum moved to Jemford Bridge to live with my grandparents. There was no room there for me, and mum wanted 'time alone to discover herself.'

The reality was, I didn't care. I was fifteen and didn't give a shit.

Besides, if I was with dad, I'd probably be allowed more freedom.

Freedom meant I could potentially see Juliet.

Either way, no matter what, life would never be the same again.

9.

She rang me every day from a pay phone near the pub.

And every day became solely about that call. So much so, that each protracted minute making up the remainder of the day became a waste of time.

Peep-peep-peep-peep-peep-peep-peep - coins dropping in, buying us another couple of minutes of her voice and breaths through a telephone line.

"Give me the number, and I'll ring you back!"

She did. I did. It worked.

We'd set times for me to call, and she'd wait by the phone box.

For three weeks we carried on like that, through to late-August. It wasn't enough. It could never be sufficient.

I barely functioned, lying on my bed in the empty house, staring at her photo, dad at work and mum gone.

As quick as that. No sense in delaying once the decision was made. They were both over forty, and having to start again.

Mum started again, at least, and dad hung around for all of the years since, waiting for her to realise she'd made a mistake and come back to him.

It never happened.

School, though. It was looming ominously.

The sense of urgency was heightened. I had to see Juliet before the summer ended. I had to fucking see her!

I boarded a train - four trains, to be precise - that would take me to her. Or close enough that I could walk the last part of the journey.

I told dad I'd be away for the night - staying at a friend's. He didn't believe me. He knew I didn't have any friends. But he had his own life to worry about.

Change at Tredmouth - more time waiting than actually moving - a rucksack and my Walkman. Always my music; my only constant companion through life.

No real plan beyond seeing Juliet. Hardly any money after the train fare - nowhere to stay. I ate a Dairy Milk from a vending machine. It melted in the heat as I sat on a bench on the platform.

She was set to go home after the Bank Holiday, and home was miles further. Half-term would be our next opportunity. Thereafter, she might be back in Warwick over Christmas and New Year. She didn't know.

It was how they dealt with school holidays since her mum had died. Juliet and Jenny were sent off to stay with their mother's sister and her husband at the pub, while their father earned the bacon.

Willing the train to go faster - wishing my life away once more.

Doubts began to creep in. Would it be the same? When you're fifteen, a few weeks was such a long time.

What if she'd met someone else at the pub? After all, that was how we met...

No!

She'd been down on the phone just two days before, wretched because I wasn't there - dreading the imminent return to her normal life.

"At least while I'm here I can visit all the places we were together," she'd sobbed.

"Marry me, Juliet," I'd asked her again, just as I asked her every time we spoke.

"I will!"

The final leg of my journey, leaving the grey concrete of Coventry and quickly hitting green countryside that felt familiar. Such a thrill to see a cut from the window. Was it our canal?

Draughts of air were drawn in, as I disembarked at Warwick and asked directions to the pub.

It was a long walk - longer than I'd thought. The day was nearly done as evening dropped her lids. Car headlights winked through hedges. It was eight o'clock at night when I arrived, but I wasn't tired. Excitement energised me.

That familiar ground beneath my feet, as I walked along the towpath from the bridge carrying the road I'd tramped along for miles.

It was all okay, I'd made it. I was back where it had taken place, and a comfort came with that. A belief, I suppose - it was embraceable and undeniably real.

The pub came into view, lit up with lights and busy with the Bank Holiday weekend trade.

Barges filled one bank, on the pub side, and I noted the spot where dad had moored, less than a month before when life had been so vastly different for all of us.

I saw her clearing a table, and my stomach kicked viciously.

She saw me walking into the garden. It was a surprise. She didn't know I was coming.

Later, she told me that she couldn't believe her own eyes - that she thought she was imagining things.

Until I said her name.

"Juliet." Just that, softly, but with so much love and relief in it.

Putting down the plates she held, she ran to me.

I dropped my rucksack and caught her, and I held her so tight it must have been painful, but she didn't care.

She cried. Huge tears, like the drops at the beginning of a storm. They ran down her face and on to my shoulder.

Her cheeks and mouth were drenched with them when she found my lips.

She brought me food. Bangers And Mash. The kitchen closed at nine. She'd be done by half past.

"Where are you staying?" she asked.

"I don't know."

"Okay. Let me see what I can do."

She took the keys to her uncle's caravan, and I slipped inside unobserved.

Despite it being in an adjacent field, I could put no lights on for risk of being spotted, so sat at a formica breakfast table with my music for company.

I waited for her. I'd waited so long, another hour was nothing.

She came to me, gently tapping the door.

"How did you get out?" I asked her.

"I climbed out the bathroom window. There's a flat roof there. Jenny will cover for me."

"How long can you stay?"

"How long would you like me to stay?"

"For ever."

We went to bed because we were fifteen and it's what you do. Isn't it? Isn't that what fifteen year-olds do?

Shit, is it what Grace does on her nights away at a friend's? What went on during her skiing trip to The Alps with the school in the winter? Was there an instructor and a log cabin, snow on the roof and a fire burning...

I think back: Was Grace different when she returned from that trip? We picked her up at the school, arriving early to see the coach pull in.

Her eyes were puffy, but that was because she'd been sleeping on the journey, wasn't it? Or did I get it all wrong, and was she hurting in the way I hurt all those years ago?

It's what my mum should have done when she was a teenager. Had she done that, she mightn't've reached forty and begun to look back on her time, full of regret for all the things she didn't do in life.

She told me later that she was a virgin the night of her wedding to my dad. Nineteen, and a virgin.

He was the only man she 'knew', in a very biblical sense, until she met Dave a short while after moving back to Jemford Bridge.

Re-met, I should say, as they'd known one another when they were young. He owned a photocopier and fax supply company out that way.

As for dad, I don't know if he had much of a life before mum. I do know he didn't have one afterwards. He married his work, essentially, until that was taken away from him. Once it was, he was left with nothing except television and tales of yore.

Ha, I scoff to myself. I sneer at him for living in the past, and here I am, having sat for the best part of two hours, doing precisely the same.

Yes, I use my records as an excuse, but they exist here because of their ability to transport me back in time.

With that I locate and play 'War' by U2. It played tinnily in the caravan that night of Friday August 26th, 1983.

It's a date ingrained in me. It was the first night we spent together. All night. Through till morning, as we pretended we were husband and wife.

I fell asleep with my drained penis inside her. She held me there through my resultant limpness, as I slept on her and in her.

We calculated that we were coupled for six hours.

At about five in the morning, I had to leave her to nip outside and relieve myself.

An hour or so on, and I was gently stirred from slumber in the most exquisite manner, as the warm cavern of Juliet's mouth wrapped around me.

In seventeen years of marriage, I wonder if Carol and I have spent six hours cojoined cumulatively in any of those years.

I know I've never been awoken by a blow-job. It's not the kind of thing you forget in life.

Sex was never very important to Carol, and I concur that there are more important things to a relationship. Particularly as you move through time, and the early fire of passion dwindles as it must.

But something must remain aglow, or what's the point? Physical attraction must surely endure. Friendship and companionship are fine and necessary, but there has to be more, or why even be together?

That's part of the enduring legacy of Juliet. The passionate side didn't have time to diminish and become staid. Ergo, I have doubts as to whether it ever would have done.

Carol, though. It was never high on her to-do list. Sex was at the end of 'Any Other Business', and usually got carried over to the next meeting.

Even now, sex isn't the purpose of her efforts with herself. Desirability is her aim. She loves to be coveted. That side of her ratcheted up as soon as she became competitive with Grace.

I re-think those words - my wife is competitive with our daughter.

It's why she takes her shopping, so that she can match her clothing and taste.

Carol is, I think, terrified of getting old. As a result, she dresses like a teenager, and has her teeth whitened and her arse bleached.

I rang dad and told him I'd be away till the Monday. He went mad on the phone. At the time, I was belligerent, ranting at him for not understanding.

But I look back on it, and know how I would react if Grace did the same at the age she is now.

I was a selfish teenager, but I don't regret any of it. Yes, my mum and dad were worried and upset, but I would still cause them that pain over and over again for that one night with Juliet.

After all, I'm not sitting here remembering me pining on my bed in my room in Oakburn. Oh, no, no, no! I'm firmly back in the time and place, with U2 transporting me there.

Take my hand, this drowning man!

We ran away, Juliet and I. Not ran away as in 'ran away', but we knew how important that weekend was. We both sensed it would be a long time before we would get an opportunity to repeat it.

"We only have one life! We might be dead this time next week," I said to her.

"Then let's go!"

"Go where?"

"Anywhere!"

So we did.

As my father drove from Brakeshire to fetch me, and Juliet's aunt and uncle berated us for our behaviour, and threatened to tell her dad, we skipped town.

It didn't matter. We were in the shit anyway, so how much more shit would we cop for if we legged it for two nights until the Monday?

Juliet took the money she saved from her work, and we walked away hand in hand. Fuck the world. If we were going to go out, we'd go out with a bang!

But there were inevitable consequences. After all, for every action there is a reaction.

The worst of which being, nobody was too supportive of our relationship after that weekend.

It's an irrelevance, though. They wouldn't have been anyway.

10.

Carol and I eat a microwaved chicken tikka masala in front of the television.

We're not together. They are two televisions in two separate rooms. She's in the kitchen, watching some reality dance programme I have no interest in. I prefer to watch something else I have no interest in.

Grace will have her veggie curry later, almost certainly in her bedroom where she can watch something I have no interest in on her own television.

That was how I ended up with the dining room as a record room. So, every cloud!

You weigh it up, don't you - record room, or family? Family, or record room?

I'm a cynic. I know that about myself.

Time was, though, I wasn't, I consider as I return to my record room and headphones.

No, I was a dreamer, and that's the opposite of a cynic, by my reckoning. A dreamer expects the best from people and the world more generally.

It's singles night in my house! It means I have to get up and down more, but I could use the exercise.

Orange Juice 'Rip It Up'.

We hopped on the first bus that came along, and, by midday, ended up in Stratford.

Upon-Avon, not east London.

Most of the Bed & Breakfast places were booked up, it being a holiday, and one with vacancies we did find turned us away. They smelt a rat.

Heading out of town towards Wellesbourne, Juliet spotted a sign indicating 'B&B', so we walked down the gravel driveway.

"Hello," she called out to a woman weeding a border.

"Hello!" came the reply.

She was a portly lady of about sixty-five, with rosy cheeks and a shock of curly grey hair that was once dark.

"I don't suppose you have any rooms, do you?" Juliet continued, "we've been camping since last weekend, and would do anything for a hot bath and a comfy night's sleep."

The lady peered at us with her rheumy eyes, as she weighed us up. A nod of confirmation to herself came, as she considered Juliet's words.

"Just the one night. is it?" she asked.

Juliet deferred to me. It was all part of the act, as she asked, "what do you think, my love? The pitch is paid for, and we can leave the tent there till Monday. Do you want two nights? It might help with your back."

"We could," I played along, pretending to stretch my back out.

"It's seventeen-fifty a night. Fifteen if you don't want breakfast."

I jumped in with, "I'd pay seventeen-fifty for a proper breakfast right now!"

That clinched it, as the lady, Monica, showed us to our room.

En route, Juliet informed her, "we're engaged, but not married. If that's a problem, Monica, we'll happily take two single rooms, if you have them."

It was a gamble.

"Oh, no, lovey, you're fine. I mean, you've been camping in the same tent all week, haven't you? I bet you zipped those sleeping bags together! No, no, don't you worry, we're not living in the dark ages here!"

"Well, between you and me," Juliet confidentially whispered to her, "that might be why my fiancé is having trouble with his back!"

"Oooh!" Monica exclaimed, before she added, "take my advice, and get him a good soak in a hot bath. I've got a bottle of addings I'll let you borrow that works wonders on my aches and pains."

"That's very kind."

"I was young once, you know?" It was wonderful to listen to them natter. Juliet had a gift for engaging with people of all ages. I think it came naturally, but she'd honed it at the pub.

"Will your husband be around later?" she continued, subtly getting all the information she required.

"Oh, no, lovey. He passed away two years since."

"I'm so sorry."

"Thank you," Monica replied, as Juliet reached for her hand and sympathetically grasped.

"No ring," Monica pointed out, glancing down at Juliet's left hand.

"I do, but not for camping," she deftly answered.

Twenty-five of our thirty-five pounds was handed over. A bottle of 'addings' came the other way.

Juliet unpacked my canvas rucksack, taking our changes of underwear and one set each of clean clothes. She folded them just as my mum used to, and laid them in the drawers in the bedside cabinet.

"You have to do this at home," I commented. "Since your mum died, I mean."

"Someone has to," came her simple reply.

"You must miss her terribly."

She stared at me for a long time, her eyes not blinking. It was as though she were trying to remember something, and blinking would interrupt and lose her train of thought.

Eventually, she said, "my life ended when she died... Not my life. My childhood ended. I had to do all the things she used to do, so that Jenny could have a childhood. I became a mother and stopped being a daughter."

"It's so sad," I said, because it was.

She smiled. "I think your situation's sadder."

"Why? My mum is alive and living in Jemford Bridge."

"Because my mum had no choice about leaving me. Yours did."

That comment has remained with me since that day in the B&B. It was typical of Juliet, and sums her up - that ability to see how something might be for others.

Empathy, I suppose it was. It explains why she could engage with Monica and others so easily.

If it was at all possible, I think I loved her even more after she said that.

"Who does your folding at home?" she asked me, coming over to the bed I was sat on.

"Nobody now."

She kissed me, before saying, "I will. I'll fold your clothes for you for the rest of your life."

I rise to change the record that has been pointlessly bumping away since it finished god only knows how long ago.

God only knows what I'd be without you.

She loved that song. The Beach Boys. We heard it on the clock radio on the Sunday morning in the B&B. Her mum had loved it. She had it on a single. Juliet thought it was a b-side.

I have it now. Not that copy, but a copy. Who knows? Maybe it is that copy. How would I ever know?

She was wrong. It was the a-side. 'Wouldn't It Be Nice?' was the flip.

Would it have been nice if we were older?

Yes, yes it would, because with age comes independence.

That was the only barrier, our age.

Fuck it! Fuck it, fuck it, fuck it! I have to stop doing this - this living in the past. I'm becoming the spit of my father.

That's the thing - if life was perfect right now, I wouldn't feel the need to revisit what's been and gone. It's the absence of all I recall in the present that's the problem.

It's the not knowing, and the what if, and the if only, and the undeniable fact that, had I not had that time with Juliet, my expectations for my own life would be so much less, because I would have no point of comparison.

If I didn't have the knowledge and experience through that relationship, would I be happier with my current lot in life? Yes! Yes I would.

But I can't undo what's done. Still, that's different to playing these records and constantly dredging it all up. But I can't help myself.

Juliet ran us a bath with 'addings'. We washed one another - every accessible part of our bodies.

With the soap as lubricant, we each reached in to the other and went to places I didn't know you could or should go.

It didn't feel wrong or dirty. It came from a desperate need to know every inch of each other - to explore every erogenous zone.

When we were ready, we wrapped our bodies in coarse boil-washed towels, and skipped back to our room along the hallway.

My erection was painful, as my blood-engorged manhood was stretched to the brink of tearing or exploding.

Juliet always took control. She knew, and I didn't. How did she know?

With her kneeling on the rug, she guided me so that my feet were either side of her, a little way in front of her knees.

Her head dropped down, rotating her undercarriage up and back. I then bent my knees, supported myself with my hands resting on her back, and we were in line.

It was ecstatically painful when I came in her. It was the most intense orgasm I'd ever experienced.

"Don't stop," she said, so I continued thrusting through the pain until I was desensitised and could begin again.

We slept for hours when it was over. And in the morning, we did it again, that time gently and sensitively, with her ankles on my shoulders and me propped up on my arms, as we tried to not let the bed squeak and the headboard slam into the wall.

11.

We went into Stratford on the Sunday. I wrote a cheque for fifty pounds, which a man cashed and gave us forty-five of.

It was my savings from the Building Society account I had. It didn't matter. What was I saving for if not that day?

Ten was set aside for Monica, and the rest was ours to do with as we pleased. We walked along the Avon, and found a patch of grass to lie on. That cost nothing.

"One more day," she sighed.

"Can you believe we go back to school next week?"

"Final year," she observed.

"Won't you stay on?"

"Probably not."

"I will. Get my A-levels, and go to university."

"What will you study?" she asked, her head resting on her open hand, her wide green eyes settled on me.

She always had a coy little smile on her lips. Not coy. I associate coyness with dishonest or manufactured. It wasn't that, her smile, but more open and approachable. It was just the way her mouth settled when at rest.

Now, when I depict her in my mind, as I frequently do, it's that day by the river that often comes to the fore. She looked so at ease and contentedly happy. It's the moment I often find myself wanting to return to.

"English. I'd like to write," I told her.

"What, like write books?"

"Yes."

"What kind of books would you write?"

"Fiction. Stories. You and me. I'd write about you and me."

"Like Shakespeare?"

"Probably a bit more modern." We'd visited a place and read about William Shakespeare and Anne Hathaway.

"I'm older than you, just as Anne was older than William," Juliet said.

"You're only a couple of months older than me."

"Still, he had to get his father's permission."

"And Anne was pregnant," I added.

"I hope it won't be a tragedy. How does it end, our story?"

"Happily ever after," I quipped.

"No, really. Tell me how it goes."

"We get married as soon as we can..."

"What about university?" she asked.

"Well, yes, obviously there's that. But we'll be together. I'll go away to some city or other, even if it's only Tredmouth, and you'll come with me. I'll have digs, so we can live together."

"It's three years away," she pointed out.

I went quiet. How would it all work?

"We can get married at sixteen, right?" I asked her.

"Not without our parents say-so," she thought. "I think we'd have to be twenty-one."

"Really? Not seventeen or eighteen?"

She shrugged.

"What about Gretna Green?" I threw in.

"There you go! Now your story begins to take shape!" she giggled, brightening as the plot developed.

"We can get married there at sixteen, right? So, you're sixteen in January, me in March. We meet up the day after my birthday, birth certificates in hand, having set off to school as normal.

"You get a train from Canterwood, and me from Brakeshire, and we meet up at Rugby, or somewhere.

Imagine that meeting on the northbound platform, both of us with a bag and..."

"We'll need money," she pointed out, "and won't it be when we're doing our exams?"

"Well, we'll pick a day when we don't have a test, and I'll use what's left of my savings. Or I'll get a part-time job to earn the money. A milk round, or similar, which I can do before school."

"Will it be a steam train?" she asked excitedly.

"Oh yes! It'll be The Flying Scotsman, and an overnight cabin."

"Mmmm, I like the idea of doing it on a train."

I grinned.

"Will you always love me?" she suddenly asked.

"God, yes," I replied instantly.

"What if I get pregnant?"

"Well, then we'd have to rethink things. I'd have to get a job, I suppose, and study at night school."

"And would you do all this for me? Would you get a job and miss university and perhaps not be a famous writer?"

"Yes!" I told her unequivocally.

I meant it at the time. I truly believed every word I said that afternoon.

We walked, never losing physical contact, never out of step. It was as if we were two purpose-built components of one efficient machine.

Fucking hell, I ached for her even when I was with her. Just the thought of not being by her side was gut wrenching.

"Marry me," I said to her for the umpteenth time.

"I will."

Being a Bank Holiday, there was an antique fair on. I paid the entry fee, and we strolled around.

Each of us pointed out objects we liked and would have in our home, our taste always matching. We planned it all, as we browsed, the comfortable home we would assemble together.

A plain silver ring she chose cost me twenty pounds. It was an engagement ring. I wished I could have got her something more expensive and fancy. But she was delighted with it, and it fitted her finger perfectly.

That was it. As far as we were concerned, we were engaged.

I think about that ring, and how it ended up on a second-hand stall in Stratford.

Did someone have to die for it to be there that day? How old was it? How many owners had it had - how many fingers did it adorn before landing on Juliet's? And what led to it having such little sentimental value that it was relinquished?

What was its story?

We ate pizza in a cafe, the smell of burnt cooking oil clinging to our clothes as we emerged into the crowded street.

A Town Crier rang his bell and delivered announcements. We stood and watched him, Juliet tight to me, enveloped in my hold.

He took a break, the man in his finery. I went up to him, as he smoked a cigarette and drank a beer at a table outside a pub.

I told him about Juliet and I. "We just got engaged. We're going to get married next March."

"Oyez! Oyez! Oyez!" he began, his bell clanking along in time. "On this very day, Juliet has agreed to be wed to Ant, and the grand union shall take place in March of nineteen hundred and eighty-four! May they be as happy and blessed for the rest of their days as they are on this day of their betrothal!"

A few people clapped, and one or two even cheered. I blushed at the attention even though I'd sought it out.

As a rule, my blushing went away when I was with Juliet. It was strange, the way she transformed me by being with me.

We went to a pub and approached the bar.

"Half a lager and lime, please," I ordered, indicating Juliet, "and just half a bitter for me. I'm driving."

"One pint won't hurt, darling," Juliet chipped in.

"You're right. Go on, make it a pint of bitter," I beamed confidently. And we got served! No questions.

My quiet nature had always portrayed a false sense of maturity, but never to the extent that I could get served in a pub.

Had I really grown up that much in the past month?

We sat in a snug corner, side by side in the shadows, the bright sun absorbed by small thick squares of glass and the dark wood of the interior.

"We have to go back tomorrow," I said heavily.

She took my hand and nodded.

"Do we have to?" I threw in.

She began to cry silently.

"Juliet, what's wrong?"

"Thank you," was all she said.

Were the tears happy tears?

"What's wrong?" I repeated.

"Nothing," she said, brightening and wiping her eyes with her hand. "I can't ever remember being this happy."

"We just have to get through this," I told her. "Then we can be together."

She slid up to me and tipped her head over on to my shoulder.

Every minute or so, I'd notice her eyes drop to look at the slim silver band on her finger.

"Do you know what I worry about?" I asked her.

She shook her head.

"I worry that you're too good for me. Too pretty. Too smart. Too cool. Someone better will come along, and..."

"Don't do that!" she snapped.

"What?"

"Put yourself down. Don't you ever put yourself down. If you really knew me, you'd know that it's the other way round. You're the one planning on going to university. I bet your house is way bigger and posher than mine. And I've met your mum and dad, remember, and I know how lovely they are."

"Was your mum lovely? Do you look like her?"

"People say I do. My nan says I'm just like her, both in my ways and in the way I look. My aunt, too."

"What about your dad?"

"I'm not like him."

"Will he like me, do you think?"

"No," she answered coldly and abruptly.

"Why not?" I was a little taken aback.

"He doesn't like me having a boyfriend. He wants me with him, to take the place of my mum, I think."

"Cooking and cleaning, and whatnot?"

"Yes, and looking after Jenny. Once mum died, I had to grow up and fill the gap."

"I wish you were pregnant!" I said. "That way nobody could stop us being together!"

She nestled even closer to me.

We nursed our drinks for the best part of an hour before heading back to the B&B.

"There you go, Monica," I said, handing her the ten pounds we owed her for our second night.

"Thanks. What have you two lovebirds been doing all day?"

"We spent the day in Stratford. It's a lovely town," Juliet said. "Have you always lived in the area, Monica?"

"Pretty much. I've never gone far. Never saw any reason to. I always loved the countryside around here. Hey, now, will you two join me for a glass of wine? I like a glass, but never bother to open a bottle just for myself."

"Of course!" Juliet chimed. "That'd be lovely."

We sat, the three of us, out in the back garden. Facing south, the August sun warmly bathed us that early evening.

"Oh, you're wearing your ring!" Monica observed as we all touched glasses.

"Yes. I thought I would, seeing how I'm not in a tent fetching water," Juliet fluidly responded.

"Let's have a look, then."

She held her hand out. Monica smiled as she took it in hers.

"Smashing! Simple rings are the best, I think. I guessed it would be a slim ring. No white mark, you see. No tan line on your finger."

"No," Juliet confirmed.

"Are you in any trouble, you two?" Monica asked without any build up. She retained hold of Juliet's hand.

"No. We love each other, and it's difficult, isn't it? When you're young, I mean."

"Parents don't approve?" Monica asked.

"No. Well, my dad doesn't. Ant's are okay about it, we think. And my mum died when I was eleven."

"Oh, my love, I'm so sorry. As for your dad, bugger him!" Monica said, and sipped her wine, the sun firing up her eyes and spectacle lenses.

We both giggled.

"No, I mean it," Monica told us, "they didn't approve of me, my husband's family. See, he was moneyed, he was, coming from near Leamington Spa, and they thought I wasn't good enough. They thought I was a gold digger, they did.

"My father was a farmer. Smallholding, and leased. Leased from my husband's family, which was the problem to some extent."

"What was his name?" Juliet asked, as the two women interlocked fingers, and sat chatting with the contact maintained.

"Edmond. Ed to me, though."

"How old were you when you met?"

"Oh, young. Too young, some would say! But when you meet the right person, you don't care, and age becomes irrelevant. I was fourteen, and he was sixteen, if you must know."

"You were very young." I winced a little at her only being a year younger than Juliet and I.

"I was. And you know what? I'm glad I met him when I was fourteen, because it meant we had fifty years together. Not that much happened on 'that front' until I was sixteen. But we spent every day together.

"It's why I'm sat here telling you about the half a century we were together. Not forty-five years, or forty-seven. Fifty! And every day was a blessing."

"Do you have children?"

"Five. Three boys and two girls. And - let me think a bit - eleven grandchildren, and two great-granddaughters.

That's why we have this big old house, so's we can fit them all in."

The women smiled at each other, Monica glowing with pride.

"How often do you see them all?"

"Oh, regular. It's funny, really, they're all away on holiday together, with it being a Bank Holiday. My eldest, Frank, he owns a holiday home down near the coast. I was supposed to go with them, but, ah, I didn't feel like travelling."

"Why not?"

"Oh, well, see," Monica began a little self-consciously, "today is two years since my Ed died. I don't know, I just wanted to be here where we lived together for forty-odd years.

"It's why I fancied a glass of plonk, tell you the truth.

"I shouldn't have had a room for you pair, really, as I should have been full, had I taken the bookings I had calls on. But I was planning on being away with the family, you see?

"Anyway, I thought, seeing how I'm here, I'll pop the sign out and see if I get any takers! Half an hour after I had, you two came strolling down the driveway!

"I knew we'd get on, the three of us, as soon as I clapped eyes on you! You didn't half remind me of me and Ed when we first met!

"I hope you two have as happy a life as we had," she concluded, and raised her glass by way of a toast.

"Look at the time!" she exclaimed. "Eight wants a quarter! Shall we have another glass, and how about some cheese and crackers?"

12.

"I'm going up," Carol informs me, her head popping round the door.

"Okay. Night."

"Night."

"Who was on the phone, someone for Grace?" I think to ask.

"Kelvin. The weather's looking good for next weekend, so we've been invited over."

Fucking hell.

"Night, then."

"See you in the morning."

It's how I came to use the former dining room as my record room. Time was, I had my collection up in the third bedroom. Carol moved in there at some point, and I had to relocate.

When was that? God, years ago.

Everything was years ago.

My records...

Can anything else so ably capture specific moments in a life?

I have a theory that many record collectors are full of regret.

It's probably true of all collectors, no matter the object. But records are different, I think.

Through the car-boot sales, I know of people who collect, for example, toy cars. Another likes annuals and comics. George from the pub has his trains.

Each of them smack of recapturing childhood - to return to those days of settled family and no responsibility, as parents took care of all the other stuff in life.

How much would I bet that George makes dandelion wine because it's what his father did? The process, smell and taste return him to his family home. The railway itself will play a part in that familiar familial setting.

Records, though: Yes, it's about the physical item, else a download would suffice. But primarily, it's about the music contained thereon.

The Walkman I had with me through that summer held no album sleeves, so there is no direct tie-in to the cover art and other paraphernalia. The sounds alone are what hold the memories.

With that in mind, I am probably a music collector, as opposed to a record collector.

I am preserving the music more than the physical item. Through it, I archive the memory, and allow myself to revisit it when I choose to. Not for some future generation, but for myself.

Grace has no interest. She considers second-hand items to be 'dead people's stuff.'

Carol doesn't collect anything. Well, clothes and shoes, but they go to the charity shop the moment they go out of fashion.

Most of my records are out of fashion. Actually, most of my records were never in fashion.

If I'm right, and other collectors seek a return innocence and childhood, then I seek to return to adolescence. I want to revisit the time in which I grew up.

We all do it, I reason, because we aren't content with our lives. That has to be true, or we'd be in the here-and-now.

Nostalgia is akin to a sort of homesickness; a longing to return to a time perceived as superior.

Juliet is the home I pine for.

The wine with Monica made us tipsy. I'd never really drunk wine prior to that evening. A fruity sweetness lingered on Juliet's breath and tongue as we collapsed into bed.

We had sex. Of course we had sex. It was lengthy and sweaty. Any air there was outside crawled in through the open window and barely rippled the net curtain.

She cried out with pleasure as I explored her with my mouth, reading her reactions and targeting the areas she responded to the most. It was the night I truly learned where and how to touch a woman.

In the morning, we washed before eating our breakfast.

Monica saw us off.

"It's been lovely having you two stay, and getting to know you both," she said.

"Thank you," we replied at the same time.

"Why so sad?" Monica asked, seeing the depression in our countenances.

"It's the end of our holiday," Juliet answered.

"Oh, don't be daft! You have a whole lifetime together. In time, you won't even remember this holiday or this place or me!"

How wrong was she?

"We'll come and see you again," Juliet said, and Monica hugged us both to her in her motherly way.

She watched us walk up the driveway, and held a curious expression as she did. It was a kind of knowing. An insight only another woman could possibly have.

I dig out and play the Fun Boy Three's 'Tunnel Of Love' on a seven inch picture disc. It's probably not a track that would render anyone else maudlin, but it destroys me every time I hear it.

The tunnel we walked through was the one beneath the main road back near Warwick, as we followed the towpath from the bus stop.

Another song - The Hollies.

...by August she was mine.

So many songs, from that time or discovered since. Recorded long after or recorded before. It made no difference. Hundreds of tunes and lyrics carry me back to her.

...someday my name and hers are going to be the same.

Beneath that tunnel I stopped walking and pressed myself against her.

A few more yards and the pub would come into view - we'd have to face the consequences of our actions.

We stood there kissing, our hearts racing in our chests - ba-bump, ba-bump, ba-bump - like the end of a record after all the tunes are played.

"Last chance," I proposed, "we can turn around and walk away again."

"I can't," she told me.

And so we walked on, arms around each other. Afraid.

Afraid of what we were about to face, but more afraid of what it might do to us longer-term.

"I'll talk to your dad and tell him it was my fault," I said to her.

The first person I saw was my dad. His face was thunderous.

Then my mum. She'd come with him, or followed him over. Was it relief I saw in her?

Next, a man I didn't know, but somehow knew was Juliet's father. Dark hair swept back, stubbly face, an angry twist to his mouth.

She was right. There wasn't much family resemblance. She must have taken after her mum. Perhaps it was Jenny I saw in him.

He strode up to us and wordlessly grabbed Juliet's arm.

A glare at me like he wanted to kill me.

"Jenny," he barked, "in the car!"

There was nothing I could do but watch them get in. Doors slammed. The engine started. A heavy plant of a foot on an accelerator. A slight wheel spin on the gravel in the pub car park, and she was leaving me.

Her head span from the back seat. A shy wave, and a hint of a smile. It was nervous, that smile, perhaps even tinged with regret as concomitance revealed itself.

A physical jolt shuddered through me.

It wasn't like before. As heartbreaking as that separation had been, as I'd sailed away with my mum and dad, there was optimism and hope. We would see each other again, no doubt.

All that remained once the car was gone from view, was an emptiness and a dread. It was stoked by a real sense that what we'd done would make it difficult for us to ever be together.

I threw up. I was physically sick on the grass by the canal.

I sank to my knees, my rucksack swinging from my shoulder. Her clothes and other things were still in it.

They would go home with me, and haunt me until they were returned to her.

"What the bloody hell have you done?" my father growled.

As he did, though, he squatted by me and I felt his hand squeeze my shoulder. There was some affection in that contact.

Here's irony. Mum had been driven over by Dave, who lived in the same street as my grandparents. It was that trip to Warwick, and the time they spent together, that led to them becoming an item.

I could fucking laugh at that.

"What were you thinking?" dad asked, breaking the silence as we drove back to Brakeshire.

"I love her, dad. All that mattered was... Is! All that matters is being with Juliet."

"You're fucking fifteen!"

"So what?"

He shot me a look that warned me not to push it.

Did my dad hit me? Often, but not that time. Even he, I believe, sensed that it would have done no good. Perhaps there was a teeny bit of the romantic in my old man. There was, I think, a little pity for me and my predicament.

"She's fifteen, son," he said, more gently and with sympathy.

"I know."

"You could be arrested."

I said nothing.

He filled the gap. "Her dad won't pursue it. If you agree to never see her again."

"No!"

"It's not a choice."

"I'd rather spend the rest of my life in prison than never see Juliet again!"

"Don't be bloody ridiculous! If you're in prison, you won't be able to see her, will you?"

"I love her," I repeated. "And she loves me."

He scoffed. "You're fifteen, the pair of you. You don't even know what love is."

"Do you?"

He let it go.

"Look," he said, in a conciliatory tone, "I was young once. And trust me, you won't remember her after a time. It's just..."

"What?"

"It's just sex, son."

I aggressively turned the car radio on.

The Golden Hour.

...loving you is easy 'cause you're beautiful...

...making love to you is all I wanna do...

Hollow on my insides.

Thirty-six years on, in a different century, in this year 2019, as the anniversary of that weekend approaches - there's still a gap.

Yes, it's been filled to some degree with 'other things'. Carol and Grace, for sure. Work and music and car-boot sales. Scrambled egg and Indian food. Beer and crisps and biscuits. Routine and getting on and making do and the company of others.

But there's still a gaping hole in me.

Rising, I raise and withdraw the tonearm, and turn off the amp, before flicking the switch on the plug.

The hum of the speakers disappears, and I pour a glass of water which I take up to bed.

Stripping, I lie and stare up at the ceiling, just a dim bulb in a bedside lamp barely lighting the room. It struggles to penetrate the thick shade, and casts distorted half-shadows.

They are like my memories.

Her face appears first, short fair hair with a long fringe swept over to one side, held away from her eyes by the open hand she props her head on.

The grass supporting her elbow is as green and lush as any I've ever seen, as it accentuates the greenness of her eyes - sparkling like emeralds as they regard me, and only me.

People around, but they are an irrelevance. Only we mattered in that moment.

From that starting point, I undress her. I try to recall the roundness of her breasts - the exact dimensions - and the precise curves of her body, as she slides down me and...

I close my eyes as I feel the warmth of her mouth on me. Her eyes are wide and shimmering with the lust and love of giving me pleasure!

But when I look down myself in the gloomy light, she's not here, and only my hand is making contact.

Perhaps we should have died that weekend.

Ultimately, what difference would it have made?

13.

I sit at my desk in the open-plan office, and scan through the new releases on a record shop website.

People wonder why I chuckle at life, and seemingly don't take anything very seriously. They say that I lack passion. There's a perception that I am shallow and dull.

I'm pegged as a bit of a nothing person.

My solitary pursuits and quietness add to the assumption.

It's the wrong way round. I find them and their lives so predictably mundane, that I shy away from engaging with them.

Material things consume. Houses and cars are measuring-sticks by which people sit in judgement.

Bragging or moaning about a life part-lived is not conversation. It is not dialogue. It is a boring fucking monologue.

If questions are asked, they are planted as segues into more self-absorbed bullshit. I'm not even supposed to answer them.

Nobody really listens. Nobody wants to hear. They pay attention just enough to be able to pick out a key word on which they can latch and attach and attempt to outshine.

Tell them something good about yourself, and they become envious and try to put it down or outdo it. Tell them something bad, and they get to laud it over you and tell you why they're so much better than you.

That's my experience, at least. So, I keep myself to myself.

Any dialogue I desire comes through my music. I've learnt more from records, and lyrical content, than I have any person I'm currently acquainted with.

And music teaches me about music, as it reveals itself.

A plethora of jangly eighties bands turned me around and pointed me back to the sixties.

Ian Dury informed me about Gene Vincent, just as The Sex Pistols did Eddie Cochran.

The Damned showed me Love.

Our love was damned.

Nine days that felt like years. That was how long it was before she called me from a public phone box.

She had to ring me. It was too risky for me to ring her.

Her dad had a lock on the home phone. It enabled calls to be received, but stopped them being made.

Bleeps and a dropping of change when I said "hello." She waited, a coin suspended until she was sure it was me.

I knew it was her before the connection could be fully completed. I made a noise. A soft throaty groan of satisfied bliss.

Her voice! Her perfect voice that sounded from that mouth I knew so well.

"Ant!" Just my name. I can never do justice to the way she said my name that day. A desperate need and all the love in the world came through that single syllable. It was a cry for help, and a relief at having established that most minimal of contact. There was something else, too. A vulnerability, I think.

She said my name in the same way she would when we had sex.

"Marry me!" I said straight away.

"I will!"

The relief was mine, then. Nothing had changed. Nothing ever would.

"Any regrets, Juliet?"

"No. None. Do you?"

"None. I have to see you."

"We can't."

"I can't live without you."

"Oh, Ant. Don't!"

"I mean it. I'm dying without you."

"Wait for me. If you love me, you'll wait for me!"

"Wait for what?"

"Sixteen, remember? Tell me the story, Ant. Tell me about us meeting at Rugby station, and catching The Flying Scotsman to Gretna Green."

"An overnight cabin," I reminded her, "and champagne for breakfast!"

"How many times will you make love to me on that train journey, Ant?"

"Once. But it'll last all night."

"God, I miss you. I miss your body!"

"I miss you so much it's unbearable!"

"Are you alone?" she asked me.

"Yes, dad's at work."

"Where are you?"

"Sitting on the stairs in the hall."

"Can anybody see you?"

"Not unless they come to the front door."

"Take your dick out."

"Okay," I said, and propped the phone under my chin as I did.

"Close your eyes, and imagine I'm there with you. Can you feel me?"

"Yes."

"Come for me! Pretend you're inside me, and that I'm right there with you."

"Hmmm," I murmured.

"Are you hard?"

"Yes. Where are you now?"

"In a phone box."

"Touch yourself."

"I can't! There are people around," she giggled, "I'm on my way home from school!"

"Are you wearing a skirt?"

"Yes."

"What colour is it?"

"Light grey."

"Is it short?"

"I took it up a bit, so mid-thigh."

"Then just reach under, move your knickers aside, and touch yourself."

"Okay, here goes."

I heard the mouthpiece rub against her face, and a slight whimper as her finger made contact.

"Are you wet?" I asked her.

"Yes. Very."

"God, I wish I could taste you."

"Come for me," she whispered.

And I did. An arc of semen shot from me and landed on the hall carpet. The phone fell from my ear, dangling from the spiral cable so that it unwound and corrected itself, repairing all of the half turns resulting from each answer and replace.

I scrabbled for it, waves of ecstacy pulsing through my entire body as I drained myself.

"Are you there?" I pleaded.

"Yes," she said.

"I made a mess!"

"Was it good?"

"Yes, but not as good as the real thing. Juliet, I think about nothing but you. Nothing matters except you. I worship you."

Peep-peep-peep-peep...

"I have to go," she said.

"No! Put some more money in."

"That's all I have. I'll ring you soon."

"When?"

"As soon as I can."

"Don't go," I begged her.

"I have to. I love you, my darling."

"I love you."

"Say it. Quickly! Before the line goes dead..."

"Marry me!"

"I will."

The phone on my desk goes. There's no long spiral cable. There's no cable at all. If Juliet rang me now, I could take it to the toilet with me and do things properly.

Not that I've ever tested that.

"Hello?"

"Anthony, could you join us in the meeting room for a few minutes? And bring the file we were discussing earlier, please."

"Yep, of course. Could you just give me a couple of minutes? I'm right in the middle of something."

"No problem."

And so I close the website of new vinyl releases this week, and pretend to type something as I wait for my erection to wane.

This is what I type: 'juliet hutchison marry me marry me marry me marry me marry me marry me why? why? why? why did it all go wrong? you broke my heart and you broke me into a million pieces you said you'd marry me and that we'd be together for all of time and i have never moved on and recovered and i know that i never will i love you i love you i love you i love you marry me marry me marry me marry me!!!!!!!!!!!!!!!!!!!'

I close the document.

Do I want to save?

No, I decide, and pull my jacket from the back of my chair, before walking to the meeting room.

I deliver the file, and answer a couple of questions to faces on a screen via a remote conferencing tool.

Unlike many record collectors, I never grumble about technological advancements. Had it been in place in the eighties, things may have turned out differently.

For starters, I have nothing against music downloads. Okay, so I prefer vinyl. Or even cassettes and CDs. Or eight-tracks. Or, at a push, wax cylinders. I even have a few minidiscs in a drawer at home.

What would I have given for a mobile phone and unlimited talk time back then? A video camera! The ability to chat via a video link...

I smirk mischievously at my vague reflection in my dark screensaver, and consider what Juliet and I might have got up to had we had that visual connection.

Is that what Grace does in her bedroom with the door locked?

I don't want to think about it...

But I can't help but think about it.

It feels so seedy and wrong, yet I know without doubt that it's what Juliet and I would have been doing had we been able.

Grace is the age Juliet was, yet there is, to my mind, a huge gulf in... I want to say maturity.

It feels as though we grew up earlier in those days. Was that because we were afforded more freedom to discover?

After all, we benefitted from a rise in liberalism, our parents having lived and matured through the sixties. Juliet and I were both born in early-1968. We were conceived in the Summer Of Love.

Is that why I have a fondness for music from that era?

Of Grace's male friends I've met, they aren't like I was at their age. For starters, I could communicate verbally with people of all ages and walks of life.

Did I, though? Or was I as closed and monosyllabic as they are with me? Don't we all shut down in front of our parents and elders?

That's probably how it should be. We have to find our own way, each generation, and move things on.

Are teenagers locking themselves in their room, either separately or in couples, and are they doing all that we did, and more besides?

Though quite how much more they could do than Juliet and I boggles my mind.

Dad said, in the car that day and later on - "it's just sex, son."

Were my hormones screaming at such a pitch that I was deaf and blind to everything and anything else? Was I thinking with my dick?

Was it just sex? Was dad right?

No, there was so much more. There was a cosiness and a belonging. A connectedness and affinity like none before or since.

Yes, sex is as physically close as two people can become, but that physical closeness brought with it an intimacy at a psychological level.

To truly love, you have to expose your vulnerabilities to another. That was what we did.

Absolute trust came as a result.

14.

Peep-peep-peep-peep.

"Juliet," I whispered, "my dad's here."

"I thought he might be, but I had to hear your voice."

"Who is it?" my dad called from the living room.

"Nobody! Just Trevor from school!"

"Well, it's not nobody then, is it? Don't be all bloody night."

I closed the door leading off the hall and sat on the third step, my feet resting on the second.

"Where are you?" I asked.

"In a phone box up the road. I only have twenty pence, so we don't have long."

"What's that noise?"

"The rain. It's hammering down."

"And you went out in that to ring me?"

"I'm heading up the shop for bread and milk," she explained.

"Any news on 'you know what'?"

"Yes, it's why I'm ringing."

"And?"

"Nothing."

I fell silent.

"Ant?" she prompted.

"I'm here."

"What will we do?"

"We'll sort it out. It's a good thing. It means we can be together, doesn't it?"

"I don't know, my love."

"How sure are you?"

"Not totally. I've missed periods before. But never two in a row. Look, I'm only a couple of days late this time. I think we should wait till the end of the week to be sure."

"Okay. How do you feel?"

"Oh, I'm physically fine..."

"No, I meant how do you feel about possibly being pregnant?"

"I don't know. How do you feel about it?"

"I don't care. If it allows us to be together, I'm okay with it. I just want to be with you, Juliet."

"Thank you."

"Have you told anyone else?" I asked her.

"No, just you. I wouldn't have told anybody before you. And there's nobody else I want to tell. What do you think your mum and dad will say, if I am?"

"I don't care what they think. What about your dad?"

"He'll go mental."

"Are you worried?"

"Yes," she said quietly, "yes I am."

"Why?"

"Because he won't let me keep it."

"You have to get away. You can come here. My dad won't throw you out. We'll be okay."

"Will we?" she asked. How our roles had reversed. In the beginning, just two months before, when we first met at the pub, she had all the control - all the answers.

She was cool and knowing and wise - unflustered and self-assured. I was the clumsy, intimidated fool next to her.

"Yes. I promise you, Juliet. We'll work it all out, whatever it is. Whatever it takes."

The pips... The fucking infernal pips!

I've detested those pips ever since. They make me anxious, as my heart rate matches them.

There are no more pips these days. Never ending call times. Only a drained battery will end the call.

But those pips, and the urgency that came with them - it was what forced the truth. It made us speak and think hastily, and, as a result, more honestly.

There was no time to reflect and consider. A question needed an answer in the moment, and that answer was truthful in the moment. There was literally no time to think.

We waited for those few days, a nervous knot inside my tummy. Something else potentially inside hers.

My schoolwork was suffering. Teachers began to notice. I was withdrawn and unsociable. Even more so than I had been the previous year. My dad was called in as a result.

It was decent of them to care.

My dad explained it all. He told them how my mum had left in the summer, and that things were difficult, but we were okay and getting used to the new life.

They misread it, all of them. It was nothing to do with mum leaving.

Juliet's potential pregnancy played constantly on my mind, but she would have been in my perpetual thoughts anyway.

They couldn't understand. And I knew that was because none of them had ever truly known love in its purest form.

I felt sorry for them. I pitied them.

She called me five agonising days later.

Juliet hadn't had her period. We agreed that she was almost certainly pregnant.

I drank. I walked to a pub outside Oakburn where a lot of students from the nearby technical college went. It was Monday, October 10th, and I should have been at school.

Along with the beer came a volley of barely thought-through notions.

I was blinkered by my desire to be with Juliet. Because of that, I could only see her moving in with me as an option.

It was never going to happen, looking back. We were fifteen. It wasn't even legal, as far as I understand things.

If it was Grace in that predicament, what would I do now as a parent?

It's difficult to be certain. One thing I am sure of, is that her boyfriend would not be moving in. And she would not be going off anywhere to live with him.

I like to think I would give her a choice, though.

With regard to the baby, I mean.

In the pub that evening, I sat alone with my headphones on. Music played, just as it always did. Always has.

A compilation tape I made of songs for Juliet and I. Two copies. One was sent to her. Not to her home. That wouldn't work. I sent it to a friend of hers after she gave me the address, and she handed it to her at school.

It was a mix of songs we both liked, and songs I heard that I knew she would like.

I'd get a job. When was the earliest I could leave school? What could I do? It was 1983. Unemployment was as high as it had been since the Great Depression fifty-odd years before.

I rang dad at some point, and told him I'd be late. I said I was going to Trevor's to work on a school project.

He didn't believe me.

That said, he didn't give me a hard time either.

"Are you okay?" he asked.

"Yes, I'm fine."

"What time will you be back?"

"About ten."

"Have you eaten?"

"Yes." I hadn't. I wasn't hungry.

"You definitely haven't done anything stupid, have you Anthony? To do with that girl, I mean?"

"No. I'm in Oakburn, dad, and I'll be back later," I assured him.

He sensed something was up, but didn't know what. It was the first time he afforded me trust and respect to that level. He knew I had to work something out.

More beer, but it had no effect on me. I don't recall how many pints I had that night. My Building Society account was ever-depleting.

It didn't matter. There wasn't enough money in there to make any real difference to anything.

A girl smiled at me. She was edgy and pretty. A Goth look about her. A Cure and Sisters Of Mercy fan, no doubt. Add a dose of Joy Division and Bauhaus. I liked that look - the dark eyeliner and scruffy hair. A bit of a punk hangover in the mix.

She wore a leather jacket and lots of silver rings on her fingers. Short black skirt and torn fishnet stockings. Doc Marten boots and a sense of fun beneath the hard look.

But she wasn't Juliet.

Three months before, and I'd have done anything to be with a girl like her.

Juliet consumed me wholly.

Stupidly, I called Juliet at home. Her father answered.

"Sorry, wrong number," I said, and hung up.

At a quarter to ten, sober as when I arrived, but bloated with fluid, I took a slow walk home.

It was damp and miserable, a heavy shroud of black cloud blanketing everything above me. No moon. No stars. No light could penetrate.

I pissed in a gateway, head tipped back, staring up at the abyss.

No answers came to me that night.

I was glad to arrive in our street, and to feel the front door handle in my grip.

Dad was in bed, but awake. I felt bad. He had to be up early for work. But he wouldn't sleep until he knew I was in.

I heard his voice from upstairs.

"That you, Anthony?" He wasn't angry in the slightest, judging by his tone. Relief was all I heard.

"Yeah."

"You okay?"

"Not really, dad, no," I said as I stood at his bedroom door, not quite daring to step over the threshold.

I heard his lighter grind, and the fizz of a cigarette taking the flame.

"What's up?"

I stepped in and aimed towards the orange glow of his smoke. He still slept on the side he always slept on.

"Have you been drinking?" he asked me, perhaps smelling it on me.

"Yes."

"Feel okay?"

"Fine. I tried to get drunk, but couldn't."

"That bad, eh?"

He flicked his ash in the glass ashtray that had appeared in the bedroom since mum had left.

"Want a smoke?" he offered.

"No, I don't."

"Good for you."

"Dad..."

"Yep?"

"Juliet's pregnant."

A silence.

Eventually, after two long draws and exhalations, he asked, "is it yours?"

"Of course."

"How can you be sure?"

"It's mine, dad."

"Okay. Then we've got some talking to do. Right now, get to bed."

And that was that. He nubbed out his fag, and lay back down from his propped position on the sheets that needed washing.

I padded away.

To my departing back, he said, "it'll be alright, Anthony. I love you."

And I burst into tears.

15.

I missed a record fair for this, I think, as a taxi ferries us to our destination.

"Is Grace happy?" I say to Carol because I can't think of anything else to say.

"Why don't you try asking her?" she snaps back. A question with a question. She's in one of those moods.

"I'm not sure she'd tell me."

"No, well, have you thought about making more of an effort?"

"You two talk, though, right?"

"What do you think? Not really, no. She's fifteen, Anthony. Think what you were like at that age."

It's all I fucking think about.

I don't tell her that.

"Does she have a boyfriend?" I go with instead.

"Nobody serious. She's too young for all that. But a couple of boys are interested, I think."

"That Callum who comes round sometimes?"

"The gay one?"

"Is he?"

"Yes."

The taxi driver glances in his rearview mirror.

"What time should we book the taxi to pick us up?" I ask.

"We haven't got there yet!"

"No, I know that. Swimming pools aren't my thing, that's all, and..."

"Shut up! We'll leave when I'm ready to leave. Anyway, we can't be too early. Grace is having a few friends from school round..."

"What? When?"

"This evening, obviously!"

"Shit, I hope they don't go in my record room."

"You're so bloody selfish!"

"I might give her a call," I say, reaching for my phone. "Tell her the room is off limits…"

"Don't you dare! Did you bring your trunks?"

"Why?"

"It's a fucking swimming pool party!" she hisses viciously. "Why do you think?"

"No. I forgot."

I didn't fucking forget.

"Oh, god help me. I expect Kelvin will be able to lend you a pair."

I pull a face into the side window. I should have sat in the front with the driver.

"Motown," I say to him.

"Sorry, sir?"

"Motown you're listening to," I clarify.

"Is it? It's just what's on the CD."

"Well, what CD is it?" I keep going.

He scrabbles in the door pocket, and emerges with a CD case. I can tell it's cracked by the crinkly noise it makes in his hand. Something rattles around inside. Probably a broken centre spindle. It'll scratch the disc…

"Motown Greatest Hits," he informs me.

"Let's have a look."

Yep, the spindle's broken and the case is cracked.

"Some good tracks on here. Smokey, Four Tops, Temptations."

"It's just noise, sir. I pick them up in the charity shops for pennies. Beats listening to the cust… Better than listening to the radio all day. Too much natter for my liking."

I hand it back wordlessly.

"Try not to show me up today," Carol sighs.

Kelvin is a first rate wanker. Carol works for him. Something to do with insurance. Carol assists him and answers his phone.

I answer my own, the lazy sack of shit. It's not difficult.

His girlfriend's lovely, though. Lovely to look at, I mean.

Beyond that, I wouldn't know. She never says much.

Speaking, I get the impression, would get in the way of her pouting and posing statuesquely.

I've tried sucking my cheeks in like she does, and it makes them ache after a few minutes. And it's hard to swallow like that.

I watched her for ages at the Christmas party, and I'm as sure as I can be that she didn't swallow once. Where does her spittle go?

Carol told me to stop staring at Sharelle.

"Do you think she swallows?" I asked my wife that December night.

She pulled a face and walked away from me.

As the taxi pulls into a large house near the racecourse south of Wrenbrook, Carol spits, "try not to stare at Sharelle all day."

"Are we early?" I ask as we make our way to the rear of the property, following a brief argument as to what time the taxi should collect us. We settled on nine thirty.

"No, why?"

"There's nobody else here."

"It's just the four of us. Who did you think was going to be here?"

Shit, there's no place to hide. I'm going to have to talk to them.

"Anthony," Kelvin says. It's just my name. It doesn't mean anything, and warrants no response. His handshake crushes my fingers. I'll never play piano again.

I'll never play piano.

"Kelvin," I say anyway.

He looks me up and down through his mirror-lensed shades. I'm uncomfortable seeing my own image every time I look at him.

And I'm uncomfortable looking at him, in his shorts and flip-flops and bugger all else. Well, aside from the gold chain winking at me from the thatch covering his rotund chest.

"Carol! Looking lovely as ever," he smarms, and they hug. He keeps his arm round her as he escorts her to meet Sharelle.

"Hello again Sharelle!" I call from a safe distance.

She's wearing a bikini. Well, half of one. Actually, it's about a quarter of one. It's just string threaded through three triangular sandwiches with the crusts cut off. Over that is a semi-transparent sarong thing.

"You have a beautiful home," Carol enthuses.

"We'll show you round later. Drink!" Kelvin proposes. "Cocktails for the ladies. Anthony, what'll you have?"

"Oh, erm, just a beer, thanks."

"Ice bucket there. Help yourself."

No bitter. Just lager in bottles. I peer at the labels for alcohol percentage, and opt for something 4.2. A session beer.

I take a seat on the patio, and listen to Kelvin and Carol laughing inside.

Oh, I can bear this, I think, as I stretch my legs out. Carol's happy, and that makes my life easier. I'll make the best of it.

She looked smashing in her little summer dress. I probably should have told her that. Still, she must have noticed my appreciative looks.

Kelvin emerges and joins me on the patio. He takes a seat alongside me, as I remove my feet from my slip-on shoes, and wiggle my toes in my socks.

"This is the life," I say to him.

"Not bad for a boy from the rough side of Tredmouth, eh?"

"Not bad at all!" I agree.

"Aren't you hot in all that clobber?"

"No, I'm fine. I'm not one for the sun these days."

"Neargh," he says in a dismissive manner, "all that ozone stuff. I think it's bollocks. Nothing better than feeling the sun on your body. Well, there are better things, but let's not go there!"

He elbows me in case I missed the fact he was using smutty innuendo.

A chuckle seems like the best response.

I don't do shorts.

The thing with shorts is, you have to start wearing them early in the season. Miss those vital first few days of sunshine, and you're always playing catch-up on the tanning.

Besides, I don't tan. I go red. Then peel. Then return to the same shade of pallid as I started with. It's not worth the pain, itchy discomfort and sleepless nights.

Oh, and the skin cancer.

Still, I unbutton my cuffs, and neatly fold back my shirt sleeves so they go half way up my forearms.

Carol and Sharelle walk out through the open patio door. I avert my eyes and allow them some space.

Kelvin doesn't. "Cor, who are you two, and what have you done with our birds?"

I can't help but glance. Carol has changed into her bikini, a bright yellow one that shows off her fake tan. She has a cracking figure, thanks to her exercise class and competitiveness with our teenage daughter.

"Hey up, you smuggling budgerigars, Caz?" Kelvin calls.

Caz, I realise, is my wife.

Caz giggles. If I said anything along those lines, I'd get an ear-bashing.

I was concerned that her dress and bikini were a bit revealing. I needn't have worried. Sharelle has lost the sarong since I last saw her. I was evidently being priggish.

"She's got Scando in her, you know?" Kelvin explains.

"Sorry?"

"Sharelle. She's half Danish."

"Oh, right."

"They don't have that British reserve thing going on."

"No."

"You know," he says, leaning close to me. "I've seen her mother's tits more times than you've had hot dinners."

Seeing how they've only been together for three years, I sit and calculate that he's seen his future mother-in-law's breasts approximately seventeen times a day. That seems a bit excessive, and difficult to explain through accidental encounters.

It's all so crass, that's the thing. I know I often think about Juliet and the sex we had, but it was never smutty.

It was beautiful and honest. And instinctive.

None of it was stereotypical, or done because that's what people did. We weren't acting out parts in some amateurish 'oooh matron' way. Every contact between us was natural and intuitive in the moment.

Carol would dress up when we first got together. That was her version of sexy. Stockings and suspender belt - lacy bra and undies - clownish makeup and a touched-up bikini line.

It did little for me, though I played along. After all, those moments were rare, so if there was sex in it, I was game.

Juliet...

Juliet was naked. No teasing. No pathetic unwrapping, like it was some reward for being a good boy - as though it were some special occasion and I should be so lucky.

We met at work, Carol and I, in the place I've worked at for the past quarter of a century, in various guises.

She was a client of mine down in Tredmouth. A city girl, born and bred. I was thirty-two, and she twenty-eight.

Seventeen years after meeting Juliet, I was just about capable of embarking on another serious relationship. That's how damaged I was.

Damaged? Perhaps not that. But I certainly set Juliet as my yardstick by which all others would be compared. They all fell short. By about a yard.

Carol was attractive to me because she was different. Different to Juliet, I mean.

She was hard next to Juliet's softness. She was decisive and regimented, unlike Juliet and her spur-of-the-moment approach. Yes, Carol is a planner. Juliet was more go-with-the-flow.

Through work, we got to know each other over business lunches and meetings. Mostly, though, it slowly developed over the phone. We wound up attending a conference together. In Stratford, of all places. We each had a room for two nights, in the hotel where it was being held.

We drank too much at the hotel bar.

Somehow, from that, we decided we might possibly be compatible.

There was a part of me that needed to bury the ghost of Juliet, if that's the right expression. Being back in Stratford had stirred up the memories and brought them spinning to the surface.

Carol was there. And she seemed nice. She was nice enough for me to ask her to be Mrs Nice some time on.

Her lack of passion was safe, I thought.

It was then, in Stratford, that she'd said to me, "I don't think sex should be the most important thing in a relationship."

"No, but it is quite important, I think. If only to bring people closer together."

"Yes, I know that."

"Particularly if you want children."

"Do you want children?" she'd asked me.

"Yes. I think I do." And I'd thought of the baby Juliet carried.

It crossed my mind to tell Carol everything, as we lay in her hotel bed watching the news on the television. I didn't, though.

"You're quiet," Kelvin observes.

"Sorry, miles away."

"Another lager?"

"Yes, please. Thanks."

"What were you thinking about?" he asks as he hands me a bottle, having removed the top with a bottle opener depicting a naked buxom woman.

"Funnily enough, about how I met Carol."

"Tell me to mind my own business," he begins, "but are you two getting on okay?"

"I think so," I answer. "It's hard, you know, having a kid, and... I think we're in a bit of a rut."

It's good to tell someone.

"You should mix it up a bit," is his advice.

"How do you mean?"

"Serve them beer all the time, and they get bored of it. Pour her a glass of wine every now and then. Or that pink stuff with the bubbles in. Offer her a cocktail, with an umbrella sticking out the top! Get her on the brandy. Brandy makes 'em randy. Whisky gets 'em frisky. Gin'll get you in!"

"Right."

"Are things alright in the, erm, bedroom department?" he asks out the side of his mouth.

"The wardrobe door needs adjusting."

"What are you saying? That it's a bit difficult to open?"

"No, it won't close, that's the trouble. It's always open."

"Really?" he says, and stares off into the distance.

Carol looks happy. At peace, I mean. She's a fretter by nature. And she's so terrified of getting old. She turned forty-seven in May, and I think 'the big fifty' plays on her mind.

Between exchanges with Sharelle, a relaxed smile curls her lips. It seems to broaden slightly every so often. Behind her dark lenses, are her eyes closed? Is she napping? What does she dream of - where does she go when her mind wanders?

Perhaps she has a secret akin to mine; some lost love who pops into her head unbidden each time a fissure opens via some tie-in or other.

She went away with a bloke called Iain before we met. The revelation came when we were chatting about places we'd been. It was in those early days of the relationship, back when we were getting to know one another.

"Mauritius," she'd claimed was the best she'd sampled.

"How long for?"

"Two blissful weeks."

"What did you do?"

"Lay in the sun a lot. Ate lovely food, and drank and swam the afternoons and evenings away!"

"How old were you?" I'd played along, watching her face as she'd drifted back to that fortnight.

"It was for my twenty-seventh birthday."

"Oh, so fairly recently."

"Yes. Though it feels like years ago."

"We'll go back, if you like?" I'd suggested.

"No. We should go somewhere else and make new memories."

"Who were you there with?"

"Oh, a friend of mine."

"A girlfriend?"

"No." There was a reticence to elaborate.

"Were you happy?"

"Yes, I was."

"With the place, or with him?"

"Both."

"What was his name?"

"Iain. With two i's."

"What happened between the two of you?" I'd asked her.

"It didn't work out."

"I'm sorry."

"Don't be silly. It's not your fault. It was just one of those things." She'd softened at that, and kissed me tenderly.

I think we loved one another back then.

We had a friendship, first and foremost. That was a good starting point, I figured. We were similar at that time, in terms of what we wanted from life. A child. Security. Safe.

I'd learn later that Iain cheated on her as soon as he'd had the holiday she'd paid for.

She reaches for her drink, and sucks a fruity-looking concoction through a day-glow straw. Sated, she lies back down, still facing me - still looking serene.

I smile at her, but she doesn't respond. Her eyes must be closed again, as Iain does to her whatever it was Iain did to her in Mauritius.

Where's the harm? We all have a past, and it doesn't hurt anyone to quietly revisit it in our minds. I'm sure everybody does, don't they?

I hope Iain's making her happy.

Because I'm not sure I can.

"You girls need filling up?" Kelvin booms to them. "A drink, I meant!"

That made her smile, my wife. She got a little kick out of that one. That's the level.

"Please," they both call back.

"I'll do it," I offer, pleased to have an excuse to pop inside for a minute where it's cooler.

"It's mixed, the cocktail, in a jug in the fridge. Don't forget to shake it," Kelvin says.

She was working as a waitress...

Not in a cocktail bar, but a pub near Warwick.

It's hardly Mauritius, but the place is an irrelevance. It's the one that got away. That's what endures, that unwritten ending.

Except the ending is written. The End.

It's not 'happily ever after'. This is real life. Carol made do with me, and I settled for Carol.

Made do. Settled for.

Is that what it is?

With the fridge door ajar, I stand before it, lit up and burning energy as the cool air soothes me. I waft it a bit.

"Are you hot, Anthony?" Sharelle asks me in her clipped way.

I jump, having not heard her enter.

"A little warm," I confess.

"Carol says that you forgot your shorts."

I nod and smile.

"I will get you some. You can go for a swim and cool off."

"Honestly, no, don't go to any trouble."

"Oh, okay. You're right, of course, we are all adults, and can go for a skinny-dipping."

I blush. I can't tell if she's joking. "I'm not really much of a swimmer."

"You cannot swim?"

"I can breaststroke."

As soon as I've said it, I wish I hadn't. Sharelle touches her own breast, as if the word subliminally triggered an involuntary reaction.

I blush even more.

It's one of those awkward predicaments, where to not look at her, as is my inclination, will make it so obvious that I'm not looking at her.

My only option is to keep looking at her, but only her face. Do not, under any circumstances, allow my eyes to drop. For some reason, I don't blink either. Even a blink might be misconstrued as a lowering of my eyes.

It becomes quite painful.

'I wish she'd turn away,' I chant silently to myself.

And just like that, she does.

Daring to look down, the cocktail jug trembles in my hand.

She pauses to retrieve something from a low cupboard. Rather than squat, she bends in the middle, resulting in the white twine becoming visible where before it was hidden from view.

God, she's attractive. A woman sculpted to physically appeal, but where's her soul and personality? My hand brushes the front of my trousers. It surprises me to discover I'm mildly aroused. I didn't expect to be.

"Do you have seven inches?" she asks as she rises empty-handed.

I have no idea how to respond.

Thankfully, she heads back outside.

16.

I pause to let my eyes adjust to the brightness before tackling the steps between the house and the pool.

The contents of the jug splash into the extravagant glasses the women drink from.

"Did you shake it?" Kelvin asks.

Bollocks, I forgot.

"Yes, I saw it shaking," Sharelle answers for me. Bless her for that.

Kelvin has joined the ladies. Carol glistens with suncream. Kelvin wipes the residue from his palms to his hirsute shoulders.

"I was telling Kelv that you used to play squash," Caz says. I realise she's referring to me.

"Did I?"

"Yes. You told me you did. Before we met."

"Oh, no, that was badminton," I clarify.

"Did you play in a league?" Kelv asks.

"No, I played in my garden. With my cousin. We'd use the washing line as a net. I'm not sure it was regulation height."

"Badminton! Squash! It's all the same. As long as you can hit the thing, you can play," Kelvin explains. "It's all about grip and coordination. It's all in the wrist!"

"Well, I'm not as…"

"Ms Nice, when we get back in the office on Monday, check my schedule, if you'd be so kind. After work work for you, Tone?"

I nod, because what the fuck else can I do?

"I'm also reliably informed that you like your vinyls," Kelvin continues.

I wince at the 's' on the end, but don't have the will to correct him.

"That's right."

"Then there are some boxes for you to have a shufty at in the garage. They're Sharelle's father's records. He was a DJ, you know?"

"Oh, really?" Just like that, I'm much happier to be here.

"On the radio?" I ask her, unafraid of her breasts all of a sudden.

"No. In clubs."

I try to calculate her age, or, more aptly, her father's age. She could be twenty-five, or she could be sixty. I'm not sure what's original, and what might have been altered.

"Nightclubs?" I fish.

"Yes. Clubs at night."

"When was that?" I ask as sensitively as I can.

"In the seventies, I think."

"How old are... How old, roughly, is your father?"

"He died last year," Kelvin picks up the explanation. "He was only seventy-one."

"I'm sorry," I say to Sharelle.

She shrugs as if it was no big deal. Still, she smiles her appreciation. As she does, a dimple appears on her left cheek.

Juliet...

"Anyway, we ended up with his old vinyls," Kelvin continues. "I was going to drop them at the charity shop, but you can have any you want."

"How many are there?"

"There's a few boxes of them."

"How many boxes?"

"About a dozen or so."

"How big are the boxes?"

"They're wooden things, about this long," he says, indicating with his hands.

My mind is running all the numbers. There must be a couple of hundred in each box. Maybe two-fifty. Possibly more. A dozen boxes, means up to three thousand seven inch singles.

A DJ would look after his records.

Seventy-one in the year 2018. He was born in 1947. At what age would a DJ start? Eighteen, nineteen? Probably about right, so he began in 1966.

Looking again at Sharelle, I see the ageing on her neck. It's not bad, she looks great, but there are telltale signs.

Carol nudges me with her knee, so I stop staring.

I think she's late-thirties.

Kelvin? He's roughly Carol's age. Possibly late-forties. He's got a few years on Sharelle, anyway.

He's definitely closer to Carol's age than he is his girlfriend's.

I suppose that's why they get on. They do get on.

You know when you know?

The overuse of his name, and the regular dismissals - "he's not my type, Kelvin, but he does make me laugh!" And how often she brings him up in conversation.

"So, are you interested in these vinyls?" Kelvin asks, bringing me back.

"I'd love to take a look."

"Come on then! No time like the present! Caz, you want that look round the house?"

"Oooh, yes! I'd love to be nosey!"

"Sharelle, are you coming?" Carol asks.

"No. I will stay and drink my drink."

They leave me in the garage, where I find the wooden trays of singles stacked in two columns.

A worktable's utilised, as my fingers go to work flicking through the factory and picture sleeved singles. Each one is housed in a clear outer with a sticker on - easier to read in the dim light of a discotheque.

A lot are chart hits of the day, as you'd expect. Certain labels cause me to pause - Regal Zonophone, and early Bowie on Deram and Philips. The ones I don't know are what get me excited.

They cover the second half of the sixties, and all of the seventies. They're immaculate, in alphabetical sequence, through punk and post-punk, before touching the next decade and Juliet...

"You like old records?" Sharelle has a knack for making me jump. At least she has her sarong back on.

"I do. Your father had good taste in music."

"What do you think Kelvin and Carol are doing right now?" she asks without warning.

"I don't know."

"He cannot help himself."

"Right. Why didn't you go with them, if you were worried about it?"

"I'm not worried. She seems nice. Why didn't you go?" she asks me.

Why didn't I go? Because the records were all I thought about in the moment.

Did I think that the 'tour of the house' line might have been a ruse? It crossed my mind. I thought I saw a small twitch of accomplishment at the corner of Carol's mouth when Sharelle refused to join them.

"It's not my thing, looking at houses."

"Your thing is seven inches?"

"Erm, yes."

"Do you know why Kelvin does it?" she asks next.

"No," I concede, as I look at her sculpted and bronzed face and body. "I'm sure it's not your fault."

"Of course not. And it has nothing to do with your wife."

"Doesn't it?"

"No."

"Then why?"

"Because of you. It is you who bothers him. So, he has to take something from you to... How do you say? Inflate himself. By having your wife, he is proving to himself that he is the better man. Perhaps the more desirable man. Do you see?"

I chuckle nervously.

"Maybe we should have some fun, if they are," she suggests.

"I don't think it would be right."

For the first time that day, and on the couple of other occasions I've met her, she laughs. It's a nice laugh that shows off her small aligned teeth, and the pinkness of her tongue and gums.

It humanises her, and I realise that she is, in that moment, very beautiful.

"That is why," she says.

"Why what?"

"That is why he will never be the better man, Anthony," she says, before turning on her heel.

I go back to browsing through records in the air-conditioned garage.

Twenty minutes later, I rejoin the others, and help myself to another beer. Carol is flushed in the face - drink, the heat, or something else?

"What do you reckon, load of rubbish?" Kelvin greets me.

"Not at all. There are some rare records there. To be honest, some are worth a few quid. You might want to try selling them."

"Nah, can't be bothered with all that. Like I said, they were going to charity, so they're yours if you want them."

"Well, let me pay you," I suggest to Sharelle.

"No. I would like to go to a good home."

Yes, I expect she would. My home isn't that good.

"Well, at least let me buy..."

"Oh, for god's sake," Carol butts in, "just have the bloody records if you want them, and be grateful!"

She drones on about how I can't accept gifts, and my attitude of 'neither a lender nor a borrower be'. I hear 'stick in the mud' and 'only child' and 'incapable of sharing' as my character is assassinated.

It's water off a duck's back to me. I'm lost in thoughts of playing those records and incorporating them into my own collection.

And Juliet. Always Juliet.

Caterers arrive at some point, and decorate a table with fruit salad and cheeses and sliced meats and quiches. It's far too much food for the four of us. Especially as Sharelle barely eats anything.

I knew there'd be little triangular sandwiches with the crusts cut off. I open one up to reveal pinky flesh. It's salmon, I realise with relief, before piling my plate with them.

"You and Kelvin seem close, Carol," I say to her when we have a moment alone.

"We have a laugh, that's all. Lighten up!"

I let it go. I want her to be happy, and she has been for our time here.

Swimming follows the food, Kelvin leaping in and splashing everyone with displaced water. Carol takes it seriously and competitively, rattling off a few lengths.

Sharelle glides in to the cool water like a mermaid, and floats around on her back, occasional flicks of her toes steering and propelling her.

I sit in the partial shade and watch it all.

"Come on in, Tone!" Kelvin calls out.

I shake my head.

"Yes. Come join us!" Sharelle seconds the motion.

Carol says nothing.

Removing my socks, I roll up my trousers to reveal my untanned lower legs. I take my beer over and sit on the edge of the pool, the cool water lapping at my feet. It is pleasant.

For a while I forget about everything. I stop worrying about Carol and Kelvin, and what Grace and her friends might be doing in my record room.

Perhaps it's one beer over the top, but I'm at that stage where things don't seem as important as they usually are.

I am, in fact, lightening up! Wasn't that the expression Carol used?

Bollocks to it, perhaps I will slip into the shorts Sharelle left on the chair for me.

Having nipped inside to change in the downstairs loo, I slather myself with suncream before stepping out.

A cheer goes up. I blush.

"Bring some cold beers with you, Tone!"

'I wish I could be the person Carol wants,' I think to myself as I pop the tops off the bottles, 'for our time here at least.'

With beer distributed, and a sultry 'thank you' from Sharelle, I leap into the air, and land in the deep end of the pool with my legs, arms, eyes and mouth agape!

Everybody laughs! Not at me, but with me.

It's fun and thrilling and cool and...

Am I the problem? Since Juliet, I've never once taken a chance. I've never let my hair and guard down.

Would I be a better person had I never met her?

17.

Kisses and hugs sent us on our way in the taxi. And promises to do it all again soon - dinner at our place - squash after work - records to collect.

It's a different car and driver. But the music seems to be the same.

Two of the boxes of records sit in the boot. I couldn't help myself. I'll get the rest later.

"Thanks for making an effort," Carol says, and she pats my knee.

"I had fun," I admit. "The sandwiches were smashing."

"Shame we had to leave when we did."

"I could have stayed longer, to be honest, but the taxi was booked."

Something bizarre happens. She slides over to me on the rear seat. She takes my hand and places it at the very top of her thigh. Her skimpy little dress has ridden up, and she wears something lacy beneath.

Blimey.

Most shocking of all is that I resist the temptation to tell her to put her seatbelt on.

It's been a long time. Beyond months, and into years. I haven't kept track of how many.

I don't do anything. I just leave my hand there, and she tips her head over on to my shoulder.

It's what Juliet did in the pub in Stratford. Same spot on the same side.

"Are you happy?" I ask Carol. Anything to get Juliet from my subconscious.

"Yes!" she says, a bit slurred; a bit tipsy.

"Good."

"Kelvin's such a laugh, isn't he?"

"Yes," I agree.

"You can see why I like working for him, can't you?"

"Yes, yes I can."

"We have such a laugh in the office. It's not even like going to work, really, with Kelv there."

"No, I bet it isn't."

"Sharelle's a bit of a cold fish, though, isn't she?"

"Oh, she's alright, once she opens up a bit. She should smile more."

"She thinks she's god's gift. Did you see what she was wearing? Well, barely wearing!"

"Oh, it's up to her. After a while, you don't even notice."

"Phurrr! Everything on show like that. It's a bit... Well, tarty, I suppose."

"As I say, it's up to her," I reply, and feel an involuntary spasm shoot through my little finger as it rests against Carol's vulva.

"Kelvin says she's a bungalow! Do you know why?"

"Yes."

"It's because there's nothing upstairs! Kelvin is funny, isn't he?"

"Yes, a laugh a minute. I must say, I found Sharelle quite intelligent, once you crack the surface."

"Really? I found her boring. I think Kelvin does, too, you know? Not that he's said that, but you pick things up when you work together all day."

"Right."

"Kelvin says that I'm a godsend in that regard. He says it's great having someone who he can trust, and bounce things off."

"Right," I try to say enthusiastically.

"It's nothing like that," she adds, and moves her pelvis slightly.

"I didn't think for a second it would be."

"Why not?"

"Well, he's got Sharelle, hasn't he?" I can't help but chuckle.

"What do you mean by that?" Her change in tone is palpable.

"Just that he's with Sharelle. And you're married. To me."

"Oh, yes, yes, of course! I think I looked better than Sharelle today. What did you think?"

"You both looked lovely."

"I'm surprised you noticed how I looked." She's fishing for compliments.

"Of course I did."

"Well, you were staring at her all day!"

"I was not."

"You were! Do you like her?"

"Yes, I already said that. Once you crack the surface..."

"I think she's had work done. On her you-know-whats, I mean."

"Right."

Silence is my best chance of surviving this taxi ride, I decide.

Sharelle's right. Carol and Kelvin are cut from the same cloth.

Carol doesn't care for Kelvin. Not really. This, now, is what it's all about, with her pushing herself against my fingers, her hand slipping inside my shirt after she unpicked a button.

It's the Sharellephant in the room.

My desiring her above Sharelle is what's at play.

Wanting to be Grace is all part of the same thing.

Confirmation comes via, "is Sharelle sooo much more attractive than me?"

She whispers the question in my ear. Her close breaths make the hairs on my neck stand up. The Temptations sing 'Get Ready'.

"Don't be daft."

"The way you were looking at her all day..."

"I wasn't, I promise you."

"Kelvin says it's all a front, the sexy thing she does. He's not said much to me, but I don't think all's rosy in that department."

"Oh, right."

"Men like real women, don't they?"

"I do."

"I mean, imagine doing it with her... Well, you may as well be with a blow-up doll!"

"I suppose."

"Still, it was good of her to give you those records."

"It was," I confirm.

"Are they any good?"

"Yes, a cracking lot!"

In my mind, I depict the sleeve from Soft Cell's 'Torch'. The track was on a cassette tape years ago, playing through tinny little speakers that I could plug in to the earphone jack.

With that, I'm in a caravan by a pub near Warwick. No lights, just stars and the moon looking down and lighting my way that night.

And her eyes, looking up at me and shining bright - my hands reaching out - both of us glowing sex - hold me, hold me, hold me!

Carol rests her hand on my groin.

My somewhat aroused state brings a sigh of satisfaction from her, before she slides back over to her side of the back seat and fastens her belt.

18.

The house is quiet. Too quiet.

There are no teenagers with their grubby, sticky fingers on my records. There's no debris littering the kitchen, and no smell of smoke and weed.

The recycling bin is as optimistically empty as when we left, and the neighbours are as absent as they usually are.

It's no different to every other time I come home.

After paying the taxi driver and depositing the two boxes of records in my room, I go and look for Carol and Grace.

There are tears.

"What's wrong, Carol, why are you crying?" I ask, encountering my wife half way down the stairs.

"She's got a boy in there with her!"

"Oh. Oh, right."

"Is that it? Is that all you have to say?"

"Well, she's fifteen. Think of what we were like at that age."

She stares at me with what can only be described as loathing, before pushing past me and continuing her descent.

"Grace, can I come in?" I call softly as I tap on her bedroom door.

A shuffling preempts the opening. Grace's angry face is all I see through the gap she allows.

"What?"

"I'd like to come in, please."

"Why?"

"Because this is my house, and I think we need to have a chat. Your mum's upset."

She opens the door and steps back with it.

"Alright?" says a sheepish lad who sits on Grace's bed nervously jigging his leg up and down.

I nod.

He's dressed, but his clothes haven't had time to settle into place. His hair is frizzy from where he pulled his t-shirt on. One of his socks is missing.

The bed, I notice, has been hastily restored to almost made, and the pillows still hold impressions of their heads.

"Grace, what are you doing?"

"Nothing. Just hanging out."

"What about the party?"

"I decided to cancel it. This is Ben," she says, indicating leg-jigger.

"What do you do, Ben?"

"Nothing," he answers far too quickly.

"I meant generally."

"Oh, er, studying and working part-time."

"Time you were going, Ben," I tell him reasonably sternly.

"Yes!" he agrees. There's a lot of relief in his voice.

He adds, "see you, Grace. Thanks for the, erm… Thanks for the chat. I hope I helped with your school thing."

Lying little twat.

Escorting him to the door, I step outside and say, "where do you live?"

"Oh, no, nothing happened, my mum and dad…"

"How far is it?"

"Oh, just ten minutes away."

"Will you be okay getting home?"

"Yes, thanks. I've not been drinking." He pulls a car key out of his pocket.

"How old are you?"

"Seventeen."

"Grace is fifteen."

"I know."

"She's fifteen, Ben."

"Ah, yes."

"Did you take precautions?"

"We didn't..."

"Did you take precautions?" I ask more forcefully.

He nods and avoids my eyes.

"Right. Go home."

He loiters, tapping his key against the back of his hand.

"What?" I ask him.

"I love Grace," he says, and blushes horrifically.

"So do I. Now, drive carefully."

He gets into a car that's a damn sight fucking better than mine.

Carol stands at the door.

"He's driving a car!" she points out.

"He's sober. I smelt his breath."

"I don't care if he's tee-bloody-total! He's driving a car!"

"Yes."

"Well, how old is he?"

"Seventeen."

"Grace is only a child! He's raped her!"

"Don't be ridiculous."

"Ridiculous? She's fifteen, Anthony! Fifteen!!!"

"She's sixteen in a few weeks."

"It's against the law."

"She's..."

"I'm going to call the police! My poor little baby girl..."

"Just shut up, Carol!"

Oh shit, what have I done?

Fuck it, in for a penny... "And get inside, so that I can have a talk with our daughter."

She does! She's so shocked, she wordlessly turns and trudges off to the kitchen - in floods of tears and with exaggerated sobs.

I find Grace in her room, morose, and sitting on her bed.

I take the chair in front of her dressing table.

"Are you okay?" I ask her.

She nods. "I thought you'd be later."

"Obviously. Look, Ben seems like a decent enough young man. I need to know: Did anything happen tonight that you didn't want to happen?"

"No," is her instant response. "No! It's not like that!"

"Okay, but I had to ask."

She relaxes a little. I sense her worry is for Ben, and not for herself.

"Was tonight your first time?"

She shakes her head. I can see the emotion in her. This is so difficult for my Gracie...

I want to stop, for her sake. I desire nothing more than to spare her all of this awkwardness - all of this embarrassment.

"Have there been others? Other boys, I mean."

"No. Only Ben. Once before at his house."

"Okay. It's okay."

Shit, now I'm the one who's awkward and embarrassed.

I want to ask her if it was perfect and loving and... I want to ask her if it was like Juliet and I.

"Are you happy, Grace?"

"Yes. I'm so happy it hurts."

And she can't check the tears any longer. Keeping my distance, I stretch and hold out my hand. She takes it and shakes it appreciatively. A thankful and affectionate squeeze.

"I do know, you know, Grace? I know exactly how you feel right now."

"Oh, daddy!"

She pulls me to her, so I go. And I sit next to her as she curls into a fetal position and sobs her heart out.

I merely stroke her hair and feel her heat through my palm as she cries herself out.

"Why do you cry?" I whisper to her.

"Because I can't be with him all the time," is her response.

She's so much better than me.

I think of all the worry I must have given my mum and dad when I was her age. I ran away, and with Juliet falling pregnant...

I've never really thought about what it must have been like for them before now.

"I can't really bring male friends home," Grace says quietly after a time.

"Of course you can."

"No, I can't."

"Why on earth not?"

"Because of mum. Because of how she is with them."

Oh, god. I think of all of it - the competitiveness and the way she was with Kelvin and Sharelle this very day.

"Your mum, I think, doesn't like herself very much at the moment, Grace. She's a little worried about getting older. And that's sad, if you think about it. It's tragically sad."

"Is that why you and her don't get on?"

"Ah, well, that's probably to do with me as much as anything. But, yes, I think that's part of it."

"I wish you could both be as happy as I am right now, dad. It's so magical, what I feel inside."

"Yes, I remember that feeling."

"Does it last forever?"

"It can, I believe. If you want it badly enough."

"You said that you knew how I felt. When was that? Was it with mum?"

Shit.

"Yes, then. But before then, too."

"How old were you?"

"Erm, about the same age as you are now. A bit younger, to tell you the truth."

"How old was she?"

"A similar age."

"So my age?"

"Yes."

"What was her name?"

I probably shouldn't do this…

"Don't worry, it'll be our secret," she adds.

"Juliet. Her name was Juliet."

So good, I say it twice. It's the first time I've said her name out loud in years. And the first time I've uttered her name to Grace.

"And you loved her?"

"Oh god, yes."

"And you still do." It's not a question.

Still, I answer it with, "yes, I do. I always shall. But I love you and your mum, so…" I don't know what to add.

"You look so sad," she observes.

"Not sad," I fib, "reflective, perhaps. How could I be sad with you as my daughter?"

"What was she like?"

"Who?"

"Juliet."

"It was a long time ago."

"I'm sorry, dad."

"Ah, you don't need to be sorry. I'll see if I can talk to your mum and..."

"No, not for that. I'm sorry that your heart's a bit broken."

I'd never noticed how alike our personalities are. I saw it when she was small, but it seemed to go away from her. She's a romantic, I suppose, and a dreamer.

"I love you, Grace."

"I love you, dad."

It's been a long time since we said that to each other.

"Here," I say, reaching down and handing her something.

Before she can wipe her eyes on it, I add, "make sure Ben gets his sock back."

Carol is in the living room, a glass of water on the table. A bottle of pills stand alongside. She slaps two prozac into her mouth, and stabs aggressively at her tablet.

"Are you okay?" I ask her.

"Oh, I'm fine," she replies curtly.

"What are you doing?"

"Nothing."

"Grace is settled. We'll talk to her in the morning. She was pretty upset."

"Yes, well, so am I, if anybody cares to notice." A dismissive humph ends the discussion.

I close the door silently, and pad along the hallway to my music room and the two boxes of unexplored vinyl singles.

19.

"Will you accept the charges for this call?"

"I will."

"Connecting you now."

"Juliet?"

"Yes. Listen, why is your dad at my house?"

"My what is where?"

"Your dad! He's at my house talking to my dad."

"Now?"

"Yes. Me and Jenny were sent outside. What's going on?"

"I don't know. It's the first I've heard of any of it."

"What do you think they're talking about?"

"My dad knows, Juliet. I had to tell him."

"He knows about me being pregnant?"

"Yes."

A silence.

"Juliet?"

"We said we wouldn't tell anybody."

"I know, but he was alright about it. He didn't rant. We talked."

"When was this?"

"On Tuesday."

"What did he say?"

"That we'd sort it out. I told him things about us, Juliet. Perhaps he's gone to see your dad to discuss you coming to live here."

"Don't be silly. My dad's not going to allow that, is he?"

"Why not?"

"Because we're fifteen, Ant!"

"So what? We'll be sixteen in a few months, and then they can't stop us. We can do what we want then."

"I can't just do what I want, can I? What about Jenny?"

"What about her?"

"She's my sister."

"What are you saying? That you don't want us to be together?" I fired back.

"No, of course not. But…"

"But what?" I pleaded.

"God, I wish you were here. Why didn't you come with your dad?"

"He didn't tell me he was going. Trust me, I would have insisted, if I'd known."

"Shit!" she exclaimed.

"What?"

"Does he know that my dad doesn't know I'm pregnant?"

"Erm, yes. I told him nobody knew."

"Will he tell him?"

"I don't know," I admitted.

"Shit."

"He's going to have to find out at some point, Juliet."

"I know. Fuck! I wish I was dead."

"Don't say that."

"You don't know what he's like."

"Perhaps my dad will still be there when you get home. He won't let anything bad happen."

"What will happen to us? Oh, Ant, I just want to be with you."

"And me you."

"And I want to wake up with you every morning, so the first thing I see every day for the rest of my life is your smile."

"That's all I want in the world. I want you next to me. Always. I'm not complete without you, Juliet. I'm restless constantly, and it's exhausting being apart from you.

"I'm like a bird, way out in the middle of the ocean, flying around endlessly, but there's nowhere to settle and rest, let alone make a nest. And I don't know which way the land lies."

"I know, my love. I know what you mean. I feel like I'm in limbo, waiting to see what happens next."

"What will happen, Juliet?"

"I think I might find out when I get back home."

"Are you worried?" I asked her.

"Are you?"

"Yes. No! No, I'm not. My dad was okay about it. He didn't go mental. He was calm and, well, okay."

"Jenny! I won't be long, just wait there," she called, and I heard the moan of the phone box door as it closed.

"Sorry. I'm going to have to go," she said to me.

"Not yet."

"I'm really worried, Ant. I'm scared."

"I know," was all I could think to say to her.

I felt a dread wash through me - an awful sense of impending doom.

"I will marry you, Juliet," I told her.

"I wish we were married!"

"Will you be able to ring me when you know what's gone on at home?"

"I don't know. It's hard to get away sometimes. But I'll try. I'll find an excuse to nip up the shop, and I'll see if I can get to a phone."

"Thanks. Look, this might not be a bad thing, my dad being there. It might speed things up," I said optimistically.

"I'd better go."

"We'll talk later. See you."

An hour passed. Two. Then three. No call. Dad wasn't back.

What the fuck was going on?"

Dad, I would learn, called in to mum's on his way back from Canterwood. He informed her of what would happen.

I would be the last to know.

The phone!

"Hello?"

"Ant, it's Juliet."

"Marry me!"

"Yes, I'm fine, thanks. I'm here with my dad."

"Oh, okay. How... How did it go?"

"Everything's fine." Her voice was flat. I heard her take a deep breath. "Ant, I don't want to see you again. And I'd like you to stop contacting me."

"What? No!"

"It's what I want."

"No it isn't. Juliet, it's..."

"Please... Don't make this harder than it is."

"I can't live without you."

"I'm sure you'll be fine. It was a mistake. You and me, I mean. It was a holiday thing, that was all. And now..."

I heard her voice falter. It was bullshit. She was being made to do it!

"Juliet, don't do this!"

"Please don't try to contact me again. Ever. Bye."

"Juliet, I lov..."

The line was dead, and so was a part of me.

But I knew! It wasn't true, any of it.

"What have you done?" I raged at my dad when he arrived home.

"Did she call you?"

"Yes."

"Then that's an end to it."

"You can't do this!"

He sat down heavily on a kitchen chair. With his elbows resting on his knees, he leant forward and ran his fingers through his thinning wavy brown hair.

"I didn't have a choice. And neither do you," he told me wearily.

"What about the baby?"

"She'll be going to a clinic soon enough."

"A clinic? What clinic?"

"To get rid of it, Anthony."

"An abortion?"

"Yes."

"Her dad knows she's pregnant?"

"Yes. I told him. The man was worried sick. I'm worried sick. Your mother's worried bloody sick. We're all worried fucking sick, Anthony! This has to stop."

"I love her!"

"It doesn't matter. You don't even know what that means. You're both fifteen, and until you aren't, that's how it is. Those are the rules. You don't see her, and you don't contact her. Understand?"

"Fuck you!"

He glared at me. I could see he wanted to clout me, but he held back.

"I know it's hard, son. But it's for the best. Look, if you two still want to be together when you're seventeen and know your own minds, I'll support you. But until then, stay away from her, you hear me?"

I stormed out and ran. I ran like I'd never run before. Aimlessly and without care. I ran hard, so hard that my heart felt ready to burst. It didn't matter - it was already broken.

Seventeen? Why seventeen? That was over a year away. Nearer a year and a half! That was a fucking lifetime away!

I followed the cut. West. Why that way? It was away from Juliet.

When I could run no more, I sat on the clammy ground and roared with frustration. Birds took flight, and a fish or toad plopped in the canal.

Canals. Fucking canals! I was plagued by the bastard things.

I analysed the call over and over, trying to recall every word said. When I asked her to marry me, she replied, 'yes, I'm fine.'

Was that a yes, she would marry me? Was it slipped in furtively?

Carol breaks into my thoughts.

"Playing your records as usual," she observes.

"I am."

"We need to have a serious talk to Grace in the morning."

Before I can respond, she's gone. Off up to bed, no doubt, to lie and think about whatever it is she thinks about these days.

Grace...

Did my past have a bearing on how I handled her tonight? Of course it did.

Every paternal instinct dictated that my reaction be a little more like Carol's.

But I couldn't do it. I couldn't be a hypocrite.

So much of my life has been taken up by thinking about what might have been.

Perhaps Ben is Grace's 'one'.

If he is, and she is his, I have to do what I can to enable and support them.

Because I know - I know what the alternative is.

That's the thing they never understood, my parents and others.

It wasn't meeting Juliet and her falling pregnant that ruined my life. That was the best thing that ever happened to me.

Losing her was what destroyed me.

And I will play no part in destroying my daughter's chance of happiness in life.

20.

Four days of abject misery crawled by before a letter arrived.

Dad was at work when the post came, so I snaffled it when I got in from school. The postmark showed Canterwood.

I don't need to search through my albums. I go directly to the section, and locate The Four Pennies 'Juliet'.

Inside is the letter.

Do I like the album? Not really. It's not my thing.

But the moment I saw it in a second-hand record shop in Millby, I had to have it. It was five pounds.

It dated from long before our time, and was discovered by me many years after, but that didn't matter. If it encapsulated, or even hinted at her, I was sold.

My hand is steady this time, but it trembled when I first opened the envelope.

I didn't know what to expect. Would it be a reiterating of what she'd said on the phone, or a retraction and explanation of that call?

No small silver ring was contained therein, my fingers told me.

She licked this envelope, as she did the stamp affixed neatly in the corner. Will it still hold her DNA?

The paper is ruled, and torn from a school exercise book. The ink is pale blue and from a biro. Did she sit in class and write it? Which class was it, and what should she have been doing?

Her hand is rounded, flowing and feminine. The letter 'A', when capitalised, is a large version of a lower-case 'a', devoid of harsh points and angles. Her writing, like her, is curvaceous and sexy.

'Monday Oct. 17th, 1983.

My Darling Ant!

You must know I didn't mean a word of it! I was made to say the things I said on the phone on Saturday.

You are the rest of my life. You are my entire life. I think of nothing but you constantly.

But...

We cannot have contact for a while. I have to let my dad think we are finished. If he does, he'll relax, and we can be together again.

My hope is, if I can convince him, Jenny and I will spend Christmas and New Year at the pub. And if that happens, maybe - just maybe! - you can meet me there.

We will need to be very clever about how we do things from now on. I'm not even sure I can trust Jenny. If I get a chance, I will telephone you. If your dad answers, I'll need to hang up. If you answer, and he's there, let me know somehow. Just say that there's nobody there by that name.

If we do go to stay with my mum's sister, we may go on December 23rd. But it may not happen until Boxing Day. Do you think you can wait that long for me? It feels like so far away.

To be honest, I think I may need that time. I am booked into a clinic. Wednesday November 2nd is THE DATE.

Our baby will be taken from me, and we have no say in the matter. I'm angry, but what can I do? I wish I was older!

We will have children one day, won't we? I am certain that I do want children with you. How many will we have?

Are you sad or relieved?

I don't want to think about it, Ant. I want to think about afterwards, and the rest of my life with you!

You do still want to marry me, don't you? I worry that you've already found someone else, because of what I was made to say. I'm frightened that you won't wait for me, and will meet someone who you can be with.

I'm glad that it's getting dark earlier, my love.

Dark evenings mean I can move with less chance of being spotted. I hope it means I can get to a phone to call you. I go without lunch and save any money I can, for the phone or for stamps. Your dad will see if I reverse the charges. And what if he answers the call!?

I wish I had the money I earned in the pub in the summer. No! No, I don't. That paid towards our nights in Stratford with Monica.

Oh, it seems so long ago!

I used to dread the winter, and now I don't mind it at all.

Since I met you, I don't seem to mind anything. Apart from being apart, of course.

When I was little, I'd get upset this time of year. My mum told me it was because of the leaves dying and falling from the trees. I thought they would never come back.

It was silly, really, but I was only little.

Dark, colder weather means I wear my coat. And that hides me. The little bump showing on my tummy is under wraps. And I get out of PE! My dad wrote a note to the school saying I was to be excused until half-term because of verrucas!

I'm not sure that this letter will reach you. Will your dad take it before you can see it? Would he do that? Mine would.

I have to get away from him, my darling love. But I have to think of Jenny, too. She is all alone, apart from me. And she's so young.

I rub my bump when I'm alone in bed and Jenny is asleep. I whisper to it, and tell it about how he or she came about. I tell him or her about you.

And I tell the bump that I'm sorry he or she will never meet you.

I ache for you...

I love you! I love you more than I ever thought it possible to love anything.

Only my mum can compare.

I wish my mum was alive right now! If she was, my life would be so different.

Well, I'd better sign off for now. I'll call you as soon as I can.

You do still want me, Ant, don't you? I'd die if you didn't!

Perhaps it would be better if I did die when I go to the clinic. You could then live your life without me and all the trouble that follows me around.

I'm so sorry if I hurt you. I wouldn't do that for the world. But we have to pretend for a while. Just for a few weeks. I will be sixteen in January, and you in March. If we can get to then, they can't stop us being together. Nobody can!

Wait for me, my love.

Know that you have all of my love for ever.

Your Juliet

xxxxxxxxxxxxxxxxxxx'

Three weeks passed. It was twenty-one days during which so much changed, but nothing happened in my world.

A life was ended.

It took place in a clinic in Canterwood. I had no say. I wasn't welcome there.

I'm not pro or anti anything on that issue. What other people do is up to them, and none of my concern. Who am I to judge?

They will have to live with their decisions, and, if they believe in a higher being, they will ultimately have to answer to them.

Having no say in the matter bothered me. Not being by her side irked me more.

Juliet had no say either. It was forced on her.

But we were so young. And we may have thought ourselves mature and ready for parenthood, but I know, looking back, that we weren't. Well, I wasn't.

All of that said, I wish we'd had a baby. Had that happened, I would have a lifelong connection to Juliet.

However painful that link might have been, and still would be, I would take it. It would be better than nothing.

When she next contacted me, Juliet was without child.

It came through a phone call on a Wednesday morning. November 9th.

It was about eight o'clock. I was getting ready for school. She was on her way to school. Dad was at work, as she knew he would be.

The peeps.

"Juliet?"

"My darling."

"Marry me!"

"Yes! Oh, you still want me!"

"Of course I do."

"Just to hear your voice..." she struggled to say.

"And yours. How are you? How did it go?"

"I'm okay, I think. I was bad for a few days. I was off school, but I went back on Monday."

"Did anybody say anything?"

"No. Not really. I think a couple of girls suspect something, but I said I had flu. My dad wrote another letter."

"Are you sure that you're, you know, okay?"

"Yes, I'm fine. Don't worry. I have to see you."

"When? How?" I pleaded.

"We're going to the pub after Christmas. On Boxing Day..."

"I'll find a way to get there."

"Wait. My dad's coming with us. He'll be staying that night, before heading back to Canterwood on the 27th. With Christmas falling on the weekend, it's a holiday, so he's off work."

"Then I'll come for the 28th!"

"How will you get away? What will you tell your dad?"

"I'll think of something."

"You can't just run away, Ant. If you do, he'll ring my dad, and then we'll be in trouble."

"I know."

"And I can't trust Jenny, or my aunt and uncle, so we'll have to be very smart. I probably won't be able to see much of you."

"I don't care. If I only get to hold you for one minute, it'll be worth it."

"I should be okay for 'you know what' by then. The clinic said a few weeks."

"Oh, Juliet, if all I can do is lie with you and cuddle you, that'll be enough."

"I could still do other things."

"Don't!" I chuckled. "Did it hurt? At the clinic, I mean."

"Not at the time. I had some pain afterwards. And the anesthetic made me sick."

"Who was with you?"

"My nan came in the end. Thank god! It was better with her there than my dad."

"Is she your dad's mum, or your mum's?"

"My dad's. My mum's family have nothing to do with him. Except my aunt and uncle at the pub. And they only see him so that they can see me and Jenny."

"Why?"

"I don't know. There was some falling out when mum was ill."

"But he's going for Christmas?"

"Yes. It was the only way they'd get to see us, I think, so they agreed."

"What's your dad's problem with you and me?" I asked her.

"It's not just with you, Ant. He has a problem with all of my boyfriends. Not that I've had many. I don't know... He's angry, I think. And he drinks a lot. That makes him worse."

"Angry at what?"

"Angry at the way his life's turned out, I suppose. He's lumbered with me and Jen, and his wife died."

"How old was your mum when she died?"

"Thirty-seven."

I thought of my own parents being older than that. "Shit," was all I could think to say.

"The cancer spread too much before they spotted it. That was why my mum's family blamed him, I think. Because he didn't make her see a doctor, even though she was ill for a long time."

"What do you think?"

"I don't know. We didn't know anything, me and Jen. She wasn't well. Then she went to hospital. Then she died."

"Did you visit her?"

"In the hospital?"

"Yes."

"Yes. I remember going to see her. She was on morphine, and pretty out of it. But she forced a smile, and told me she loved me. She made me promise I'd look after my sister, and do as my dad told me."

"I'm sorry, Juliet. I'm sorry your mum died."

"Thank you, my darling."

"Am I really going to see you?" I asked excitedly.

"I hope so."

"How many weeks is it?"

"Seven," she answered unhesitatingly.

"You counted them?"

"Yes."

"How long is it since I saw you?" I further asked.

"Ten weeks and two days."

"You counted those too?"

"Every single second," she answered. I had no doubt that she had. "I have to go," she said, the pips sounding.

"Try to ring me soon," I implored her.

"I'll try. I love you."

"I love you."

I went to school, my confidence restored.

It wasn't a confidence that altered me outwardly. I was always quiet, even during that time of Juliet. Most conversations I had were with myself in my mind. I thought of things that would make me inwardly laugh, but felt no need to share them and win friends.

It did manifest itself, though, that self-assuredness. It must have done.

Why else did the bullying stop?

Perhaps it was simply on account of me becoming less of a swot at school. Lessons and tests didn't matter all of a sudden. That attitude made me more likable or accepted.

Or was it because I didn't give a shit, and bullies are adept at honing in on vulnerabilities that make us victims? In short, nothing they could do would bother me. There were easier victims for them to target.

I'm unsure whether I was mature enough for the kind of sexual relationship I had with Juliet. At the beginning, I probably wasn't.

Did the sex make me more mature? I don't know how it works, but there must be some kind of chemical reaction that comes with it - some release of hormones that had an affect on my mind and body.

I was more surly and somewhat aloof. More introspective, I suppose.

It was no surprise that I discovered The Smiths right around that time.

21.

An after-work game of squash with Kelvin turned into this. There was no squash.

There was no Kelvin.

I bought a racquet. That was when I discovered how to spell it.

He cancelled at the last minute. Something cropped up at work. He was very apologetic, and overstated how sorry he was.

I wasn't.

The Red Lion is hardly heaving at five on a weekday. A few men in suits dot the bar, staring into phones or the tops of their pints. None of them, I sense, want to be here. It's simply better than going home.

I include myself in that.

Things have been grim since Grace and Ben were rumbled.

Speaking of illicit sex, I'm as sure as I can be that Kelvin is with Carol right now. That was the 'something that cropped up.'

Should I be angry? Should I be tearing round to the office, and fighting for... My honour? Her honour?

That answers my own question - I don't even know what I'd be fighting for.

Being a Thursday, Carol is supposed to be at dance class. I could go there, and prove a point through her absence. At least then I'd know. Well, not for sure, but it would leave little doubt.

What will any of it achieve?

"Here he is! The man I owe my life to - the gentleman I attribute my wellbeing to - the reason I am above ground!"

"Hello, George."

"Now, I insist - adamant, I am - and shall not take no for an answer - I am buying you a drink - procuring you a beverage - furnishing you with a pint of Jemford Best!"

"Thought you'd never offer."

He returns with two pints, sets them down, and sits opposite me.

"Now, I must apologise to you for my lack of gratitude, I fear, on our last encounter," he begins.

"Oh, there's no need," I assure him.

"No. I told you something daft - something I wish I could take back - something I didn't mean. I didn't want to die that day, Anthony lad."

"No, well..."

"It was the shock, I think, made me talk peculiar like - the near-death experience left me befuddled - a lack of oxygen rendered me somewhat confused."

"I understand."

"Cheers," he says, touching my glass with his. "It's been difficult adjusting, you see? My wife, Angela, she left me a while back."

"I'm sorry to hear that, George."

"Yes, well, not as sorry as I was, I can tell you that. Gutted, I was - cut to ribbons by it - mortified!

"But you have to ask yourself, see - you have to step back and take stock. What do I want more than anything in the world?

"Well, what I want most of all in life, is for Angela to be happy. That's all I've ever wanted. Since Engelbert, her happiness has been my primary concern - my number one aim in life - my dearest wish.

"I know I can be an awkward character - a man with peculiar ways - not the easiest to be around, perhaps. And that was fine when I was working.

"Suddenly, I'm on the scrapheap - put out to graze - a man lacking purpose, I dare say.

"That was hard, that was. Bloody hard! A lot more difficult than I imagined it would be, to make that adjustment - to find my feet - to settle in to retired life.

"I was bloody selfish, to tell you the truth. I didn't chip in - didn't pull my weight - didn't play a part in home life!

"And what about her life? Angela's? Her workload increased because of me being there all the while, moping about - maudlin - miserable. Getting under her feet - in her way - making demands. I was carrying on like I was still supervising at work, see? That was my mistake!"

"So, what will you do?" I ask him.

"Win her back - reclaim her - recapture her heart!"

"How?"

"By being all that she needs me to be - all she desires - all she wants in life!"

"O-kay, erm, how?"

"Trains are going to have to go!"

"Trains?"

"Model railway. oo Gauge - 1:76 scale - sixteen point five millimetre."

"And you don't mind getting rid of them?"

"For Angela, I don't mind getting rid of anything. I'll make a batch of dandelion wine, and..."

"Not dandelion, George," I jump in, recalling Carol mentioning it as being one of the problems. "What about a nice drop of elderberry?"

"Hey, that's a thought - there's a notion - worth considering certainly. You understand women," he says to me.

"I wouldn't say that exactly. It takes a while, though, making wine..."

"It does. To do it properly - to get it right."

"You should buy some bottles, next time you're down the shops getting your dinner."

"Buy it? I haven't had to buy wine in years, lad!"

"No, but perhaps Angela would like a different wine. One made by someone else. I'm just thinking out loud."

"Yes, I see where you're going. Because that would be drinkable now - instant - a ready-to-serve libation!"

"There you go. What will you do with your trains?"

"Sell them, I expect - hock them off - flog the lot. And I'll use the money to book us a holiday some place. Tinbury Head or somewhere. Perhaps Skegness..."

"Or abroad?" I gently suggest, and worry I may have overstepped the mark.

"She did always fancy a train holiday. A real train, I mean - one that carries people - Orient Express."

"There you go. Be apt, that."

"It would, wouldn't it? Trains for a train."

"Or a cruise, perhaps," I toss in to the mix.

He drifts off, imagining his trip with his returned wife. I use the gap to fetch us two more pints. I'm appreciative of the company, and to engage with someone whose life is even shitter than mine.

Misery loves company, I guess.

"Here," he says, "you like your music, as I recall - fond of a tune - keen on a ditty?"

"That's right."

Shit, he's going to sing again.

"Bet you won't know this one - before your time - from back when songs meant something!"

He takes a sip of his pint by way of lubrication.

"...aaaa-you gotta ride it like you find it get your ticket at the station of the rock island liiiine!"

Good fucking grief. And it was going so well.

Mostly to stop him, I break in with, "hey, here's a thought, George. I read in the paper something about Engelbert Humperdinck touring in 2020. Now, that would be a treat for Angela, I bet."

"Is that right? I took her to see him, you know, and our special song was by Engelbert?"

"I know. That's why I suggested it."

"I shall look into that. Do you have a special song?"

"Several."

"Ah, there's always one that gets you."

"I was listening to The Four Pennies, 'Juliet' recently. That one always..."

"There was a love, I knew before, a-she broke my heart, a-left me unsuuuure..."

"Yep, yep, that's the one. Close enough."

"Here, this is what I want to know - this is my confusion - the thing I'm struggling to comprehend and make sense of."

"What's that?" I reply.

"Why aren't you at home with this Juliet? Because, I can tell you now, if Angela was waiting for me, I should not be sat here with you! No offence meant - no disrespect intended."

"None taken. Ah, if Juliet was waiting for me, I would never leave her side."

"Out and about is she? You have to give them space - let them do their own thing now and again - allow them a bit of breathing room. That's what I failed to do with Angela in recent times, and it cost me dear."

"I think my wife is having an affair," I say to my total surprise.

"I'll tell you something, man to man - between us - not to be repeated," he says, leaning closer to me.

"Go on."

"All the things you worry about when you're young - forget them. You get older, and you won't give a toss about those things.

"To tell you the truth, I kept Angela on a tight rein - a short leash - and I did that because I knew she was too good for me, deep down. I was the luckiest man alive, to be with her. And I was always terrified of losing her, see?"

I nod.

"I stopped her living her life, to some degree. Especially after I retired. I wanted her there with me all the time, and she wanted to be off doing what she'd been doing.

"Take her Dancing Class, for example. I bet she's there now, jumping around and having a merry old time. And where's the harm? What's the worry in that? How can it hurt?

"But me, being a daft old sod, I tried to stop her - tried to keep her close - attempted to harness her.

"I should have bloody gone with her. That's what I should have done! And I shall, if I get another chance.

"This Juliet you mentioned - you said how you'd never leave her side. Well, that's the wrong way to go about things, if you'll pardon me saying so.

"All that'll do is drive her away. I know! Look at what's happened to me."

"It's different."

"Are you sure? Angela had an affair, you know?"

"Really?" I say.

"Yes. It was years ago - in the eighties. With a man she met in a shop she worked in. Spitting image of Engelbert, he was. Dark hair and a moustache."

"What did you do?"

"Nothing - not a thing - absolutely bugger all."

"Why not?"

"Because it made her happy. She needed it."

"Even so, she cheated on you."

"Cheated? Who said anything about cheating? She came to me, and we talked about it. I told her to go ahead, if it would make her happy - give her a lift - brighten her world!

"Her mum had died, and she was very low. I couldn't lift her out of the doldrums - raise her from the pit of despair - restore her to her former glory. So, I let Engelbert do it, in a way. It was a bit of a fantasy thing for her, I suppose."

"Did you worry about losing her, though?"

"No. I knew it was an itch she needed to scratch - something she had to do while she was young enough. She'd only ever had relations with me, you see?"

"My mum was the same."

"And what happened there?"

"She left in 1983."

"There you go - there you have it - there you are!"

"But Angela still left you," I remind him.

"She did - I can't deny it - I have to agree. But not for those reasons. She left me because I didn't treat her right. Truth is, I reckon she might have left me thirty-five years sooner, had I not given her that bit of freedom.

"And I'll tell you something else for nothing. Once she'd scratched that itch of hers, we were a lot better in 'that department', if you follow my meaning. Yes, her having that comparison, I think, helped us both.

"Now, listen to me, an old man.

"This woman of yours - this Juliet - if you love her, and I mean really love her - do whatever you have to do to make it work!

"And if you can't be bothered doing that, then you don't deserve her!

"But if you release her - let her go - give her all the freedom she wants - and she decides not to come back to you...

"Well, in that case - if that happens - if that's how it pans out - then she doesn't deserve you!

"Either way, at least you'll know."

And I remember. I recall years before, precisely where and when I'd met George.

22.

"How was your dance class?"

"Fine. Same as always."

"Carol, we need to talk."

"I'm tired," she says, and goes to walk away.

"Don't go. Please."

"I need a shower, and I have to get changed."

She doesn't usually bother with a shower after her dance class. It's not that rigorous.

"Have you eaten?" I ask her.

"I had something earlier. I might just have a sandwich. What about you?"

"The same. I'll make us both a sandwich. What do you want in it?"

"There's some ham in the fridge needs using. And a bag of salad."

Will she strip, and see her body in the mirror, or does she avert her eyes? Can she stand to look at herself?

I've not done a very good job of making her feel desired. When was the last time I paid her an unprompted compliment? I think it, but I don't say it.

I struggle with receiving praise, Because of that, I don't value it.

It stems from childhood. Mum and dad were hardly lavish with praise and encouragement. But other events in my life have also made me wary of it.

At school, being praised and getting good marks made me a victim. Thus, I shied away from them in order to survive. Not to be popular. Merely to survive and have a tolerable time there.

I dumbed and dimmed myself down, lest I should shine too brightly and attract attention.

Anonymity suited me.

The Town Crier in Stratford was so out of character for me. With Juliet by my side, I wanted everybody in the world to see me.

Her shining so bright made it okay for me to shine alongside her, because I would never be able to put her in the shade.

"Thanks for the sandwich, Anthony."

I encourage people, even my wife, to call me by the full name I've always disliked.

Ant was someone else. That name belongs to Juliet, and my time with her.

Detachment. Separation. I compartmentalise every facet of my life in order to keep her all to myself.

Adultery? In my mind I've been committing it for all of my time with Carol. And others before her.

So many times, when having sex with other women, I've shut my eyes and held my breath and cast Juliet in their places.

And in the flush of passion, I've tried to summon my special power.

In my head, I've implored - 'I wish I was with Juliet!'

I wonder - did they see the disappointment when I opened my eyes?

We have no special record, Carol and I. If we did, I'd dig it out now and play it loudly. For once, it wouldn't be underhand, secretively playing through headphones so that it might take me into a world of my own.

Not a world of my imagining, because it was real. It was so very fucking real.

I stopped being a dreamer when I met Juliet. Yet, I've dreamt of her ever since.

The other dreams, the ones before her, were aspirational. They were achievable. Did I think they would all come true one day? No, I wasn't naive. Still, they only depended on me to make them happen.

As soon as you begin to dream of something that is reliant on another, it becomes so much more difficult.

It's why I'm a loner. It's why I have no aspiration at work. It's why I'm a record collector.

Leave me alone to get on with it, and I'll be okay. Don't make me put my faith in others.

"Shall I put some music on? What do you fancy listening to?" I ask her as she eats.

"Anything. I don't care."

She listens to chart music. I can't make head nor tail of it, all the 'featuring' and 'remixed by'.

It's what she dances to at her classes - middle-aged and elderly women boogieing away to music that should belong to Grace's generation.

Grace? I have no idea what she listens to. It isn't the shit in the charts, I'm pretty sure of that.

Does she lie in her room, ear-buds in, and listen to the lyrics and apply them to her life - her love with Ben? Do they sometimes break her heart and have the power to reduce her to tears?

And not always sad. Often happy or erotic.

Ultimately sad, though, because harking back to the past, by definition, always must be.

No better memories have come along to supercede them.

There is no music I can play for 'us' - for Carol and I. So I go with the record already on the platter.

The Smiths debut on Rough Trade with the cursive logo.

"I popped in the Red Lion today," I tell her. "I saw George in there."

"That must have been fun."

"It was alright. He's not so bad, when you get to know him."

She's disinterested.

I push on, though. "He wants Angela back."

"Well he would, wouldn't he? Men only appreciate what they have after they've lost it."

"Am I losing you, Carol?"

"Pah! Where would I go?"

"I don't know. To be with somebody like Kelvin perhaps?"

"Don't be ridiculous. Is that what all this is about?"

"All what?"

"Talking and music and making me a sandwich!"

"I suppose so, yes," I confirm.

"You have nothing to worry about on that score."

"I'm not worried. I just want you to be happy. And I don't think you are," I say, and sit next to her.

She lifts her legs on the sofa to form a barrier and distance herself from me.

"It's not me you should be worried about. It's Grace!"

"Grace will be fine. She's in love. And she's fifteen. Don't you remember what it was like?"

She doesn't answer.

"Do you remember, Carol? Was there someone you thought you loved when you were Grace's age?"

She smarts at the 'Grace's age' line.

"I don't mean to imply you're old. You're not. You're in great shape, and you make such an effort with yourself. I do notice, you know? And I think it's wonderful. I think you look fantastic."

I feel my face colour ever so slightly. Praise again, prickling at me.

"Of course I had boyfriends at fifteen," she concedes. "But the world was different back then."

"Was it?"

"Yes. And Grace needs to focus on her education. She needs to go to university, and get a degree. She won't get anywhere nowadays without a degree. It's not like it was, Anthony."

"What does it matter?"

"Of course it matters."

"I just want Grace to be happy," I say.

"And you think I don't? But getting banged up and her head turned by some lad so much older than her - where's that going to lead her?"

"She's not daft, Carol."

"Really? Well, what do you know about this Ben she's seeing?"

"Not much," I admit.

"No. Well I do. He works down the town, in a shop selling computer games. He's not going to university, is he? And if we're not careful, nor will Grace. He'll spoil her opportunities in life, you mark my words."

"What if he's the only thing she'll ever find in life that will make her happy?"

"You're being ridiculous."

"No, I'm not. I don't want her living her life with a regret."

Carol looks at me curiously.

"Are you talking about Grace, or us?" she asks me.

"All of us. Everybody."

"Oh, Anthony," she sighs wearily, "you need to get over things that happened years ago. This music - how old is it?"

"It's from the eighties. Eighty-four, to be precise."

"Right. When you were sixteen or so?"

"Yes."

"That's your trouble. You live in the past, and you think everybody else does the same. What's done is done, and can't be changed."

"We're all clinging on to something from the past, it defines us to some extent," I say. "Lately, I've been thinking a lot about past relationships, and..."

"How long have you known?" she interrupts me.

"A long time."

"Why didn't you say something?"

"I don't know. The time never seemed right."

"Oh, Anthony. Is that what's been bothering you? Stuff from the ancient past?"

"It is."

"Look, Kelvin and I went out for a few months when I was about seventeen. Things happened, and we split up. I connected with him through the internet - through the school site. I hadn't seen him in years. We got chatting, realised he had an office in Oakburn, and he asked me if I'd go and work for him."

"Erm, right. Kelvin."

"Yes. I should have told you, I know. I'm sorry for that. But what difference does it make?"

"None, I suppose. Did you love him?"

"I was fond of him, but it didn't work out. We all have a past, Anthony. It isn't worth getting upset about."

"No, I suppose it isn't. What about Grace, though? Shouldn't she have a chance to create her own past?"

"Like I say, times are different."

A stab of the remote control signals the end of our chat.

"It's nine o'clock," she informs me, "and I want to watch the rerun of 'Bangkok Hilton'. Do you remember it?"

"No."

"Nicole Kidman."

"Right. How old is it?"

"1989, I think. God, I was sixteen or seventeen when it came out originally!"

Well, at least we communicated.

Is that her way of travelling through time? Via a television series dating from when she was with Kelvin.

Did they watch it together, or did she watch it at home with her parents and siblings, and think of him throughout?

I slink away to my music and my own secret garden of rich pickings and hidden corners.

In a way, I envy Carol. She has her memories back in her life. They're accessible and touchable to her.

If Juliet reappeared in mine, I know with certainty that I would seek and embrace every part of my history with her.

Moreover, I would walk away from all I know, simply to be with her once more.

And that would be easier now. Now that I know about Carol and Kelvin.

23.

I summoned my special power, though I can't remember precisely what I wished for. The crux was for something to chance along that would enable me to illicitly, but seemingly legitimately, meet Juliet at the pub.

A school trip was my opportunity. Well, that, and dad being distracted by a new romantic interest.

I couldn't stand her, the woman he met. But I was appreciative of her arriving on the scene when she did, it being late-November of 1983.

Her name was Rosemary. She had three kids. Two boys younger than me, and a daughter a year older. They didn't move in per se, but they practically fucking did.

In the short term, it removed privacy, and the ability to speak freely with Juliet on the phone. Our conversations became more coded as a result.

The school trip was due to begin on the 27th and run through to the 2nd of January. Six days in the Lake District doing god knows what, weather permitting.

It was dishonest, taking the cash dad gave me for it, but that money would afford me accommodation somewhere close to Juliet. That was all I could think about.

Mostly grey and damp, but mild on the whole, is how I remember that winter of 83-84. Christmas dragged by, Rosemary and her brood ever-present. She cooked the dinner. The boys were young and still 'believed'. The daughter was as quiet and introverted as me. She wanted us to be friends, but I wasn't interested.

I forget her name. That's how little attention I paid. She offered to help me with the exam studying I was pretending to do locked away in my room.

In different circumstances, I might have explored some kind of relationship. She wasn't unattractive, but I could see that she would turn into her mother at some point. A gnarled, pushy, busy-body who, once she got her claws in, would never relent.

I kept my distance and rode it out till the day of departure.

On the evening of the 26th, I packed my rucksack having spent the day with mum over in Jemford Bridge.

Dad came to see me in my room. "Are you going to be alright?"

I nodded.

"It's good," he said, "you going on this trip. It might take your mind of that girl you met. Cheer you up a bit."

I shrugged.

"Here," he added, holding out a twenty pound note. "Part of your Christmas present."

"Thanks." I felt guilt then, knowing the money for the trip was hidden in a sock I'd packed.

I thought about telling him the truth. But I knew he'd stop me from going if I did.

"Hey Anthony," he said as he reached my bedroom door.

"Yeah?"

"Be careful, alright? Just... Be careful."

The way he said it, I wondered if he knew the truth after all. Or suspected. Still, if he did, he wasn't stopping me.

It was a risk, all of it. Not that I was concerned about the repercussions. My primary worry was Juliet not actually being there.

We hadn't spoken since the Thursday before Christmas - the 22nd. At that time, her stay at the pub was still on, heading up there on the 26th. Her father planned on leaving on the 27th.

Being a holiday schedule, it was set to be an arduous train journey. And so it proved. By the time I reached the final leg to Warwick, I'd missed the connection, and there were no more trains that day.

It wasn't as late as it felt, but was pitch black as I marched those miles along the road, stepping to the verge every time a car came. I walked into the traffic, headlights blinding me, the hood of my parka conically protecting my face from the chilly damp blasts each vehicle displaced.

A line of cars and vans pulled away from a red light, so I skipped up the bank.

I saw him as he crept by, Juliet's father. A van coming the other way lit him up as he drove past my narrow view through my hood.

Had he seen me?

There was no option but to carry on. I was only a couple or three miles away. Another hour perhaps.

I had nowhere booked to stay the night. If need be, I'd sleep rough somewhere.

On I walked, chipping away at the miles, having to pause every couple of minutes as traffic came by.

In the village, I rang the pub from a phone box.

What would I say if her aunt or uncle answered? A panic set in.

"Hello?" Was it her?

"Hello. I wondered if you were open this evening?"

"No, sorry, we're closed for the holiday. We're open again from Saturday."

"Juliet?"

"Ant?"

"Yes."

"Oh! Where are you?"

"Five minutes away. I'm at the phone box by the Post Office."

"I was terrified you'd get here too soon. My dad only left about an hour ago."

"I know. I saw him on the road."

"Did he see you?"

"I don't think so."

"He can't have done, or he'd have come back."

"Where should I go?" I asked her.

"Here! To the pub. I'll tell you everything when you get here."

"Meet me by the caravan in ten minutes."

"No need. The caravan's not here. Just come to the pub and knock the door."

"Really?"

"Yes!"

She didn't wait for me to get that far. I knew it was her, despite the dark and the fact she was wrapped up in a long coat. I knew by the way she moved.

And my stomach rolled over and over itself in a sickening yet blissful way.

She ran to me. I was too exhausted to reciprocate. My feet were sore and blistered, and I hadn't eaten anything since leaving home all those hours before.

Such was the power with which she connected, and with my rucksack on my back, I almost toppled backwards.

"Marry me!" I said before her mouth found mine.

And she nodded emphatically that she would, her hands clamping my cheeks, and moving my head up and down in time with hers - her eyes glistening wet, staring into mine beneath the yellow light of a lamppost.

Nothing and nobody could keep us apart!

"Come on," she said, leading me by my hand back to the pub.

"What's going on?"

"Last minute changes. Dad went back to Canterwood as planned. I pretended I wanted to go because of a party at New Year. Of course, I didn't."

"Anyway, dad agreed to me staying here. My aunt and uncle are away in the caravan till Friday, seeing his family in the Lake District. Jenny went with them. They left just after dad."

"So, we have the place to ourselves?"

She nodded and grinned. "For three nights."

She further explained, "I offered to be here to take deliveries ready for New Year. It couldn't have worked out any better. I could have gone with them, but I said I needed to revise for my exams anyway."

"Ha!" I cackled as we entered the warmth of the public house, "we might both have ended up in the Lake District at the same time."

"I know! I thought that. We were meant to be together, however it might have gone. I think my mum's looking out for me!"

"You're so cold," she added, and began warming my ears in her hands, her breath and mouth thawing my nose and eyes.

"I'm so hungry," I told her.

"I'll put a couple of pasties in the oven."

"In a while," I replied.

She read my meaning, and directed my hands under her red wool jumper. They found her breasts, as the heat of her radiated into me.

"Are you okay?" I asked her pointedly.

"I'm fine, my darling."

"After the operation, I mean?"

"I knew what you meant. And, yes, everything's fine."

"How do you know?"

"How do I know that it's fine for us to make love?"

"Yes," I confirmed.

"I just do."

"Because, if it isn't, I'm happy just to be with you."

"Ant, it's absolutely fine. Trust me. Anyway, I'm on the pill now."

"Really?"

"Yes. My doctor started me on it. He said it was to help regulate my periods, but it isn't really for that. Food," she announced, "I need you fit and strong!"

We ate our pasties and drank hot tea in front of the fire in the living room. I was edgy that first evening, expecting someone to come back and discover us. The longer it didn't happen, so the more I relaxed.

"Hey," she said, "tell me about this new girlfriend of your dad's! Is she as horrible as you said on the phone?"

And so I did.

When I got to her daughter, Juliet said, "is she pretty?"

"No. Well, if she is, she's not my type."

"What colour is her hair?"

"Dark brown."

"Has she got a nice figure?"

"I don't know. I haven't really looked. Anyway, she hides her figure in baggy dark clothing."

"So you tried to look then?"

"No! She's a bit stick-like. And a bit weird."

"She's there, though, isn't she? Available, I mean."

"Juliet, stop. Don't…"

"Men can't help themselves. Has she tried it on with you?"

"No. We've barely spoken. She offered to help with my revision."

"Is she doing A-levels?"

"Yes, I think so."

"Don't cheat on me, Ant. It's the one thing."

"Never! I never would, Juliet. Don't even think it."

She settled against me again.

We went to bed at some point. We slept in her room, pushing the two single beds together. It was where we'd first had sex, almost five months before.

I was so gentle with her, worried about her healing after the abortion.

"Thank you for caring," she said to me afterwards.

Only under cover of darkness did we venture outside. The nights arrived early in late-December, so we went for strolls and avoided the village. The cut and the countryside were enough for us.

On our walk on the Wednesday evening, I pointed out, "I'll need to find somewhere to stay from Friday night."

"I've been thinking about that. About how we can be together, I mean."

"How?" I asked eagerly.

"Well, obviously overnight is a problem. But if you had something more like a hotel, we could at least go there during the day. I have some money I got for Christmas. How much have you got?"

"Over eighty pounds, with the money from the school trip, the twenty dad gave me, and some I had. All I've spent is the train fare."

"Okay, so we have over a hundred between us. You have to be home on Monday, so three nights."

"If we need more, I could use the last of my savings," I suggested.

"No, it's too risky. Your dad will want to know why. And he'll be able to see that you got it here."

"How much will a hotel be?"

"It's New Year, that's the problem. The pub will be packed, and so will everywhere else. Even so, you might get a room for thirty a night."

"What are we going to do, Juliet?"

"Monica?"

"I thought of that. But won't she wonder why you aren't staying with me?"

"Unless I did stay with you," she suggested.

"Your dad will find out. And he'll tell my dad."

She went quiet.

"We can't run away, Juliet. I can't put my parents through that again."

Everything's so 'in the moment' when you're young. Something happens to us as we get older. We feel a need to plan everything, and preempt every eventuality.

The closer Friday got without anything in place, the more likely we were to do something rash.

Ah, but those two and a bit days in the pub! They were flawless, as we played husband and wife.

We cooked and ate together. We bathed and showered together. We slept together. And we had the most perfect sex imaginable three times a day at least, such was our insatiability for one another.

The rest of our lives would be like that, we vowed.

24.

On the Friday morning, I packed and left her.

I stayed with Monica because I couldn't bear the thought of being alone in unfamiliar surroundings.

"Where's your young missus?" she beamed at me on arrival.

"Around. She's staying on campus at Warwick University, but I thought I'd come and see you. Nothing much for me to do there."

"Oh, well, that's smashing! It's lovely to see you."

She put me in the same room Juliet and I had shared. I soaked in the tub we'd used. It all helped me cope with not being with her.

Did she know, Monica? Did she sense it?

We met, Juliet and I, in Stratford on the Friday afternoon. Everything felt preordained, as she gave me a slab of Kendal Mint Cake her aunt had got for her. I could give it to my dad when I got back home.

Juliet was my best friend. Yes, the passion and sex are where my mind goes when I think back. But we were so close. I felt that I could tell her anything.

And I did. I told her everything about my life - past, present and my dreams for the future. It was a shared dream.

On the Saturday - New Year's Eve - it was so cold we had to find somewhere indoors. She couldn't stay long, as her services were required in the pub. We sat in a cafe in Warwick, and drank coffee, making a cup last forty minutes.

New Year's Day was our focus. Monica would be out all day seeing her family, so I'd have the B&B to myself. The pub was closed until the evening. It was our final chance to be alone together.

That Saturday evening, I sat with Monica and shared a bottle of wine.

Once she'd loosened me up, she asked, "what's going on, Ant?"

"Nothing. Why?"

"I didn't come down with the last shower, you know?"

"I don't know what you mean."

"Now, you do know that Warwick University isn't in Warwick, don't you, Ant?"

I blushed. I didn't have a clue.

"It's in Coventry," she informed me. "You and Juliet - there's more there than meets the eye. She's not at Warwick University at Christmas and New Year. Now, what's really going on? Why don't I pour us the rest of the wine, and you can tell me?"

With glasses replenished, I began. "I love Juliet more than I've ever loved anything in my life. Everything else doesn't even come close. And I know that she feels the same about me. But we can't be together."

"Why not?"

"Her dad won't allow it."

"Okay, you told me that before. And I told you - bugger him! If you want to be together, be together. I told you about me and my Ed. Nothing would have kept us apart. And people tried, believe you me."

"It's not that easy."

"It is. I see the love between the pair of you. You don't even see the world when you're together. And I remember that feeling."

"Next year, things will be easier," I told her.

"Next year is tomorrow," she reminded me.

THE CUT

"It is, isn't it?"

"Right, so don't waste a day. I look back on my fifty years with Ed, and I regret every single day we spent apart. There weren't many, but if I could turn back the clock, I'd have spent them with him.

"I mean it, Ant. You might think me a daft mare, but I'm right on this one, so you pay attention to batty old Monica!"

I grinned at her, as she glared at me over the coffee table.

It dawned on me then. She wasn't messing around. She was so serious that it made her a little angry and emotional.

"It's all I want in the world, Monica, to be with Juliet every day of my life."

"I had a feeling, you know, when you left together last time you were here. I had a strange sensation about Juliet."

I recalled the knowing expression on her face.

She continued before I could say anything. "I had this overwhelming thing about a baby, and Juliet carrying one. Was I right?"

"Yes."

"Is that what happened? Is that why her dad is so against it?"

"I think so."

"When's she due?"

"She's not. He made her get rid of it."

Monica stared hard at me through the dim light.

"Made her, you say?"

I nodded.

"How old are you?" she asked, and I felt a dread rise to my sternum.

"Sixteen," I fibbed.

"And Juliet?"

"A couple of months older than me." That was true, at least.

Silence reigned. Monica held her wine, the stem suspended between two fingers, the bowl cradled in her palm, but she didn't drink it. The little finger on that hand stroked the wedding ring on her other hand rhythmically.

I didn't drink my wine either. It didn't feel right.

"I could get into trouble, you know?" she said eventually.

"I'm sorry."

Monica placed her glass on the table, stood and left the room.

Was she ringing the police? I thought about running, but where would I run to at that hour on New Year's Eve?

She returned after a few minutes.

"Here," she said, and held out the money I'd paid her.

"I'll go and pack my things. I'm sorry, Monica," I said, standing.

"You'll do no such thing! Where are you going to go? Besides, you won't find another place to stay this time of night. Sit back down!"

I sat back down.

"We've both told a bit of a tale," she said, picking up her wine again. "Now, you take that money. There's nothing in the ledger, so you're here as my guest. I have a feeling you might need that cash at some point, so hang on to it.

"When my son picks me up tomorrow morning, you stay out of sight. Understand?"

"Yes."

"See, now, I met my Ed when I was fourteen, as I told you in the summer last. I also told you that we behaved ourselves till I was sixteen. Well, did we heck as like!

"We were at it like rabbits from the off! And, you can guess, I fell pregnant when I was fifteen."

She takes a sip of wine. I mimic her.

"Well, you can imagine the scandal in those days - the shame! But I wasn't ashamed. Oh no! And there was talk, from Ed's family, about entrapment, and me deliberately getting 'in the club' to ensnare their son. Load of twaddle!

"Money was offered for me to disappear and start afresh elsewhere. And there was talk about a back-street termination!

"We were having none of it, Ed and myself. He stood by me, that wonderful man. He gave up any inheritance he had coming, and told 'em to shove it!

"He told anybody who'd listen, and quite a few who didn't want to hear - he told them that he loved me, and that we'd be wed as soon as we could!

"Frank came from that. My eldest son. He's in his fifties now, as you'll have worked out. He'll pick me up tomorrow, and I shall have a cracking time with him and the rest of the family.

"He's a rock, is Frank, just like his father. And there's not a day gone by that I've ever regretted that decision to have him.

"I see so many people, making life decisions based on this and that - money and bloody houses and god only knows what else. Even the kids they have aren't born from love. They're planned bloody pregnancies - fashion accessories with their whole lives mapped out for them before they've so much as taken a breath in the world!

"It'll all count for nought when you get to my age. The only precious things I own are in here," she said, tapping her head. "and them things that came from my life with Ed. Five kids - now, let me think a bit - eleven grandchildren, and two great-granddaughters!

"He lives on, you see? He's here, every day, through them. Because every single bit of it came through love!

"So, you keep your money, young Ant. And I expect you've already made plans to take advantage of my not being here tomorrow?"

I blushed again, nodded, and offered her a shy smile.

"Good for you! Now, ten wants a quarter. Shall we open another bottle, and see if we can make it to midnight?"

When the hour arrived, we were both squiffy with drink.

It was Monica's suggestion to phone the pub.

"Hello? I was in there earlier, and I think I may have left my shawl behind! Oh, there's been nothing handed in - what a shame! The girl might remember. A pretty thing - short fair hair. She was a smasher, she was. Really looked after us. You should pay her a bonus!"

I giggled, and made a sign for her to not overplay her hand.

"Would it be possible to have a chat with her?" Monica pushed on. "Oh, thank you. Juliet, I think her name was. Is that right?"

It took less than a minute for her to come to the phone.

"Hold one second please caller!" Monica said, and handed the receiver to me.

"Juliet?"

"Ant!" she whispered.

"Happy New Year!"

"Happy New Year, my sweetheart!"

"We'll be together this year, Juliet. This is the last New Year we'll spend apart."

"Oh, my darling, I hope so."

"Monica knows everything," I told her.

"What?"

"I'll explain tomorrow. Come as soon as you can."

"I will. I love you, Ant!"

"I love you, Juliet."

I heard her giggle quietly before the receiver was replaced.

25.

Knowing we were in such close proximity somehow made it harder to be apart. At least when she was in Canterwood, and I in Oakburn, the distance quelled the urge to some degree.

That new year's day, with the radio for company, we stroked, caressed and tenderly licked every inch of one another. Nobody, to this day, has known my body as intimately as Juliet did, and vice versa.

It's no exaggeration to say that she knew me better than I knew myself.

We made love four times in seven hours. Juliet was never closed to me. We pleasured each other, and climaxed together time and again.

We both knew that it might be a while before we could be together once more.

"I wish I could live inside you," I quietly informed her.

We shared a bath, and lay in bed afterwards, the hour of her departure and Monica's return beginning to close in. The buses were running, but on a hugely reduced schedule, given the day.

She rested her head on my chest.

"I don't want there to be any secrets between us, Ant."

"I don't have any. I've told you everything about me."

She spoke without engaging me. Her voice seemed to reach me through my body, rather than through the air and to my ears.

"My dad wasn't worried about you getting me pregnant."

"I'm sure he..."

"He was worried that he might have got me pregnant."

Silence.

Absolutely nothing as her words sank in.

I didn't breathe. She must have heard me not breathing. Was there a spike in my heartbeat that she listened to as I remained perfectly still?

"I thought about telling you in writing, because I can't bear to see and hear your disgust."

An avalanche of thoughts collided in my brain...

All the while, he'd been having sex with her - he'd been where I'd been - that was how she was so versed - so experienced - so knowledgable - the baby might have been his - not mine at all - did she know when we first met? - did she use me...?

No - No! - NO!!!! - this wasn't her fault - this was wrong - he was the other person she'd had sex with, the one she'd mentioned - the mistake that went on for a while - the mistake that was still going on...

She should have told me - she should have told me - she should have told me...

Oh, but imagine what it must be like - her mum dead - her dad doing that - Juliet, my beautiful Juliet...

She wanted me - she didn't want him! - the fucking bastard - the fucking pervert - the fucking...

That's why she can't leave her sister - why she's worried about her being alone with him...

What does it change? - what does it change? - what does it change?

Something did change in that moment.

I felt it, that fractional almost imperceptible shift.

"I'm terrified that I'll lose you," she sobbed, and I became aware of her tears running off my torso.

The sex - the sex - the sex - what we did that very day...

And the next day - she'd be home - would he be with her?

I wanted to kill the cunt.

"Say something, Ant. Please, anything. Do you hate me?"

"No, no, no, no," I replied, and twisted to find her face with mine. "This isn't your fault..."

"I was thirteen when he started. As soon as my periods began. Jenny's coming up to that now."

I didn't know what to say.

Now, I see. I thought I was mature enough for what we were doing. But I wasn't. Not really. The sex, yes. But an actual real relationship, with all it might entail - I was nowhere near to being ready for that.

I think of all I could have done - all I failed to do.

For Juliet.

And Jenny, too.

Monica spoke with me as a new year approached, and talked of regrets.

The year had barely begun before I started down a path that would cause me the biggest regret I believe it's possible to carry through life.

At times it's been unbearable, my failure to act on what Juliet told me that day.

But I was fifteen...

So was she. She was just fifteen years of age.

Her mum had been dead for over four of those.

She could have told someone. She could have told someone other than me!

"I love you, Juliet," I said, because I did.

"I love you, Ant. We will be okay, won't we?"

"Yes," I assured her.

"Ask me," she pleaded.

"Ask you what?"

"To marry you."

"Oh, of course! Will you marry me?"

"I will."

26.

We dressed. We kissed. We hugged. We tried to be normal. We said the things we always said. And I meant them. Every word.

But it wasn't the same. I wasn't sure it ever could be.

Could it?

Perhaps I needed time to get my head round everything.

Did it matter?

After all, it had been going on all the time I'd known her. Why did knowledge make such a difference?

Juliet must have sensed my reaction, and how must that have made her feel?

Thirty-five years on, and I know I would handle it so differently. Three and a half decades later, and what her father did to her is inconsequential to me. I cannot find any fault in Juliet.

Because there is none.

I could cry every time I think of her.

Her love for her sister, and protecting her from him... I'm not worthy of being with her.

I never was.

That early-evening, I walked with her to the bus stop. We saw the headlights and the sign lit up at the front - the number indicating it was the service that would take her away from me.

There was sadness as always at her departure. But a tiny piece of me - the very smallest part in a place I didn't know existed - simply desired to go home to familiarity and an uncomplicated normality.

I wanted to run and hide.

"I love you, Juliet. I'm so sorry."

"You have nothing to be sorry for, my darling. I love you more than ever. Thank you for still wanting me."

"Marry me!"

"Oh, I will. As soon as we can, we'll be together. But I must take Jenny with me."

"I know. We'll find a way."

"We always do, don't we?" she said brightly.

The bus pulled up, and the door hissed open.

"Oh, Ant, you are my whole life."

"Phone me as soon as you can!" I begged her, slipping five pounds of the refund from Monica into her hand.

"I will."

She skipped onto the bus. The doors closed. I watched her walk towards the rear, and choose a seat on my side, as far away from the other three passengers as she could get.

I waved her all the way down the road. Her eyes followed me, looking back.

By the time Monica got in, I was in bed.

And in the morning, I headed back to Brakeshire.

No music accompanied me on that journey. My world was silent, apart from the chatter of passengers and the rhythm of the train on the tracks.

What should I have done? All these years on, I know I should have encouraged her to report him. There were people who would help, even in 1984, right?

What would have happened? I presume Juliet and Jenny would have been taken into care. Her father would have been arrested. Is that how it would have gone?

Proof, though. There has to be proof.

With her being fifteen, was I as guilty of a crime as him? Even though I was only fifteen myself.

Is Ben in the same boat, by having intercourse with Grace?

Where's the line?

Take age out of it, and isn't it about consent? Without consent, it's rape.

Father and daughter is incest. That's illegal.

I did nothing. I told nobody. We carried on, Juliet and I, and I hoped it would go away.

I didn't want to talk about it, so rarely asked her. There was something within me that... It made me focus on the impact it had on me. It was selfishness, and, as a result of it, I didn't consider Juliet enough.

She'd say things in our sporadic phone calls, but I couldn't respond in the way she needed. I believe she wanted someone to take care of it all for her - for someone to step in and make it all go away.

Men, even young men, like to fix and solve. I wanted a solution, but couldn't see a way of achieving it.

On my arrival home, dad and Rosemary sat silently at the kitchen table awaiting me. Dad's face told me I was in trouble.

What did they know?

I feigned ignorance, waiting for them to show their hand, making a scene of dropping my rucksack to demonstrate fatigue.

The Kendal Mint Cake was handed over, and received with a grunt.

"What's going on?" I asked.

"Sit down," dad instructed me.

"What's wrong?"

"Did you take your father's wedding ring?" Rosemary asked.

"No. Why would I take dad's wedding ring?" I said to her, before switching my eyes to him.

"It's gone missing," he said.

"I have no idea," I replied. It was the truth. "Where was it?"

"In my bedside drawer."

I shook my head and went to stand. "I'd better unpack."

"You didn't touch it, did you Anthony?" dad asked.

"No. I told you that."

"You promise?" he asked me, as seriously as he'd ever asked me anything.

"Yes."

"He's lying," Rosemary chipped in. I shot her a look.

"I haven't touched your ring!" I angrily replied.

"Well, it's missing. The only people who have set foot in this house since Christmas are myself, Rosemary and her three, and you. One of you took it."

"It wasn't me."

"If I find out it was, Anthony…"

"It wasn't!"

"And I can assure you it wasn't me, and my children are not thieves!" Rosemary wailed. "And they aren't liars, either!" she added, before pointing her painted finger in my direction.

Dad nodded. He stared at me.

I could see in his eyes that he knew something. He looked down at the Kendal Mint Cake on the table.

"I didn't go to the Lake District," I confessed. "I went to see Juliet back at the pub. Now, you can punish me for that. I don't regret it and I don't care. I'll suffer the consequences. But I did not take your wedding ring, dad. I give you my word."

Again, he nodded.

"I'd like you to leave my house," he said quietly in my direction.

I fixed my eyes on him, and saw him turn to Rosemary.

"Me?" she shrieked.

"Yes. I'd like you to get out of my house now, and never come back. I don't want to see you or your children ever again. Is that clear?"

"Now hang on a bloody minute!" she fired back. "He's just admitted that he's a liar. He probably took the ring to sell so he could spend the money on this girlfriend of his!"

"I'll deal with my son. He may have told a fib, but I can understand why. He's no thief."

"Oh, really? Is that bloody right? Then where's the money from his school trip? Because, if he didn't go, he stole that from you..."

"Get out!" my dad roared, and brought his fist down on the table. Or, more aptly, on the slab of Kendal Mint Cake.

She left, slamming the door as she did.

"Do you want a coffee, dad?" I offered.

"No. I want something stronger." He went off to get a bottle of Scotch.

Two glasses appeared on the table, joining his ashtray, his fags and lighter, and the crushed bar of mint cake.

He poured the golden fluid into the tumblers. One was slid over to me.

"What the fuck's going on?" he said, and took a swig.

"I didn't touch your ring, dad."

"I know."

"But I had to go and see Juliet."

"I know. You should have told me. I had a feeling, but..."

"If I'd told you, you'd have stopped me."

He nodded. "You're both fifteen. It's going to get you in trouble. It already has. You're wasting your education, your head's all over the place... She'll be the ruin of you, that one."

"No! She's the best thing that ever happened to me."

I took the tiniest sip of the whisky. I loathed the smell and taste. It burnt my throat as it went down.

That moment was the closest I ever got to telling dad about Juliet and what was going on. Again, as with so many things, I wish I had.

"I can't stop you," dad said, "and you'll be sixteen soon enough. Just be bloody careful, son."

He lit a smoke, the yellow nicotine stains on his fingers showing the extent of his level of stress.

"I will. Juliet's on the pill now, so she won't be getting pregnant again."

He nodded to let me know he'd heard me. He could hardly condone underage sex.

"I knew a girl when I was about your age," he began, "a short while before I met your mum. I thought she was the one. I'd have done anything for her."

"What happened?"

"She met someone else."

"And that was it?"

"That was it. Then I met Miss Anthea Pleasant at a friend's house, and I saw that it was all for the best. If I'd been with the other one, I wouldn't have been at my friend's that day. We would never have met, your mother and me, and you wouldn't be here causing me all this grief."

"I'm sorry, dad."

"So you should be. Do you love her?"

"Yes. I think so."

"Think's not good enough! Be sure, if you're going to throw your bloody life away over her!"

"I do. I do love her."

"And it's not just sex?"

"No."

"Okay. Then I'll turn a blind eye. But watch yourself! You hear me? And no more lies. My blind eye in exchange for your honesty. Deal?"

He raised his glass looking for an agreement. I tapped it with mine, and risked another sip. It wasn't quite so bad second time around.

"How did you get this bloody Kendal Mint Cake?" he suddenly thought to ask.

"Long story."

"Well, there's the best part of a bottle here, so you can keep me company by telling me."

He went to refill the glasses. I put my hand over mine. "Mind if I have a cup of tea?" I said.

He shook his head, and I filled the kettle as I began telling him about Juliet's aunt and uncle.

And I gave him back the money for the school trip. Well, most of it, thanks to Monica's refund.

Life drifted for Juliet and I, despite dad's partial support. Protecting Jenny was Juliet's primary concern. She would... not offer herself as a sacrificial lamb. But she did ensure that she was chosen ahead of Jenny.

Chosen.

Fucking hell.

With Juliet being on the pill, I know the abuse became more frequent.

A month passed. Juliet turned sixteen. Nothing changed. Nothing happened. We were both preparing for exams.

My quietness and disengagement was again flagged up at school. The headmaster called me into his office for a chat.

I thought about telling him everything, but held my tongue. I'd promised Juliet I'd not tell anybody, and I kept my word.

He assumed that my pensive and withdrawn state was a result of my parents separating, and I was okay with him thinking that.

A Valentine card arrived. The Canterwood postmark told of its journey. It arrived on the Saturday prior, and dad picked up the post from the mat. He handed it to me with a wry smile.

It was my first ever Valentine card.

I find it inside The Cure's 'The Love Cats' twelve inch, the envelope long since lost.

It's pink and red, showing a heart with a silhouetted couple walking into it, their arms wrapped around one another. It could be her and I.

Inside, her undulating handwriting arrests me again. It looks like she looked. Flowing and curvy - open and honest. It's so easy to read.

'My Darling Ant, I crave you! Just to walk by your side is all I desire in life. I am truly forever yours. And soon shall be yours alone. All of me is waiting for you, and all of my love you already hold. Juliet xxxxxxxxxxx.'

Even that has a reference to her father, and the fact I was having to share her with him.

How did I feel?

Confused. Torn. Powerless. Rudderless. Afraid. Happy. Sad.

It's an irrelevance how I felt. How must it have been for Juliet?

We'd talk on the phone at least once a week - always her having to ring me.

I'd listen to her cry with frustration. No words. Just her crying.

I had a strong urge to want to rewind to the previous August, or the days in the pub before I went back to Monica's.

Even to revisit that afternoon just before she told me.

I knew I was hiding from it. We were both drifting along, and waiting for something to happen.

As a result of that, I also drifted through everything else in my life.

I wasn't revising. My mind couldn't settle. Other thoughts were constant invaders.

Dad told me later - by not opposing Juliet and I, he hoped I might settle down and not squander my chances.

It didn't work.

My sixteenth birthday came and went. Another card in a record, depicting a couple lying in a summer field, her blowing a dandelion clock.

'Birthday Wishes For You!' the front reads.

Inside, she wrote, 'My Darling Man! My wish this day is for your happiness, because if you are happy, I know I shall be! Every second of my life is spent wishing you were with me. All of my love is yours. Come and claim it, if that's your wish! Your Juliet xxxxxxxxxx.'

The fucking exams. When would I see her again? My appetite to see her grew and grew, ever more avaricious.

Easter was April 22nd. It was our only chance before the summer.

Everything we'd planned - all that we'd spoken about as soon as we turned sixteen - none of it came to be.

We were limping from one thing to the next, always finding an excuse as to why we couldn't, rather than pushing ahead with what we both desired.

It made it more imperative that I see her. I knew, as soon as I was with her, we'd reset and focus on what was truly important.

But I didn't want her sister being with us. It was supposed to have been just she and I.

The rules of engagement had changed.

Still, every call, I'd plead with her, "marry me!"

"I will!"

For us to be together I needed a job. A decent job. And to land that, I needed the qualifications I was set to fuck up.

It was 1984. There were no jobs. The country was a mess.

There was no fucking hope!

I had to see her! I was wasting away without her.

And we were sixteen. Nobody could stop us.

"I can't leave Jenny," she protested.

"But I need to see you, Juliet."

"How?"

"I'll come to Canterwood. Even if it's only for a day. If we can just spend an hour together, it'll be worth it!"

"Yes! Yes! Come to me, and we'll work the rest out like we always do."

I told dad. No secrets. He shrugged and said it was fine.

"Besides, you'll go anyway, so what can I say? Thanks for at least telling me this time," he added sourly.

As Easter drew closer, so the familiar tingle of anticipation grew stronger.

A weekly phone call was all we had. If dad answered, he'd hold the receiver out to me wordlessly, before leaving me in peace.

I masturbated on an almost daily basis. It had always been Juliet that I imagined at such times, conjuring up one of the occasions we'd been together and effectively reliving it.

After a while, an image began to creep into my mind, and once it was present it was difficult to erase.

It would be Juliet beneath me or on me. But it wasn't really me with her. If I held myself in frame for too long, I'd be darker and older - I'd morph into something that I knew was her father.

As a result, I began imagining sex with someone who wasn't Juliet.

To my shock, the goth girl from the pub began to pervade my fantasies.

I don't know why. She wasn't a patch on Juliet. Nobody was.

27.

A bus from Oakburn took me to Birmingham, whereafter another deposited me in Canterwood.

Songs on tapes were my travel companions for those ninety miles. They were all I needed. I sought no other interaction.

All those hours I could have spent revising, but didn't.

She met me at the bus depot, and the instant I saw her sitting in a shelter, all of the old feelings rushed back and churned my stomach.

I'd begun to have doubts. Everything was too difficult. Too many things were stacked against us. But seeing her removed every obstacle.

She saw me, and self-consciously used her fingers to flick her fringe over and behind her ear. Her hair was a little longer than the last time I'd seen her. And her lips glimmered with the minty balm she always used.

She stood and ran to me, and we made contact with force enough to bruise. It was akin to a remerging, as our mouths keenly sought the other's, and a rush of emotion and adrenaline and something I've never felt with another person, swamped me.

And I knew it was exactly the same for Juliet.

There was no imbalance in our love. None. Every other relationship I've known has that disparity one way or another.

My dad loved my mum more than she loved him.

Carol loved me more than I loved her in the beginning. Until she dropped to my level and beneath.

How did I know? It's something you feel, that sense of balance. It was as if I was floating in the air. I felt weightless and carefree. As a result, I could never fall.

That gave me a feeling of invulnerability.

I was nervous at the prospect of visiting Juliet on her turf. All other contact had been on neutral ground, generally speaking. As soon as I held her, my trepidation disintegrated.

That greeting alone was worth the journey. I could have turned, re-boarded the bus, and gone immediately back to Oakburn, and I would have been happy.

Juliet showed me the sights. Canterwood is a small city. It was a large town until recent times, its name coming from a wooden perimeter wall, long since perished.

The old part of town was quaint, with black wood beams showing on white painted frontages. Rapid growth radiated out from that hub, through grey concrete before hitting red brick.

She showed me her school as we walked to the town, hand in hand, fingers intertwined, and we kissed as we walked along, perfectly in harmony.

She looked divine, in faded jeans that nibbled at her crotch, but weren't skinny and stretch. Yellow leg-warmers sat atop black suede pointy boots, and a long pastel-yellow jumper hung to below the pockets on her jeans, her hands partly covered by the sleeves.

We sat and drank tea in a cafe, and she explained that she took her mum's old clothes, and altered them accordingly, such was her lack of funds.

"Dad doesn't ever think to give me any money," she explained, and I felt a jolt when she used his title.

I nodded my understanding.

"How's the Saturday job?" I asked her, keen not to dwell on her father.

"It's good, actually. At least I have my own money. I can ring you!"

"I love you, Juliet." I didn't know why I was suddenly sad.

"What's wrong?" she perceptively asked, and took both of my hands in hers.

"I don't know. I've missed you. It's been nearly four months since I saw you. It feels like all the time is being wasted."

"I know," she said, "but we have our whole lives ahead of us. Look, we've made progress. Your dad is okay with us, at least." She always saw the bright side.

"He knows it's pointless trying to stop me seeing you. I'm not sure it's the same thing. Hey, will you be back at the pub in the summer?"

"I don't know."

"I was thinking I might see if I can get a job out there. Anything would do. That way I could be close to you for six weeks."

She smiled.

"Just six weeks?" she asked softly.

"Well, it depends on my exam results, I suppose. I might need a job for longer than six weeks."

"If you do A-levels, it'll be another two years of this."

"I know. But what can I do?" I asked rhetorically.

"Something'll come along!" she chimed, and I met her dimpled smile with a grin.

"What if someone sees us?" I asked her as people passed by the cafe window.

"Dad's at work. My nan is at home with Jenny. Anybody else doesn't matter."

"God, in Oakburn everybody knows everybody, pretty much. You can't get away with anything."

"Where will we live, do you think?"

"I don't care. As long as I'm with you."

"I need to get away from Canterwood," she announced. "Away from dad, I mean."

I nodded.

"I'll come to Brakeshire, Ant. He won't be happy with Jenny moving away, but he can't stop me."

I thought of the practicalities and implications of it - a thirteen year-old girl running away from the family home to live with her sixteen year-old sister and her slightly younger schoolboy lover.

No, don't think about it! Not then. Not at that moment.

"Do you want to see where I live?" she asked.

"Er, yeah!"

"Obviously we can't go in, but we could walk round the back fields, and get pretty close."

As we walked, we planned my stay.

Her schoolfriend, Sarah, was away for Easter with her parents. Juliet had a key and was tasked with looking after the cats. I would stay there for two nights.

Jenny was staying at her nan's for the week because her dad was at work.

To cover that night, Juliet told her father she was babysitting for a woman she knew through her Saturday job. Because they wouldn't be back till the early hours, she was staying over.

"Does he suspect anything?" I enquired of her.

"Not as far as you're concerned. He thinks we drifted apart after I got pregnant. But he always thinks I'm up to something."

"So, what, he suspects you're seeing someone else?" I said in a slightly accusatory way.

"You have to understand, he doesn't want me seeing anybody, so he's constantly checking up on me. Oh, Ant, there's nobody else!"

"Sorry. It's just, with us being so far apart, and me hardly seeing you..."

"That's the one thing I would never do. You have to trust me."

We joined our bodies again as we strolled along a path through a copse on the fringe of the estate she was born in.

That path ran parallel with a train track that sat a few metres up on a ridge. A metal fence with warning signs screwed to every second post kept people out.

Being April, it was squidgy underfoot, so we kept to the narrow grass verge, and sidled along holding hands.

Juliet dropped my hand without warning. Looking round her, I saw two lads strutting towards us.

She knew them, and they exchanged greetings.

"Who's this?" one of them asked, tipping his shaved head in my direction.

"Just a friend," Juliet replied.

"Got a name, has he?"

I went to answer, but before I could Juliet said, "Mark."

"Alright, Mark?"

"Alright."

"Not seen you round here before," the bigger of the two said. He wore the skinhead garb of the times, with DMs half way up his shins where they met turned-up jeans. A Fred Perry badge was evident beneath his blue bomber jacket.

My eyes were drawn to the tattoo on his neck - 'cut here' and a dashed line.

I shrugged.

"Got any smokes?" was the next question.

"No, I don't smoke."

"Where are you from?" he asked, registering my accent.

"Br..."

Juliet shot me a look.

"Where?"

"Braunston," I quickly corrected.

"What are you doing here?"

"Nothing," I said.

"Good. Keep doing nothing, and you'll be okay."

"Leave him alone, Dougie," Juliet jumped in.

"Why? What do you care? Your boyfriend, is he?"

"No. He's just someone I know. But he's alright."

"What's in the bag?"

"Just some clothes," I replied.

"Why do you carry your clothes in a bag? Are you a fucking gypo?"

The rain saved us - one of those sudden April showers that come from nowhere and pelt down without warning.

"Fucking hell," Dougie moaned, and they jogged on along the path looking for shelter.

"Come on, quick!" Juliet said, and we leapt over the path to the other side of the trail.

We ran for a minute, before Juliet pushed through a gap at the bottom of the metal fence. We scrambled together up the bank.

"Mind the rails!" she shouted, and skipped across the line.

I followed her, my eyes straining to see along the track in both directions.

A hut offered sanctuary, the door unlocked, long since kicked in. The window was boarded up and the inside smelt faintly of urine.

Whatever function it once performed, it no longer did. Wires hung from ripped out panels, and there was nothing to sit on. Still, it was dry.

"Why did you deny who I was?" I asked her as I recovered my breath.

"They live in my street. What if they told my dad?"

"Would they?"

"I don't know. But they know him from the pub."

"How old are they?"

"Eighteen, nineteen."

"You're soaked," I pointed out, her yellow jumper stretched and baggy from the deluge.

I dug into my bag and emerged with my spare top. It was a blue zip-up. A towel followed it.

"Here," I said, "put this on."

She peeled off her jumper, as unabashed as she'd been that previous August.

My eyes drank her in, as if for the first time, despite me knowing every millimetre of her body.

I didn't want to do it there, in that grotty place, but I desired her to such a desperate extent.

She whispered, as I wrapped her in the towel, her exposed breasts pressing against me, "I'm at the end of my period, so there's a little bit, but it's okay to make love to me."

I didn't. Instead, I dried her, and marked the towel with the make-up she had around her eyes. A little pink came off her lips.

When she was warmer and dry, I dressed her in my spare top, drawing the zipper up through her cleavage.

"Thank you, my love," she said so softly it was like a tickle from within, as if she was physically stroking the inside of my body.

We felt the vibrations coming up from the ground long before any sound reached us.

And no sooner did we hear it, than it was on us and blasting by, just a few yards away. A train full of people going to wherever from wherever, for whatever reason. And they were oblivious to us and the, in the great scheme of things, insignificant encounter taking place in that seemingly boarded-up hut.

Yet, it is one of the most important snapshots from my life.

I can close my eyes, and I see her so vividly, her arms raised, and the yellow jumper turning inside out as she removed it.

Her fair hair darkened by the moisture, water dripping between her breasts, her nipples protruding with the cold, threatening to break off, her areolae flecked and textured, goosebumps evident on her charming skin.

Her face, just emerged, the brief covering of her eyes catching her pupils in mid-dilation, and the green of her irises wild and excited as though it was the first time she'd ever seen the world.

And she was looking at me.

Her mouth was ever so slightly open, those pink lips of hers, still glistening, the balm repelling the water, a breath half drawn, the bottom of her top teeth just showing, and her pink tongue set in the midst of it.

That, right there, was Juliet at her most naturally beautiful.

It was as if I fell in love with her all over again every time I saw her.

She was like a song or a book you think you know. But each time you listen to it or open the pages, you notice something you'd never spotted before.

And you can't comprehend how you ever missed it.

28.

The rain passed as quickly as it had arrived, and left the greenery smelling fresh with new life.

A less muddy but more circuitous route took us through an industrial park. A potholed lane cut through to the estate Juliet called home.

From a distance she pointed out where she lived - a small brick house with three bedrooms, and a tiny kitchen at the rear, allowed for by an extension. As was the bathroom above it. It was semi-detached by virtue of being at the far end of a short terraced row.

"Which is your room?" I asked her.

"The one on the right."

"And Jenny's?"

"Jenny sleeps with me most of the time. It's safer that way."

We didn't talk about that. I didn't talk about it.

Even so, I asked, "has he never touched your sister?"

"I don't think so. She says not, anyway."

"Why you?"

"I'm older."

"But he'd started by the time you were Jenny's age."

"Yes. But I'm more like my mum. Looks-wise, I mean. That's part of why, I think."

"I'm sorry, Juliet. I'm so sorry for everything you've been through."

She squeezed me, pulling me closer to her.

"Will you wait here? I won't be long, but I need to go and get some things for tonight."

I would. I'd have waited for ever for her in that moment.

We played 'house' again that night, just as we'd done in the pub in the winter. A Chinese takeaway was our dinner. After eating, we washed up and replaced everything back where we'd found it.

Even household chores, such as washing and drying up together, were enjoyable. There was something captivating in observing her perform everyday tasks. Just watching her drink a glass of water was mesmerising to me.

It was so easy. I realise it's different living with someone twenty-four hours a day, seven days a week, but Juliet and I slotted together like two custom-cut segments.

When we came together, we formed an arch or a ball - something strong and impenetrable. Whereas separately we were two unstable pieces that didn't quite fit anywhere else.

Despite her light period, we had sex. Afterwards, we washed in the bathroom sink, cautious of using anything that might betray our presence.

She washed me with such care before we returned to her friend's bed. A cat jumped up and joined us, curling behind my knees. It added to a sense of homeliness, and gave an insight as to what life would be like. One day.

We were in a very different part of Canterwood to Juliet's estate. Tall hedges and acreage afforded us some privacy, though we were mindful of putting lights on and potentially having the police called on us.

Sleep came easy after the day of travel. To close my eyes with her pressing against me was heavenly. I woke, had a fleeting second of panic at the strange surroundings, before I saw Juliet and all was ideal again.

She made me feel so secure.

She slept on as I watched her - so at peace, as I studied the veins on her eyelids, and a trace of a smile played on her lips.

"Juliet," I whispered.

Her eyes snapped open, a panic. She cried out for half a breath.

Before she melted back to herself as her eyes focused and recognised me.

How many times must she have awakened to be confronted by him?

Sneaking out the rear of the property, we hopped a fence unobserved, and walked through dewy grass to a park. On the far side stood a ring of evergreen trees, with benches dotted around the perimeter.

Plentiful rainfall rendered the grass green and lush, and it was well tended. Recent cut marks showed a diagonal pattern.

"This is Canterwood Memorial Park," Juliet explained as we took a seat. "There was a siege here about a thousand years ago. Virtually the whole town starved or were killed in the fighting."

"Really?"

"Yes. They called Canterwood the 'Childless Place' as a result. Not a single person under thirteen survived. The bodies were buried here, in a mass grave. Well, those that weren't eaten."

"Is that true?"

She nodded and snuggled against me.

"I want to live somewhere else," she said. "Tell me about Oakburn."

"It's a market town. Medium sized, I suppose. There's lots of countryside around it, which I like. The Brake Canal runs through it, and the river Tred sits just to the east."

"Are there nice places to walk?"

"Yes, but it's very flat out in the west of Brakeshire."

"What about shopping?"

"You can get most things you need. The record shops are good. But you have to go to Millby or Jemford Bridge for some things. Or Tredmouth, which isn't far away."

"Where do you like to go?"

"I ride my bike down to Norton Basset sometimes. There's a lake in an old quarry, and you can walk or ride round it."

"Is it quiet there?"

"Very."

"Hmmm," she purred.

"Shall we live there one day?" I proposed.

"Would you like to?"

"I always thought I'd live in Tredmouth. Or Millby. Somewhere with a bit more life. Millby might be best. Like Oakburn, you don't have to go far to be in the countryside."

"I'll live anywhere with you, Ant. As long as it's not here, in this childless place."

"Was it a happy life when your mum was alive?"

She considered her response. "I think so. I'm not sure she was happy. But she sheltered us from it all, I think. I remember walking down to the old part of town, where we were yesterday, and going to the market every Saturday. She'd let me have anything I wanted from the sweet stand.

"They were mine, those sweets. She'd never even take one when I offered. She told me that we all needed something we could have just for ourselves. It was important to have one thing in life that we never had to share.

"They'd have massive arguments, my mum and dad. It was mostly about money, from what I remember. He's such a tight bastard.

"Whenever I picture her, I go to those Saturdays at the market. The men on the stalls would all give her a look, and be a bit flirty. She just smiled at them, and walked on. But I'd feel a little skip in her step through her hand I was holding.

"At home, though, she always looked sad. I think if she hadn't died, she would have left him. And she would have taken us with her."

"Where would she have gone?" I asked.

"Her sister's."

"At the pub?"

"Yes. My aunt told me the last time I was there, that she'd mentioned it. But then she got ill."

"So, we would still have met when we did?"

"We would!"

"I'd give you everything I have, Juliet. It's not much, but I'd give it to you. I'll never be like your dad."

"I know that. I think meanness is one of the most unattractive traits in a person. Not just money. But people who are mean with money are always mean in other ways, too.

"I knew the day we first met. You handed over the fiver you carried, and trusted me with it. And your dad slipped you another fiver when he came back from a walk with your mum. Do you remember?"

"Yes." I chuckled.

After almost nine months, we had that intimacy that comes from shared experience - moments only the two of us knew about.

"What's the time?" I asked her.

"I don't know. I don't care," she said, and adjusted her position against me.

Neither of us had a watch. There were no mobile phones to tell us. It was 1984, and the world was incomparable with now.

We weren't cold despite the chill. We each buried our hands inside the other's coat, and soon found flesh to explore anew.

Without warning, she pulled away and locked her eyes on me. "If anything ever happens," she said with more seriousness than I'd ever seen in her before, "meet me here on this bench. Our bench! Come here on a Sunday at two in the afternoon."

"Why? Nothing will..."

"Promise me, Ant. If something happens, and we make a mistake, or someone gets in our way, we meet here. On a Sunday at two o'clock. Promise me!"

"Okay, I promise. You're scaring me, Juliet. What's wrong?"

"Nothing, my love. Nothing at all," she said, as she softened once more. "What day of the week and what time?"

"Sunday. Two o'clock."

"Good. Never forget."

"I won't."

"I love you, Ant. Fuck me."

"Sorry?" It threw me, her use of the word. Juliet always referred to it as 'sex' or 'making love'.

"My period ended. I want you to fuck me here, on our bench."

"Someone might see!"

"Let them. Anyway, they won't. There's nobody around."

She sat astride me with her knees on the bench, her long coat covering us. We pulled apart and re-met, sharing the workload and minimising movement.

"Come," she begged me.

So I did.

It was as though she were marking the bench, and claiming it as ours - cementing it in my head as somewhere special I could always go to reconnect with her.

Our taste in music had gone away from the charts in the months we'd been together. By April of '84, the alternative scene held more appeal. Cocteau Twins, Nick Cave, Sisters Of Mercy and The Smiths were what we listened to.

I have a closer relationship with my record collection than I do with any person currently in my life.

It knows and holds secrets I've never dared to share with anyone.

Those inanimate, yet animated records act as confidante and therapist - memory jogger and familiar old friend I've had for as long as I can remember.

They never alter and never judge. They wait for me to rediscover them, and can provoke such strong emotions within me.

My record collection doesn't just hold the good bits of my life. It can't. It has to hold everything.

As a result, also contained within it is the means and power to destroy me.

29.

I slept alone that second night at her friend's house.

She waited until her dad went to work before six, and came to me over on the other side of town. She ran those three miles just as the sun rose. She would, she vowed, be with me until it set.

My bus was booked for half eight that evening, and would get me home around midnight.

She let herself in. I heard the key in the door, followed by her footfalls on the stairs. A doubt crept in to me. It was her, wasn't it?

I sneaked a look, and saw her undressing in the half-light the curtains allowed. And she slid into bed with me, her body cold yet sweaty from the exertion of her run. Her breathing was rapid, her pulse hammering in her chest.

Neither of us uttered a word.

My leg draped over her, as I attempted to expose as much of my body to hers as was possible.

We fell asleep like that.

An hour and a half passed, and when I awoke, neither one of us had moved an inch.

To know that feeling - to sleep wrapped around someone, and have no inclination to adjust position or find a little space...

She stirred as I stroked her arm. She wriggled in an attempt to get even closer to me. I kissed her neck with feathery lightness, before tracing the contours of her ear with the tip of my tongue.

She shuddered as I did, and I whispered, "I love you."

At that, she twisted to find my mouth with hers. A film of sweat coated our bodies where they made contact. As the bond was broken, and air rushed between us, I felt the cold invade.

Juliet loved having sex with me. She is the only person I am certain of in that regard.

My worry is, and always was, did she love having sex? As a result, was I largely an irrelevance?

I think of Carol, and how she paid lip service to sex when we first met. Not that she used her lips.

But she saw sex, I think, as something she had to endure as part of a relationship. At least, in those early stages. And again when we tried for a baby.

Also, it was always my impression that she thought of sex as being a bit naughty and not as something to be particularly enjoyed. She could never let herself go and relax.

It was Juliet, given what she suffered, who should have had issues with it. She simply didn't.

For years, I've thought about it. Did she enjoy sex so much because of a desire to supplant the sex she'd been made to endure?

By loving what she had with me, did it somehow diminish what her father did to her - in a 'that's not real sex, this is' kind of way?

I don't know the answer. It didn't occur to me to ask at the time.

There are so many unasked questions I wasn't ready to hear the answers to.

Juliet fed the cats and double-checked the house as I packed my bag. We left over the rear fence again, and walked through the park.

A cafe towards the town centre served us a tea and toast breakfast. It wasn't much, but we didn't need much.

"What would you like to do today?' she asked me.

"We've never seen a film together," I replied, thinking back on my first ever date with Lucy. It had only been four years before.

And that was what we did. Unlike with Lucy, I remember what we saw. It was 'Splash'.

In stark contrast to my only other date at the pictures, we sat at the back and may as well have only paid for the one seat.

"She's very beautiful, isn't she?" Juliet observed as we walked out into the bright daylight.

"Daryl Hannah?"

"Yes."

I looked at her to see if she was testing me. She wasn't. "She's very nice. But she's not a patch on you."

She scoffed. "I wasn't saying it for that."

"I know. But I also know that if Daryl walked down this street right now and asked me out, I'd choose you."

She laughed and shook her head.

Again, I wonder about people. Could she not see herself as I saw her, and did I not see myself as she saw me? Are we all too drawn to our own perceived imperfections?

There was nowhere to go before my bus left. I detest that time when a departure is imminent. It reminds me of dropping someone at the airport. Don't linger. Deliver them to the terminal, and leave.

But she couldn't leave. We had to take advantage of every vital second together. Who knew when the next chance would come?

"The summer," we decided. But we'd see each other somehow before then.

Whatever happened, we would finish the school year, and spend those six summer weeks together while we waited for exam results and next steps.

Jenny, as always, was Juliet's only concern.

Had it not been for Jenny - or, more aptly, Juliet's worries regarding her father - I believe things would have turned out differently between us.

We whiled away the time by returning to the ring of trees in the park, and our bench. She reiterated the agreement. Two on a Sunday. She added to it. The last Sunday of the month.

"Why do we need a plan like that?" I asked her.

"Just in case."

Did she know something was going to happen?

I carved our initials crudely in the back of the bench with a key. 'J + A LOVE'.

When the time arrived, we reluctantly made our way to the bus station.

The number of days on which we saw each other total twenty-nine.

Sixteen of them were whole days. The others perhaps just an hour.

Less than a month was the amount of time I was actually in her company.

How is it possible for so much to emanate and endure from such a short period?

Sometimes it feels as if they were the only really important days of my life. And whilst each time we met was exhilarating, so every time we had to part was soul-crushing.

I rode the bus back home, and stared at a smudge of myself in the window. I saw anguish and stress. It was like suffering a bereavement every time we were parted.

The simple act of ending a phone call was difficult enough, but having to break contact, not knowing when the next time would be - that was physically painful.

I've never been addicted to anything. Not drink, nicotine or drugs. Yet, I imagine the withdrawal is similar. And despite the awfulness of it, so many relapse and put themselves through it time after time.

We can't help ourselves.

Was it healthy for me to be with Juliet? No. Oh, but yes! The greatest high I've ever known came from being with her, just as the greatest low was being apart.

I travelled home on the bus, depressed yet euphoric at the same time. I was consumed by my next fix as I suffered the come-down from the last, it still coursing through my body.

Her smell lingered on my fingers, and I sniffed them obsessively, mindful of touching anything that might diminish the scent.

I closed my eyes and attempted to snooze, but to no avail.

Music. Music was the only thing that could bring me out of it, so I turned on my Walkman, and played the songs that carried me closer to her.

30.

I don't know why I did it.

Because my exams were finished, perhaps, and because of the uncertainty.

On a late-June day, beneath a sun that appeared happy to stick around for three months, I returned to the pub by the technical college I'd visited eight months before, back when Juliet had been pregnant.

She was there when I arrived, the goth girl. Her name, I would quickly learn, was Sam, short for Samantha.

We recalled one another immediately, and she came over and said hello.

"Hi," I replied. "You alright?"

"I am now."

"How do you mean?" I asked, wondering if she meant because I was there.

"I just finished my last test, so I'm celebrating." She was Scottish, her accent told me.

"How'd it go?"

"Ask me in a few weeks, and I'll tell you."

She took a seat and told me what she was doing at the college. It was something to do with land surveying, I think.

I was vague about my situation. Waiting for exam results, and then decide on the next step, was all I divulged.

Music was a safer topic, and we were both happy to stick to that. Siouxsie Sioux was her idol. I could have guessed it from her clothes and make-up.

"Are you seeing anyone?" she asked me.

I couldn't lie. "Yes."

"Where is she?"

"She doesn't live round here. What about you?"

"Nobody serious. Is yours serious?"

"I think so."

"You think so?"

"Yes," I smiled. "It's difficult, with the distance, you know?"

"Aye, I know. Let's see a picture, then?"

I pulled it out of my pocket, the same one she'd given me the previous summer.

Sam took it, laid it in her palm and studied it. "Pretty wee lassie," she reported, and handed it back to me with such care once her survey was complete.

She was twenty-one and attractive. The leather jacket and short skirt captured her perfectly - feminine, yet robust. Her choice of profession was traditionally male, and I could ably see her in a hard-hat, out in a field with the rain pelting down, as she took measurements and did whatever it was she did.

There was a strength and a confidence about her that appealed.

I believe it was my increased self-confidence that appealed to her. I wasn't in the pub with a group of mates. I was there alone, content to sit quietly and drink a beer, with just my thoughts for company.

I'd noticed it before that day. Ever since Juliet and I had met, I carried myself differently. There was an assuredness that led to me being noticed.

But whereas the bullies left me alone, so women - girls, more accurately - would pay me attention.

As we sat in that pub chatting, I had no intention of having sex with Samantha.

Right up until I entered her, as she knelt before me with her skirt flipped up to her waist, I was adamant that I would not, even if she wanted to.

I couldn't blame the drink. I wasn't out of my head. I was fully in control.

Yet, there was something about it - an older woman; a woman without the baggage and ties Juliet carried; a woman I could fuck without commitment.

For that was all it was.

Neither of us spoke of love or a repeat performance. It was time and place and in the moment.

She was the second girl I had sex with.

It was just sex.

It wasn't making love.

There was no build-up - no foreplay.

It was a celebratory shag on the floor of her digs at the college. It wasn't worthy of messing up the bed.

I opened her up with my hands on her buttocks, and slipped inside her.

Once there, I didn't spare the horses, and she didn't want me to. Her pale flesh rippled at every slapping impact, and we grunted in unison until it was over.

And as soon as it was over, I dressed, told her I'd see her soon, and left.

An oppressive blackness hung over me, despite the clear sky above. Every pace closer to home ratcheted up the guilt and regret I felt.

I had an urge to tell someone what I'd done - to confess.

And the person I most wanted to tell was Juliet. She was my best friend. She'd understand.

It was a mistake.

Fuck me, was it a mistake.

31.

I had the greatest thing in the world, but it wasn't enough.

Why did I do it?

Because I was sixteen, and sexually active. Sex leads to more sex. Juliet wasn't there. That was it in a nutshell.

But there was more to it than that. Samantha was more on my level. Juliet was way above.

There was a constant feeling of Juliet only being with me until someone better came along for her.

I don't sit here listening to Siouxsie & The Banshees, and think of Samantha. When I played Captain And Tennille, it didn't swamp me with any kind of emotion regarding Lucy.

They are not the important tracks in the soundtrack of my life.

All of those pertain to Juliet exclusively.

Carol and I don't have a special song. It's because I've never permitted it. There's no room. The tape is full. And to allow a new one would mean recording over an old one.

How does it work? Is the original tune still there on magnetic tape, hidden beneath whatever is laid over it? Is it similar to artists reusing a canvas?

Peep-peep-peep-peep...

"Juliet!"

She was talking, attempting to come up with a way we could see each other over the summer.

"Juliet, there's something I need to tell you," I spoke over her.

A dreadful silence. Three seconds of nothingness that spoke volumes.

I thought about it. It ran through my mind to say, "I love you, and I just had to say it."

"I met this girl. Juliet, I'm so sorry..."

Not a word.

I continued. "It was a mistake, and if I could undo it, I would. I love you, Juliet. You're all I want in the world, but I just found myself in a situation... I had to tell you. It's been killing me not to."

"When?"

"Last week. Friday."

"Who is she?"

"Nobody. Just a girl I met in a pub. Juliet, I didn't..."

"Had you met her before?"

"No. Yes. Once. Last year."

"After we met?"

"Yes, but nothing happened. Not then."

"But now it has. Funny, you didn't mention her. Will you see her again?"

"No. Never."

"I'd better go."

"Juliet, don't go. I'm sorry. I'm so terribly sorry."

"Why?"

Why was I sorry?

"Because... Because I love you, and I've cheated on you. I don't want to hurt you. Not for anything."

"Well you have."

"It's why I told you. I couldn't live with it."

"Am I not enough for you, Ant?" she asked, showing the first hint of the emotion bubbling just beneath the surface.

"Yes! It's just... It's so difficult sometimes."

"I'm hardly having an easy time here."

"I know. I know that."

"We just had to get to the summer," she said quietly.

"But what will that change?"

"I'll leave school soon. I thought I could leave here, take Jenny and..."

"And what?"

"Something."

"I have to do my A-levels, Juliet. I need to get a degree. Get a good job."

"I can't wait that long!"

"Nor can I."

"No, well, you've proved that," she said bitterly.

"It was just sex!" I shot back. "You've been having sex..." Oh, if I could take that back.

I would give my life to be able to take that back.

"I have no choice," she said so quietly I almost missed it.

"I'm so sorry. I didn't mean it like that."

The peeps. The fucking peeps.

"I'd better go."

"Juliet..."

"What?"

"Call me soon. We'll talk. We need to talk."

"I need to think," she said, and the line went dead.

32.

I'd been meaning to get around to it. I didn't call ahead. I cleaned out the boot of the car, dropped the seat, and set off to Wrenbrook to collect the rest of the boxes of singles.

It's a Saturday afternoon, and the roads are busy with traffic, it being a delightful September day.

They rush, the other cars, seemingly desperate to get to wherever it is they decided to go. Or to return from the place they visited. It smacks of resentment, and time being wasted.

They sit on my bumper, peering round me to see if it's safe to overtake, before leaving me in their wake.

The whole world, it feels like, moves at a different speed to me. It passes me by, and I'm happy to let it do that.

"Hello, Sharelle. I was in the area, and thought I'd call in on the off-chance to collect those records."

"This is fine," she informs me.

She's wearing a red tunic dress that hangs to her mid-thigh. Her feet are bare.

"Is Kelvin home?" I ask as I enter the house.

"No. Work."

"How have you been, Sharelle?"

"I am fine. Everything's fine. Would you like tea?"

"Er, yes. Please. Thank you."

She sets about making it. I'm struck by her movements. Everything she does is so measured and precise - the kettle filled to an exact point, and the cups set squarely and centrally on a tray with the handles pointing to the right.

"Sugar?"

"One," I reply.

She measures it, returning to the bowl three times to add just a few more grains until she's satisfied.

"I am lonely," she says suddenly, still facing the window above the sink.

"So am I," I'm shocked to hear myself reply.

"I know. I recognise it from myself."

"Why are you lonely?" I ask, as we wait for the kettle to boil.

"I have no friends. This place," she says, waving her arm at the outside, "is not for people like me."

"Why not?"

"Nobody talks to me, because they think I have nothing to say."

"I'm sorry. What would you like to talk about?"

"You."

"Me?"

"Yes. I am interested in people. I like to hear about their lives, and what they have done. But it is hard to ask people about themselves if you cannot get to know them."

"I haven't done much, I'm afraid."

She looks at me curiously. "There is something inside you. Something I cannot understand. It is as if you carry something heavy, even though you carry nothing."

"I'm full of regret, Sharelle."

"What do you regret? Things you have done, or things you have not done?"

"Both."

"Tell me," she invites, and pours water into the cups.

"I cheated on someone. I don't know why. And I worry that it cost me so much."

"Your wife?"

"No. It was long before I met Carol. I've never cheated on anyone since that one time."

"How old were you?"

"Sixteen."

"And you loved the girl you betrayed?"

"Oh, god yes."

"Sixteen is so young. We all make mistakes, I think, when we are sixteen." She gathers her long straight blonde hair, and snaps a tie around it, so it hangs droopily by her cheeks. It instantly softens her.

"But I knew I was making a terrible mistake when I made it. And I didn't stop."

"How did she find out? What is her name?"

"Juliet." It hangs in the air, that name. I say it so rarely out loud, but constantly in my head. For years I'd not uttered it to a soul. Yet, recently, I've said it to Grace, George and now Sharelle.

I continue. "I told her about it."

"Why did you tell her?"

"Because of the guilt."

"But you lost her because you told her?"

"Not exactly. But I don't think it helped."

"So, better not to tell?"

"I don't know the answer to that. If I could go back, the thing I would change is having sex with someone else in the first place. The fact I told Juliet would then be irrelevant. There would be nothing to tell."

"She could not forgive you?"

"She did forgive me. But it was complicated, and that added to it. I think it bothered me more than it bothered Juliet."

"That's the sadness I see in you?"

"That's a part of it. So, why are you interested in people?"

"I am trying to learn psychology. I am studying for a degree at home."

"That's wonderful."

"Thank you."

"How's it going?" I ask, taking the tea she hands me, the liquid still rotating from her stirring.

"I like it. I like to understand. It is why I wish to meet people. To see those things in them. They make us what we are, I think, the experiences in life."

"They do," I concur, and take the high stool she indicates at the stone countertop.

I talk to her, and she listens. I tell her things as we drink our tea, and continue long after it's finished.

They're things I've never spoken of. But, I begin to understand, they are also things I needed to share.

I tell her about how Juliet and I met, and how we ran away, and I tell her about the pregnancy.

But not everything. There are some things I can't tell her.

In a lull, Sharelle says, "I think, perhaps, Juliet was not as committed as you were. It is always you going to her, Anthony. Did she ever come to you?"

"Yes!" I snap defensively.

"You are so quick to defend her."

"She ran to me that morning in Canterwood. She ran away with me to Stratford. Of course she was committed."

"Did she ever visit you in Brakeshire?"

"Once," I inform her.

"How long for?"

"Three nights. I met her half way, and..."

"It is always you making the running. That is what I see."

"She couldn't come to me."

"Why not?"

"Because she couldn't."

"Of course she could. It is a simple thing to..."

"She couldn't leave her sister."

Shit! Don't make me go there. Don't make me betray her by telling you.

"Why not, Anthony?"

"Ant!" I'm shocked by how much aggression is in my voice. "My name is Ant," I add more calmly.

"Okay. Why couldn't she leave her sister, Ant?"

My head drops and shakes. I pick up my cup, even though it's empty.

Oh, the fucking lump in my throat - all the years of never telling.

Sharelle's hand finds my forearm and rests there.

"Tell me why she couldn't come to you, Ant?" she says so softly.

"She couldn't leave her sister," I whisper in reply.

"You said that. But why not? If she loved you as you say, she would have come to you. Perhaps she didn't love you as much as you think she did," she adds.

"She fucking did!" I throw at her, my eyes snapping up and locking on hers. But she doesn't flinch.

Still, she holds my arm.

"She couldn't leave her sister alone, because she was terrified of what her father might do," I say.

"What did he do, Ant?"

"To Juliet..."

"What about her? It's okay, Ant. It's okay to tell the truth."

"He sexually abused her."

Oh, the relief!

All the years of not telling...

Sharelle places both of her hands on my arm. Her eyes drop down, and I see her adam's apple bob as she swallows heavily.

"Who was the father of the baby?" she asks after a few seconds of thought.

"Who knows? Juliet was sure it was mine. But she couldn't know. Not really."

"Was it a boy or a girl?"

"I don't know."

"Now I understand the weight you carry."

As I look at her, it's as if I truly see her for the first time.

Perhaps the smudges on my vision allow me to perceive things I'd not noticed before.

It further softens her, and adds a warmth and depth.

"You are such a good man, Ant Nice. Such a nice man."

"No, I'm not."

A chuckle leaves me. It's self-depreciating and dismissive.

"I'd better be going," I announce.

"Yes."

She watches me as I load half the boxes in the back of the car.

"I'll have to come back for the rest," I inform her.

"No problem."

I could have double stacked them. Yes, I was worried about the weight, and them shifting. But I think I may have done that to offer me an excuse to return.

We hug, and I kiss her - a little peck on her face; on the side of her mouth. I feel her lips part ready for more, but I pull away.

And I drive back home, the traffic pushing in front of me and taking the place on life's road where I might have been.

If only I was bolder and not so nice.

33.

"Shall we go barging again, dad? Just you and me."

He stared hard at me before he shook his head.

"Come on," I cajoled him, "it was good fun last year."

"You only want to go so you can see her at the pub."

Of course, he was right.

He added, "what'll I do all week while you're with her? No, I'll stay here. It's all the same to me."

"Dad, we can..."

"Go see her, if you want," he snapped, and went back to the darts on the television.

My exam results were not what was hoped. A's were B's, and not numerous. B's were C's. C's were fails.

It wasn't enough. I went to see the headmaster, to plead my case for staying on. He was dismissive.

I'd gone from top of the class to below mediocre in the space of a year.

Peep-peep-peep.

"Hello. Juliet?"

"How are you, Ant? Did you get your results?"

"Yeah."

"And?"

"Not great. You?"

"About what I expected. Not that it makes any difference," she stated.

"Juliet, I love you. You do know that, right?"

"Yes, I know you believe you do."

"Don't say that."

"What do you want me to say?"

"That you love me. That we're... That we're okay. That you'll marry me."

"You haven't asked me."

"Marry me, Juliet! I'll leave school. We can be together now."

"I will, Ant. If you're sure."

"I am! Any news on the summer?"

"I'm not going to the pub. Jenny's going. I'll stay here. He'll be worse if Jenny's not around."

"Fucking hell."

"I can't carry on like this, Ant."

"Fuck this. We'll just go, Juliet. If Jenny's safe, we can go to Gretna Green. Anywhere! We'll just go and be together, and work the rest out as we go along. Come here, to my house. I'll talk to my dad. It'll be okay. I have to spend these six weeks with you."

"Six weeks?"

"The summer holiday."

"What about after that? I can't just go for six weeks, and expect to come back. And what about Jenny?"

"I don't know! I don't fucking know…"

"And I have a job now. I've been offered a full-time position at the place I was working on Saturdays."

"Right. And what will you do?"

"It's ninety pounds a week, Ant. Plus overtime. I might be able to rent a flat, or something."

I could feel her slipping away from me.

"I have to see you!"

"It doesn't start till the second week of August. The woman I'm replacing is leaving then."

"Then we have a week. Let's go away, Juliet."

"I need to think about it."

"Okay, yes. Have a think, and call me."

She hung up before the pips came.

A day later, dad called out from the living room.

"I was thinking."

"What about?"

"That holiday you mentioned. I suppose we could go for a week."

"Ah. No. I'm not sure it's such a good idea."

"I thought we could invite your mum. Give you chance to spend some time with her."

"It's not going to work, dad."

"Please yourself," he muttered, and went back to the cricket on the television.

I think of that as I walk over to visit him. He lives in a small ground-floor flat these days. He does okay. Feeds himself, cleans up. Survives.

An hour every week is all I see of him. We have a drink. Depending on the time of day, it's coffee or wine.

I usually time it for the coffee. The wine takes him back, and stirs up the lingering indignation.

Strange, then, that I head over for six in the evening - prime wine time. He has his food at five-thirty precisely. I find him outside having an after-dinner smoke.

"Didn't know you were coming." He always says that. "Everything alright?"

"Not bad, dad. You?"

"Same as always."

"Any more trouble with your stomach?" I ask him.

"No. Right as rain now. I reckon it was that sandwich I had."

Not the endless coffee, wine, cigarettes and greasy food, then? I don't say that.

"Will you have a glass of red?" he offers as we head inside.

"Go on. A small one."

He pours a large one.

The television's on. The television's always on.

"Heard from her?" he asks, because he always asks that. He means my mum.

"I spoke to her in the week."

"Still with that prat?"

"Dave? Yes, she's still with him."

"Bloody biggest mistake of her life, that was."

"She seems happy enough. And has done for thirty-six years." I mumble the last bit.

He looks at me incredulously.

"See the football scores?" he asks.

"Yes. Tredmouth did well."

"They did. They were one down at half time."

"I saw."

"How's work?" he asks. A safe topic of conversation.

"Same as ever. Anything happened here?"

"They cut the trees down at the back."

"Oh, why?"

"Getting too big, they reckoned. They were worried about them coming down. Small root balls, or something. Here, the bloke who did it - have a guess how old he was?"

"I dunno."

"Eighty! Older than me, and still working doing that. He drove the machine. They mulched up the lot. Hell of a job he did. Eighty!"

"Hope for you yet, dad."

"They were fools getting rid of me at the work. I had years left."

"Hey, I was up by the cut today," I interject, keen to get him off the work and retirement rant.

"What for?"

"Just walking. Remember that barge holiday we had in 1983?"

"I do. We drove down to Oxford."

"That's right."

"Me, you and her." I see the sadness swamp him, as he connects the dots and recalls it was just before she left him.

He's so thin now. And shrunken more generally. He doesn't take care of himself - diet, exercise and lifestyle.

"We should have gone on that holiday, dad."

"What holiday?"

"That barge trip. The year after mum left."

"Ah, ancient history, that."

"Even so, we should have gone. Just you and me."

"That was the year you left school, wasn't it?"

"Yes."

"You wasted your chances there. You could have gone to bloody university! I blame your mother for going, I do. It disrupted you."

"It wasn't that, dad."

"No. Well, and that bloody girl you got mixed up with! Like I say, a bloody wasted opportunity."

"Juliet. Her name was Juliet."

"Yep, that one."

"I loved her, dad. I still do. I think about her all the time."

"Phurrrr! Better off rid."

"Why?"

"She'd have been the ruin of you, she would. As I said at the time, it was just sex you saw there. You've landed on your feet with Carol. Mind you, you should have stuck with that other one. Emma, was it?"

"Dad, you remember when she got pregnant?"

"Carol? Of course, I'm not bloody senile!"

"No, I meant Juliet."

He crinkles his brow, and allows his eyes to focus on that part of the past.

"Yes. A mess that was. You daft sod."

"You drove over to Canterwood to see her dad - remember?"

"I did. Someone had to sort it out."

"What did you do?"

"I slipped him a few quid. To take care of it - private, like. To get you off the bloody hook."

"You ruined my life, dad."

"Ungrateful shit! I saved you from ruin, is what I did!"

"No. I know you thought you were doing right, but you were wrong. The only person you got off the hook was her dad."

"What are you talking about?"

"He was abusing her, dad."

"What? Sexual abuse, you mean?"

"Yes."

He looks into the top of his wine glass and processes what I just said. He's not daft, my dad. He forgets things - names, mostly. But he's as sharp as he ever was.

"Serious?"

"I wouldn't make it up, would I?"

"Poor girl. And you knew?"

I nod.

"Back then, I mean - you knew?"

"Not then. She told me a few weeks afterwards."

"Bloody hell."

"Yeah."

He pours more of the wine, even though we're not half way through the first pouring. He needs something functional to do - something to engage the left side of his brain, and shut down the more creative right side.

"I'm sorry, Anthony. I'm sorry you had to contend with that."

"I loved her, dad."

"Fucking hell."

"Yeah."

"She was a lovely looking girl."

"She was. And she was so kind and smart and... She was perfect, dad."

"Fucking hell," he repeats.

He mutes the telly, but doesn't turn it off. I see the dark nicotine stains on his fingers as he presses the remote control.

"That bastard took my money. He must have been laughing at me," he says eventually.

"Probably."

"I remember her like it was yesterday. We were at that pub near Warwick, and I took your mum off for a stroll. I was wasting my breath trying to get her to change her mind.

"And when we came back, you were sat with the waitress. I remember thinking, 'fair play, Anthony, you've done alright there, son!'

"And when I went over to see her father, she answered the door. Well, she lit up at the sight of me! She looked so...

"I suppose she was happy to see me, because she thought I might be there to help her. And I thought I was. Helping her, I mean. And you. I believed I was doing the right thing. 'Hello, Mr Nice!' she said. So polite!

"That's our trouble, Anthony. We live up to our name. We're too bloody nice sometimes.

"I asked her if her father was at home. He was, it being a weekend. And I see it now - with hindsight and knowledge. I saw the fear on his face when I told him his daughter was up the duff.

"And I thought it was concern for her. But it wasn't. It was concern for his bloody self, the sick bastard.

"And he took my fucking money, and never let on!"

"There's something else I want you to know, dad."

"Go on."

"I never touched your wedding ring."

"No. I reckon she had it. That daughter of that woman."

"Rosemary," I remind him.

"That was her."

"What makes you think that?"

"Just a feeling. She was edgy when we asked the three of them. Anyway, I never saw it again. And perhaps I'm better off without it hanging around in my life."

"She's not coming back, dad. Mum, I mean."

"No. I don't believe she is, son. I don't believe she is."

Another silent period as we drink and think.

Dad breaks it once more. "What's brought all this on? Juliet and barging holidays from prehistoric times?"

"Carol and I are... We're struggling."

"How bad?"

"Pretty bad."

"Because of Juliet?" It's a logical question, given the conversation thus far.

"No. She's not in my life."

"Well, she is, isn't she?"

"No, I've not..."

"In here, she is!" he snaps, and taps his head. "You love her. Inside yourself. And you can't love two people in that way. It's why I've never really been with anybody after your mother. It wouldn't be fair, Anthony. It wouldn't be right."

"Grace is only fifteen, and..."

"Grace will be fine."

"I'm not so sure..."

"She'll be fine!"

"How do you know?"

"Because you were."

"Was I?"

"Yes. You've done alright in life. And now I know what was going on, I think you've done more than alright. You're a good man. You come and see me every week! That's more than a lot of people round here get!"

"What would you have done differently, dad? Knowing what you know now, I mean."

He drifts away again, as he depicts the man he was then, in his early forties. A fit, strong, quite angry man. "Got her out. I'd have got her away from him."

"And what about her sister?"

"Her too! And I'd have brought them here to Brakeshire and rung the police. That's what you do, isn't it?"

"I don't know, dad. But I know I should have done something."

"You were a kid."

"We should have gone on that barging holiday, dad. Just the two of us."

"Not too late, is it?"

"What do you mean?"

"I mean, it's not too late, if I'm not mis-bloody-taken!"

Perhaps he's right. It might not be too late.

34.

We met at Rugby station, just as we'd once said we would. Juliet had arrived first, and remained seated as I walked towards her.

How things had changed compared to our prior meetings. We'd be okay, though. I was confident that when we were together, we'd fit back into place. We'd pick up where we left off.

Dropping my bag, and taking a seat on the bench next to her, I said, "I'm sorry. I'm so sorry. I made a terrible mistake."

"It's okay," she responded, and warmed a little. "It must be hard putting up with me and my..." She didn't finish the sentence.

"I love you," I told her, because I absolutely did.

"I love you. Don't hurt me again, Ant. Please."

"I won't. I promise I won't. What did you tell your dad?"

"That I was going away for a few days."

"And what did he say?"

"Nothing. I threatened to tell, Ant. I told him that I would go to the police if he ever touched Jenny. And if he carried on doing what he's doing to me."

"Shit! And how did he take that?"

"He was scared. I could see that, but he tried to hide it. Look," she said, and lifted her hair to show a bruise on the side of her head.

"He did that?"

She nodded.

"The cunt."

I opened my arms to her then, and she fell in to me.

As she did, I understood. Every ounce of energy she possessed was being used in holding herself upright. It had shattered her to confront her father, and to walk away and come to me.

More so, given what I'd done and the broken trust.

"Where are we going?" she asked.

"I have no idea. Where do you want to go?"

"The seaside. I want to go to the seaside."

I smiled at her, and kissed the welt on her head.

I'd withdrawn the rest of my savings, apart from a couple of pounds just to keep the account open.

Juliet had her wages saved. We were as flush with cash as we'd ever been.

"Happy anniversary!" she said cheerfully.

"Happy anniversary, Juliet."

A year had passed. A year to the day since I saw her for the first time at the pub, carrying Scampi In A Basket.

Three-hundred and sixty-six days with it being a leap year - and on that bonus day, she'd asked me to marry her in the way I always did her. My instant reply was "I will!"

I would have, if only I could have found a way. If only I'd been brave enough.

Because there were ways, but I shied away from them. I failed to recognise the immediacy - the urgent need.

At sixteen, we don't think of the future to any real extent. Or, at least, I didn't back then.

The future was the summer holidays, and then the next stage of my education. Two years ahead was about as much as I could cope with.

Her hand in mine was an anchor. With her, I didn't think about anything but being with her in the moment. There were no serious thoughts of next moves on my part, beyond maintaining a hold on her hand.

A year before had been so different, because all of what we faced was twelve months away.

We looked at the map on the station wall - a national network. We were in the centre, the coast an azure outline in any and every direction.

"Here's a thought," I proposed. "Birmingham's not far away. From there we can get to Tredmouth easily enough, and I know that route. There's a direct train to the coast around Tinbury Head. Here," I pointed out, tapping the glass covering the map.

"Hmm," she breathed. "I would like to see where you're from."

"We could stop off there on the way back. Perhaps have a night or two in Brakeshire."

Thus, a rough plan was devised.

With tickets purchased, we boarded a train north, and settled into a seat.

All of my concerns melted away - my exam results and my mistake with Samantha. I knew we'd be fine once we were back together.

The weather was exemplary again. It was as if nature herself approved of our love.

With it being a Saturday lunchtime in the summer, the train to Tredmouth was busy. There was an energy that came with it, as we felt a part of something bigger.

So much of our time together had been spent hiding and isolating, it was refreshing and exciting to be part of a crowd. And I was so proud for those hordes to see me with the most ravishing girlfriend I could imagine.

Total strangers would nod a greeting and smile as they made their way along the aisle for whatever reason.

The whole world felt like such a happy place that day. And we belonged to it.

Alighting at Tredmouth, we ran to make our connection, and squeezed on to a throbbing train to the coast.

All seats were taken, and we sweated amidst the throng of humanity. Red-faced children refused to sit still, as vexed parents gave up trying to contain their excited energy.

We were heading to the seaside!

Sitting on the floor between two carriages was fine. Juliet was within my reach, and I clung to her as we rode the twists and bucks induced by every uneven point on the line.

We moved together, in time with the rodeo, because we were young and indestructible, our baggage acting as armrests.

"I will marry you, Juliet! I always told you I would," I cried over the roar bouncing off the land rushing by through the open window, as people sought a cooling breeze from outside.

She found my lips with hers, and we each placed a hand on the cheek of the other to maintain contact as another lurch passed along the train.

Unusually, we both had our eyes open as we kissed, and I looked wildly into the green of her irises, and saw the same vim looking right back at me.

For we were still part children, in a way.

Ah, but mixed in with that look was something more adult - a lust and passion at what we both knew lay ahead over the coming days.

A year had flown by, yet had dragged agonisingly across each and every day.

We'd only had that five times.

Five.

That was how many segments of time we'd actually spent together - the two the previous August, around New Year, Easter, and then.

But, I consider, I felt it on that very first day, sat on a bench by the canal outside the pub. An energy. A pull like magnetism.

And nothing had changed. Nothing ever would. We were meant to be together. I made a mistake, but we were too strong to be broken by one error.

We got lucky, but one makes one's own luck. A free bus sign ushered us on board outside Tinbury Head station. We followed a group of people, thinking it would deliver us to the town, where we'd find lodging.

Rather, it headed west, winding along the coast, dropping people en route at their destinations. We sat nervously, never sure whether we should hop off or wait and see the next place.

Half a dozen remained, and when four of them rose, we followed suit.

A sign welcomed us to Haven Bay Caravan Park near the village of Wishaven-Next-The-Sea.

"Hello," Juliet chimed when it came to our turn to approach the desk and check in. I'd learnt to let her do the talking.

"Have you got your booking form?" the lady asked.

"No. We were hoping you'd have a vacancy."

"It's your lucky day!"

"Is it?"

"Yes. We should be full, but we had a cancellation this afternoon. Do you want it?"

"Yes please!"

"Only five nights, I'm afraid. Until Thursday morning. We have a reservation for next weekend. Is that okay?"

"Perfect! How much?"

"Sixteen a night. And that gets you use of the showers and pool. And the club's open for drinks and food, twelve till two and five till eleven."

"Bedding and towels?" Juliet sensibly asked.

"All included. And there's a laundry by the showers, but that's extra."

Juliet looked to me. I nodded and grinned.

"We'll take it. Thank you." And we did, handing over nearly half of the cash left after our train fares.

Oh, the blissfulness of having our own little home for five days and nights, as we located our caravan and sank down on the bed, breathing a comforting cocktail of calor gas and seaweed and... That aroma only a caravan emits!

We couldn't lie still, despite our fatigue. Even the sex could wait a little longer, as we delved through cupboards and explored every inch of our home.

It was our home!

I worked it through in my head - sixteen a night, a hundred and twelve a week, perhaps a bit less out of season when demand wasn't so high. Five thousand a year. Juliet was set to earn nearly that, and if I could do the same...

Perhaps it was possible.

We ran to the beach, sliding down a sandy trail - emerging to be confronted by gaudy towels and greasily tanned and dry red bodies.

We'd had our fill of people for the day, and sought solitude once again.

To that end, we strolled, holding hands, pausing to remove our shoes and roll up our jeans so that the sea could bathe our feet as we made our way.

We found a rocky outcrop and sat, silently staring out into the massive expanse of ocean that winked at us teasingly, and stretched the sun from a ball to a ribbon.

"We can do this, Juliet. We can be together."

And her dimple showed as her smile formed, disappearing as that smile became something broader and magnificent.

A ribbon from a ball, I thought again.

35.

A trail led us away from the beach. A walk along the coastal road delivered us to the village of Wishaven.

Bread, butter, eggs, bacon, sausages, dried pasta, tomatoes, baked beans, soup, cheese, milk, tea, biscuits, wine, beer. Nobody checked our age.

"What about sugar?" I asked as Juliet filled a trolley.

"There's half a bag in the caravan."

As I was looking through every cupboard for curiosity's sake, Juliet was doing it for practical reasons.

She was planning meals and how we'd live.

It was what she'd been doing since her mum died; since she was eleven.

"There's a fridge, but no freezer, so everything has to be fresh," she informed me. I'd not even thought to check.

She then asked me, "do you need any bathroom stuff?"

"No, I don't think so."

"What about soap and shampoo?"

"Ah, yes. I didn't bring any."

"You can use my shampoo," she smiled, and added a bar of soap to the load.

Back at the caravan, I helped her put things away as she directed.

"Hungry?" she asked when we were done.

"I'm hungry for you," I replied.

She came to where I sat on the bench-seat at the dining table, and sat astride me, her knees either side of my thighs.

"This folds down in to a bed, you know?" she said.

"Does it?" I retorted suggestively.

"I'll take this one, if you like, and you can have the main bedroom."

I looked at her to check if she was teasing. Her face was set. My smile withered and died.

"Juliet..."

"I was joking!" she said, erupting into laughter, and my hands went to her ribs and tickled.

She winced and cried out.

"Hey, what's wrong? Did I hurt you?" I asked, pulling my arms away.

She stood and peeled off her orange top. And she picked the button on her jeans, and trod on the hems to lever them from her legs.

And I looked at her - at her perfect shape.

I touched her - standing to unclip her bra and slide it down her arms.

I kissed her body, then.

I kissed every fading bruise on her form.

From the ones on her ribs where he kicked her as she lay curled up on the floor...

To the ones on her arms where she sought to protect herself and her major organs...

To the one on her head that began the assault, as his fist connected with her skull and rattled her brain...

To the ones on her legs where he forced them apart...

That was when she'd snapped and stood up to him.

That was enough.

She'd told him. Either it stopped, or she'd stop him.

Whatever it might take.

The law. He was afraid of the law.

He hadn't touched her in the days since. Not since the night he'd returned from dropping Jenny at the pub.

"He cried, you know?"

"Your dad?"

"Yes. He cried when I stood up to him, and threatened him with the police. He wept and whined like a baby, going on about mum dying, and leaving him all alone with two daughters."

"What did you do?"

"Nothing."

"What did you say."

"Absolutely nothing."

"You can't go back, Juliet. Ever, I mean."

"I don't have a choice, Ant. I'm not leaving Jenny with him."

"Is she away all summer?"

"Yes. The same as last year."

"What would your aunt and uncle do if they knew?" I asked her.

"I don't know. I've thought about that."

"Would they look after Jenny?"

"I look after Jenny. I promised my mum. I tried to tell my nan," she added.

"When?"

"A couple of years ago."

"What did she say?"

"She told me that I was a disgusting girl, telling filthy lies like that. And she said we'd be sent away, and I'd never see Jenny again if I carried on telling tales."

"Shit."

"It's okay to touch me, Ant. Unless you don't want to."

"Oh, no! I'm frightened of hurting you, that's all."

"I need you to show me that you love me. I need that right now."

I took her hand and led her to the bedroom, and I made love to her as tenderly as I knew how. I forbade her from touching me. Everything that evening was about soothing her.

An hour on, we walked to the showers and I waited while she checked the ladies block. It was empty, so she hissed for me to come in.

With the door closed on us, I washed every molecule of her skin using nothing but my hands and the soap we bought.

I shampooed her hair, and massaged her scalp, before rinsing and applying the same to myself.

I loved smelling as she did.

So gently did I dry her, squeezing her hair in my grip, and sliding the edge of the towel between her toes.

I'm sure those bruises had faded a little more when we were done.

"Thank you," she simply said before I helped her get dressed.

"No," she stopped me as I took her foot in my hand, ready to insert into her panties. "I want to feel free."

I nodded, and put her clean underwear back into her bag.

She stood from the bench she sat on, and I levered her dress over her damp hair. That was all she wore, that one item of clothing, and her open shoes.

"I feel better," she whispered, stretching up on her toes to find my lips.

Her arms wrapped around my neck so that she could hold herself at that height, and she kissed me in a way she never had before.

I don't know why it was different. It was fuller, and contained more depth, is how I describe it.

There was more feeling in that kiss than any sex I've had since Juliet.

As I sit here listening to records in my room, my mouth opens as I replay it in my mind. My tongue moves forward, as she massages my mouth with hers, and then fills me with her own tongue, threatening to pull away, forcing me to chase after her, but then returning and filling me again.

"Juliet!" I say aloud and hear the sheer longing in my own voice as it echoes in my headphones.

My head shoots round.

The door is closed, and I'm alone.

We ate in our caravan that night, Juliet preparing it all in her beguiling way. I watched her beat eggs and grate cheese as toast browned under the blue gas flame, and beans bubbled in a silver pan. She refused my offer of help.

"Shall I butter the toast?" I suggested anyway.

"I'll do it. Put some music on, Ant."

There was a radio in the corner, so I played around with it until I discovered something decent.

I know the song that played as we sat at the table and started our meal. Someone requested it on the station I found - The Dickies 'Nights In White Satin'.

It took me a verse and a chorus to work out what song it was, despite the opening line telling me. I'd never heard it before, only knowing the Moody Blues version from those school discos a lifetime before.

We ate as we listened to those Saturday night requests, each one sent in for a reason - each song connecting one person to another, and holding a memory of a time and place.

Who were those people, and what happened to their memories? I sometimes imagine them sitting as I do, furtively playing the songs that take them back to some utopia.

Or just something better.

That night in bed together, as we lay facing each other, our faces an inch apart, I asked her, "are we okay, Juliet, you and me?"

"Hmm," she hummed in that way she did. "Just for the things you've done today, I will always love you. Never forget that."

Everything was okay. She loved me. I loved her. That was all that was important. We'd work the rest out.

Sunday morning...

I slid from the bed and left her sleeping so prettily. I couldn't bring myself to wake her. I made us tea, and carried it back to the bedroom.

Juliet was awake, having heard me clanging around as I struggled to light the stove and boil the water.

"Marry me!" I begged her.

"I will!" she said through a sticky mouth, as she pulled the cover tight to her chin.

God, I was so happy.

She cooked breakfast - sausage sandwiches - as I made more tea, and the radio played ABC and Frankie Goes To Hollywood and A Flock Of Seagulls. It was chart music, but it was fine because it was of that very time in that caravan on that day.

The sun poured warmth and light through the window, and irradiated her so her figure showed through the plain white dress she wore.

We ate and drank, and planned our day. We'd go into Tinbury Head for a look around, skip lunch and eat back at the van to save money.

Our plans were delayed, as we made love rabidly, with the radio playing along and the sun on our bodies.

Twice without pause, because once wasn't enough. Nothing could ever be enough.

It was still early - ten o'clock - because I'd been awake since the sun rose before six. At home, dad wouldn't see me until mid-morning on a Sunday, if he was lucky. Often, whole Sunday mornings were lost to me.

On our way down to the beach, Juliet suddenly stopped walking. Her hand covered her mouth, and caught the most delightful little shriek, followed immediately by a giggle.

"What?" I asked her.

"I just dribbled," she whispered.

Sounds carry memories like nothing else. To this day, I hear the shocked squeal she gave when that happened.

She washed herself in the sea before we walked east towards Tinbury Head.

New levels of happiness outstripped seemingly unsurpassable levels continuously during our stay.

"You look so content," I observed, as we paused to look out at the sea.

"I am."

"Why?"

"Because you make me so. You make me laugh, and you make me think. And, yes, you've made me cry. You make me better, and you make me confident.

"You make me," she ended with.

"I wish I could undo what I did, Juliet. I don't know why I did it."

"It wasn't just what you did. It was also what you said."

"I know. I was stupid."

Making amends for my mistake made me myopic. As a result, I failed to see the bigger issue.

Yet, I have no excuse. It was laid bare in front of me - the bruises and welts and fear.

The abuse.

"I've applied for college," I told her as we walked inland to the town. I'd been waiting for the right time. "To do my A-levels."

"Where?"

"In Jemford Bridge. I'll live with my mum during the week, and dad at weekends."

"Your dad will miss you." Typical of her - thinking of others.

"No, he won't."

"I'm pleased for you, my love."

"Are you?"

"Yes," she answered, and paused to apply her minty lip balm.

36.

I think she knew. The week we had in August of 1984 was likely to be as good as it would ever get.

That day in Tinbury Head, we lived our dream amidst the crowds of people. We walked through the fairground, and rode the big wheel. We strolled the market, and I bought her a stick of rock. A record shop beckoned, and she bought me Spear Of Destiny's 'Liberator' single.

Even that, I've thought for three and a half decades, must have been a cry for help I failed to heed.

I play it now in my room.

"I'm sorry," I say aloud as I do.

I talk to her. It's fucking mad, but I always have, either in my head or aloud when I think I'm alone. I ask her advice sometimes.

Does she ever give me a thought? I doubt it. I doubt she'd even remember my name. That said, Nice is hard to forget.

"Alright?" a voice penetrates.

My head swivels. "Hello, Grace. Come on in," I invite her, as I drop my headphones around my neck.

"You're in here a lot lately."

"Am I?"

She nods.

"Ah, you know me and my music," I say lightly.

She picks up the red sleeve to 'Liberator'.

"Never heard of it," she comments.

"Here," I say, and offer her the headphones.

She puts them on and listens. Her foot taps and her body sashays in time.

"It's not that different to the stuff me and Ben listen to," she says when it's finished.

"Right. That's good, then!"

"How old is it?"

"The record?"

"Yes."

"Erm, it came out in 1984."

"Wow!"

"How are you and Ben getting on?"

"Fine, I suppose. I haven't seen much of him lately."

"Exams?"

"That. And other things."

"It's a big year, Grace, with your GCSE's, and..." It drifts, my sentence.

"What?"

"Nothing."

"Go on, what?" she pushes, and lifts the needle off the record before returning it to its cradle.

I note the steadiness of her hand. So assured. She hands me my headphones.

"I want you to be happy, Grace. That's all I care about, really. There's such pressure, you see? Pressure on you to achieve. And pressure on me to be a good parent, and encourage and support you in becoming a great success."

"And?"

"And... And the truth is, I think it's all bullshit, Grace."

She pulls a face of mock shock.

"No shit, dad?"

"No shit, Grace."

"What would you do differently, if you could be my age again?"

"You don't want to know."

She sinks to the floor and sits there waiting for my answer. I've dug myself a bit of a hole, I can't help but think.

Fuck it. "I'd have left school and got a job as soon as my O-levels were over. I'd have lived my bloody life, Grace, and seized every day. I would have been more selfish then, so that I might be less selfish now, if that makes sense."

"Are you happy, dad?"

"With you, I am."

"But what about with yourself?"

What a clever daughter I have.

"Not really, Grace, no. Please, don't think I regret having you in my life, because I don't. I'm just telling you this, because I don't want you to end up like me."

"I think you're pretty cool, dad, actually," she says kindly.

I blush slightly. My old issues with praise and compliments highlighted once more.

"Meh," is all I can manage to almost say.

"Seriously. You like your music, and you're pretty laid back. And you listen, dad. You haven't forgotten what it's like to be my age. That's brilliant!"

"Thank you."

"Is this about that girl you loved? Juliet?"

Shit, she remembers her name.

""Yes, that's part of it."

"What year was that?"

"!984."

"When that record came out?" she astutely asks.

"Yes. Exactly then."

"Do me a favour, dad?"

"Of course. What do you need?"

"Don't be miserable because of me. Don't stay on my account. You said you wanted me to be happy. Well, that's hard when you and mum aren't."

She rises and sets my turntable in motion. She brings the tonearm across, and drops it on the run-in groove of the same record. I hear the crackle in the one ear I have covered, the other left open for my daughter.

"Dad?"

"Yep?"

"You can still call me Gracie, if you like."

"Oh! Okay."

"I'll leave you to your memories."

Gracie. My special name for her.

Just as Ant was for Juliet, from there and then.

For others to use it would somehow dilute it, and make it less specific - less special.

"Ant!" she called that first day we met.

"Ant!" she squealed as we rode a ride at the fairground.

"Ant," she said, before asking me something.

"Ant," she cried with such relief, after we got separated in a market and re-found one another.

"Ant," she breathed as we made love.

"Ant," she began when it all came to an end.

Except, of course, it never really ended for me. It carries on through records and the memories I can never move on from.

On the Monday, we made sandwiches together, side by side, me spreading butter, Juliet slicing cheese. We took crisps and went for a walk in the nearby Wishaven Woods.

A clearly marked path ran for five miles, delivering us back to the start point. A lake occupied the middle ground.

As we walked, Juliet told me the species of every tree we saw, and pointed out characteristics, whether that be the bark or leaves.

"How do you know them all?" I asked in awe.

"My mum taught me. She loved being around trees. So do I. Is this what it's like at that place you said we might live?"

Juliet asked me as we strolled easily, the canopies offering ample shade.

"Norton Basset? No, there aren't so many trees there. There are plenty in Oakburn, though. It's why it's named Oakburn, I suppose."

We stopped to read a sign at the lake. In the twelfth century it had been a site for punishment, specifically for women of loose morals.

The gist being, it was a sin for women to be in any way dominant in the bedroom. Only subservience was acceptable, in order that their husbands could impregnate them.

Further, it was believed a woman must reach orgasm for a child to be conceived.

As a result, victims of rape who fell pregnant were judged to have 'enjoyed the experience', and 'punished accordingly'.

Along with common whores and other adulterous women, they were brought to the lake, where their noses and ears would be cut off to 'uglify and render them less desirable.'

In addition, certain pious women would have the procedure done voluntarily, to protect their virginities by discouraging sexual overtures.

The noses and ears were then tossed into the lake. Many of the women died from infection.

The expression 'cut off your nose to spite your face' was believed to have emanated from the practice.

Juliet quietly read it and shuddered.

"I can't wait for two years, Ant," she said.

"I know," I replied.

We ate out that Monday night, in the club house on site. The guy working the bar was early-twenties, dressed in black from head to toe, and with hair longer on one side of his head than the other.

He was good-looking, with George Michael stubble and a self-assuredness that allowed him to show chest hair through the three unpicked buttons on his shirt.

"What can I get you?" he asked Juliet, all beaming smile and open-mouthed pouting.

"Half a lager and lime," she requested.

"What about your kid brother?" he beat out by way of putting me down and determining the relationship.

"He's not my brother," Juliet said, slipping her arm through mine.

"Oh, sorry, mate. What do you want?"

For me, it was what I wanted. For Juliet, it was what he could give her.

"Pint of bitter, please."

He looked at me, and I knew he was thinking of asking me to prove my age. I felt myself blush a little under his scrutiny.

With a nod, he set about pouring my pint.

"Where you from?" he asked when the drinks were in front of us.

"Brakeshire," I answered.

"Canterwood," Juliet said a moment after.

"Canterwood, eh? I know it well. I was up there last year playing a gig. Do you know…"

And he was off, mining that common ground established, knowing that I couldn't join in the conversation.

He knew we were underage, and that we lived miles apart. From that, he reasoned we weren't properly committed and living together - that he had a chance.

Kelvin does it all the time, mentioning places and people in Tredmouth that Carol might know, fully aware that I probably won't.

Jez, his name was, the barman. And he played guitar in a band I'd never heard of.

We went and got a table, and ate burgers and chips.

Overweight, middle-aged men; younger men with kids with buckets and spades; even younger men who were there to pull; not yet men who were there on one of the last holidays they'd spend with their parents.

It didn't matter about stage of life - they all looked at Juliet in a way that showed their desire.

And whilst that gave me a thrill, because she was with me, it also terrified me - that ever-present prospect of someone better coming along and taking her from me.

Someone like Jez.

Sex was ubiquitous between us. Every opportunity we had, we made love. During that week in the caravan and elsewhere, I would estimate we did it at least twenty times.

To put that into perspective, when Carol and I first got together, we probably took several months to reach that number. And that was at the very beginning of the relationship.

Carol has never once made me ejaculate orally. She's never used her hand on me. She's never made herself climax in my presence. I've never made her climax.

Even when Juliet and I weren't having sex, we were sexy around each other. Contact was constant. Caresses were ceaseless. Looks between us were lustful, like starving animals looking at a potential meal.

"I love the fact I turn you on," she said on the Tuesday as we walked along the cliffs to the west of where we were staying.

I laughed at her comment. "You could turn anyone on."

"But I only care about you, Ant."

I suggested we go back to the club that evening, despite my worries about Jez. There was music on, and her comment made me feel more secure.

She wore her white dress, and I was a foot taller as I walked by her side, our arms proprietorially around the other's waist.

Jez served us without any problems, and we sat chatting and drinking for a while.

Juliet never left my side - we never once broke contact. There was no opportunity for anyone to invade.

Eventually, though, I had to use the toilet and get us another drink. That was when the vultures swooped.

As I stood waiting to be served, I turned back in time to see her smile and shake her head at an older man who asked her to dance.

She looked at me with a certain pleading in her eyes.

I walked over to her before I'd got the drinks.

"Are you okay?"

"It's fine," she said, and I noticed she'd laid her left hand on her knee to show the silver ring.

"Do you want to go?"

"No. I want to dance with you."

And so we did. To OMD's 'Talking Loud And Clear'. And then to Wham! and Frankie Goes To Hollywood and even Neil's 'Hole In My Shoe'.

We danced for an hour at least. To The Beatles and The Animals and Yardbirds.

For your love...

We laughed and smiled and, as things slowed down, we swayed together, Juliet's head resting against my collar bone, as I stroked her hair with my thumb.

"My god, I love you," I said to her.

And when we were gagging for a drink, we went to the bar together, hand in hand.

"On me," Jez said, and slid us a pint and half a lager and lime. "You earned it!"

We went to our caravan buoyant. The second the door closed on us, I slid my hands up her legs and lifted her dress to her hips as I sank to my knees.

The following day, it was too hot for the beach, so we lounged around the van and talked for hours on end. We chatted about anything and everything, because being with Juliet was so easy.

"It's our last night here tonight. What shall we do?" I asked her.

"I don't mind."

"Do you want to go into town?" I proposed.

"No, not really. Will we be able to sleep together at your parents?"

"Shit! I meant to ring them," I remembered. "I'll do it from the phone box up the road."

"Will we be able to share a bed at night?" she persisted.

"Probably not."

"Then this could be our last full night together," she pointed out.

37.

We lay on the bed, too hot to be beneath so much as a sheet.

Our bodies glistened with sweat long after our breathing had recovered to normal levels.

Music drifted in to the bedroom from the radio, the sun a few hours from setting, and not a wisp of a breeze moved anything outside the window.

The DJ told us the time - "five forty-five, and it's great to be alive, here on Tinbury Sound."

"Six wants a quarter!" we said in unison, and smiled as we thought of Monica, and being with her a year ago.

Other than that, I heard no noise and saw no movement. A lull had descended, as people had returned from the beach to relax before heading out for the evening.

Birds were still, waiting for the heat to abate before industriously collecting their dinner.

I was the most contentedly relaxed I'd ever been in my life in that moment.

My ears strained and retuned themselves, deciphering the rhythmic shush of the ocean a couple of hundred yards away. No gulls shrieked, and no children squeaked with joy.

Had the world ended?

It shocked me to think that I didn't care if it had. Mum and dad... Everything I knew could be gone, and I didn't care. I could have remained in that caravan with Juliet for the rest of my life, never seeing another soul.

My hand reached out and felt the moisture and the warmth of her body. As long as she was alive...

I was in that state of limbo, where I'm a second away from sleep, and nothing is quite real, as everything is open to interpretation, and thoughts slide from the grip of the mind before they can be processed and understood...

The music played on, soothing me.

And Juliet sang so delicately and beautifully.

"I go to sleep, sleep, and imagine that you're there with me..."

Forcing myself awake, I turned to her and rested my head on her pillow.

"Don't stop," I implored her.

"I love this song," she said between verse and chorus.

"Why?"

"It makes me think of my mum."

And when she turned to face me, a cascade of tears tumbled from her eyes to be absorbed by the pillow.

The sun picked them out as they fell, turning them to jewels. And as the light danced through them, I saw her mother, or an older version of Juliet, because she was just like her mum.

She sang on, her voice unaffected, every syllable patting my face gently. It seemed to come from her very spirit.

It jarred me. It jarred me to see her in such agony, yet be powerless to alleviate it, let alone make it go away.

I'd never lost anybody. I couldn't understand. Yet, I did. I felt some of her pain.

Just some of it.

"I think I'd have liked to have met your mum. Would your mum have liked me?" I asked her softly when the song was finished.

"Yes. If for no other reason, she'd have loved you because I do. And because you make me happy."

And I was happy, knowing that.

"Do you want to see a photo of her?" she offered.

"Of course."

I gazed at the small colour picture, and saw in it what Juliet would be like in a few years. It was remarkable, how similar they were.

"It's the only photo I have of her. My dad destroyed the rest after she died."

I browned the last of the bacon, cut up into little pieces, as she cooked pasta and made a sauce from the milk and cheese.

Tomato was added, and the last of the cheddar grated on top of the dish.

"All ready for when we get back," Juliet said, putting it in the fridge.

"Where are we going?"

"Let's go for a walk on the beach," she suggested, "and watch the sun set."

We followed the shoreline east, walking lazily hand in hand. As the sun dipped, we turned back west and walked into it.

An older couple, perhaps in their seventies, strolled towards us as we did. They too grasped hands and were in no hurry.

"There's a golden light around you two," the lady said when we met.

"It's just the sun," I replied, and smiled.

"No. No it isn't," she softly informed us, and they passed on.

"Sixty years from now, do you think we'll be like them?" I asked Juliet.

"I hope so."

38.

A square package stands propped against the wall by my music room door.

Perhaps Grace picked it up. Or Carol.

She never says much now. The odd grumble, but long gone are the days of bothering to take an interest, even if that interest was merely to find out how much I'd spent.

This one was forty-five pounds and change, plus postage, registered and insured. Postage isn't cheap these days, especially from abroad. It came from Portugal, even though the record inside is Italian.

Sometimes I think it would be cheaper to fly over and pick them up.

Tag on a bit of a holiday.

It's well packaged, with cardboard slices laid inside the seven inch mailer. The record itself has been removed from the picture sleeve for transportation, to stop it cutting through the edge if dropped. It's tucked in a new plain white sleeve.

The original is housed in a cheap but new poly outer. I'll switch it for something more sturdy, and re-use this one on a lesser record.

It's as described. The picture sleeve has faint ring wear, a little feathering along the open side, and a crease on one corner. VG-plus is accurate.

The labels are clean, with just a small 'x' marked on one side in biro. I don't know why. Perhaps it was at a radio station once, and that was to indicate the play side.

The vinyl is shiny with very light marks, probably caused by the insertion and removal from the sleeve. It certainly looks EX on visual grading.

Still, I've had records that look mint, but play like they've been lobbed in a fucking blender.

To be fair, I've also had some that look like they've been dragged behind a tractor, and, amazingly, they play absolutely fine.

The record is, I remind myself, fifty-three years old. It's older than me.

I'm a little marked and worn. I don't play as well as I once did.

My creases are around my eyes and mouth, and a slight sagging runs along my jawline.

The scratches and marks would no doubt show, if viewed under a bright light, with me tilted at an angle to best expose them.

The Fingers is the name of the band.

'I Go To Sleep' is the lead track.

I still hear her singing it in the caravan that early-evening.

I'll play my new arrival later, after I've changed and eaten. I'll delay the moment for as long as I can.

After all, it's not as if it's the first time I've ever heard it. I have the UK single, also from 1966. In truth, I have more than one copy of that. And the UK demo copy I overpaid for, at a record fair in Tredmouth about fifteen years ago.

Then there are the other one hundred and thirteen copies of the song I have on singles.

There are more, if I include twelve inch, albums, CDs and cassettes.

I'm not even a Pretenders fan, despite having their version of 'I Go To Sleep' about thirty times.

There's a Page One promo copy by Marion, that I paid over two hundred pounds for. That was my most expensive purchase.

I have a Dutch language version in a picture sleeve single by Conny Van Bergen, and a USA only single by Adrian Pride.

I'll need a new single case soon. With a lock. It was why I wanted those records at the car-boot the day Yellow Hat beat me to the booty.

Before he got run over.

Perhaps another half a dozen could be added without cramping them. Each case holds roughly forty singles in high-grade plastic outer sleeves.

There are three such cases, kept locked and stored in the sideboard my record player sits on.

It's fucking tragic when you think about it.

As a result, I try not to think about it.

And I keep buying copies of 'I Go To Sleep'.

39.

We switched trains at Tredmouth on the Thursday afternoon, and didn't alight when we reached Oakburn. The line continued on, running parallel with the Brake Canal all the way to Jemford Bridge.

Mum, I believed, was going to be more accepting than dad. After all, she was living in sin with Dave at his place a few doors down from my grandparents. To deny us would be a little hypocritical. Still, separate rooms awaited us.

We do the same with Grace, allowing her to take 'friends' to her room during daylight hours, but forbid it at night.

Really, what the fuck is the difference?

As a result, we had sex all the time during the day, and then pretended that my recently pregnant girlfriend and I were innocent virgins between midnight and nine in the morning.

"She's absolutely lovely, mate!" Dave said to me when we were alone, and Juliet was down the garden looking at flowers with mum.

She was a bit down when she returned to me.

"What's wrong?" I asked her.

"Nothing."

"Is it being here with my mum, and thinking about yours?"

"A bit, I suppose. Your mum's so excited about you living here when you go to college."

"During the week. I'll go back and spend time with dad at weekends and holidays. And I'll see you, of course," I hastily added.

"On weekends and holidays," she echoed sadly.

"What else can I do, Juliet?"

"I'll be working from next week. I won't get six weeks in the summer, Ant, and every weekend off."

"I know. I know that."

She smiled and snuggled up to me on the swinging seat, with its floral canopy shading us.

"I love you, Ant," she said with such torment in her voice, but I failed to read it. I believed it was passion in the moment.

"This week has been the best week of my life."

"I'll never forget it," she replied. "Thank you for loving me despite all my problems."

I wish she'd been angrier and more direct with me. I wish we'd argued about it. It might have opened my eyes, and forced me to act.

I wish she'd given me an ultimatum.

But it wasn't in her nature to be like that. I don't believe she had anger in her. And, of course, that was part of the attraction.

We walked, and I showed her the sights, just as she'd shown me Canterwood. Crossing the Jemford Road, we strolled up the hill to the south of the town, and entered a clearing beneath a big old oak tree.

Surrounded by a ring of high brambles, we sat on the even plateau looking out over a park at the base of the hill. It was busy with children playing football, their voices reaching us as excited squeals.

They weren't much younger than us, some of those kids playing.

The change from childhood to adolescence seems to happen overnight almost. We will it, and seize it, that growing up. Until we reach a stage whereat all we desire is to return to our youth.

One day at work, I looked up the weather for 1984. August was sunny, warm and mostly dry. September started well, but became overcast and wet after a few days. It was, on the whole, a miserable month.

That's precisely how I remember the year.

"We should go and see your dad," Juliet suggested that Friday afternoon on the hill.

"Why?"

"Because we should. And I want to see where you were born, and where you've lived your whole life."

I sighed. "Okay. We'll go over on Saturday, and stay one night. We have to get to Tredmouth on Sunday, anyway, for your train. It's on the way."

Her train home.

It momentarily killed the mood, that thought. Six days had passed since I'd met her at Rugby station. Over that time, I couldn't imagine her not being with me.

Juliet must have felt similarly, as she came to me and kissed me.

"It's pretty private here," I pointed out suggestively.

I gazed up and around to make sure we were alone, and couldn't be overlooked, and spotted what looked like a hollow in the tree.

Climbing up, I explored. A thatch door had been fashioned, and covered the hole in the trunk.

"There are tools in here, and drawings. There are things carved from wood," I called down to Juliet.

"Really?"

"Yes."

"Leave it, Ant."

"Why?"

"They're someone else's private things."

"Well, they're just left here."

"Perhaps someone left them for a reason. As a shrine. You don't know what happened."

I peered through the leaves at her. She looked sad and serious.

"Okay. You're right," I agreed, and replaced the door before hopping back down.

She hugged me tightly when I was back on the ground.

"Hey, what's wrong?" I asked her.

"Nothing. I was just worried about you falling."

"Really?"

"That, and I have a feeling."

"What kind of feeling?"

"I don't know. It's like our bench in Canterwood. It feels like this is someone else's special place. Can we go, Ant?"

"Of course. Are you sure you're alright?"

She nodded. "I felt as if someone was watching us, and listening to us," she further explained as we made our way back down the hill.

As we walked through the town, we met my grandparents.

"This is my girlfriend, Juliet," I informed them.

And they insisted on us all going for tea and cake in a cafe in Jemford. It made me feel so terribly proud.

40.

Dad was okay. He drank his whisky and smoked and made an effort.

I took the sofa, Juliet had my bed. She left her scent and presence there to haunt me for the few weeks before the sheets were washed.

She came down to me in the dead of night. I couldn't sleep, knowing she was in the room above me.

If dad knew, he chose to ignore the creaking stairs and door dragging on the carpet.

She wore a t-shirt of mine, just long enough to cover her. And she lay with me, tight, facing, almost merging beneath a single quilt and one pillow.

We didn't do anything.

It was enough to just be together and to fall asleep.

When I awoke, she was gone. Dad was up early as always, even on a Sunday, the kettle being filled - cigarette smoke drifting through from the kitchen.

"Cuppa?" he asked, seeing me sit half upright.

"Please."

"What about her?"

"Juliet, dad. Her name's Juliet. She'll have tea. Same as me."

He put the radio on, because that's what he always did.

Yazoo. 'Don't Go'.

"You'd better take it up to her," he said, placing two mugs on the table.

"Thanks."

"She's leaving today, right?"

I nodded.

"Right. Good," he said.

What on earth did that mean?

"What time's her train?" he added.

"Three o'clock."

"No rush, then?"

"No."

"Good."

What the fuck was he talking about?

"I like her, you know," he further felt a need to say. "It's not that I don't like her. This Juliet, I mean."

"Right."

"I've got to do some things. I'll be a few hours."

"Okay."

I took her tea up. She was awake, but still in bed. In my bed.

We heard dad go out the front door. The car door closed with a cushioned thump, and the engine sparked to life.

Peering round the edge of the curtain, I watched him reverse off the drive.

And I had sex with Juliet for the final ever time.

Unless I count the thousands of times I've had sex with her in my mind.

"Can I keep this t-shirt?" she asked me, holding it to her face.

"Why?"

"Because it smells of you."

"Yes," I chuckled.

We walked along the cut, as we'd done so often before. Except the occasions weren't that numerous. When you relive every minute so many times, it feels like more.

Skipping down steps without letting go of one another, we emerged in Oakburn town centre. I saw people I knew, from school or elsewhere, and it was so gratifying for everyone to see Juliet, and the fact that she was glued to me.

Why didn't I go with her on the train? All the way, I mean. I went as far as Tredmouth, and stood waiting with her. An awful sensation ripped through me as the train approached the platform.

I thought about buying a ticket. I thought about doing lots of things.

But I didn't do any of them.

I could have gone to Canterwood with her. But then what? Our money was mostly spent, and I had nowhere to stay. She began work the next day, so I'd be on my own until she finished.

"Don't go," I said, and almost lost it there on the platform.

Something inside me told me it would never be the same again.

"I have to, Ant."

"No. You don't. Don't go. Don't ever go."

"Don't make this harder than it is."

"My dad likes you. He told me. You can stay..."

"Shhh," she bade me, and kissed me - the train pulling to a stop.

"Don't go," I said again, the tears beginning to blur my vision.

"I have to, my love. I have to start work. And I have to be there when Jenny comes back."

"Don't..." was all I could manage.

"I'll ring you as soon as I'm back in Canterwood. From the station. I'll ring you."

She was edging away from me, towards the train as people began to stream off.

"I love you so much..."

"I love you, Ant. With all my heart, I love you."

I held her hand through the lowered window until the last second.

It was excruciating to let go and say goodbye.

A hollowness entered me.

Marry me, I mouthed to her as the train pulled away.

She nodded and smiled in her plaintively beautiful way.

Sunday, August 12th, 1984. Three in the afternoon. Platform two. Tredmouth station. Brakeshire.

The sun shone.

But her face put it in the shade.

I never asked her, but I know she cried as soon as I disappeared from her view.

There were so many tears between us.

She knew, I think, that day.

She knew what was coming.

41.

We carried on, speaking every other day on the phone. Her work was going well. She liked it. The other women were great.

A week passed. And another. And I didn't act.

I went for my interview at Jemford College Of Further Education. Two years of studying for A-levels. Maths, English Literature, History.

Why? I don't know.

I didn't care for any of it. All I cared about in the world was Juliet.

Yet, one I bothered to pursue, and the other I let drift.

I'd change it all if I could go back. Every single life decision I made during that summer of 1984, I would alter if given the chance.

I've wished for it countless times.

"I wish I could go back!" But my special power can't do that. It can't undo what's done. It only works on the immediate future.

September 27th, 1984. A Thursday. Around six in the evening.

Peep-peep-peep...

"Juliet?"

"Hello Ant."

"Marry me!"

"How are you?"

"I'm fine. What's wrong?"

"Ant... I met someone else. I'm so sorry."

"What? What are you talking about?"

"I met someone, Ant. Through work. He asked me out, and I said yes. And I really like him."

"Juliet, no. Don't do this, please..."

"I won't lie to you. I won't cheat on you."

"Juliet... Just... Give me time. Just give me time."

"You have a life to live, Ant. And you should get to do what you want to do."

"I want you. That's all I want in life."

"I'm sorry."

"Juliet, don't!"

"Be happy, Ant. I hope you can want that for me, too. I'll always love you. But I can't..."

"You love me! I love you! That's all that matters."

"No. I wish that was true. All things come to an end. Good and bad."

"Juliet..."

"I have to go. Bye."

"You're still there."

"Yes."

"Why?" I asked her.

"I don't know."

"I love you."

"I... I'll never forget you, Ant."

And the line went dead.

42.

The next day, I didn't go to college. Nor did I attend a class the following week.

Inside, I was irreparably broken.

I said I was ill, and everybody believed me. I looked ill. I sounded ill. I was pale and shattered - weak and hurting.

I was, I believe, depressed.

And utterly heartbroken.

Thoughts of ending my life occurred to me. I'd fantasise about how I'd do it. Pills. A leap. Cut wrists. Hanging.

"It's just a bug," I told my parents, and remained in bed for days on end.

Soup was as much as I could manage to eat. Water passed my lips when thirst became uncomfortable. It didn't matter. Nothing could fill the void in me.

Except Juliet.

Dad noticed first.

"She hasn't rung you this weekend."

"No. We broke up."

He thought about it.

"When?"

"Last week."

"Well, maybe it's for the best. You can concentrate on your education now."

Fuck off.

Mum's take was, "oh, you were both too young, anyway. Plenty of time for all that later on."

Dave got it, though. We bonded a bit over it. "It's hard, Ant, isn't it? I do know, you know? But I also know it'll get easier in time.

"Anyway," he added, "I loved your mum back in the day, and we ended up together. If it's meant to be, it'll happen."

A glimmer of hope.

I did nothing. I sulked and waited. Waited for her to change her mind.

For months, I lived a partial existence.

Around Christmas, I went to find Samantha. She was still in the area, and still drinking in the pub where we'd met previously.

I'm unsure why I went. Because I wanted sex, I think. She didn't want to know me. I was a shy boy again, without Juliet in my life to inflate and promote me.

We barely spoke, as she stuck with her group of friends. Eventually, I slipped away unnoticed, and trudged despondently home.

My time at college lasted a term and a bit. They were happy for me to leave. It was clear to everybody I was wasting my time and theirs.

I thought about contacting Juliet. They were constant, those notions. But, as is my way, I didn't act on them.

Several times, I part-dialled her dad's, before hanging up. I researched and found her nan's number and did similarly.

The risk of humiliation and further rejection stopped me.

The job I got was the only thing I could get. I worked at a poultry processing plant. It was abysmal.

I derived something from punishing myself through the sheer brutality that came with the work.

They didn't expect me to last a day, but somehow I stuck at it. As I did, I got physically stronger and immune to the shit and death I was surrounded by.

And as I proved myself, so the bullying stopped. Until, one Friday after I turned seventeen, I was invited to join the others for a few pints.

Our working day started early and finished early, so we were in Oakburn on the piss by early-afternoon.

They stuck to the cheaper pubs and working-men's clubs, where nobody baulked at the stench of death and crap that got ingrained in your hair and skin.

I was on a hundred and ten pounds a week. Some of it went to dad for board and lodging. The rest went on drink and records. Clothes were purchased only when I had to.

Work dictated I move back to Oakburn, and my old room in the only real home I'd ever known.

We fought a lot, dad and I. He was disappointed in me, for squandering the opportunities he was never afforded.

Juliet...

I ended up doing all she needed anyway. But only after it became pointless.

The best part of a year passed. Suddenly, without me noticing, it was January 1986.

At work, a bloke called Paul took me under his wing. When I'd joined, he'd been the cruelest to me.

He explained it during one of our snooker games on a Sunday evening. "Make or break, Ant. That's the best fucking way. If you aren't cut out for the work, I need to know that sooner rather than later. So I pushed you, and you anted up. Fair play to you, mate."

He sank a red in the top corner. "Oooof, that wiped its fucking feet!"

Paul was mid-twenties, married with a young kid. He was as hard as nails, but had a soft side to him. It was Paul more than anybody who brought me out of my depression.

"Never seen you with a girl," he said, as he lifted the triangle off the pack of reds.

"Ah, I was with a girl for about a year. But we broke up."

"When was that?"

"A year and a half ago. I loved her, Paul. I suppose I can't get over her. Your break."

"Why'd she dump you?" he asked, as he sank down on the baulk end of the table.

"Who said she dumped me?"

"It's fucking obvious, you twat!"

"She met someone else. She was... I was young, and she wanted more than I could give her, I think."

"Want me to sort him out?"

"No," I laughed. "She was pregnant."

"When she dumped you?"

"No. Before," I explained, as I tried a long pot along the cushion that rattled in the jaws of the pocket before staying out.

I'd never told anybody else.

"What happened?" Paul asked as he tapped it in and got position on the black.

"She was made to get rid of it. Her dad made her, I mean."

"Shit. I'm sorry."

"Do you want to see a picture?"

"Go on then," he said, and paused to swig his pint.

I tugged my wallet free and retrieved it, the photo she gave me when we first met.

He studied it for a while.

"She's fucking gorgeous," he commented.

"Yeah. That's why I don't have a girlfriend. Nobody really compares, you know?"

"She from round here?"

"No. Canterwood."

"Canterwood?"

"Yes," I confirmed.

"Fancy a trip on Wednesday?" he said, trying to break the pack of reds as he sank the black, but nestling in them and leaving no pot on.

"Where?"

"Canter-fucking-wood!"

"Why?" I asked, tapping the top of the cushion by way of applause for his safety shot.

"Thirty-odd thousand broilers need loading. Overnighter. Work's paying for a night away."

"Are you going?" I slammed a stunning long red into the bottom left corner, and flukily evaded any cannons to settle perfectly on the blue.

"Shot! No, but I'll get you on it, if you fancy it."

"Okay," I agreed, and set about making my first ever fifty break.

A minivan picked me up from home just after eleven on the Tuesday night. Chickens were caught at night, to be at the plant for first thing in the morning.

There were six of us. I knew the guys through the drinking after work. I'd done a bit of catching when I'd first joined, and it made the processing plant look like an office job.

Except for the driver, everybody snoozed in the van, knowing it would be the last chance we'd have for twenty-four hours.

I couldn't sleep, though.

The radio played hypnotically through the darkness. Amidst Pet Shop Boys and A-Ha, there was an underground scene emerging with jangly guitars and sensitive lyrics that appealed.

DId Juliet still listen to music?

I didn't even know if she was in Canterwood. There had been no contact between us since that phone call sixteen months before.

There wasn't a single day when I didn't think about her. Or, more aptly, think about what I lost. Her birthday was coming up.

Eighteen.

My workmates awoke from time to time to smoke a cigarette. The reek of that was preferable to the stench of shit and rotting flesh that caked their boots and the inside of the van.

Around one thirty in the morning, we rattled along a bumpy lane a few miles from the city. Flasks were opened, as the aroma of coffee accompanied the smoke.

It takes a certain type of person to do the job full time. None of the guys were big, but they were lean and knotted, with senses heightened from constantly working in the dark.

There was a wildness in their eyes, like animals on the hunt. Scars marked their hands and arms, where beaks and claws had dragged and opened up their flesh countless times.

All had hardened skin on their palms and thumbs from the constant friction of carrying chickens by their legs to a lorry stacked with plastic crates.

Fuck, it was cold when we emerged from the minivan to greet the first of the six lorries we would load that night. A light freezing rain fell noiselessly from above.

No gloves. I'd learnt that the hard way. They snag when you hand the birds over to the packer on the back of the truck.

Inside the shed, a long hangar of a building, with a low slanting roof about four feet high at the sides. Just the minimal amount of light permitted, so as not to alarm and scare the birds, and make them more difficult to catch.

They're fat and ugly, their bones allowed to develop just sufficiently to support their body weight. A low humming came from them - all twelve thousand of them in that one shed. Two other identical structures stood alongside.

Feeders and drinkers ran in a grid throughout, difficult to see in the near blackness, and constructed from sharp metal.

Any air there was held particles of sawdust, feather, skin, dead rotting flesh and fecal matter.

You got used to it.

Down we went in unison, fingers blindly doing all the work, as legs were located and stacked into the palm in such a way as they wouldn't be squeezed together and broken.

A broken leg meant a dead or rejected bird on delivery. Each one counted.

They weighed five and a half pounds each, having grown at a tenth of a pound a day since hatching.

They were eight weeks old.

Seven at a time they went, four in one hand and three in the other.

By early-afternoon, eighteen of the thirty-six thousand would be dead. Twenty-four hours on, and they would all be gone.

Sixteen tons I would handle.

Sixteen tons of living creature.

It shames me when I think back on it.

And all so I had an excuse to visit Canterwood, and perhaps be closer to her.

The ideal moment to catch something is when it is in suspense and has no energy. It isn't when it's falling or ascending, or flying towards or away from you. It's when it has no desire to escape.

Toss something lightly in the air, and catch it at the point of zenith. There's a feeling that comes with it, as your hand closes around it - a feeling of comfort and immense satisfaction.

It's not trying to evade. It comes from a sense of real feel - of it being simply what it is, without external force. A perfect meeting.

But the only way to maintain it is to keep hold of it.

Let it go, and it will fall or rise, or otherwise escape. External forces will come to bear.

So, if you find that ultimate embrace, never let go. Never relinquish your grip.

Because to recapture that moment will mean running the risk of throwing it away. Do that, and you may never catch it again.

43.

We were done by ten. Eight hours to load eighteen thousand chickens on to six lorries. A break was taken after two and four were loaded. Liquid poured down scorched throats. Sandwiches eaten from hands that couldn't be cleansed.

A buzz at the end, at having completed the shift. Because, as had been proven over and over, not many people could.

The workload did for plenty. But the conditions did for more.

That frigid clean air became the only respite between handfuls. Oh, and that shockingly bitter night was so welcome every time I emerged from the heat of the shed.

Back to the accommodation. A cheap hotel on the edge of the city. I didn't care, as long as it had hot water for washing and cold water for drinking. A bed to lie on. Hard as slate, but I didn't notice.

A shower. Scrubbing every cell that constituted me. Snorting and rubbing the inside of my nose until it bled slightly. Shifting the shit and piss and ammonia.

My legs ached with the miles covered. My hands cramped from the constant gripping and releasing.

A tenner bonus sat in my pocket for subsistence. Or beer, to be more precise.

I headed out at midday. Fourteen hours until it began again.

Ten minutes on, and I emerged by the bus station and added the filthy diesel fumes to the poison already inside me.

She met me there.

She ran to me when I stepped from the bus...

I sat for a minute where she'd sat that day.

Following the route she took me on, I found the cafe we'd visited, and ordered a tea and a pie. A seat by the window allowed me to forlornly look for her amongst the shoppers that passed by.

Leaving, I met the other catchers entering a pub.

"You coming, Ant?" one called out.

"Maybe later."

"We'll be here for a while. The food's meant to be good."

I nodded.

Despite my painful limbs, I covered the miles, locating the path by the railway line. My plan had been to revisit the hut we'd sheltered in, but the fence had been repaired.

Instead, I emerged in the industrial estate, and found her house. It appeared unoccupied but lived in, not that I ventured too close.

I was so tired. I had two choices, as far as I was concerned. Go to the park on the other side of town, or meet the guys in the pub.

One lay en route to the other, so I began walking that way undecided.

A phone box attracted me.

"Directory enquiries. What town or city, please?"

"Canterwood."

"And what name?"

"Hutchison. Juliet."

"Do you have an address, sir?"

"No. No I don't."

"Sorry, sir. There's no Juliet Hutchison listed."

"Okay. Thanks for looking."

I rang her dad's number, having retained it. It was no longer valid.

For all I knew, she was married, moved and had changed her name.

The hotel was my aim. A couple of hours sleep before heading out for a hot meal and a few pints. Then some more sleep, work, home. Fuck it.

I blushed at my failure and sense of loss.

"I wish I could just see her!"

Back through the old part of town, with its white paint and black beams, none of it as picture postcard as it had once been.

A miserable greyness muted everything, not least of all, my mood. It was a mistake going there, I told myself. I was okay. I was moving on - getting on with my life - working and playing snooker and drinking with the guys...

"Ant?" her voice said.

I span to see her emerging from a shop.

My eyes drank it in, that scene.

There she was. It was her. A little older, but the same. Her hair longer and tied back. She looked pale and tired, with little dark patches beneath her eyes.

I saw her face flush slightly as she realised it was actually me.

She pulled a pram behind her, as she struggled with the door.

I stepped over and held it open for her.

I smiled at her.

"Thank you," she said.

I almost burst into tears.

"What are you doing here?" she asked.

"Working. Just for two days."

"You're still in Brakeshire?"

"Yes. Still at dad's."

She seemed more nervous than me, her questions coming at me rapidly.

"How is he? And your mum and Dave?"

"Fine."

"Your grandparents?"

"Everybody's fine."

"What are you doing for a living?"

"Farm work," I replied, because it was better not to be too specific.

I glanced inside the pram. A little wrapped-up cherubic face slept soundly. Perhaps she was nannying.

"Not college, then?"

"No, that didn't work out."

"It's good to see you," she said, relaxing a little. Was there a flicker of emotion around her eyes and mouth?

"And you. How are you, Juliet?"

"Okay. Yes, I'm okay. You should have let me know you were coming."

"How?"

"Ah. I don't know."

"You never called me. I presumed you wanted to be left alone," I said a little bitterly.

"I thought it would be better. A clean break."

"Better for who?"

"Both of us, I suppose."

An awkward silence ensued, which we both filled by nervously glancing at one another. Neither of us knew whose move it was.

"Look, it's cold and I'm tired. Do you want to get a tea or coffee?" I proposed.

"I'd like that. Let's go to that cafe we went to when you visited me."

"You remember that?"

"Of course!" she said.

"I was there earlier. But I don't mind going again."

"Did you go there because we went there?"

"Yes. And then I walked along the railway, and saw your house."

"I don't live there any more."

"No."

I ordered tea for us both. "What about...?" I asked, pointing at the pram.

"She's got her milk if she wakes up. She won't, though. She always sleeps after her lunchtime feed."

"I'll get these," I insisted.

"Thank you."

"So, you're doing okay? And Jenny?" I said as we waited for our drinks.

She nodded. "It's not what I wanted from my life. But I don't have to worry any more."

"Do you see your dad?"

"No. He knows where we are, but he stays away. He played the granddad card, but I don't want him near."

So, the baby was hers.

"Is he still in the same place?"

"Can we not talk about him, Ant?"

"Yes. Sorry."

The pram dictated we take a different table to the one we'd shared previously. My nervousness showed through the rattle of the cups on their saucers.

I absorbed her figure as she removed her coat. I wondered if her breasts were the same, or had the child altered them? They looked a little bigger. And what about the rest of her? Would she feel the same as she once had?

"You've put on muscle," she observed, and I realised that she'd been checking me out as I removed my coat, just as I had been her.

"It's physical work."

"I thought you were going to be a writer."

I chuckled scornfully. "No. That was a different life. A different story. A different person, in a way."

"I've thought about you," she said, the first chink in her armour.

"And me you."

"Do you remember..." she started to say.

"Let's not do that," I cut her off.

"You're right. I'm so sorry, Ant. I must have hurt you terribly."

"You did," I admitted. "You still do."

"It's good that we can be friends, though."

"I don't think we can, to be honest," I informed her, and regretted saying it.

"Oh."

"I love you, Juliet. I always have. And I always will."

"Ant, stop..." she pleaded, and touched my hand. "So many scratches," she noticed, and enfolded my hand within hers.

I looked down, and saw the thin silver ring I'd given her. It was on the ring finger, but her right hand.

She drew a breath and prepared to speak, but she swallowed the words - something held in check.

"I have a different life now," she eventually said.

"So I see. How old is she?" I asked, tilting my head towards the pram.

"Four months."

She's not mine, then.

"You didn't hang about," I snapped.

Oh, that was cruel.

"Ant, don't!"

"Who's the father?"

"His name's Steve. He's a kind man..."

"I don't care."

"Ant, let me try to explain, please."

I nodded and dropped my eyes to the table.

"I had to get away. And I had to take Jenny with me. You know that. I couldn't ruin your life, Ant. Your parents would never have forgiven me, if I'd made you leave college and give up everything.

"I met Steve at work. He's older than us - late-twenties. But he's a kind man. Gentle. And he has a house and a good job, and he was willing to take Jenny in."

She grinds to a halt.

"Do you love him?'

"In a way, yes."

"Not like us? Not like you did me?"

"No. Not like that," she answered honestly.

"I've been dead without you, Juliet."

"Oh, my love!"

"Don't call me that unless you mean it!"

"I'll always love you. I told you that. It's because I love you that I did what I did."

"Do you do with 'Steve' all the things you used to do with me?"

"No!"

"Bollocks."

"I know you don't believe me. It's not like that. It's not like we were. Nothing will ever be like that."

"You're pushing a baby in a pram, Juliet."

I couldn't keep it up, the anger. I couldn't hurt her any more. I thought I wanted to - that it would help me, to make her feel some of what I'd been feeling for sixteen months.

"I'm sorry," I said.

"So am I. What are you sorry for, Ant?" she asked, and took my hand again. Our first ever contact had been that, as I'd taken her hand at the pub.

"For not providing what you needed. I should have got a job, and we could have rented a place. You, me and Jenny. I wish I'd done more. I needed more time, Juliet."

"I didn't have any more time."

"No, I know. What are you sorry for?"

"For losing you. For hurting you. For ruining your prospects anyway, despite trying not to."

We both sipped our tea. It was arbitrary, the tea. An excuse to spend a few minutes together out of the cold.

"No sugar," I observed.

"No. I'm trying to lose weight and get my figure back."

"You look great."

"Thank you."

"You look tired, though, Juliet. And stressed."

"Hmmm," she purred, "I could go to bed now and sleep for a week."

"I'm game."

She laughed lightly, but we both flicked our eyes at one another to see if it was a serious offer.

"I miss you so much, Juliet. I don't really live."

"Are you seeing someone else?"

"No."

"Have you, though, since... Since us?"

"No. Nobody. What's her name?" I asked, pointing a thumb at the pram.

"Annie."

"After your mum," I said rhetorically.

Annie, I'm not your daddy.

Her hand remained resting on mine. I didn't know what to do. I knew what I wanted to do.

"What's it like, being a mum?"

"Tiring. But she's great, really. I wish you could hold her."

"I don't want to hold her."

"Oh. Sorry, I shouldn't..."

"Do you ever think about our baby, Juliet?"

"We couldn't be sure it was yours, Ant," she pointed out, and touched her face as an excuse to remove her hand.

"No. Of course."

"I should probably be going," she announced, and I saw that I'd pushed too far down that path again.

"Not yet," I almost begged. "Finish your tea, at least. Are you hungry? Do you want anything?" I knew the offer was made to keep her there.

"No, thanks, my..."

Love.

The radio playing in the cafe had escaped my attention, being quiet and nonintrusive. It was a different version of the song.

'I Go To Sleep'.

The Applejacks. They had a big hit with it back in the sixties.

"It reminds you of your mum, this song," I reminded her.

"It did."

"Not any more?"

"Yes, it still does. But it makes me think of you every time I play it now. I see us in that caravan at the seaside."

"Do you think of me when you lie in bed, Juliet?"

"Sometimes," she admitted warily. Then, "quite often."

More than half of me wanted to pursue that. I've often thought - had I pushed at that moment, she might have come back to me.

But there was a reluctance. I dress it up as me being 'nice', and not wanting to take her from her new life. But the truth was, I couldn't see myself being responsible for another man's child.

It was trite, but I was seventeen, coming up eighteen.

Again, I wasn't ready. And when I think about it in those terms, it wasn't trite. It would have been cruel to take that on and fail.

However, within a short time, I would have taken that on in a heartbeat.

"I think about you constantly," I admitted to her.

"I'm not worth it."

"To me you are."

"Ant..."

"What?"

"If things had been different."

"I know. But I can't help loving you, Juliet. I can't just erase how I feel."

"Nor me. But we have to get on with our lives. Both of us."

Another period of tea sipping silence.

"Are you glad we met?" she asked me.

"Now or then?"

"Oh, erm, both, I suppose. But I was thinking about now."

"I don't know. I was looking for you, on the off-chance, you know? But I've thought a few times, that I wish I'd never met you, to tell you the truth."

"Why?"

"Because it wouldn't hurt, if I didn't know it. I wouldn't know it to miss it."

"I wouldn't change anything we did," she countered.

"Not even the end?"

She smiled bashfully.

"I hope you can be happy again," she said kindly, and I knew she was ready to leave.

"I'll survive."

"I really have to go, Ant. I'm sorry."

"Do you want to meet later? I'm here for the night. Heading back in the morning."

"I don't think it would be a good idea."

"Fair enough," I replied, backing away in the face of rejection.

I didn't stand to see her off. I wasn't sure my legs would support me.

Was a kiss appropriate? A peck on her cheek. Perhaps a hug.

No. I did nothing.

Bundled up in her coat, she turned and settled her eyes on me. "I'm glad I saw you again," she said.

"Take care, Juliet."

"You too."

"I love you," I told her.

"I know."

With that, she gripped the pram handle and set off.

When she reached the door, she applied the brake and strode back to me.

She leant in close, her minty breath hitting my face.

"Ask me!" she commanded.

"Marry me!"

"I would have!"

And she kissed me in the way she always did - full on, mouth caressing.

My hand reached up and found her waist, and I gently gripped.

"Bye, Anthony Nice," she said, and cupped my cheek.

My grip wouldn't release. I held her, but she pulled away and I lost contact.

And I numbly sat and watched her push the pram up the slight hill.

I sat there for an hour, but she didn't come back.

44.

"So, how did you find her?" Paul asked as a huge kick messed up his position on the green having dropped the yellow in its own pocket. He'd struggle to get on the brown.

"I bumped into her in the city centre."

"Just like that?"

"Just like that."

"And?"

"And nothing. We talked."

"You didn't shag her?"

"No. It was busy, being in the city centre."

"You're not back on then?" he probed, as we both watched the cue ball run the full length of the table and back again, giving him a straight pot on the brown.

"Shot. Sink this and the blue, and I'll need a snooker. No, she's with someone else. She had a baby, and whatnot."

"Fuck. Sorry, mate. How do you feel?"

"Surprisingly alright. She was okay. That was the main thing. We talked, and she explained a few things."

"Good," Paul said, before he slammed the brown in with far more force than he needed to, and over-screwed back for the blue. It was a fine cut to the middle as a result.

"Why is it good?" I asked.

"Because I've lined up a date for you with a girl called Emma. Friday at mine."

"Paul, no, I'm not... Ooooh!" I interrupted myself as the blue came back off the angle of the pocket and left me on.

"Just fucking be there. She's a nice girl, mate. About your age. Eighteen, I think. Maybe nineteen. She's tidy. Not a badger's arse."

"Alright. What time?"

"Six."

A little top and left spin allowed the cue ball to bounce clear of the cushion for a chance at a straight pink off its spot.

"Fucking hell," Paul muttered, and finished his pint. "Stevie Wonder could clear these."

"That's her new bloke's name."

"Stevie Wonder?"

"No. Steve."

"Sounds like a wanker."

The pink rolled in to the corner pocket, with just a little follow-through to leave me on the black.

"What's her name again, this girl?" I asked him.

"Emma."

"What's she look like?"

"Like something you'd want to shag. Come on, sink this and I'll get us another drink while you rack the balls. And give the table a brush. I'm getting a lot of dodgy rolls."

I dispatched the black for an unassailable two-nil lead. We'd still play the third frame, though.

It's what we always did. Three frames.

You have to play on. Re-rack and go again.

Paul knew that. Even though he'd lost, and couldn't win, he understood that you had to have another go.

She was lovely, Emma. Dark haired and petite, with large sad brown eyes and a shyness akin to my own.

She made such an effort for the blind date, wearing a short silver dress and boots that almost met it. Dark mascara served to make her eyes look huge, and the rest of her face smiled throughout, almost at odds with her eyes.

I fancied her. There was no doubt about that.

When I caught her looking at me, as I sat on the sofa holding the baby, I blushed at my lack of effort. It was shirt and jeans, as usual, for me.

We got on right off the bat, chatting about music and life in general. She was nineteen, and lived in Millby. She had a car! A red mini, to be precise. I was taking driving lessons, and she offered to help out.

She liked The Cure and T Rex, Bowie and Roxy Music. Older brothers affected her taste. She told me about Brian Eno. I didn't know much about him.

I kissed her goodnight when I left around midnight. It was good, but it wasn't Juliet.

Paul caught me up. "Told you she was alright, didn't I?"

"She is. I like her."

"She likes you, too. She told us."

"Thanks, Paul."

"No problem. See you Sunday for snooker."

"Actually, no. I'm going out for a lesson with Emma."

"The fucking bitch!"

"I can tell her no."

"I'm messing with you, you tit! Get in there. I'll see you at work on Monday."

"Yep. Thanks again."

I had a little skip in my step again that night, as I walked the few streets to dad's.

Half way home, I saw a man staggering down the middle of the road. He veered towards me, obviously drunk. He wielded an open bottle of wine.

"Have you seen Engelbert?" he called to me.

"Who?" I called back, keeping a line of parked cars between us.

"Engelbert! He's with her - with my wife - the love of my life!"

"No, sorry, mate."

"If you see him, you tell him to release her - let her go!"

"Will do," I said, and jogged away laughing.

Until I remembered it was actually Saturday morning, and therefore Juliet's eighteenth birthday.

Despite the late hour, I grabbed a beer when I got in. Dad was in bed, so I popped a record on with the volume low.

The Cure, 'Head On The Door', because it was close to hand.

Close to me on a night like this.

I wanted the record to be about Emma.

But it wasn't.

In my head, I heard a baby scream, and wondered if she was awake as I was, and what she might be doing? Perhaps she sat rocking and feeding little Annie, singing a song about going to sleep...

Did she feel me invade her mind, as she always fucking did mine?

Screw!

I was sinking again, disappearing beneath the oily water where she took me and held me - all green reeds and algae, the latter blinding me, the former tethering me, and not allowing me to push away and break through to something fresher - something in which I could actually fucking breathe!

I picked the lines of scabs the chickens left on my forearms, and made them bleed all over again, and I bit through the hardened blister on the skin between my thumb and finger to open it back up. And I gnawed at my thumbs, biting off particles of my own flesh. I did it because I wanted to carry on feeling the pain.

The pain was all I had left of her.

The blood - iron tasting in my mouth - so I swilled it away with beer, and switched off everything and went to bed, where I thought of Emma - pretty, enchanting Emma, in her silver dress and long boots, and dark eyes and shiny almost-black hair...

And I went to sleep.

45.

The car-boots are done for the year. There's an indoor one every other Sunday, but it's miles away near Tredmouth, and is more like a market.

Sheer desperation takes me to the jumble sale.

Fuck me, Yellow Hat even beat me here. He's probably looking for a new hat. I hope not. What would I call him?

He walks with a stick and a limp, and uses his disability to his advantage, ensuring clear passage to each trestle table without the need to do battle with women with reinforced elbows.

It's a vicious fucking game, the jumbles.

Church summer fetes, even, are a richer seam to mine.

It's all about percentages. That's what destroys you. One in twelve jumbles might actually deliver something. Eleven other times, I'll walk out with nothing to show for the cuts and bruises.

Beneath a pile of women's nylon clothing, I spot a box, and wrestle my way in.

A well timed handbag to my ribs knocks the wind out of me, but I struggle on, warily swiping aside a pair of navy blue trousers that are too crusty to crumple at the crotch.

What have I become?

My fingers go to work, pulling up the first seven inch square...

Knitting patterns. For fuck's sake.

There's nothing. I leave, back out into the rain, and jog to my car. It's a waste of time. Everything's a waste of time.

Still, I have time to waste. I think about visiting dad, but he'll know there's something wrong if I go on consecutive days.

As I sit in my shit car, the steering wheel held even though I haven't yet started the engine, I decide to pay Sharelle a visit, and collect the remainder of her father's records.

I've been putting it off - afraid of what might happen.

My marriage, I think, is over.

Except it continues. Carol's rarely at home these days, as work and spending time with Kelvin have become her priority.

The worst thing about it is, I know but don't much care. I thought I would, but I don't. As a result, I turn a blind eye, and continue to chuckle and be nice old Anthony Nice.

Well, no more Mister Nice Guy!

With a certain driving ambition, I start the engine, and set about weaving my way south across country to Wrenbrook.

On reaching it, I don't take the turn. Instead, I keep bearing south to Tredmouth. And when I reach that, I take the bypass, and pick up the main route eastward.

At some point, I stop for petrol and a sandwich, which I consume on the road.

Ninety miles lie between Oakburn and Canterwood. I've often thought that I could walk them in thirty hours, but never did. The bus takes three and a half, allowing for changes. The train a little less.

To drive it, though, takes about an hour and forty, traffic allowing.

I know that, because I've driven it quite a few times.

On arrival, I don't bother entering the city centre. I hang a left a mile or so before, and skirt a housing estate. On it is a house I stayed in for two nights. Juliet spent the first of them with me. On the other, I slept alone nervously, and she came to me as soon as she could in the morning.

She ran the miles between us in the cold and dark. She undressed without a word, and slid into bed with me, seeking the warmth and comfort of my body. All of which I was eager to give to her.

I've never been right. Not since Juliet. It was wrong of me to even attempt a normal relationship. I can't blame Carol for looking elsewhere. I simply don't love her in the same way.

I like her. I did, at least, before we drifted apart. And I respected her. That was important.

In time, though, she altered the things I liked and respected her for. It was a relationship based initially on friendship and common circumstances.

We'd have been exposed sooner, had she not fallen pregnant. But planning and anticipating Grace's arrival, and the aftermath of having a baby were all consuming. Because of it, we didn't notice the cracks opening. Or, if we did, we presumed them to be caused by the life-changing experience of bringing a life into the world.

We could have prolonged it further, by having another child. But we were well in our thirties, and didn't want to go through it again.

School and baths and meals and homework and stories and tears and laughter were the next dozen years and some, as life blurred by and suddenly I was fifty.

Fucking fifty!

How did that happen?

How does anything happen? I'm not sure.

How did I end up in Canterwood again, heading towards a bench in a ring of trees in a memorial park?

Dead children, I always think when I come here.

The journey is a microcosm of my life since Juliet. I wasn't even fully aware of it, or truly conscious of a single thing I encountered. I was on autopilot, because all I could see was the destination.

That objective to everything is Juliet. Even when it isn't, it still is.

Every single place I go, I look for her.

For years before dad moved from my childhood home, I waited for her to contact me there.

I didn't leave home until I moved in with Carol when I was thirty-three and a third. I remained there because it was how she could find me and reconnect.

Except she never did.

Well, apart from once.

The rain stops and the sun emerges as I pull up in the car park at the entrance. I take it as a positive sign. Just as I do the rainbow arcing overhead, indicating that its treasure sits in the ring of evergreen trees.

I'm early. An hour early. But it doesn't matter. I'll sit and wait for her. What's another hour added on to all those years?

I play music on my phone; a compilation I made for her decades after I last had any contact with her. They're songs I think she would like, or tracks that have something, either in the sound or lyrics, that remind me of her.

There are a lot to choose from.

'I Go To Sleep'. The Kinks version - the Ray Davies demonstration recording.

The original, and therefore the best, because that's what Juliet will always be.

I didn't hear it until fairly recently. When I say fairly recently, I mean in the past ten years or so. I picked up a Kinks CD boxed set with a live seven inch single included.

There it was, track three on disc two, all two minutes and forty-three seconds of it.

The two piano notes after 'sleep' make the hairs on my neck stand up.

It's so much easier nowadays to hit the back arrow and play the track again. And again.

No more rewinding tape and hope you drop lucky on the beginning.

To rewind.

That's what I have wished for countless times, but it never comes to pass. I wake up every morning, either alone or with the few other women I've had relationships with, and my first thought is to look for her.

Because I went to sleep imagining she was there with me, and that sense of her must have remained with me all night.

It's so exhausting to wake up every single morning, and to be faced with disappointment.

So I drive here every last Sunday of the month. And I sit and wait on our bench at two in the afternoon, just as she made me promise I would.

But she never comes.

46.

Emma gave me a driving lesson that Sunday. She was patient and kind.

I decided it best not to tell her that I wanted to pass my test and get a car so that I could drive to Canterwood every last Sunday of the month.

We drove out near Norton Basset, and I recalled Juliet and I talking about the lake, and perhaps living there one day.

Afterwards, we went to her place - a lovely little house in Lower Millby. She had money and support from her family. Not to mention a job in an office at one of the distribution companies in the area.

I liked her. A lot. For the first time, I began to imagine that I could perhaps have a life after Juliet.

Nothing amorous happened that afternoon and evening. We sat and talked as we listened to records. Right from the off, we connected as friends. She felt comfortable and familiar.

Just as Juliet had.

The difference being, after several hours in Juliet's company, we'd explored every inch of one another, and consummated our relationship.

With Juliet, something told me that it would be fine to slide my hand beneath the waistband of her washed-out denim skirt. And so it proved to be.

Yet, with Emma, I held back.

Why?

DId Juliet exude something that spoke of her availability? Sickeningly, did that emanate from the abuse she suffered?

Or was I more drawn to Juliet, and so couldn't help myself? Similarly, was she drawn to me, and so couldn't resist? Was it irresistibility, perhaps?

I don't know the answers.

"Shall we walk to the pub?" Emma proposed, as opening time at seven approached.

"I need to get the train back to Oakburn," I pointed out.

It was a convoluted journey due to no direct line. It involved having to head in the opposite direction on the branch line, and then loop round, either via Jemford Bridge or Tredmouth.

"I could drive you."

"No. It's too far, there and back. Besides, you wouldn't be able to have a drink then."

"True," she agreed.

After a pause, she suggested, "you could stay the night."

"I've got work in the morning."

"So have I."

"I'd still have the same problem of getting back."

Why was I looking for excuses? I should have bitten her hand off.

"We could call in sick," was her next idea.

"We could. But Paul knows I'm with you. He'll work it out."

We sat there, not even touching. Emma rose to put another record on. I don't recall what it was, which speaks volumes.

It had been less than two weeks since I'd seen Juliet - since she'd kissed me and offered me hope.

I played the cafe meeting over and over in my head, poring over every word she'd uttered, in an attempt to decipher something that I felt sure was there.

The thing was, I knew Juliet still loved me. Circumstance was all that kept us apart. If I could change those conditions...

'Ask me! Marry me! I would have!'

Would have. Past tense.

But that kiss that followed.

That fucking kiss.

Her hand on my cheek.

Mixed messages.

"If you just want to be friends, that's fine," Emma said gently.

"No," I blurted. "I mean yes! I want that. I want more than that. It's just..."

"Is this your first time?"

"God, no!" Okay, I'd take that back. "I mean, I've had a couple of relationships."

"I know you're younger than me. But I like you, Ant."

"Thank you. I think you're beautiful. And patient and kind."

"Then will you stay tonight?"

"Yes."

"Shall we go to the pub then?"

"Yes. Good idea."

So we did, and we drank and lost our inhibitions. I stopped thinking about it being a Sunday - two in the afternoon long since passed.

It was quiet that night, the January cold keeping people in their homes. As a result, we could comfortably walk side by side along the narrow pavement in that quaintly antiquated part of town.

Her hand brushed mine, so I took it, and she moved closer to me.

"Your hand's so cold," I said, and grasped it more fully.

We bore left on Mill Lane, and cut across a triangle of grass that crunched beneath our feet, the day's moisture already frosted.

It was nice to simply walk comfortably with someone again.

A warmth tingled our extremities the moment we stepped inside the Old Mill pub. An open fire glowed in the cosy bar area, orange flames flicking tongues up the flue after every crackle.

She had a glass of white wine, and I a pint of Jemford Best Bitter.

Juliet drank beer when I did, and wine when...

Don't think about it, I urged myself.

Sour grapes.

We took seats on opposite sides of a small round table where the heat from the fire could reach us. Her booted foot rested against my shin beneath the wood.

I took her hand, and we talked and smiled across the oak. She was known there, and a couple of people said hello.

"This is Ant," she introduced me. "A friend of mine."

Hands were shaken, and cheeks pecked. And it was so good to be able to meet her friends and be a part of her life.

That had never been possible with Juliet.

In the Old Mill that night, it felt normal. I felt like a part of something bigger, as opposed to the 'us against the world' life I'd known before.

Everybody liked Emma. It was obvious. She was so decent and approachable.

I was aware that Emma and her friends were a little above what I was used to. Still, she knew what I did for a living, and it hadn't put her off. She knew that I worked with Paul before she even agreed to the date.

Again, the word 'comfortable' came to mind. I fitted there that night with people who wore clean shirts to work, or were students at university.

Yet, something was missing.

When she returned from using the toilet, even though she'd only been gone for a couple of minutes, there was no little churn in my stomach as there had always been with Juliet.

It was something over which I had no control - that chemical or biological reaction to another person.

But it was fine, that missing element. It would come, perhaps, in time, as we got to know each other and feelings deepened.

Did Emma have a churn, though? Or was that not possible? Did the churn only come to two people simultaneously?

At nine, we said our goodbyes, and ventured back out into the cold again. The grass crunched more toothily as we re-crossed the triangle, Emma tight to my side, her arm around me and her hand buried in my pocket.

I stopped her when we were half way back, and ushered her round to face me. She was so cold.

Opening my coat, I brought her within the folds, and wrapped it around her. She was small - about five-three - so I leant down and gently kissed her nose, allowing it to find the warmth on the inside of my mouth.

We kissed, the wine sweet on her tongue, and I felt myself becoming aroused.

I think she felt it too, as she pressed against me.

"Let's go home," she said shiveringly.

Home. It was said in a way that implied it was a shared home.

Music soundtracked our thawing out, as we both sought a warm drink. Was it a delaying tactic, and who instigated it? Juliet and I would have thawed out in bed in a very different way.

But there had to be more to a relationship than sex.

We kissed and cuddled as we defrosted, and I found her pert little breast through her jumper with my thumb. She gave a soft whine as it passed over her nipple.

"Shall we go to bed?" I suggested.

She nodded, too reserved to say the word.

Was it reserve? Was it a coyness or a demureness?

Coy was dishonest in my book - a pretence.

No, she was demure, as she modestly disappeared into the bathroom, saying, "I won't be long."

I had no toothbrush I realised, as I heard her brushing her teeth through the door. Water ran and I heard splashing. Then the flush of the toilet, the water used to mask the sound.

By the time Emma reemerged, I was stripped to my boxers and sitting on the bed. It seemed a shame to get in to it, so neatly was it made; the sheets and quilt freshly laundered.

Did she do that because she anticipated that happening?

She was in her underwear.

The curves weren't the same...

"I'll just use the toilet," I said, and stood so that my arousal was obvious.

She blushed, because she was genuinely shy when it came to sex.

By the time I returned, she was in bed, a dim bulb in a lamp on her side being all that illuminated the room.

As I'd stood in that pristine bathroom, I'd decided something. I'd be honest, and behave as my instincts and experience dictated.

I contrasted everything taking place with the uncomplicated openness of my first time with Juliet - every time with Juliet.

And I considered what Paul had said, about make or break, and it being better to know sooner rather than later.

So, without ceremony, I removed my boxers, and turned to face her.

She smiled. She was fine with it all.

Rather than sidle in alongside her, I pulled back the covers to expose her naked body. I would play the Juliet role, because, I knew, I was the more experienced of us.

Beginning with gentle kisses around her neck and shoulders, my lips covered her entire body.

It was different. Everything was slightly different to the person I knew so well.

Her hairs were denser and coarser. She didn't respond in the same way.

I found the places Juliet had guided me to, and I did all that would have had Juliet arching her body off the mattress...

Don't think about that, I willed myself.

I slid up her body, lining us up, and dropped my hand ready to guide.

"Contraception," she whispered in my ear.

I'd never had to think about that before.

"I don't have any."

"In the drawer!" she said urgently.

Leaning over, I rummaged, finding the pouch and tearing it open with my teeth. I knew the basics, but I'd never actually put one on before.

First attempt was the wrong way round. I was clumsy, the light dim, in a hurry...

Back in position, lined up, smoothly entering.

She didn't move with me. There was nothing coming back.

It had been such a long time. Almost eighteen months. Since Juliet...

I erupted inside her - inside the rubber - white light and sparks, a moan of pleasure as the first wave exited me...

Breathless, despite the short staying power, my pulse racing almost as rapidly as my mind.

I didn't pull away. I stayed there as everything settled. If we did it again, would I have to get a new condom, I wondered?

"Juliet?" I began to ask.

"Who?" Emma said, and I felt her tighten around me a little.

"Sorry."

"That was the girl you were seeing, wasn't it?"

"Yes. Yes it was."

"Paul told me."

"Okay."

It was bizarre, having that conversation while I was inside her.

I withdrew, and rolled on to my back.

"I'm sorry," I said again.

"It's okay," Emma said kindly.

"No, it isn't."

She did something then that I will always appreciate. She sat up, her bashfulness gone, and she removed the condom.

She knotted the open end, wrapped it in a tissue, and took it with her to the bathroom. I heard her washing her hands, and wondered if I'd blown it.

"Are you over her, this Juliet?" she asked when she returned, and joined me back on the bed.

I blushed awkwardly and kept quiet. I didn't want to lie to her.

She perceived something from that. "I'd rather not continue this," she said, "if you're waiting for her, and you're just using me in the meantime."

"No. It's not like that. It's over." By way of showing her how over it was, I played with her nipples. She didn't stop me.

"It doesn't sound like it's over."

"Well it is. She's with someone else. She has a child."

My blushing burnt my face and neck.

"What do you want, Ant? From me, I mean. What do you wish for right now?" Emma asked.

"I wish you'd help me move on from her, because it's destroying me."

"Okay," she said, and that was that.

I moved on, and passed my driving test, and got a Ford Fiesta, and left the processing plant for a job in a warehouse that would eventually lead to a job in an office.

Emma and I were best friends who had sex a couple of times a week. And that was fine and dandy.

She'd come out of her shell on that front, and we'd found one or two things that got her juices flowing.

I stayed at her place most weekends, and kept a toothbrush there.

Paul and I switched our snooker night to Thursday.

47.

"Happy Valentine's Day!" Emma chimed, and handed me a twelve inch square package and a card as she stood at the door of dad's house.

"Thank you! Happy Valentine's Day!" I beamed back and kissed her, before showing her in.

It was early. A Saturday. We had plans for that special weekend. It was to celebrate both the day, and the fact we'd recently reached our one year anniversary.

I was happy. Juliet was always there, but she was more in the shadows, and not prevalent in my mind. Time, I understood, was indeed a great healer.

My life was on the up, and I couldn't complain.

Dad stood when she entered the living room. He didn't do that for anyone else, but he liked Emma.

'Done alright for yourself there,' was his way of expressing that to me.

We opened our gifts before we set off.

I got her The Bangles album. On cassette, so she could play it in her car. And chocolates and flowers.

'Manic Monday', because it signified the end of the weekend and our time together as the working week dawned.

She got me the Sisterhood LP, and Robyn Hitchcock's latest. She could have stopped there. That was enough.

No, though, because Emma was so generous and thoughtful. I didn't deserve her.

She had to go and get me a Japanese promotional copy of 'The Very Best Of The Pretenders', with the name misspelt 'Pritenders'.

I wasn't even that keen on the band, but she knew I liked the track 'I Go To Sleep', and she'd noticed it was on there.

We didn't have time for me to play it, but seeing it listed kindled something in my brain. A still frame of a girl lying on a bed in a caravan. Another of her leaning on her hand by the bank of the river Avon.

Yet another of her face as she orgasmed...

Shake it away. Don't go there.

'She'll be the ruin of you, that one.'

'Done alright for yourself there.'

Move on. Keep moving on.

"Where are we going?" I asked Emma. "You still haven't told me."

"It's a surprise."

"I know. But if I'm driving, it would help to know where!"

She laughed.

"Tinbury Head! I've booked us a great restaurant for dinner, and a night in a plush hotel."

"Wow!"

"So, let's go!"

"Bring me some of those strawberry biscuits you got last time!" dad called out.

I'd forgotten about those biscuits, and how Juliet had made me buy them for dad, as well as a different flavour for mum and Dave.

Everything felt as though it were pointing me at Juliet once more. Just as I was beginning to break free.

How could somebody who I spent so little time with retain such a hold on me?

My future was there, right in front of me, smiling and happily bouncing on the balls of her feet - a night away paid for because she cared and was so lovely.

Everybody I knew - everybody! - thought I was the luckiest bloke in the world. Except me.

Emma was lovely and loving and lovable. And I did love her.

"I thought you'd never been to Tinbury Head before?" she asked once the front door was closed.

"I was near there once, and popped in to the town."

"When was that?"

"Oh, a couple of years ago."

"On your own?"

"No."

Emma said no more as we dropped our bags in the boot of my Ford Fiesta.

"Hey," I said pulling her to me, "that's all in the past. This weekend is about you and me."

That was my genuine intention as I drove south.

The hotel was the most upmarket place I'd ever stayed in, and our evening meal was four courses from a set Valentine menu, each oozing quality.

Prior to that, we wrapped up and strolled around Tinbury Head. It was out of season, so a lot of businesses were closed, but there was enough to do and see.

Just being by the hoary sea was energising, and I was glad it wasn't summer as it had been on my previous visit. That fact made it feel like a different place.

Emma liked to be talked to. In the bedroom, I mean. She got turned on through me making up little sexual fantasies that, I quickly learned, worked best when there was an element of risk involved.

Again, years later, I think back on it, and see that there was a desire in her to be more adventurous and unconventional.

To look at Emma, versus - oh, I'll pick someone at random - Juliet, on the surface, Emma looked like the less inhibited.

Juliet was 'girl next door' to Emma's boots and big-eyed sex-appeal. Emma was sexy black underwear and push-up bras - immaculately made-up and quick with a suggestive comment.

We stumbled across the story telling. She was reading a book in bed one night, and I noticed she was very turned on. Thereafter, she'd get me to read out passages that she liked and aroused her.

Over time, I began making things up. I'd whisper them to her, and she'd play with herself until she reached a point at which she would climax.

Public places and being discovered were the topics that got her there quickest, I learnt. In addition to voyeurism.

In Tinbury Head, I noticed she was a little more liberated and frivolous than usual. It was probably because she was away from Brakeshire. She knew nobody, and so judgement didn't matter so much.

In a clothing shop, Emma seemed keen for me to try something on.

I remembered the story I'd made up for her, where we were in the changing rooms, and one thing led to another, before the assistant came over to see if we needed any help.

The assistant on that occasion was a fair female I'd based on Juliet, as they so often were.

Anyway, the door had been conveniently left unlocked, and her tapping swung it ajar. As a result, a thoroughly enjoyable threesome commenced in both of our minds.

"You should get a suit," Emma suggested. "They're in the sale."

"I don't need a suit."

"Everybody needs at least one suit. You could wear it for dinner tonight."

"I've got a pair of trousers and a jacket. They almost match!"

"Just try it on. For me, please," she implored, and gave me a saucy little look.

I glanced around. Despite it being a Saturday, it was just us and the assistant. She was a Madonna type, with shaggy blonde hair and a crop-top. Bangles adorned most of her forearms, and she looked to be late-twenties. She wasn't my type, but neither was she not.

"Okay, I'll try it on," I agreed.

The cubicle had a simple curtain across it, and a full-length mirror screwed to the back wall.

I removed my shoes, coat and jeans, leaving my shirt on. Emma poked her head round the curtain and crooked her finger. I stepped to her and she whispered, "take your boxers off."

Doing as I was told, she took them from me and put them in her handbag.

"Try the trousers," she ordered, once I'd slipped the jacket over my shirt.

I did.

"They're too big. Here, give them to me, and I'll get you the next size down."

I could hear her talking to the woman in the shop, cooing about something she spotted, and asking if they had the suit trousers in a different size.

And I knew the assistant was bringing them over, her bangles ringing out metallically as she moved.

"Here are the trousers," she called, and her hand and arm pushed through the edge of the velvet curtain.

I took them and said, "thanks."

That was it. I ended up buying that suit.

We left the shop, Emma very pleased with her little game. "Did she see you?" she wanted to know.

"I don't think so. She might have, though, in the mirror."

"I think she did. There was definitely a smile on her face when she came back out. Did you fancy her?"

"Not really. She was okay."

"Would you have screwed her, if she'd wanted you to?"

"I don't know," I said, and laughed.

"You've got no underwear on," she reminded me.

"I know. It's cold with the wind."

We leant on the wooden railing on the pier and stared out at the gunmetal sea with its flecked white waves.

That night in bed she got me to tell her a different version of that event in the shop. In it, bangle lady sucked me off, as Emma browsed the goods.

Wondering what was taking so long, she went to the changing cubicle and peered round the curtain. She watched on and played with herself, as I had sex with the woman.

"Did you come in her?" she asked me.

"Yes."

"Was it nice?"

"Yes."

"Do you fancy her more than you fancy me?"

"No."

"Do you want to come in me?"

"Yes."

And so I did. It was the first time, that Valentine's night, just over a year after we met, that we didn't take precautions.

48.

It was Emma's idea to go for a walk in Wishaven Woods after breakfast on the Sunday. I should have come up with a reason as to why we shouldn't.

Passing the caravan site, I'd kept my eyes fixed firmly ahead.

It was a bright, crisp day, where the pale blue sky looked to be a very long way away.

Every step made me think of Juliet. I suggested we take the circuitous trail in the other direction - anti-clockwise - just so it wouldn't be quite the same as where I'd walked with her.

The trees were bare and brittle, the wind that close to the shore having stripped them of the brown clusters of dead leaves. They littered the ground, many still on the twigs they were born to.

We walked hand in hand and chatted, because it was easy with Emma. She was easy to be around. We made plans for the year ahead, and my nineteenth birthday a month away.

Emma would be twenty-one in the October, and we talked about a holiday somewhere abroad. I'd never been abroad. Emma had. She'd been to Spain and France and America. Other places, too.

We had the woods to ourselves that day, it seemed. There was no life whatsoever. Not just people, but no birds or woodland creatures. The lake was devoid of the ducks and geese that Juliet and I had fed with our sandwiches.

"That's a birch. That's oak," I pointed out as we walked.

"How do you know?" she asked me.

"I just picked it up over the years."

"From your mum and dad?"

"Some of it," I lied, because how could I tell her that I knew it all through Juliet?

We rested at the lake, and studied the same sign Juliet and I had read.

Emma's reaction was similar - a mild disgust at the noses and ears cut off women - an anger at the victims of rape being punished for falling pregnant - a mild pleasure from learning where the expression 'cut off your nose to spite your face' might have originated.

"You've been here before," Emma suddenly stated.

"I have."

"With her?"

"With Juliet, yes. How did you know?" I asked, wondering if I'd betrayed myself in some way by scanning the sign.

"You didn't ask where it was. You drove here without having to look it up."

"Ah."

She still had her arm threaded through mine. She hadn't pulled away.

"You could have told me."

"I didn't think it was right to."

"I always have a feeling there are things I don't know about you. Like you're holding back all the time."

"You know more than anyone, Em."

"Did you have sex with her here?"

"In the woods?"

She nodded.

"No."

"I might be pregnant, Ant. After last night."

"I know."

"What would you do if I was?"

"It wouldn't change anything," I said.

"It would change everything!"

"No, I know that. I meant, it wouldn't change how I feel about you."

"How do you feel about me? Because I'm never quite sure."

"I love you. You know that." I meant that. I did.

"And I love you."

"Juliet..." I began, and almost fucked up because I used the wrong name. I covered myself by hastily saying, "Juliet was then. It's over. I won't lie to you, I loved her. And now I love you."

"Make love to me, Ant."

"Here?"

"Yes."

"Anyone could come..."

"I don't care."

"It's cold."

"I don't care," she said adamantly.

So I did. I lifted her up on to a picnic table, and I truly made love to her, as passionately as I ever had. I slammed into her, my flesh slapping against hers and resounding through the frangible woodland.

She came in huge shudders, her whole form glowing beautifully, and I matched her.

And just in that instant, for the briefest of moments, I could have sworn I was back with Juliet.

As we walked to the car on jittery legs, Emma happily said, "see, next time we come here, you'll think of me."

We drove home, as much a couple as we'd ever been. It was as though a weight had been lifted, as we laughed in the car, and Emma squirmed in her seat and relived the shop game and the passion in the woods.

I'd tapped into something in her. Or, perhaps, she had me.

We were still smiling when I used my key to open the front door of dad's house that Sunday evening.

He was there, the television on as always, a drink by his side, and the smell of smoke. Some of it from his cigarettes, and some of it from the fire he'd lit on that cold night.

Emma gave him the biscuits Tinbury Head was known for, amongst other things - pink shortbread-type circles with bits of fruit in them.

He had one right away, and made a show of not sharing them. But he offered, and we declined. They were his.

I thought of Juliet's mum telling her how everyone should have something they didn't have to share.

"What would you like to drink?" I asked Emma. She was staying the night, before heading to work in the morning.

"Wine, if there's any open."

There wasn't, but I'd open a bottle of red I had in for her. Fuck it, I'd have one as well.

"A couple of letters came for you," dad said.

I found them in the kitchen on the table where we always left post that wasn't for us.

One was my bank statement. The other was...

The other was a card in a red envelope.

The postmark read Canterwood.

Emma was there before I could react.

"What's that?"

"A card, I think."

"Who from?"

"I don't know, I haven't opened it." But I knew. I knew from the writing, and those rounded letters - the A on Ant being devoid of any point.

Wine! I'd open the wine to show Emma that she was my priority. The card could wait. It was less important.

Except it wasn't.

Tremulous. I physically shook as I poured into two glasses and handed one to Emma. Did she notice?

We joined dad and his television. Emma brought the envelope with her, and laid it on the table. I resented her touching it.

A red-letter day for me.

A red flag to Emma.

"Who's it from?" she said eventually.

"I don't know." Liar, liar, pants on fire.

"Is it from her?"

"Who?"

"Juliet."

Don't say her name!

"It could be."

"Why don't you open it?"

Dad glanced over, stood, and left the room. He wasn't daft.

"I will. Look, we've had a brilliant weekend. Let's not spoil it."

I didn't want to read it in front of her. It was private. Whatever it was, it was a very personal thing.

"I'll open it, then," Emma stated calmly, and leant forward.

"No!" I snapped too harshly - too abruptly - and took it before she could. I wanted to smell it and savour every millisecond of the experience. I wanted to break the seal, and inhale air that she had exhaled.

"What are you hiding?"

"Nothing. Look," I said, and tore across the top haphazardly, feigning nonchalance.

A quick glance at the front: A couple snapped from behind as they sat on a bench, her resting her head on his shoulder and whispering something in his ear. Two birds perched on the back rail, kissing as hearts flowed upwards. Green grass, evergreen trees, blue sky. Two bees hovering in that blue area, kissing and so in love...

'A buzz and a flutter...' the silver words on the front read.

I opened it, my hand positioned to cover Emma's view as she sat at my side cradling her wine glass.

'...each time we're apart, and I think of the love I hold in my heart. For you!'

She'd written above and beneath it: 'My Love, my Ant, I bumble around and shall never be whole without you. I will always love you. Juliet. xxxxxxxxxxx.'

A jolt shot through my shoulders, before shifting down and settling in my stomach. My mouth went dry, any moisture sitting behind my eyes.

"Well?" Emma said.

I couldn't speak. To speak would have betrayed everything I felt. Instead, I handed her the card.

She put her glass down, took it and stood. As she read it, she paced back and forth. I watched her, not knowing what to do or say - not knowing how I would respond to the inevitable question that would follow.

I saw it, then, the blue ink on the back of the card. I recognised the layout - an address, and possibly a phone number.

"You say you love me," Emma muttered flatly as she turned the card over and read the address I hadn't seen.

"I do." It was true.

"And I love you. So we can't have this," she said, and waved the card in front of her. I caught a breeze from it.

With that, she tossed it on the open fire, and I sat and watched it burn.

Oh, I wanted to leap up and grab it as I saw the flame flatten around it. I would have thrust my hand into those glowing coals.

"That was mine, not yours," I said quietly, as it ignited.

"Why would you want it?" she fired back.

"I didn't," I lied.

"Then it doesn't make any difference, does it?"

I shook my head.

She tossed the envelope on the fire as well.

"Ant, I need to know whether you really want this. You and me, I mean."

"I do."

"Then I think we should be together. Why don't you move in with me? And we could get engaged. If you're serious, I mean."

"I am."

"Then will you think about it?"

"Sure. I'm at yours half the time anyway."

It made sense. I got on with her. And her family. They liked me, and I liked them. It was normal and comfortable.

I thought of all the issues that had beset my time with Juliet. It would never have worked. Too many things were against us from the outset.

It was all too complicated.

"Are you happy, Ant?"

"Yes. I'm sorry, Em. It jarred me seeing the card, that's all. It's the first I've heard from her in a long time."

"Okay. And I'm happy. That's all that really matters."

She sat on my lap, and kicked her legs up on the sofa.

And I stared at the ash in the fireplace.

"You're quiet," she observed that night in bed.

Even that irked me - the fact she was permitted to share my bed in dad's house, whereas Juliet never was.

"I'm tired, that's all." It wasn't all.

"Do you want to tell me anything?"

"Erm, no. Not that I can think of."

"I meant... You know? Do you want to tell me a story?"

And I did. I told her all about the day she and I went for a walk in a park, and there was a ring of evergreen trees on one edge. We walked up to them, and through a gap spied a young couple on a bench.

"The girl was kneeling, her legs either side of his, her coat open and her body on show. And they moved as one, her face showing her pleasure as she rode up and down on his lap."

"Could we hear them?" Emma asked me as her hand went to work on herself.

"Yes. We could hear her moaning blissfully every time he was fully inside her. And the little slaps as her breasts tapped together."

"What did we do?" she asked next.

"We stepped further into the trees, and you did to yourself what you're doing now."

"Did you have your dick out?"

"Yes. And you sank down and sucked it." She wrapped her hand around me.

"Mmmmm! Did they see us, the couple on the bench?"

"Yes. The girl did, and she waved us over."

"What was she like?"

"Fair and very pretty. With a body to die for."

"And him?"

"He was young and slim, and quite shy. At first he tried to cover them both with his coat. But we went up to them, and you told them it was okay - that it was beautiful to see.

"They were younger than us, so listened to you when you suggested I join him inside his girlfriend."

"Oh! Both of you inside her?"

"Yes. They stayed where they were, and I lifted her coat and pushed in from behind on top of him."

"Oh my god! Make love to me, Ant. Now!"

But it was too late, as I felt a hot creamy discharge run down her hand and on to my stomach.

49.

We lasted another year and three months, Emma and I. It was my longest relationship, prior to Carol. During the time, I turned twenty and stopped being a teenager.

We never did get engaged, but I did move in with her shortly after our trip to Tinbury Head.

I should have ended it the night of the card burning. A resentment crept in as that card went up in smoke. And once it was there, it never went away.

I'd bring it up in every argument, dressed up as an example of her controlling nature.

Also, I began to tire of the sexual fantasy thing. It all seemed so disingenuous.

It spilled over to everything else. She was a great talker, but would rarely act. Fear of failing, I think was at the heart of it.

She was probably too much like me for us to have stood a chance.

For her twenty-first in the October, we went to the Canary Islands. It was my first trip abroad. The weather was beautiful, high seventies every day, and we lounged on the beach or at the bar.

It was chilled and relaxed, and reminded me of the trip we'd taken to Tinbury Head for the way she loosened up somewhat when away from familiarity.

Perhaps we should have moved away, and left all of the baggage behind.

I was never unhappy with Emma. Her only problem was that she wasn't Juliet. And there was nothing she could do about that.

"Hello George," I say, his flushed face rising from its downcast position, as I walk through the town.

"Oh! Hello Anthony lad," he replies, and I see and hear the misery in him.

"I haven't seen you in the Red Lion lately."

"No, true - that's a fact - I can't deny it."

"Are you okay?"

"Me? Oh, yes, I'm fine - tickety-boo." He's not.

"Fancy a pint?"

"I'd like that very much. Smashing, that'd be. Thank you."

We walk there in silence, his bag hanging limply from his hand.

"Bitter?" I ask him.

"Very perceptive of you. Can't deny it. I suppose I am a bit."

"I meant to drink."

"Yes, yes, pint of bitter - Jemford Best - in a dimpled pot."

"What have you been up to since I last saw you?" I ask once we're sat at a table.

"Well, I've not been out and about so much - been maintaining a low profile - keeping my head down."

"And Angela?"

"Yes. Her too."

"So, she's back with you?"

"No. No she's not. She decided that she didn't want that after all."

"I'm sorry to hear that. Did you make the changes we talked about?"

"Yes. All of them, and then some. But it wasn't enough. I can't change who I am, you see?"

"Who are you, George?"

"A man very set in his ways - not one for adventure - not a risk-taker. I made those changes, see. I got rid of the things I loved in order to hang on to the thing I love."

"That's a good thing to do, isn't it?"

"Honestly? No it isn't, as I have come to learn. I mis-read it, Anthony - I misinterpreted the situation I was faced with. I failed to see the facts that were staring me in the face!"

"I don't understand."

"No, well, you won't. You're young, you see, still full of vim and what-do-you-call-it? Full of spunk, as they say across the pond - the Atlantic Ocean!"

I glance around to see if anyone heard him say spunk. Nobody looks in our direction.

"Yes," he continues, "if I had a bit more spun..."

"You talked to Angela. Did you book the holiday and get some wine in?"

"I got rid of everything. All my wine making equipment went to a man who was very pleased to have it. As he said, they don't make tubes like that any more!

"And I got brochures on cruises for us to peruse and have a gander at over a glass of grape wine, as I call it."

"And the trains?" I dare to ask him.

He shakes his head mournfully.

"That's the bit that destroys me," he begins ruefully. "I dismantled the whole set up. I had it all, you know? Trees and roads and stations and a mile of track! All the little people, I had, and a bridge that ran over a canal with barges on it. Some of it I made myself - with my own hands - many years ago - back when I was a teenager.

"At Christmas, I'd add snow, and frost to the windows on the little buildings, and I'd run a red steam engine with presents in an open carriage being hauled! And fairy lights, and a Christmas tree in the station itself!"

"What happened to it all?"

"I sold it. Flogged it. Hocked it off. Every last bit."

"You must miss it," I said sympathetically.

"I'm heartbroken, lad, she was the love of my life!"

"I was talking about the trains."

"So am I!"

"Ah."

"It was as he struggled to lug it all down the stairs and out to the van he'd hired that it dawned on me! That was when I realised - that was when the penny dropped!

"The fact of the matter was - I was more upset about my trains leaving than I had been Angela!

"She wants a divorce, does Angela. She wants to get on with the rest of her life. Without yours truly. With someone else - another chap! A chap she met at her dance class. And she wants half the house. When I say that, I mean that she wants half the money from the house.

"Well, I don't mind telling you - no shame in admitting it - I'm worried, Anthony, and that's why I've not been out and about so much of late. I'm worried about the roof over my bloody head!

"I'll tell you this now for nothing! We all need something in life. Men, I mean. We require something we can lose ourselves in, and go back to times long since gone. It's our way of keeping them alive, I suppose - of hanging on to things. Memories, I mean to say.

"When Angela left, I helped carry her case. When my trains left, I couldn't bring myself to assist the fellow as bought them.

"I'm sure he didn't give me a fair price, but I wasn't thinking about the money at that time. I'm still not! It's the physical things themselves I miss. The holding them, and maintaining them, and just simply looking at them."

"Have you been in touch with the buyer to see if you can get them back?"

"No, I haven't. I've not had the impetus - the oomph! - the spunk!" he says, and drains the froth from the bottom of his glass.

He gets them in as I sit and think.

On his return, I say, "why trains, George?"

"Ah, well, that's a good question that is. I'm from Yorkshire originally, and we lived near a railway line. Well, every day we could, me and my brother would run across the fields and watch the steam trains racing in and out of the tunnel under the hill.

"Either that, or we'd head on down the canal, and climb the bank to the railway bridge, so we could feel the heat and wind off them when they sped by!

"Oh, the smell of them! And the sparks shooting out, as those pistons drove these metal monsters at a hell of a rate. The power in those machines, and the beauty of them - well, it would take your breath away!

"And we loved them, me and my brother. So we saved up, and bought our very first engine. OO Gauge - 1:76 scale - sixteen point five millimetre.

"It wasn't cheap, even back then - even in the nineteen fifties.

"And we got a ring of track to run it on. Well, we'd watch that train run around on the days we couldn't get to the real ones on account of the weather.

"It was such a simple set up, but it kept us entertained for hours on end, as we'd make up stories and adventures. They were the happiest days of my life!"

"Was that first train one of the ones you sold, George?"

"No. I didn't have that one. Long since gone, that one was.

"You know," he continues, "I've not told anybody about this in years. Even Angela only knew half of it.

"The trouble is, the people who knew my brother... Well, most of them are in the ground now.

"Ah, the train got broken. My brother broke it. By accident, I should point out. And I was angry with him. I shouted things, and told him that I would never forgive him.

"Well, he went off on his own, tears in his eyes, sort of thing.

"The daft bugger must have slipped - that's how I always reckoned it, despite what was said to the contrary.

"Over by the tunnel, he was, sitting on the grass as we always did. And he must have gone too close to the edge, trying to get a better view of the train as it emerged.

"Aye, I reckon he just slipped.

"I repaired that train. Good as new it was, when I was done. Bit of solder, and it ran just like before. Maybe even better!

"He never got to see it run, my brother."

In a faltering voice, he adds, "it got buried with him. It was the only way I could let him know that it was okay - that it didn't matter.

"That I was sorry."

I've never seen my dad cry.

I've never seen a man of George's generation weep.

That fact alone makes it more gut-wrenching to witness.

I blush at my own discomfort.

"I wish I could help you get them back," I tell him.

"Ha!" George scoffs once he's recovered, or, perhaps, as a means to recovery. "He had terrible trouble lugging it all down from the attic! I didn't help him. I couldn't. I'd boxed it all up, and it was down to him. I wasn't going to assist him in that."

"How long did it take him?" I ask, happy to stick with a subject that brightens George's mood.

"A couple of hours. I told him it was a two-man job, but he didn't want to pay someone. His look-out - his problem - not my concern.

"What made it worse, was the fact he'd not long since suffered a broken leg!"

"He wasn't wearing a yellow hat, was he?"

"Now, how the blazes do you know that?"

50.

I find him at a jumble sale in Millby, the yellow hat bobbing up and down as he milks his condition.

"I've got some records, if you want to take a look," I inform him.

He looks at me dubiously.

"What kind of records?"

"Round ones."

"How many?"

"Fifteen-hundred or so. Singles."

"What era?"

"Sixties to eighties."

"Why don't you want them?'

"Not my thing. Besides, I've picked out the ones I want and didn't already have."

"Right. So you've had all the good stuff, and now you're trying to shift the crap."

"No. There are two boxes in the back of my car, if you want to take a look. And more boxes somewhere else."

He takes a look, trying to play down his interest.

"Bit mixed," he sniffs disinterestedly, but I saw his nose twitch excitedly as he picked through them.

"We both know there are some rare records in there."

"Condition is everything, though. How much you looking to get?"

"Nothing."

"Nothing?"

"Well, not nothing exactly. You bought a load of model train stuff recently, up in Oakburn."

"What about it?"

"Have you still got it?"

"Might have. What's it to you?"

"I want them."

"There's some collectible stuff there, and I've barely even looked at them yet."

"So you've still got them, then?"

He scowls at the way I cleverly caught him out.

"Yes, I still have them. They're not my thing, but like I said, I know enough to know there's some stuff in there worth some money."

"And there are some records here worth some money."

He shrugs.

"A straight swap," I throw at him.

He's sceptical. "I'd need to see the rest of the records."

"I know. Give me your address. I'll bring them to you. If you're in agreement, I'll take all the train gear away on a van. How does that sound?"

"Okay. I might want some money to make up the shortfall."

"So might I."

I drive directly out to Wrenbrook to see Sharelle and Kelvin.

She's on her own again. For some reason, it saddens me, the fact she's always by herself.

"Hello Ant. A nice surprise." She neither sounds surprised, nor nicely so. It occurs to me that it may have been a joke - a pun.

"Hello. Sorry to drop by unannounced. Is it convenient for me to pick up the rest of those records?"

"Yes."

"Is Kelvin around?"

"Working as always. Is Carol not with you?" she asks, and I think I may detect sarcasm.

"No. I don't know where she is."

"Shall I call Kelvin and ask him if he knows?"

"No. Thank you."

I look at her in her loungewear, her alluring body hidden beneath thick cotton fleece.

"Will you stay for a tea?"

"I'd love to," I say, because I think she needs me to.

"How's the psychology going?" I ask as she prepares the cups in her compulsive way.

"It is good. I like it. I should get changed. I look like a scruff."

"No you don't. You look... Natural, I suppose. Comfortable."

She scoffs. "One sugar, correct?"

"Please."

As before, she measures it out, this time taking a few grains from the cup and shaking them into the sink. I get a feeling that she'd like to count them, in order to make things perfect.

She's trying so hard to please, it dawns on me.

I think about the pool party, and the catering. How wonderful it all was. How perfect she tried to make it.

What is it I see?

"Why did you want to get changed when I arrived?" I ask her.

"I don't know. To be more presentable, I suppose."

"Sharelle, you look beautiful just as you are."

She colours at my comment, and shakes her head.

"Look, tell me to mind my own business," I begin, somewhat tentatively.

"Go on, please," she encourages me.

She turns her back to tend to the drinks.

"Why don't you like yourself?" I ask her.

The spoon stops rotating in the liquid.

"I don't see anything to like. So I let other people tell me what they like, and I try to become that."

"Why?"

The teaspoon is rinsed, dried and laid on the tray.

Turning to me with a cup in each hand, she answers, "because nobody ever loved me when I was me. Well, my mother and father did. But nobody else."

"I'm sure they did."

"No. I never had a boyfriend all through school. I am quiet, I suppose, so nobody would even talk to me. Do you know why I got with Kelvin?" she asks me.

I shake my head and take my drink.

"Because he asked me."

"That's it?"

"That is it."

"Thank you for the tea," I say, threading my fingers through the handle of the cup.

"When I was young, my father would tease me. He would tell me that I was fat. My brothers, too. They would call me names, and say that I was stupid. I became a tom-boy, if this is the phrase? I did it so that they would include me in their games.

"I never dressed like a girl. Always a boy. And I would go to the discos with my father, and no boy ever asked me to dance."

I picture myself dancing to Captain And Tennille with Lucy Michelle Patterson. And with Juliet at the caravan park.

"Have you ever thought that it might be because you were too attractive? I know I'd have been terrified of asking you to dance, because the chances of you accepting would have been low."

She looks at me blankly.

Eventually, she says, "you know, I saw you watching me at the Christmas party last year. And again at the pool party. But what got your attention was Kelvin's version of me."

"I like you for what you are. What about right now? Which version is this?"

"This is plain boring me," she answers, and shrugs before hiding behind the rim of her cup.

"Well, the version of you I like is stood in front of me."

She blushes again.

"Sorry, I didn't mean to embarrass you," I tell her.

"Enough about me. I have been thinking. You love Juliet?" she asks.

"That's right. Loved," I correct her. "I've not seen or heard from her since the eighties."

"No, you still love her. Anyway, perhaps she could not be with you because she needed to forget what happened to her, and you were in her life at that time. You were a constant reminder."

"No, I don't think so. She sent me a Valentine card in '87. But I was with someone else. She put her address on it, but my girlfriend destroyed it."

"Would you have contacted her, if you'd had her address?"

"Yes," I reply without hesitation.

"And would you have been with her, no matter what?"

"Yes."

"What was she like?"

"She was perfect. Perfect for me, I mean. Ha! But too good for me at the same time. I always knew that. She would have found somebody better at some point, so it was probably for the best that it ended when it did."

"You make me angry, Ant Nice!" She even sounds it. A bit.

"Sorry."

"I will be Juliet for you. Tell me about her. How was her hair? What colour are her eyes? Describe her to me, and I will become her."

"Why?"

"Because, perhaps, she will be somebody who I would like to be. And it will help you to move on, I think, by going back."

"No," I say, shaking my head.

"Why not?"

"Because... Because you won't be her."

"Use your imagination."

"No. It won't be the same. I'll know."

"How?"

"I know every cell of her."

"So, nobody can match up?"

"No."

"Then there is only one thing you can do."

"What's that?"

"Find her!"

I stare at her. I can't. I'm married with a daughter. It's been too long. I'm not even sure I'd recognise her.

I would. I'd know her just from touch. I'd know her from a silhouette.

From smell, I believe I could differentiate Juliet. The colour of her eyes. Her smile. Her voice alone...

"I envy you, and I pity you," Sharelle tells me.

"Why?"

"Because you can do something about your unhappiness. And because you're too nice to do anything about your unhappiness."

51.

"Hey, Gracie. Not out with Ben tonight?"

"Obviously not."

"Okay. What's wrong?"

"Nothing."

"They broke up," Carol informs me once Grace is out of earshot. "Thank god."

"Oh no," I sigh.

"What do you mean, 'oh no'?"

"Well, she's going to be hurting, Carol."

"Don't be pathetic. She's sixteen. She'll get over it."

It's not worth my energy arguing, I decide. I look at Carol, reclined on the sofa, the television on, her tablet in her hand. Her fingers click away on the screen, sending messages unseen by me.

Kelvin?

"What time did you get back?" I ask her.

"About five."

There's no, 'where have you been?' She doesn't care.

I tell her anyway. "I went to see Sharelle today. About those records."

She glances up. Was that distaste around her mouth?

"That must have been fun for you."

"Kelvin wasn't there."

"No, well, he was working. Earning the money that pays for her idle life."

"She's studying psychology."

"Fascinating."

"It is."

"Fine. Just go and be with her then, if she's that fascinating."

It's pointless, the whole conversation. I trot up the stairs and tap on Grace's door.

"Are you okay?" I ask, peering round the edge.

"Come in, dad. Close the door."

I do as bidden, and sit in the chair as I did before.

"What happened, my love?"

"Nothing. We decided it wasn't what we wanted."

"It's okay, Grace. You can talk to me."

"I am talking to you. Stop worrying."

I see then. I see that she's not teary eyed. She's not upset. Is it a brave face she's putting on?

"Grace, I know how hard it can be when relationships end."

"It's not that. It's mum. She's so happy about it."

"And you're not?"

"I'm a bit sad, but it's no big deal."

"Why did you split?"

"I was a bit bored by him. That's all, really. I don't want to be tied down, and he was getting quite serious."

"I thought you loved him."

She shrugs. "It was never going to be the rest of my life, dad. I'm too young to be settled."

"As long as you're okay. As long as you're happy."

"I am."

"You don't look it."

She glances at me, wondering if she should say any more. I see her chew the inside of her cheek.

"I met someone else," she mumbles eventually. "I've fancied him for ages, and he asked me out."

"Ah. So you finished with Ben?"

"Kind of. He found out. I was going to tell him."

I sigh.

"Just... Just do what makes you happy, Gracie. But be careful, okay? And be decent about it. Be honest, I mean."

"Is mum fucking that bloke from her work?"

Shit, where did that come from?

"Er, no. I don't think so. I don't think she'd do that."

"She can't help herself. With men, I mean. It's embarrassing sometimes."

"Look, she just needs to feel attractive. I don't think there's anything more to it than that."

"I'm not like her, am I?"

"In some ways you are. And in other ways, you're like me. I think you got the best of both of us." I smile at her.

"Thank you."

"Stop worrying so much."

"I know why you look the way you do now," she says, as I stand ready to leave.

"What do you mean? How do I look?"

"Not what you physically look like, I mean how you are."

"No, you lost me."

"I felt it in myself. It's something that comes from the heart constantly being somewhere else. I was with Ben, but I wasn't really."

Smiling again, I close the door softly as I step from her room.

52.

I cue up a record. It's a reissue.

Does that matter?

Somehow it does. Having the record from 'then', exactly as it was at the time is imperative, depending on what record it is.

It explains why reissues don't detract from the price of the original. Often, it can increase the value and desirability.

I think about that - how something brand new can enhance something from years ago.

Sharelle becoming Juliet dances around my head along with the music.

The record plays flawlessly in my headphones. I broke the shrink wrap myself, and carefully handled it by its very edges so as to not mark the playing surface. I then brushed it as it sat on the platter, to ensure there was no debris in the grooves.

It's a fine repress, on thick black vinyl, and with some remastering process having been undertaken that I am incapable of discerning.

I have the original stored away. So why buy the reissue?

There are no bonus tracks, so all it offers that the original can't, is the clean sound I'm hearing.

Why did I get a reissue?

Because I'd played the original so many times that it was tired and worn out.

Yet I miss the pops and crackles and degradation in sound.

It's the imperfections that tell half of the story.

Lucy, Juliet, Samantha, Emma - they have all been in my thoughts lately, but none more than Juliet.

And now Sharelle makes a presence, as I think of her as some extension of Juliet. That, despite her being nothing like her.

Yet they do share certain things.

The dimple in their left cheeks. A blindness to their own beauty.

Juliet is my past and my future and right now. She has always been all consuming.

Are all of my thoughts of the past coming because I know my marriage is failing? Do I sense that I'll soon be free to pick things up again?

It probably explains my nonchalance. It's as if I want it to happen. I desire, I believe, to be set free.

George tried. He let his wife sleep with another man years ago. All so she might stay with him. He might tell himself, and me, that he was supportive. But I saw him that night on the street, swigging from a bottle of homemade wine, and in utter turmoil.

He removed from his life all the things he held dear. All so she might return to him.

It didn't work. He's bitter and broken. She left him anyway. And she didn't come back.

I know things have escalated between Carol and Kelvin. She went from mentioning his name all the time when it was flirtatious, to hardly ever saying his name when it became something more.

She does that, I think, because she's worried some involuntary reaction to his name will betray her true feelings, and I might see it. She still cares enough to not want to hurt me too badly.

She couldn't. I don't have much capacity to be hurt left. Juliet took it all.

And I can't be angry. Partly because I'm too nice, as Sharelle said. And partly because I simply don't care enough.

Ultimately, what can I do about it?

Yet nor am I comfortable with sitting by and allowing it to go on, either till it runs its course, or they decide they want to be together. I refuse to be some kind of cuckold. I have enough self-worth left to not want to be humiliated.

My daughter suspects.

That's wrong. For her sake, I should probably act.

Still, though, I know a lot of what is happening is my fault. It was my lack of achievement that led to her taking the job. In a way, I pushed them together.

My reminiscing about Juliet isn't anything new. It's always been there. It's in the way I look, as Grace described it.

Sharelle knows, and she's okay with it. Perhaps I should have been more honest with Carol. And Emma before her. And others - those handful of fleeting relationships I had between the two.

Juliet was my first edition. My original.

It might be painful to listen to at times, where nicks and marks intrude. But each of them are true, and tell a tale of a journey.

From start to end. From Scampi In A Basket in a pub garden, to a Valentine card burning on a fire.

I stand and raise the stylus, returning it to its cradle, and flip the record over.

The tonearm comes back across, held on the pad of my finger. And I place it gently on the clear black run-in groove.

As I sink down in my chair and set the phones on my ears, I think about records - how they have two grooves, one on each side.

I've only ever heard side one.

It's just been buffering for years, because nobody flipped it over.

It's pristine, that other side. Untouched. It's never been explored.

53·

"Carol doesn't mind you going away for a few days?"

"No, dad. We both need some space, I think. It'll do us good," I tell him as I drive to Oxfordshire.

"Must be bloody bonkers," he mumbles, "going barging this time of year. The weather forecast is terrible."

"Ah, as you've always said, you can't trust the weather people."

"Cold, windy, with heavy rainfall."

I ignore him and increase the speed of the windscreen wipers.

"Can you not smoke, dad?"

"I'll open the window."

"In this weather?"

He puts it back in the packet.

Half an hour on, I pull into the Services so he can have a smoke. He spots an overhanging roof to stand beneath. He actually runs to it through the storm. My dad - running!

Dripping wet, he gets back in the passenger seat.

"Shall we just go home now?" he asks miserably.

"No! We're going to do this, so you may as well accept the fact."

As we pull onto the motorway once more, for the third time since we left Brakeshire, he informs me, "you need some new blades on your wipers."

Fuck off!

Partly to drown him out, but also to mask the sound of the wipers grinding, I turn the radio up.

Of course, that's his cue to become fucking chatty.

"Where are we launching from?"

"Oxford. Just like last time."

"And what's our bearing?"

"Erm, north."

"In this weather? Into the eye of the storm? Be better going south, I reckon. Where are we sailing for, anyway?"

"Warwick way. Same as before."

"Can't you just drop me at a hotel?"

"No. You said you wanted to do this."

"No I bloody didn't!"

"You did!"

"I didn't!"

"You did!"

"When?"

"A few weeks back, when I came round yours. You said how it wasn't too late."

"For you! Not for bloody me. How are we going to navigate the locks? I can't be winding them at my age..."

"I'll do them."

"Who'll be on the helm?"

"The what?"

"Who will be skippering the vessel?"

"Well, you'll have to."

"Some bloody holiday, this."

"Yes! That's what I thought when I was fifteen. But it was actually okay."

I can feel myself getting stressed.

"Only 'cause you met her."

"Who?"

"That girl. You think I don't know what this is all about?"

"It's about you and me spending time in..."

"In a gale."

"...in one another's company, I was going to say. Besides, she's not going to be there, is she?"

Is she?

Something dissipates from both of us when we set foot on the barge. Dad becomes, to some extent, the man he was the last time we did this. As soon as his hand rests on the rudder control, he turns into Captain Jolly Fucking Roger.

'I'll be skipper!" he shouts over the wind. "You can be first mate. Right! Splice the mainbrace, and with a favourable wind we'll be in Banbury for teatime!"

The deluge abates to a light drizzle that can't quite extinguish his cigarette.

And in no time at all, we find our sea-legs.

As he sails north, I duck into the cabin and take stock. I work out what meals I can cook, and that there's a fridge but no freezer. I unpack everything, before rejoining him outside.

"I remember this stretch," he says at about four in the afternoon. "We'll smell the coffee factory in a bit."

And sure enough, the town of Banbury begins to unfurl itself on the horizon.

"Oliver Cromwell was here you know?" dad calls out.

"Was he?"

"Base of operations!"

And I remember him telling me that the last time we came. I'd forgotten. He hadn't.

He salutes a barge as it passes, heading south, and I smile at him when he looks in my direction.

A shake of his head and a widening of his eyes are intended to portray his wish to be anywhere else but here. As he turns away, though, I see a smile stretch his cheeks.

"Right, mate!" he shouts. "Get down the galley, and brew some coffee!"

"Aye aye, Skip," I reply, and head inside.

We berth close to the town, and I fetch us fish and chips. It's around six when I return, and already dark.

I put some music on - a folk-rock compilation, because I think dad might like it - and he produces a bottle of rum, of all things.

"Zero seven forty launch in the morning," he says, "make the most of the daylight hours."

"Roger, Roger!" I quip.

"Made good time today, son," he says, and raises his glass.

"There's no rush, dad."

"Clocks change next week. The days get shorter."

"Yep," I concur. "You missing the television?"

"I haven't even thought about it. You missing your wife?"

"I haven't even thought about her."

"That's not good."

"No."

"I watch the television at home because it keeps me company. It's better than being on my own."

"Did you never want another relationship, dad?"

"I thought about it," he says after thinking about it. "Who'd put up with me? Anyway, your mum was the love of my life."

"Really?"

"Yes. She was. I never met anybody who came close."

"Remember that Rosemary woman?"

"Oh dear! Don't remind me. You know something?"

"What?"

"I only started seeing her to make your mum jealous."

We both chuckle at that.

"Who knows where the time goes," he sings. I've never heard my father sing before. He's not very good, but there's something incredibly moving in hearing him in this place at this time.

"Sandy Denny," he says, and I look at him aghast.

"How do you know that?" I ask him, not even attempting to hide my incredulity.

"Because of you."

"What do you mean?"

"You were a baby still, when this came out. I remember you were having terrible trouble getting to sleep. To give your mum a break, I got up in the night on certain days if you cried. And you could bloody cry for England!

"Anyway, I worked out that you liked music. It seemed to quell you if I popped the wireless on.

"Well, this one night you were really bad. Teething, I think. Your face was bright red, and you were in an awful tizz.

"I span the dial on the receiver, and this song was just starting.

"Well, it calmed you down like a charm! You hushed up, and I saw you smile up at me. When it was finished, I looked down, and I saw your eyelids close.

"You went to sleep."

I've never heard that story before. Would he have remembered it, had the song not played?

By the same token, would he have been able to name the song and Sandy Denny had he not recalled the moment?

It's the two elements in tandem that make it so evocative. Visual and audible, as one informs the other. I bet dad can remember how I smelt that night, just as I do with Grace.

I watch him drink his rum before he stares at something only he can see. I know it's a memory playing out on the screen. And I think he watches television all the time to supplant them - one screen obscuring another. One drama or romance edging out the ones he's lived.

My thing is music, because it allows me to still visualise.

He has to be seeing a memory of mum. The tale of me as a baby would have logically taken him there.

"You're miles away. What are you thinking about?" I break in and ask him.

"Nothing," he says dismissively.

"Do you have regrets, dad?"

"About what?" he snaps defensively.

"It's been over thirty-six years since we were last here in a barge. She left when we returned."

"I know when she bloody left. What's your point?"

"It's as if you've been waiting for all of those thirty-six years. Waiting for her to come back, I mean."

"And you're asking if I regret that?"

"I suppose."

"No. See, the thing is," he says with gravity, "when you really give a shit, you don't give a shit."

I think about that. "That makes absolutely no sense whatsoever."

"It does!"

"It doesn't."

"Look," he tries again, "you don't give a shit when you really give a shit."

"Right. I'll make that my life mantra from now on."

"I'll tell you about regret. I'd have regretted it more if I'd settled down with someone else, and remarried and whatnot."

"Why? You've been alone for all that time."

"You don't understand, do you?" he barks.

"I'm trying to."

"What if she had changed her mind, and had decided to come back? And I was off gallivanting, or with someone else! Well, she wouldn't have come back to me then, would she? I'd have lost her all over again."

"But she never did come back, dad."

"That's not the point."

"I suppose Juliet was my equivalent."

"Bollocks!"

"What?"

"I was there, if you recall! When you were with that Emma girl, I was there that day the Valentine card arrived. You don't think it occurred to me to do what she did, and destroy it so you'd never know?

"Of course it bloody did! But it wasn't my place to. And when you let her destroy it, well, I knew then. I knew you didn't want the other one enough!

"She'd have been the bloody ruin of you, anyway, that one. That Emma was a smasher, she was."

He continues the lecture with, "but you're you, and I'm me, and we're all different.

"And I'll tell you now - if it was me, and I was in love with that Juliet like you claimed to be, I'd have been gone! You wouldn't have seen me for bloody dust!

"Neither hell nor high water would have stopped me!"

"I know, dad. I think about that all the time. That was the moment."

"She rang a couple of times, you know?"

"Juliet?"

"Yes! I always knew it was her, on account of the beeps from a phone box."

"When was this?"

"A bit later. You'd moved down to Millby with Emma."

"You never told me." A tiny pang of anger jabs at my flank.

"I barely saw you. Anyway, after the card, I figured you didn't want to know. Why put the cat amongst the pigeons?"

"You had no right!"

He shrugs.

"What did she say?" I ask him.

"Nothing. Just, 'is Ant there?' And I told her that you didn't live there any more - that you were with your girlfriend in Millby."

"Dad, for fuck's sake!"

"What? She was always very polite. I do remember that. 'Thanks, Mr Nice,' she'd say, 'I hope you're doing okay?' So I'd tell her I was fine, and that was that.

"It still rankles with me, what you told me a few weeks back. About her dad, I mean. I should have probably done something about that. But I didn't know, so what could I do, eh?

"She was a stunningly pretty girl, though. I could see why you were smitten! She'd have broke your heart, though, that one."

"She did!"

"Yep, well, I'm not surprised. Anyway, you've done alright for yourself. You've got Carol and Grace."

Fucking, fucking, fucking, fuck!

"But I think about Juliet all the time, dad."

"Tough!"

"Hang on. You were just telling me about waiting for mum for thirty-six years."

"It's different."

"No it's not. Bloody hypocrite!" We're both shouting now.

"I never bloody married! I never moved on! I didn't have a kid with someone else. I remained loyal! Haven't you been listening?"

"So, what? I have no right to go after the thing I love?"

"If you loved her, you would never have put yourself in a position where she couldn't come to you!

"If you really love someone, you bloody well wait!

"For the rest of your life, if needs be! You fucking well wait for her!

"And given what you told me about what she was having to contend with, I'm beginning to think you're a bloody coward, if you want to know the absolute truth!"

I'm up and heading outside. I can't be around him.

Oh, and it's fucking raining again. Fan-fucking-tastic.

54.

Dad hits the bank quite hard. It tips me off balance, so I make a leap for the shore. Handfuls of grass come away as I scramble clear, soaked to my knees in freezing water.

"Bloody idiot," I mutter.

"Clumsy fucking oaf," he mutters.

We haven't been getting on since Banbury.

The rope is sodden, and hardened as a consequence. I manage to bind it to the post with my frozen hands.

It wasn't the way I imagined arriving back at the pub.

Changes arrest me. It's funny how we see what's different more than we notice that which remains the same.

The pub name has changed, and heaters outnumber people. Still, it is almost winter.

Dad shuffles off in the direction of the 'Smoking Area'.

"I'm going to get a drink," he informs me.

"I'm going to get changed," I respond.

Nobody's eating outside. It's too cold.

No waitress carries baskets of scampi to a table.

I peel my trousers from my numb reddened legs, and look down at my pathetic self.

Before Juliet, I was like this. It's not quite self-loathing, but there's a distinct lack of confidence. She removed it, that doubt, and I carried it for a while, the residual effect of her presence in my life.

It enabled me to meet Emma, and even Carol. It lingered for that long.

But over time, it eroded. Life saw to that, along with people in general. I know, deep down, that I'm not even the person Carol met, let alone what I was three and a half decades ago.

It was as if Juliet instilled in me a power source, and it could only run for so long before, cell by cell, it died.

Dad's right about me. I didn't want it badly enough.

It's the story of my life. At school, in sport, I never had the determination to be good enough. I never became an author, because it took a long time.

I looked for excuses.

I blamed others.

Or circumstances. My bad lot in life.

Add in the mix that a compliment would elevate me so little, whereas a criticism would always floor me.

It was supposed to have been so different, my life.

With dry jeans on, I head off to find dad. As I make my way, I spot every place where she was with me. It makes me feel so terribly sad.

I don't know what I expected. It crossed my mind that I would find her here. But even if not, I thought that perhaps revisiting the place might make me feel happy in some way.

When I reset my course for the pub, I see dad watching me from a window.

I wave a hand, but he doesn't notice. Was he away with the fairies, picturing him and mum walking along the cut during that final week they were together?

My time with Juliet was so much shorter than his with mum. They had twenty-three years together, 'including courting'.

They were married for the majority of them, and lived together for all of that time. They had me.

I didn't once consider dad when I planned this trip. It was all about me. It must be hard for him, being back here.

"I'm sorry," I say as I join him at a table, two drinks in my hands.

"What for?"

"For being a miserable twat."

"I saw you walking over, Anthony."

"I waved."

"I know. I saw how much you hurt."

I nod and smile.

"Have you felt like that for all this time?" he asks me.

Again, I nod. I drop my head and blow a breath through my nostrils.

"We're a pair, eh?" he says.

"Yes. Cheers."

"Cheers," he replies, and taps his glass against mine.

"What do you want for dinner tonight?"

"Not bothered," he says. "We could get something here. Unless you fancy doing that pasta dish you make. I do like that."

I smile. "Yes, let's do that. I'll nip up the shop and get some bacon. We have the cheese and tomatoes."

"You used to make that for us after she'd gone off to be with that prat."

"I might go in to Stratford tomorrow. Do you want to come?" I propose.

"No. I think I'd like to stay here."

"Fair enough. Does it remind you of mum, being here?"

"It reminds me of when we were a family. It all changed around that time, with your mum leaving. But you, too. You grew up, I suppose. You stopped being a kid on that holiday."

"You were happy on that trip, dad. I'd never seen you so happy."

"Was I?"

"Yes."

"I didn't do a very good job of it all, did I? Life, I mean."

I don't say anything.

He carries on. "I've been a bit selfish, I think. I was so pleased when you moved back in with me, after you lived with that Emma for a bit. It's probably why I didn't tell you about Juliet ringing, as well. It was... You were all I had. All I had of your mother, I mean.

"I stayed in that house for all those years. I was waiting, I suppose."

"Waiting for what, dad?"

"Something to happen."

"But it didn't," I point out irrelevantly.

"No, it didn't. Don't do what I did. Don't waste your life waiting. Don't make yourself miserable.

"Thanks for the drink," he adds, as I gaze at the pub interior, and locate the spot where I had sex with Juliet when her aunt and uncle were in the Lake District.

"I love her, dad. I always have."

"So you say. But how do you know?"

How do I know?

"Because..." I begin. "Because nothing else matters as much as her."

"That's what I said. When you really give a shit, you don't give a shit."

I think that might actually make sense after all.

55.

Stratford was pointless. Well, almost. My saving was finding a copy of Lesley Duncan's 'Hey Boy' on the Mercury label from 1966, with 'I Go To Sleep' on the flip. It's only VG at best, but for fifteen quid, I figured it was worth a punt.

Aside from that, there was nothing there to be revealed. I'd done it all before, during the conference when I'd hooked up with Carol.

With time on my hands, I walk down to the B&B once owned by Monica.

The driveway is now asphalt, not grit, and houses have sprung up on the land around it.

A dog barks from a window as I approach the door and ring the bell.

"Hello, sorry to intrude," I begin.

"How can I help?" asks an Asian man of about forty.

"I was looking for someone who used to live here. It's many years ago. Her name was Monica. I don't suppose you know what became of her?"

He shakes his head. "No, we've only been here for a few years. I know her name from the deeds to the house, that's all. But that was two owners ago."

"Ah, I see. Sorry to bother you. Thanks anyway," I say, and turn on my heel.

It was silly to come. Monica would be a hundred, if she was still alive. Still, it was good to revisit the place.

"Funny," the man calls out after me, "you're the second person to ask about her this year!"

"Really? Who was the other?" I say turning and walking slowly backwards.

"A woman. She was probably about your age."

"You didn't get her name, did you?"

"No, sorry."

"Was she fair haired? Did she have green eyes?"

"I can't remember," the man says, and smiles apologetically.

I match his expression and call out, "my name's Ant."

"Bye, Ant," he chimes back, and I look up at the bedroom window where Juliet and I spent two nights together, going to places I've never been to with another person.

Is it possible? Did Juliet come back here earlier this year? Is she looking for me, just as I look for her?

No. I would be easy to find. My name alone - Nice, Anthony - would hardly be difficult to locate. More so, given that I've never left Brakeshire. Fucking hell, apart from that year with Emma in Millby, all of twenty miles away, I've never left Oakburn.

That's always been my deterrent, the undeniable fact that, if she wanted to find me, she would have.

Now, though, I think of my newly acquired information. Even after the Valentine card, she called the house at least a couple of times. Dad would have been working, so how many other calls went unanswered?

And if dad told her I was living with someone else, did she presume that I wouldn't want contact with her?

In Millby, the place I told her I always thought I might live.

I can see how she might have got the wrong impression.

A train and a taxi deliver me back to our temporary home.

"You should play with your woggle," dad decides to say for absolutely no reason I can discern as I step into the cabin.

"What?"

"The woggle!"

"I have no idea what that means."

"The woggle! On the thing!"

"Point! Point at what you mean!"

He points at my genitals.

He's finally lost it completely.

"Phone!" he rants at me. "Woggle it on your phone!"

"Google! It's fucking google!"

He looks at me like I'm the mad one.

Still, I tug my phone out of my trouser pocket.

"What do you want me to look up?"

"Her! The girl! Juliet."

"Oh, shit. You don't think I've tried that a thousand times?"

"And what did you look for?"

"Her name. What do you think I looked for?"

"What name was that, then?"

"Juliet Hutchison. Because that was her name. She probably married and changed it."

"Not according to my information," he says smugly.

"What information?"

"I got chatting to a bloke in the pub. He knew her aunt and uncle from years ago. And he remembered the two girls that used to come and stay every summer."

"Okay," I say, paying attention all of a sudden. "And?"

"And he told me that she changed her name to her mother's maiden name."

"But I never knew her mother's maiden name."

Did she tell me? Did she ever mention it?

"Oh, well, you're buggered then."

"And even if I knew it, she could be anywhere in the country. Anywhere in the world. I mean, she probably changed her name to distance herself from her dad, so it's unlikely she'd have stayed in Canterwood."

"Right."

"What?"

"Good job one of us had the sense to ask the bloke in the pub if he knew what that name was."

"And did he?"

"He might have."

"Well?"

"What's it worth?"

"Dad, don't fuck about!"

"We're nearly out of rum."

"I'll get a bottle! I'll get a fucking barrel!"

"Agreed."

"So, what's her name?"

"Smith," he says, and actually looks pleased with himself.

"Oh, for... And where is she?"

"No idea. The last he heard, she was in the Canterwood area. But that was over twenty years ago. Nearer twenty-five. Hey, at least you have something to go on!"

Oh, bless him for trying.

56.

"Will you be alright?" dad asks, stepping outside with me.

"I'll be fine," I assure him.

He lights a smoke. I've given up trying to make him stop. It would be as fruitful as me trying to forget Juliet.

Addiction.

I have two addresses and a hire car. One is a Juliet Smith. The other a Ms J Smith. Both are in Canterwood. It wasn't so many as I thought it would be, once we'd whittled the possibilities down.

The hire car is better than mine.

It's a long-shot, but it's the best shot I've had in a while. Besides, I'm half way there. I can be there in an hour.

"Right," he says, "here." He hands me a tenner.

"Dad, I'm fifty-one. I have a job, a mortgage and a credit card."

"Just take it," he insists.

I chuckle and slide the note in my back pocket.

He shakes my hand then, but he keeps a hold of it for too long. It throws me, him doing that. He's not that kind of a man.

"I'll see you later," I tell him.

"Good luck."

I feel like the British Expeditionary Force in 1939. Or Captain Scott in 1910.

It's fucking cold enough.

The radio remains silent. I don't need that now.

What if it's her?

Well, if it is, then I'll talk to her. If she's married, or whatever, I'll...

I'll tell her how I feel - how I've always felt about her. And I'll apologise. I'll tell her I'm sorry for not doing more back then.

That's as much as I can do. The rest will be up to her. Just knowing that she's happy will be something.

I'm tired of the unknown element in it all. It's time to be honest, and then see what falls out of that.

But a secret part of me, tucked way down lest I should embrace it and be disappointed - that part of me aches for us to pick up where we left off.

Everything else can be sorted out and dealt with.

Ms J's address arrives first, because it's on the west side of town. Strangely, it's close to the house of her friend that we stayed in. It's not far from the park with the memorial and our bench in it.

Perhaps she chose to live there because of that.

The house is fairly new, and large - at least four bedrooms. A BMW sits on the drive.

If it's Juliet, she's done well for herself.

I thought about phoning, but decided against it. I need to see her.

It's very wooded around the property. Juliet always did like trees.

Strewth, my legs are like jelly as I walk to the door.

A button and a sing-song chime.

A shape through the mottled glass in the door.

It could be her.

I set my face to a relaxed smile, as an arm extends to the handle.

"Oh, hello," I say, scrutinising the face and attempting to add on the years and the ageing.

"Hello."

"Sorry, I think I have the wrong house. I was looking for Juliet Smith. She was Juliet Hutchison once."

The woman shakes her head. "Sorry, nobody here by that name."

"Okay. Thanks. Sorry to disturb you."

'Smith, Juliet' was always the more likely, I console myself.

The navigation guides me around the city centre to the east. My car doesn't have satellite navigation.

I weave through tight streets. Small front yards, literally a yard long, separate the terraced houses from the pavement.

It's a grotty part of Canterwood, where indecipherable graffiti adorns just about every surface. The only shops I pass are a bookies, an off licence, and a small newsagent and general store. All have wire grilles over the windows.

I find the address, but there's nowhere to park, so I pull into a space two streets away. I'm supposed to have a residents permit, but when you really give a shit, you don't give a shit.

The house is a jewel amidst the squalor. The gate and door are recently painted, and bright net curtains hang in the windows. Hanging pots of flowers still bloom either side of the door. Drips tell me they were recently watered.

It's promising, I think.

My hand grasps a brass knocker, polished and shining. I hold it in suspension for a second, and set my face as before.

Tap-tap-tap.

There's no window in the door, but I hear a rummaging on the other side.

Despite the cold, I'm suddenly warm. Blushing.

The door opens and a child gazes up at me - a girl of about five. I look at the face - mixed ethnicity - eyes are brown, hair is dark. Do I see anything of Juliet in there? Maybe. Perhaps something in the shape of her chin.

"Hello! I was looking for Juliet Smith."

"Hang on a minute, please." So polite, and a smile that... Something.

The smell of baking. Perhaps a cake. It leaks out of the almost closed door and finds my nose.

It smells of home.

The door opens again, and a happy face greets me.

"You're the wrong colour," I stammer.

"I beg your pardon?"

"Oh, I'm so sorry! I was looking for Juliet Smith. She was known as Juliet Hutchison once."

"I'm Juliet Smith."

"I have the wrong person. Sorry to bother you."

She watches me warily as I skulk away.

Of course it was a waste of time. It was always unlikely.

"No permit!" someone shouts at me aggressively.

"Sorry. Just moving it now," I say, and wave an apologetic hand.

In the car, seatbelt on, engine started. I pull away, and weave back through the maze of tight streets, turning into a cul-de-sac by mistake, and having to seven-point turn at the end.

Dead end.

Eventually I find the main road, and follow signs for the city centre.

The bus station lies ahead. I pull into a car park and wait while someone takes an age to reverse out of the space I then occupy.

At a loss, I sit in the car and stare at my phone.

It's only ten o'clock. Five to. I left early, so I could spend the day with her.

I need a drink. A hot drink and something to eat. An hour on the meter should be ample. I lay the sticker on the dashboard. As I close the door, it flutters off and falls into the footwell on the passenger side.

Leaning over, I retrieve it, and peel back a corner so I can affix it to the side window. I resent the loss of time.

In to Canterwood, not even bothering to visit the bus station. Neither do I head for the cafe I went to with Juliet all those years ago. What would it achieve?

A chain place near the car park will do. I'll sit and have a drink and a sandwich, before heading back to the barge and dad.

The clock tower chimes the hour.

A man looks up at it as he walks towards me.

As he does, his neck stretches from the collar of his coat.

And I see the tattoo, 'cut here' and a dashed line.

57.

"Hello again," I say pleasantly. "Dougie, right?"

"Alright?" he says, and I see him trying to work out who I am. He doesn't have a clue.

He wears a black wool hat on what I imagine is a bald head. He's overweight and in poor condition, his breathing laboured.

"Been a long time. Are you still up on the Eastbridge estate?"

He relaxes a little. "Nah. Left there years ago. Are you from there?"

"I was once."

"Oh, right. What's your name?"

"Mark," I say, but I'm unsure why. "I was a friend of Juliet's."

He shakes his head.

"Juliet Hutchison," I remind him.

"Oh, I remember her."

"Have you seen her lately?"

"No. Not in donkey's years."

"Nor me. Ah, shame, I'd love to see her again. See how she's doing."

"She was lovely, she was." He smiles as he depicts her.

"She was. So what are you doing with yourself these days?" I push on. I don't want him to go. It's a connection. It's loose. But it is a link.

"Nothing much. Work. Family. You know?"

"Yes, I know."

"Look, I'd better be going," he says.

"Yes, of course. Anyway, good to see you."

"And you. Take it easy."

And we head off in different directions.

It takes a second to register, the name. "Hey, Mark!"

"Yes!" I reply, spinning to face him.

"She had a sister, didn't she, Juliet?"

"That's right. Jenny."

"Someone saw her recently. What was it now?" His hooded brow furrows. He scratches his head beneath his hat.

"I remember! Someone made a joke about me having no reason to go there," he says. "She has a hairdressing place. In Juneton Water."

"Do you know the name of it?"

"Not a clue. But there can't be that many hairdressing places in Juneton!"

"Thanks, Dougie. See you, mate."

"See you."

While I wait for my takeaway tea and sandwich, I look up Juneton Water on my phone.

It's about fifteen miles to the north.

58.

It's a quaint village that calls itself a hamlet, because it once was.

A large pond, or small lake, sits at its centre. Ducks leave v-shaped trails in the water as they paddle over to the remains of my sandwich I broke up and tossed in.

In the small parade of shops on the shore to my left, I see the sign for the hairdressing salon I seek.

It's simply called 'The Cut'.

I wonder who chose that name. Did Juliet name it, steered by memories of me?

This is as close as I've been in all this time. I don't rush. There's no hurry now.

I think of the last time I saw her, pushing a pram up a hill after she'd kissed me and told me that she would have married me.

We were seventeen. Almost eighteen.

I finish my tea as I walk the long way round the water.

What do I want to say to her? What do I hope to achieve?

The perfect scenario would be that I don't have to say a word.

I'll swing open the door, and she'll look over and recognise me. And she'll run to me as she used to, and we'll melt into one another. No words will be required.

The shop's lit up - an open sign in the window. As I approach, I see a woman near the rear working on someone's hair.

Is it Juliet? I can't see. The counter and a shelf unit holding products obscure my view.

It could be. There's something about her movements that feels right.

There's a florist two doors up. Should I get a bunch of something? No. It's too over the top.

After dropping my cup in the bin, I open the salon door and step inside. My glasses steam up.

A whiff of hair dye and minty shampoo fills the air. She always used a mint lip balm...

"Take a seat, love. I'll be with you in a few minutes."

She called me love. The accent's right, but it doesn't sound quite like her.

"No problem."

Music plays. A track from after we were together - Duran Duran, 'Come Undone'.

She did like Duran Duran.

There are magazines, but I can't focus. My hands are sweaty, so I wipe them on my thighs before polishing my lenses.

"Do you want a coffee or tea while you're waiting?" she calls over the hairdryer.

"No thanks. I just had one."

My seat is on the side where she can't see me. Why did I do that? I think about moving, but before I can, my phone rings.

"Back in a minute," I say, and step outside.

"Hello?"

"Dad?"

"Yes. What's up Grace?"

"Her!"

"Who?"

"Mum!"

"What?"

"I came home from school because... I wasn't feeling well. And I caught her!"

"Caught who doing what?"

"Mum! She was with him!"

"Who?"

"Kelvin! They were at it on the sofa!"

"Give me that phone!" I hear Carol say in the background.

"Fuck off, you... Slag!" Grace screams at her.

"Give me the phone!"

"It's my phone! Get your own!"

I hear a lot of scraping in my ear.

"Anthony!" Carol screeches. "Don't listen to her! I was giving Kelvin a massage because his back was playing up, and she showed up with some boy, and..."

"That wasn't his back you were massaging!"

"...and..."

"Carol!" I interrupt. "Carol!"

"Yes?"

"I don't give a shit."

And I turn my phone off.

A woman leaves the salon, a happy smile as she looks sideways at herself in the glass shopfront and admires her new hair do.

Stepping back inside, she's at the rear of the shop again brushing up hair cuttings.

"Come on back," she instructs me. "Just a cut, is it?"

As I step round the display, she rests a brush against the wall, and turns to me.

"You," is all she says after a few seconds elapse, during which she makes the connection.

"Me," I confirm.

"It's been a long time."

"It has. How are you Jenny?"

"Erm, okay. She always said you'd come."

"Juliet?"

"Yes. Hang on."

She walks by me, up to the door. She locks it and flips the sign over to closed.

Jenny was never too like Juliet. She took after her father more. Darker and... I don't know what. Harder looking, I suppose. Not so soft and rounded. Not so comely.

But you could always tell they were sisters. It's the bits of Juliet that captivate me in her.

"Are you sure you won't have a drink?" she says. "I think I might."

"No. Thank you. Honestly, I'm fine."

"Did you want a hair cut?" she thinks to ask as she pours coffee from a glass jug.

"No. Thanks."

"It's been a long time," she repeats.

I nod. "What... How's your life, Jenny?"

"Okay. Great, actually. I have this place. I'm happily married with two kids. Life's good. I have no complaints."

"It's a lovely village."

"I like it. It's a bit different to where I grew up."

"Do you see your dad?"

She pulls a face as if there's a bad taste in her mouth. A shake of her head tells me all I need to know.

"What about you? How are things?" she asks.

"I'm doing okay."

"And your mum and dad?"

"You remember them?"

"Yes. From the pub. And from when your dad came to our house."

"They're both fine. I'm on holiday with my dad at the moment, as it happens. It's kind of what led to me tracking you down."

"Have you been looking?"

"Yes."

"She always knew you'd come. I expect you'll want to visit her?"

I nod and smile. "If that's okay."

"I can't come with you. I have a client due in twenty minutes. But I can give you directions. It's not far."

"That'd be fine. Thank you."

She writes on a notepad on the counter.

"Jenny, will you do me a favour?"

"Sure. What do you need?"

"Don't tell her I'm coming."

She stops writing.

"Ah, she's with someone else, isn't she?" I realise.

"You don't know."

"Know what?"

"Juliet died."

59.

The world shifts under me.

I think I might pass out.

"Are you okay?" Jenny asks, but her voice is woozy and a long way away.

She touches me, her hand on my elbow, and she steers me to a chair. It's a chair clients use when she cuts their hair.

I feel myself drop as she presses a lever with her foot.

In a mirror I see myself. Or someone like me. A ghost. A white face and dead eyes staring back at me.

"I'll get you some water," she says, and jogs to the dispenser.

"When? What of?" I manage to ask.

"Cancer. She was thirty-seven."

"The same age as your mum."

"That's right."

"I love her. I always have."

"And she loved you."

"Did she?"

"Always. She never married, you know? She had her daughter. Annie lives in the village, and helps me out here a couple of days a week."

I nod my understanding.

Jenny squats in front of me and takes both my hands in hers.

"I'll cancel the appointment. We'll go and visit her grave together. Okay?" she proposes.

"Okay. Thank you."

We walk together, her arm threaded through mine. It's done, I think, to stop me from falling.

"She always wore that ring you gave her," Jenny says.

"Really?"

"Yes. She was buried with it. You know, when she was too ill to go herself, in the weeks before she died, she made me go to Canterwood every last Sunday of the month."

"To our bench at two in the afternoon," I say for her.

"That's right. As I said, she knew you'd come one day. When you were ready."

I think back. When would that have been? Fourteen years ago. It was when Grace was a toddler, and I'd look after her on Sundays to give Carol a break.

I'd take her to the car-boots with me, and let her mum sleep in.

It was the time when I didn't go to Canterwood.

"There's a letter for you at my house," Jenny informs me.

Again, a nod is all I can manage.

She's buried close to a tree. An oak. She knew all the trees, and how to identify them. The oak tree, with its leaves like hands.

Flowers are present. Jenny tidies them and picks out two dead blooms.

"I'll give you some privacy. I was always doing that. Back then."

"Thanks, Jenny." She strolls away.

I kneel on the damp ground.

A moan sounds from deep inside me as I try to hold it all in.

I growl to reset my larynx.

"I love you. Every single second since the first day we met, I have loved you.

"Marry me!"

Something catches my eye. A leaf flutters down from the branch over us. I hold out my hand and it lands in my palm without me adjusting. It's still slightly green and holds a bit of life. Her hand in mine.

She would have.

And I smile through my tears. It takes me by surprise, to discover myself able to smile.

A stream of images play before me. Snapshots of love, as she looked at me a thousand times over those few days we actually got to spend together.

I see her the first day, reclined on a bench by the cut near Warwick as she rubbed her face against me. And in her bedroom later that day, her eyes gazing up at me. And on the bank of the Avon in Stratford, and when the Town Crier announced our engagement, and in a bath at Monica's, and sitting outside the B&B drinking wine with the sun lighting her up, and running to me as I alighted from the bus, and washing and drying up together, her cooking our dinner, and drinking a glass of water, and walking through the woods, and the top of her head as we danced, and every detail of her ear as I traced it with my tongue, and a yellow jumper just peeled from her body as rain trickled between her breasts, her eyes shining as they looked at me, and so, so many more.

Until I settle on one - Juliet sleeping in a caravan near Tinbury Head.

On the headstone is her name, and the dates of her birth and death.

And four words.

'I Go To Sleep'.

60.

The ring of trees and our bench are my destination. It's not our bench any more. It's been replaced three times that I know of, over the years.

My crude etching has long since disappeared.

Tucking my coat beneath me, I sit and carefully draw the letter free of my pocket - her curvaceous hand that matched her body and open nature. Her writing is as beautiful as she was.

'Ant x' is all she wrote on the front.

It takes strength to open it. I try to pick the point of the flap to preserve it, but it tears upwards jaggedly. One side lifts, though, and I draw my tongue along the line where hers went, as I breathe in the air that touched her inside.

And I read...

'My Ant, my only true love.

Did you ever write our story, I wonder? I imagine it would be a chapter in your life, rather than the whole book.

For me, though, you are the complete tale.

And I'm now on my final chapter.

When you get to the end, and time is so precious, it focuses the mind on what is truly important. I find myself desirous of writing just three letters.

One is for Annie, my daughter. You met her in Canterwood when she was just a baby. I've told her all about you, and that she is the reason I've lived a happy life, despite not being with you. She made it worthwhile, the loss.

I hope you'll get to know her, and find yourself able to love her a little bit. Both for the parts of me that she shares, and also for the bits of her that are not like me, for those are what make her special.

The second letter is for my sister, Jenny. She knows everything now. And when I look at her, and how wonderful and successful she is, I know that I did the right thing by protecting her from my father.

Even though it ultimately cost me your love, and the life I might have lived, being with Jenny and seeing her shine and thrive, and become a mother to my niece and nephew, have been consolation enough.

Keep an eye on her for me, Ant. Keep a watch over both of my other loves for me!

The third letter? You're holding it! For I know you shall come one day, and you'll read these words.

I know that with certainty, because true love never dies.

I know, because I love my mum as much right now as I always have. It's twenty-six years since she died, and nothing has changed!

I'm torn, Ant. Just as I've always been. I'm torn between wishing things could have been different, and, because of what I have, not wanting anything to change. I would not be without Annie, and I could not have abandoned Jenny...

Oh, but what of us!

How different my life could have been!

I've played it out a million times, and imagined how the story might have gone.

Yet, my love, I'm glad you're not here now to see me like this. I wouldn't wish for you to have to witness and to be burdened with my demise. I fear it would break your heart, and that leaving you would make this even harder for me.

Because, my darling 'husband', no matter what, I would still have got this cancer, and I would still be dying.

I wonder when you will collect this letter, and what circumstances have brought you back to me?

I know that you married and still live in Oakburn. The internet can be quite revealing!

Are you happy, my love? Oh god, I hope so! But a piece of me knows - if you're reading this, you probably aren't.

Well, you must find happiness, Ant! You absolutely have to. Do that for both of us. Because, if you can't, then all of the sacrifice and being apart was for nothing.

For all these years, I've left you alone so that you might live and enjoy a better life. The best life!

Oh, but let me be selfish for a moment! I think I can be now, as I write my final pages. I think I've earned the right.

My time with you - our adventure - our love - know that it has sustained me for all the time since. I never loved another.

Steve was so good to me, and offered me a way out. But I'm not writing a letter to him. He is the father of my daughter, and is in her life. He's a good, good man, Ant, but he was never you.

After Steve, I dated a couple of men, but my heart was never in it. I had no heart to offer them. You have always held it.

I wish you could look at yourself through my eyes, and see what I see. Just as I wish I could see myself through yours.

We made each other more than we would ever have otherwise been, my darling.

That was why I waited all these years for you.

I go to sleep dreaming of you every night. Each day, I ask myself what you would do in any situation I face.

And many of the remaining hours are filled by remembering all that we did.

It satisfies me in every sense to relive our love and passion.

There are so many songs that bring you to life inside me, whether that be in my head or in my body.

If I wish to visit you, I go to the canal (or cut!), and I walk along for a while, and you seem to appear by my side.

Sometimes, I swear, I feel your touch!

I feel your hand in mine, and then your arm around me. I talk to you, and hear your replies in my head.

I love you. Now, lying here, I love you, Ant Nice.

Never ever forget that!

They say I don't have long left.

I'm resigned now. I'm tired of fighting.

I'm so terribly tired.

Oh, I wish you were here...

Forget what I wrote before! I wish you were here now, to hold me, and perhaps...

Just perhaps, if you were with me, I'd have more strength.

Strength enough to hang on. Strength even to beat this disease!

No! I couldn't put you through this.

I will die, and I don't know what will become of me.

All I know is, I will save my strength so that I can hold on to you, and take you wherever I go!

Marry me!

That's my dying wish! That we could be married, if only for a day...

...and a night! Oh, one more night!

Goodbye, my darling.

You've always had all of me.

You are the love of my life, and soon the love of my eternity.

For that is how long I'll wait for you to come to me again.
Your Juliet.
xxxxxxxxxxxxx'

I place the partly green oak leaf inside the envelope, and slip it gently back into my coat pocket so it rests against my heart.

61.

I've trudged through my life like a leaden-footed automaton, such is the weight of my regret.

Because of it, I have been a shackled man.

Opportunities lost. Opportunity. Singular. Juliet.

I cast my eyes back on my time on earth, and despite what I have in the here and now, it shall never come close to compensating for what I lost.

It'll never be enough.

And perhaps that's because I can idealise the past, whereas the present is starkly flawed.

I don't want it to be this way. I love my daughter. I loved my wife. I married her for the right reasons. But I simply cannot help how I feel, and how I've always felt about Juliet.

I've been deluding myself, and even though Juliet is gone, the memories aren't.

A rouge of anger - a heat of angst - colours my face.

"I wish I was dead!"

And nothing happens. Because that would be too fucking simple. I don't have any special power.

But the truth is, I wish I was dead because she is, and that's the only chance I have of being with her again.

It's a gamble - heaven, and life after death - but I'll take it right now.

"Well, did you find her?" dad asks.

"I did," I say, and mechanically hand him a bottle of rum.

"And?"

"She died fourteen years ago, dad."

"Fucking hell. I'm sorry."

"Fancy getting drunk?"

He nods. "Been a while since we got half-cut."

"And tomorrow we'll leave here."

"No rush," he says. "It's not like I have much to go back to."

"You've probably got more hope than me right now."

I step onto the barge, and feel it shift on the cut.

Dad pours the drinks while I sort out some music. I give in and leave it silent.

There's no song I desire to hear. It's as if the music stopped playing.

And for the first time in my life, I tell my dad everything.

62.

"I'll tell you what they're going to do," George says.

"They're going to lock everything down, and…"

"We're headed for a lockdown - stuck inside - no going out!"

"Morning, Grace," I say, glad to have someone present to share the load.

"Morning. Happy birthday, dad. Hello George."

"You need to get supplies - get ahead of the game - stock up on essentials."

"What's he going on about?" Grace asks.

"The virus."

"Oh, right. Kelvin has hundreds of toilet rolls, mum says. He's got them all in his garage."

"Well, he'll need them. Kelvin's full of shit," is my observation.

"Yes," Sharelle confirms as she makes a glorious entrance.

"Hello, Sharelle. Are you alright?" Grace asks.

"Yes." And then, "how are you?"

"Fine. You changed your hair," Gracie says to her.

"Yes."

"It's very eighties."

"Yes. Short here, and swept over at the front. Your father likes this style."

"It suits you. Where are you lot going?"

"Car-booting. First one of the year!"

"Oh, god."

"Are you ready George?"

"All set - ready for the off - chocks away!"

"Are you coming, Grace?" I ask her.

"What do you think?"

"Come on, it'll be fun."

"Yeah, dad. It'll be great fun looking at dead people's stuff."

"So, are you coming or not?"

"I'll get my umbrella."

And it's okay, life, I think, as I sit at the lights before the roadworks at the bridge. Or is it an aqueduct?

The oak trees, for which Oakburn is named, are budding into new life. It goes on, that cycle. No matter what.

"What time are they coming?" Grace asks me.

"Lunch time."

"And what are their names again?"

"Jenny and Annie."

"Annie, you say? Here, I bet you won't know this one - proper song..." George jumps in.

Oh, for fuck's sake.

"A-you fill up a-my sennnnses..."

"Like a night in the forest," Grace joins in. I didn't know she knew the song. I didn't know she could sing so well.

"Like the mountains in springtime," Sharelle goes next.

"Like a walk in the rain!" they all belt out.

A barge chugs by, catching my eye.

Over the top of the blue brick wall, I see a young couple walking along the towpath at almost the same speed as the boat.

He has his arm round her shoulder, and she leans into him. They kiss as they walk, and he says something that makes her gaze into his eyes, before her head nods in acceptance.

I wonder what he asked her?

Will lockdown stop them being together? Will they survive it all, and emerge intact?

I grin, and recall a holiday I had when I was fifteen.

And I reach over and rest my hand on Sharelle's thigh.

She turns to me, and smiles beautifully. Naturally. A little dimple appears in her cheek, before her smile broadens and obliterates it.

We listen to records, and I tell her why they're important to me. Sometimes, I ask her to dance to them with me.

She knows that if Juliet was here, I wouldn't be with her. But she also knows I am what I am because of Juliet and all that happened. And, amazingly, she's fine with it all.

We got together in February, around Valentine's Day. And, as of last night, she moved in with me. The virus forced us into making a decision. Perhaps it's hasty. Time will tell.

I think Juliet would be okay with it. I hope so.

'Come fill me again.'

"Dad, the lights have changed," Grace says from the back seat.

I move on, passing through a dark moment before reemerging into the light.

And I leave the cut behind for now, watching it diminish in my rearview mirror.

The end.

Worldly Goods

***** What a lovely, uplifting, heartbreaking, funny, wistful and wise story. I fell headlong into this book - the characters were believable and human, and I found myself identifying with each of them - their joys and sorrows, their longings and regrets.

There were moments that brought me near tears (I actually wiped one or two away on the second to last chapter). I recommend this book to anyone, especially any of us who still collect records.

Thank you so much for this wonderful volume! Easily worth more than 5 stars!

***** 'Worldly Goods' is simply fantastic! Any vinyl collector will feel right at home with the tale Andy spins across its 290 pages.

It will make you laugh. It will certainly make you cry. Andy is skilled at slowly letting the reader become familiar with the characters and watching them grow and mature. And this growth is so subtle that you admire characters like Danny Goods and his father Bill Goods. And you only learn about Bill through his letters to Danny six years after his father's passing, what a beautiful and poignant journey of discovery!

Folklorist - The Tommy Histon Story

***** 'Worldly Goods' was full of charm, nostalgia, warmth and a sense of belonging to one's family, but 'Folklorist' is a tale of mystique, darkness and magic.

A story of a loner; a loner with inexplicable innovative talents that belonged to another time, a time ahead of his own.

This is an engrossing read, and the writing, the pace, the decision to inject interviews, stories etc. on Tommy from the future at regular intervals, before returning to Tommy's own time, enhances the legend brilliantly.

There is a troublesome darkness in Tommy's soul that sets him apart from others. He is one almost not of this world. And yet, deep inside, lies a sweet soul who desires no other purpose in life than finding someone to love for the first time.

All cool music lovers and followers of cult musicians, myths & legends must read this!

A truly superb book and one which left a huge impression on me.

***** In an ideal world, 'Folklorist: The Tommy Histon Story' would be a #1 seller. It's a great story, extremely well written. It's emotional and moving, and you won't be the same after you read it. At least for a while.

It's about a musician who was never understood (well, barely noticed, actually) in his time, and was always ahead of the game. We have the privilege of reading about a unique talent written by another unique talent; the writer Andy Bracken.

This is the fourth book by this author I've read. And they keep getting better. There's no way that you won't identify, somewhere in his books, with some of the characters' thoughts and attitudes.

Bracken's capacity to write about feelings and emotions is compelling. And he knows how to tell a story; always a good story.

His previous book, 'Worldly Goods', was my favourite book of 2019. If someone loves records and has a record collection, well, 'Worldly Goods' is unmissable.

And now we have 'Folklorist'. This book must be read by every serious music lover. And, by the way, any serious reader of modern literature.

Book of the year, again!

Thank you for taking the time to read this book. It is very much appreciated, and I sincerely hope you enjoyed it.

A **Morning Brake** Publication.
Contact: morningbrake@cox.net

Other works by Andy Bracken:

Novels set in Brakeshire and elsewhere:

- The Cut
- Equilibrium
- Folklorist: The Tommy Histon Story
- Worldly Goods
- Across The Humpty Dumpty Field
- Reflections Of Quercus Treen and Meek
- The Book Burner
- Clearing
- The Decline Of Emory Hill
- What Ven Knew
- Gaps Between The Tracks
- Beneath The Covers

Non-Fiction:

- Nervous Breakdown - The Recorded Legacy Of Eddie Cochran. (unpublished)